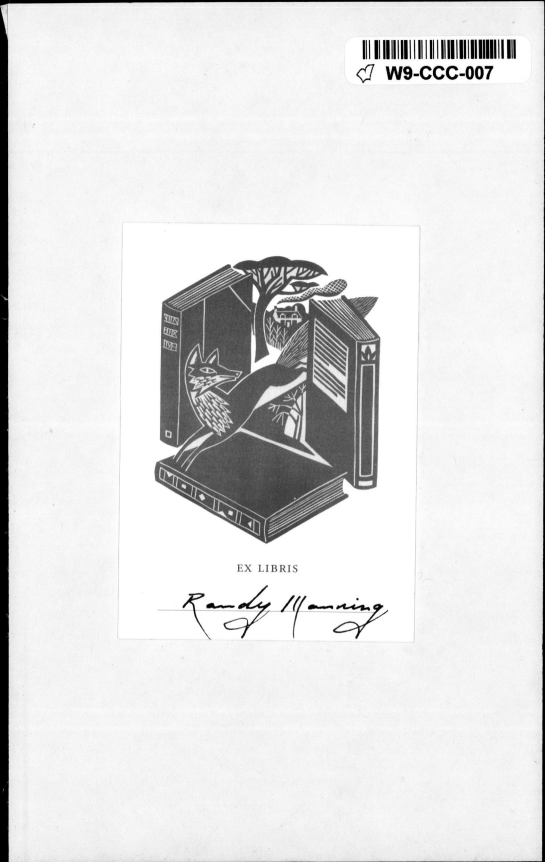

EX LIBRIS

BY SARAH DUNANT

• • •

IN THE NAME
OF THE FAMILY

IN THE NAME OF THE FAMILY

A Novel

SARAH DUNANT

HARPERCOLLINS PUBLISHERS LTD

In the Name of the Family
Copyright © 2017 by Sarah Dunant.
All rights reserved.

Published by HarperCollins Publishers Ltd

First Canadian edition

HarperCollins books may be purchased for educational, business,
or sales promotional use through our Special Markets Department.

HarperCollins Publishers Ltd
2 Bloor Street East, 20th Floor
Toronto, Ontario, Canada
M4W 1A8

www.harpercollins.ca

Library and Archives Canada Cataloguing in Publication
information is available upon request.

Book design by Liz Cosgrove

ISBN 978-1-44340-647-5

Printed and bound in the United States
17 18 19 20   LSC/H   10 9 8 7 6 5 4 3 2 1

For Professor Roy Porter, 1946–2002
Because the way he thought, taught and wrote
history made it as exciting as any novel.

. . . As an eagle may fly carrying a tortoise in his mouth, then drop it to the ground so that the fall smashes open its shell . . .

—Niccolò Machiavelli
on the vagaries of fortune

IN THE NAME
OF THE FAMILY

Prologue

You couldn't call him tall; he was barely an inch bigger than her and wiry in stature. His soot black hair was cut unfashionably close to his head, and his face, broad at the eyes, tapered via a thin nose to a sharp clean-shaven chin. The word *weasel* had come to mind when they first met. But strangely it hadn't put her off. Marietta Corsini had known already that her future husband was clever (he had a job in government and everyone knew men like that needed a wheelbarrow to carry their thoughts), and within a few minutes he had made her laugh. He had also made her blush, for there had been something in his bright-eyed concentration, his almost animal quiver energy that seemed to be half undressing her. By the time they had said their goodbyes she was smitten, and six months of marriage has done nothing to change that.

He leaves for work each day at dawn. In the beginning she had hoped that her nest-ripe body might tempt him to linger. The city is rife with stories of married men who use early risings as excuses to visit their mistresses, and he had come with a reputation for enjoying life. But even if that were the case, there's nothing she can do about it, not least because wherever he is going, this husband of hers, he has already "gone" from her long before he gets out of the door.

In fact, Niccolò Machiavelli doesn't leave the warmth of his marriage bed for any other woman (he can do that easily enough on his way home), but because the day's dispatches arrive at the Palazzo della Signoria early and it is his greatest pleasure as well as his duty to be among the first to read them.

His journey takes him down Via Guicciardini on the south side of the city and across the river Arno via the Ponte Vecchio. A maverick winter snowfall has turned into a grimy frost and the ground cracks like small animal bones under his feet. On the bridge fresh carcasses are being unloaded into the butchers' shops. Through their open shutters he catches glimpses of the river, its surface of the water a silvery apricot under the rising sun. A feral dog streaks across his path, going for a gobbet of offal near the wheel of a cart. It earns him a kick in the ribs for his daring but his jaws remain firmly clenched over the prize. Scavenging opportunist, Niccolò thinks, not without a certain admiration. Stick a feathered hat on him and give him a sword and you've got half the country. How long ago was that business in the city of Fermo? Christmas, yes? He'd opened the dispatch himself: the duke's "loving" nephew had invited his uncle to a seasonal dinner, then locked the doors and slaughtered him and his entire council, taking the title for himself. In the chancery, his staff were laying bets on how long it would be before the next murderous dinner invite, but Niccolò's money is on the usurper. While the man may be a thug, he's also a mercenary leader in Cesare Borgia's army, which makes him a thug with powerful allies.

Across the bridge, he passes by the side of San Pier Scheraggio church out into the open space of the Piazza della Signoria, dominated by the handsome crenellated palace of government. To the left of the main doors is a weathered bronze statue; the figure of Judith, calm, concentrated, a raised sword in her right hand poised to slice through the neck of Holofernes, who sits painfully twisted at her feet. Niccolò gives her a silent salute. He knows men in government who find it unnerving to be greeted daily by the sight of a woman administering justice to a man, but they are missing the point. Donatello's statue, plundered from the Medici palace and placed here eight years before, stands as a deliberate reminder to the republic of Florence that she would never again allow the dictatorship of a single family.

Alas, the gap between the ideal and reality in politics is enough to give most men vertigo. If Judith were to lift up her eyes now, she would be looking at the place in the piazza where they had burned the Dominican friar Savonarola, whose fanatical devotion to God's laws had made him another kind of tyrant. Every time he passes a tavern where some idiot cook has burned a carcass on a spit, the sick-sweet smell of caramelized fat and flesh has him back inside the crowd, straining to see the stake over the shoulders of bigger men. He had never witnessed a public burning before—Florence has little fondness for such barbarity—and Savonarola had been garroted before the faggots were lit, but the spectacle, and the stench, had still turned his stomach.

He'd known then that Florence had a challenge ahead of her, re-establishing a working republic after so much madness. And if he is confident in public—for that is his job—in private he has grave doubts.

He slips into the palazzo through a side entrance, exchanging a joke with a sleepy guard, before climbing a spiral staircase that takes him through the great central hall, up a further flight into the council rooms and offices above. His desk is in a small antechamber set off from the main salon, with its gilded wooden ceiling and patterned fleur-de-lis walls. The temperature is almost as cold inside as out. When the elected members gather there will be braziers and fires lit, but as a hired hand he has his own clay bottle and must send out for regular refills to stop his feet from turning to ice. He will do it later: once the seals on the day's dispatches are broken he won't feel the cold.

It is Niccolò's business, as head of the second chancery and secretary to the Council of Ten for Liberty and Peace, to keep abreast of every shift and change in the political landscape of the country. For as long as he can remember such things have fascinated him. He was barely thirteen years old when his father had placed a newly printed copy of Livy's history of Rome in front of him, and like every first great love affair, it has colored the way he sees the world ever since.

"This is the most treasured possession this house now holds, you hear me?" Such dry humor his father practiced. *"In a fire you had better took to yourself, for this will be the man I save first."*

He wonders sometimes what the great Livy would make of this

modern Italy. In his own mind he sees the peninsula as a great ragged boot hanging off the Alps, the leather mottled and discolored by the vicissitudes of history. In the north, for the second time in a decade, a French army is in occupation, ruling Milan and overshadowing a dozen smaller states close by. On the Adriatic coast, Venice is puffed up with her own wealth and battles with the Turks, while the wild lands of the south are under the control of the Spanish, with a few old French strongholds inside.

But it is what is happening in the middle that would have surely fascinated Livy the most.

The speed and ferocity of the rise of the Borgia family have taken everyone by surprise. Of course Rome has had unscrupulous popes before, men who quietly favored the fortunes of their "nephews" or "nieces." But this, this is different. Here is a pope, Alexander VI, who openly acknowledges and uses his illegitimate children as weapons to create a new dynastic power block; his eldest son Cesare, once a cardinal, marches at the head of a mercenary army conquering a line of city-states historically owned by the Church, while his daughter, Lucrezia, is the family's prize marriage pawn.

Two of the day's dispatches bring further news of the Borgia project. Lucrezia is now halfway across Italy with an entourage the size of a small army en route to her third husband, the Duke elect of Ferrara. Meanwhile, the Pope and his son, on a lap of honor to celebrate their latest conquest—the state of Piombino and the island of Elba—are making an early departure by boat back to Rome. How long till they arrive? If the wind obliges, the water will carry them faster than any road in winter, though it's not a journey that he himself would choose to make. At least the rest of Tuscany will breathe easily for a while; a soldier at sea cannot be a duke leading an army on land.

He is filleting the dispatches ready for the council morning briefing when he hears the sounds of the great bells from the Cathedral of Santa Maria del Fiore marking the starting hour of the day. His thoughts move briefly to the cathedral workshop where the Florentine sculptor Michelangelo Buonarroti has spent the last nine months chiseling into a block of flawed marble, commissioned by the state to produce a great statue of David to be placed on the façade of the cathedral. No one has been allowed near the work, but the leaked gossip talks more of its emerging size than its beauty. It remains to be seen whether it will be powerful enough to shield the city from the Borgia Goliath.

As the last chimes die away, a series of contorted male shrieks rise up from somewhere nearby; a late coupling between the sheets or a few early knife thrusts into a belly? He smiles. Such are the sounds of his beloved city, the sounds indeed of the whole of Italy.

WINTER
1501–1502

There is no outrage or crime that is not openly practiced in the Vatican Palace. The Borgia Pope is an abyss of vice, a subverter of all justice. . . . All fear him and his son Cesare, who from being a cardinal has made himself into an assassin and at whose orders men are killed, thrown into the Tiber and despoiled of all possessions.

—Anonymous letter circulated in Rome
December 1501

CHAPTER 1

❖

*I*t is late afternoon and papal galleys are becalmed under a scrubbed blue sky. They had left Piombino with the dawn, pushed on by a temperamental wind that changed its mind too often for comfort, until it deserted them entirely, leaving them to drift like dreamers rocked on a gentle sea. To starboard, the Tuscan coast is a thick charcoal line on the horizon. The two vessels are separated by a hundred yards, Pope Alexander behind, Cesare, Duke Valentine, in front.

Despite the cold, Alexander, swaddled in furs on deck, is greatly enjoying himself. A magnificent trip this has been, a pope embraced by his people, from hermit monks with stinking breath to hosts of pretty women eager to kiss his robes and hang on his every word. He could happily have stayed longer, but Cesare, as ever, is pushing the pace. Alexander would relish another sunset over the water, though it could scarcely rival the one that had accompanied them into Piombino harbor five days before. Despite a lifetime in ill-lit rooms thrashing out Church politics, this bear of a man still has wonder in him when it comes to nature and had watched entranced as the sun descended slowly into the sea, like a giant red-hot metal disc pulled by some powerful lodestone beneath the surface. Such delight he had felt at his own flourish of poetry! He should leave Rome more often. Even the Prince of Christendom deserves a little leisure amid the burden of work.

On the galley in front, Cesare is less even-tempered. Italy's most feared warrior is not at his best on water. When the weather is benign he is uncomfortable with the infinity of emptiness, and when the wind rises, slicing the sea and making the deck lurch beneath his feet, his stomach lurches with it. To be at the mercy of his own gut is a humiliation that can easily shade into aggression. What he needs is a little danger to get his nerves singing louder than his innards.

He crosses to the port deck, where the captain is standing, studying the western sky. He places himself next to the man, bracing his legs and resting one hand on the rail in unconscious imitation. "What do you see out there?"

"Nothing, my lord. Only weather." Burned bronze with a bush of black curls, the man looks as if he has been hewn out of a trunk of Indian ebony. If it wasn't for the papal insignia on his back, one might take him for some kind of infidel.

"What weather? There is none. If it stays this calm we will be stranded here all night. Why aren't we using the oars still?"

"The oarsmen are tired. They need a rest," the captain says, his eyes never wavering from the horizon.

The air is still, not even a hint of breeze. Apart from the lazy slap of water against wood, it feels as if the world has stopped moving. Cesare falls silent, squinting out into an endless nothing. His only experience of such stillness is the anticipation on a battlefield before the first cannons are fired. Could it be that there are sails somewhere out there, just beyond his eye's reach? Is that what the captain is seeing?

These last days his thoughts have been running on piracy. Stories of how the citizens of his new state of Piombino and the island of Elba live in constant fear of attack from infidels, descending out of a clear sea, overrunning villages, slaughtering the men and carrying the screaming women and children back to their ships. Years later one might hear of children taken in this manner coming up for sale at the slave market in Venice and finding their way into a house where, through the mist of time, they would recognize the lilt of a mother's lullaby or words of the Lord's Prayer, though by then they worship only heathen gods. At this point in the retelling, his father's eyes had been glistening with pity. Cesare, in contrast, had been boiling with fantasies of revenge.

My God, how he would like to take them on. To slice open their pagan Turkish bellies and set fire to their sails halfway to Constantinople. If their galleys were to appear on the horizon now, they would see what even a handful of Christian warriors could do. He has already studied the guns mounted on the hull, knows their range and capacity, and has quizzed the crewmen on the business of aiming over water. He would like to see the damage done when a cannonball rips through a wooden hull. Had not his namesake Caesar taken on a whole Egyptian fleet and sunk it into the depths? Or was that Emperor Augustus? Recently his grasp of history is becoming blurred inside the accelerated creation of his own myth.

"Do pirates sail this far south?"

"We are in no danger, Duke Valentine. The papal galleys are built to outrun anything on the sea if the men put their backs to it."

"We wouldn't stand and fight?"

"No."

"Afraid of a few infidels?"

"Fear is not the issue, my lord," he says evenly. A ship's captain shares command with no one, and he is finding it hard to conceal his dislike for this young papal bastard who thinks he knows better than everyone around him. "It is the value of the cargo we are carrying."

A cockroach skids across the boards close to their feet. Cesare, an expert at detecting criticism in compliment, stamps fast, relishing the crunch.

"Why don't you steer closer to the shore and launch the rowing boat? Corvetto can't be far away. My men and I could be back in Rome by morning."

"It is not safe, my lord. The coast here has hidden reefs. The boat could be blown onto them."

"By what? The sea's as flat as a nun's chest."

"Now, yes," the captain says, his attention also on the deck and the sight of a second cockroach scuttling wildly. "But in these waters it can change without warning." Behind it comes another, and another.

"Your vermin have good sea legs," Cesare says angrily as his boot comes down again. "Or maybe they too are bored with waiting."

The captain, ignoring the insult, lifts his eyes back to the horizon and moves off quickly down the boat.

Has he sensed it already, this man who knows the sea better than the body of a best-loved mistress? What is it? A certain tang in the air? A muscle movement of water in the distance? Or perhaps the cockroaches have told him, for God often gives unexpected gifts to His most despised creations.

Whatever it is, he knows they will not outrun it on the manpower of these oarsmen. He has never seen such a scrawny bunch of galley slaves. He sends a message to the sailor in the crow's nest to unfurl a flag requesting that the Pope's boat make up speed to join them. It would be safer if the two vessels were closer together.

Alexander registers the jolt as the oars start dipping and pulling at the water. He has been halfway across Italy in his thoughts, traveling with his daughter as she moves from town to town, her smile seducing everyone she meets. His sweet Lucrezia. It has been only a few weeks since they took leave of each other, but already her absence is a wound inside him. My God, her husband had better appreciate her or he will send an army to get her back.

The galley is picking up speed, and he turns to watch the oarsmen at work. From the raised deck he can make out their bowed heads and shoulders, hear their grunts, almost feel the stretch and heave of muscle and sinew. The fleet had been in dry dock when the late decision was taken to do part of the journey to and from Piombino by boat (Cesare's whim as ever), and his Master of Ceremonies had spent hours fretting about having to pull men from Rome's prisons to make up the bulk of the labor. Poor creatures. Even criminals who serve their Pope deserve to keep their arms in their sockets, he thinks. I shall bless them all when the trip is over. He, who would stitch up a dozen cardinals if he could bleed more money out of them, has always had a soft spot for those manifestly weaker than himself.

But it is not the moment to dwell on tender feelings. A slap of wind on his cheek pulls his eyes toward the horizon. In the west, where once there had been a spotless sky, a glowering band of cloud is now rising, heavy with rain. It is moving rapidly, lifting, spreading, darkening, so that even as he watches the low winter sun is swallowed up inside it. The temperature is dropping and the water is now an iron gray, the surface whipped up into flurries by the worsening wind. As the agitation grows the galley starts to roll under his feet. He braces himself against the rails. How fast the change! It is as if Neptune has filled his giant cheeks, and with one enormous breath is blowing a fully formed storm over the rim of the world.

His chaplains are already at his side, hurrying him toward the deckhouse as the first raindrops hit, fat as bird shit, soaking everything they touch. Above their heads a jagged line of lightning slices the sky. He grips the rail tighter. He is a man who knows about storms at sea and the havoc they can wreak. On a journey back from Spain as papal legate twenty—no, surely it must be thirty—years ago now, his fleet had been not far from this same coast when the water had started to rise and hiss and he had watched helplessly as his companion galley was blown toward shore only to be smashed like a bunch of kindling twigs on a submerged reef of rocks. For months afterward in his dreams he could hear the sound of the wind mixed with the screams of drowning men. The Lord had gained a brace of churchmen and courtiers that day, may their souls rest in peace. He can still recite most of their names and see a few of their faces. God damn Cesare's impatience, he thinks. It is the disease of youth to mistake speed for strategy. They should have stayed in Piombino for another day rather than giving in to his insistence on returning to Rome.

"Get your men under cover." On the boat in front the captain shouts to Cesare as he moves past him to reach the wheelhouse. "I need the deck clear for the crew."

"I told you we should have used the oars! We could have been halfway to Rome by now," Cesare spits back, the mast above them creaking under the whip of the wind. "How long will it last?"

"As long as the Lord decrees," the captain mutters, making a rapid sign of the cross as he turns in to the force of the gale.

• • •

In her room in the ducal palace of Urbino, Lucrezia's feet hurt. When she walks her soles burn and when her toes are released at night they still feel pinioned together. The pain is more than the bondage of fashion; her wedding dowry shoes, twenty-seven pairs of the finest perfumed Spanish leather made from a template of her feet, each one hand-sewn, gilded, jeweled, perfumed and shipped from Valencia, had arrived too late to be fitted and tested before they were used.

It would be better if she did not dance so much. But how can she resist? She, who loves to glide and twirl and skip through feasts and celebrations night after night, so applauded that after a while her partners fall away, clutching feigned stitches in their sides, to show off her grace and stamina. No, Lucrezia Borgia must dance; it is one of the joys of her life. And more than that, it is what is expected of her.

Perhaps if there were fewer miles between festivities. In the twelve days since they left Rome they have visited almost as many towns and are still only halfway to Ferrara. It would be a punishing schedule even in the best weather, for this is not so much a journey as a campaign trail, the Pope's daughter conquering city after city with charm rather than cannons. In the beginning, she had wrapped herself in furs and battled the freezing air. Those first days it had been snowing—snow in Rome!—and she had been amazed how people flocked out to see her. She had waved and smiled and smiled again. If they could brave the weather then surely so could she. But the snow turned into heavy rain and ugly sucking mud, so that recently she has retreated to her litter. It is comfortable enough on the open roads, but when it comes to the slopes of the Apennines and towns like Gubbio and now Urbino, the steep winding paths have her lurching and jostled until her bones have started to protest.

She settles herself into the cushioned window seat in this latest bedchamber. There is a fire in the grate and tapestries on the walls. How delicious to be warm again. Outside, she hears the traffic of chests pulled along flagstone floors. It takes an age to settle the household of courtiers and servants who travel with her. Tonight's accommodation is particularly magnificent. The palace of Urbino is famed through Italy as a treasure-house of the new culture. They will have precious little time to appreciate it, she thinks with a small sigh. The trunks will barely have been opened before they must be packed up and loaded again, and this evening will merge into all the others, an orgy of goodwill and gifts, bowing, kissing, sweet words, compliments and of course dancing. Her feet sing out in sympathy. She longs for a day when she can sleep later than the dawn, or pass a few hours reading or washing her hair; the chance to be alone, sullen, even sad for a while.

Above the marble fireplace is a sculptured frieze of naked cherubs, parading joyfully, clutching golden horns and tambourines. The miracle of chubby flesh hewn out of stone. Before she gave birth to Rodrigo she barely noticed such creatures. Now she sees babies and cherubs everywhere. The sculptor must have had boy children of his own to breathe such individual life into each body. She imagines one of them clambering onto her lap, fat little arms thrown around her neck. The marble skin grows soft and warm in her mind. She bends her head involuntarily to smell the perfume of his scalp, such a mass of fair curls already, so different from the dark hair of his father.

"Madonna Lucrezia? Do I disturb?"

"No, no, Signor Pozzi," she says, brushing the imagined little body off her skirts as she regains her composure. "I am savoring my surroundings. I still don't understand why we can't stay longer. The Duke and Duchess of Urbino are so magnanimous in their hospitality, moving out of their own palace to make room for us. It seems impolite to remain for only one night."

The Ferrarese envoy shuffles his feet. This is a conversation he had hoped was over.

"My lady, I assure you they understand very well the constraints that the journey and the weather put upon us. We have a great many miles to travel to Ferrara and the date of your marriage is—"

"Oh, I know the date as well as you. It is engraved upon my heart and I would give anything for it to have arrived already, as I am in a fever of expectation to meet my dear husband." And it is said so prettily that who could doubt its sincerity? "But." She pauses. "If I am to please him in the way I would wish, then I must be allowed to catch my breath."

Born Gian Luca Pozzi, this seasoned diplomat is known to everyone in the Borgia entourage as Stilts, because his legs are unnaturally long for his body so that when he walks he must take stilty little steps to allow the ladies to keep up with him. He has been at Lucrezia's side for months, sending back reports to his master, the Duke of Ferrara, on her character and worthiness for marriage into the House of Este. Now it is his job to get her to the wedding ceremony on time.

"Also, not only is Urbino joined in dynastic marriage to my new home in Ferrara," she continues with a pointed seriousness, "but it is in alliance with His Holiness Pope Alexander. I think both of my fathers would see it as politic for us to enjoy more of the city's welcome, wouldn't you agree?"

The envoy munches at his cheek. When the Pope is brought into play, it is always a sign that this delicate young woman, who often appears to have no thought in her head past the choice of her next outfit, is digging in her heels. Outside, the rain is a percussion of nervous drumbeats against the leaded windows. Urbino is famous for its modernity, and not all her rooms have been so finely protected against drafts.

Throughout the palace there is an air of people shaking out their wet clothes and settling in to stay.

"My dear lady, you must help me here. I—"

"And"—her voice remains sweet despite the rise in volume—"you will have noticed that a few of my ladies are at war with phlegm and fever. This morning Angela was almost too sick to travel. If she should pass such an ailment on to me . . . well . . . Duke Ercole, my new father, would never forgive you if I arrived in Ferrara weak as a kitten."

Pozzi smiles bleakly. His employer will forgive him even less if she gets there late, since the astrologers singled out the date six months ago and half of Italy is on the move to be there in time. As for Madonna Lucrezia's health, there are things he could suggest: she could dance less and sleep more, or cut down the time spent on her daily toilette. But there would be no point. The Pope has made it clear to all that having paid a fortune to marry off his daughter, he intends to gets his money's worth, using this journey as a way to show her off.

Not that she will disappoint. Of that he is sure. There may be more beautiful women in Italy, but there is something in the mix of grace and vivacity, especially when she is on the dance floor, where her feet seem barely to touch the ground, that seduces whoever is in her orbit.

Like many others, he had arrived at the Vatican court, his ears ringing with gossip, expecting to find some vain vixen, racked by lust and cruelty. Yet within weeks his dispatches were filled with descriptions of her sweetness and modesty. It has taken him a little longer to come upon the metal under the softness. But then it has been years since the state of Ferrara had its own duchess, and it's possible he has forgotten the subterfuge of clever women, how stubborn their gentleness can be. If the lady will not be moved, then what can be done? He lifts his hands in submission.

"Excellent." She laughs, victory lighting up her face and making her look younger than her twenty-one years. "We shall leave the day after tomorrow well rested. My brother's emissaries will guide us through his cities to Bologna and from there we can travel by barge. Which will be kinder to all of us and"—a hint of the coquette now—"once I am caught on your glorious river Po, well, I shall not be able to get off. Isn't that right, my dear Pozzi?"

He bows, his smile as professional as his frown. Tonight's dispatch is already written in his head: in battles of diplomacy no skirmish is too small to fight and no defeat so big as to mean the loss of the war.

He is barely out of the door before she is on her feet calling to her ladies. "Angela, Nicola, Camilla. . . . Leave the unpacking. The palace of Urbino is waiting for us!"

◆ ◆ ◆

Off the Tuscan coast, both galleys are now playthings of the storm, though the Pope's ship, farther out to sea, is taking the brunt. The rain is a sheet of water driven horizontally by the gale, with waves rising high as a fortress wall so that as each one hits it is impossible to tell freshwater from brine. The vessel is equally confused, one moment pushing forward, climbing up a cliff of water to a crest, where it seems to stop like a gasped breath before crashing down with a force that feels each time as if it must shatter the hull. Then everything shifts and suddenly the boat is yawing and what is not nailed down yaws with it, careering from port to starboard and back again. The deck is a death trap; any man losing his footing will save himself only when he slams into something nailed down, and unless his grip is iron tight he will be ripped up by the next wave and thrown into the sea. In the stern, the oarsmen are lying flat, their oars tied under their bodies; in such violence any untethered object becomes a battering ram or a flying club.

The crew, who earn free liquor onshore by telling shipwreck stories that have landlubbers' eyes popping out of their heads, are paying dearly for every embellishment uttered. Each lashing, smashing wave brings another emergency: a shred of canvas, yanked from the furled sail, a bucked timber, more bailing as the galleys take on yet more water. It is an old torture, sticking a man in a prison pit where the water never stops rising so that the only way to survive is to keep on pumping. In their nightmares they will be bailing water for years to come. As the next wave hits, a few start to wail and cry out, their voices barely heard against the mad shrieking of the wind and the snarls and groans of splintering wood. The storm is discordant with its own orchestra of suffering.

And in the midst of it all, inside the deckhouse, the Holy Pontiff of Rome, vicar of all Christian souls on earth, wedged in his chair, encased in furs, is singing psalms loudly.

Fortune, a wayward goddess at her best, is at her most capricious at such moments. When events spin out of control she will happily abandon men who daily practice only unfailing kindness and virtue. Equally, she takes perverse pleasure in protecting those who, merciless in life, show a natural magnificence when the dragon roars in their faces. Rodrigo Borgia has always been such a man. Faced by enemy guns outside of Rome, he opened the gates and invited them in. When a thunderbolt split a chimney in the Vatican, pulling a ceiling down on his head, and the palace went mad bewailing the death of the Pope, he had sat calmly under a mountain of rubble until they pulled him out unscathed, saved by a miraculous conjunction of two fallen rafters that had locked a few inches above his head. His beatific smile as he emerged had been something to see.

He is lucky in another way too: inside that cart horse body sits the stomach of a merman. So while others are emptying their guts onto the cabin floor, it is now, with the storm at its height, that he sees fit to take himself out on deck.

Inside the howling rain, Cesare's galley is nowhere to be seen. Still, Alexander is sure it is out there, somewhere close. For so many years he has been working for this moment of his life: the founding of a Borgia state in Italy through the muscle of his son and the loins of his daughter. They have come too far and are too close for it to end here. He would never feel such calm if at this moment Cesare was sinking under the waves. Not even the most righteous God would be that cruel.

The captain, lashed to the wheel, sees the outline of the papal bulk in the rain, and starts yelling and gesticulating for him to go back inside. But Alexander, flanked by two chaplains, only lifts his hand in blessing. Two nearby sailors register his presence, and in the lull before the next wave hits, they throw themselves at his feet, burying their faces in the wet silk of his hem, crying out for him to save them with his prayers. He gestures for the chaplains to raise them up and blesses them individually, taking their sodden bodies into a deep embrace, like a father to his sons.

As the next blinding wall of water hits, the chaplains use their own weight to pin the Pope against the deckhouse to shield him from the worst. When they see him emerge from the soaking still standing, other sailors start calling out in prayer.

"Do not fear, my sons," he bellows into the wind. "The Lord shows the violent Majesty of His work to those He loves most. You have His greatest servant on board and He will not let you down."

They can barely make out a word he is saying, but the fact that he is there at all is a thing of wonder. Sailors know the scriptures of the sea better than any man: Jonah given shelter in the body of a whale, Moses parting the waves with his hands, and the Lord himself, choosing only fishermen to follow him, calming troubled waters and walking upon the sea as if it were the land.

The Lord is my rock, my fortress, and my deliverer.

The Pope bellows out the words of the Eighteenth Psalm.

In my distress I called upon the Lord.

His chaplains' practiced voices braid together with his, and for a moment the sound seems to find a pathway through the gale. Or could it be that the force of the wind is dipping just a little?

To my God I cried for help
From his temple he heard my voice.

The next waves soak, but the punch they deliver seems less angry. A few of the sailors who recognize the words of the psalm start yelling them out in wavering voices; even the captain himself calls into the wind.

> *The Lord reached down from on high, and He took me.*
>   *He drew me out of many waters.*

There is no question: the force of the rain is lessening and the boat is holding her own inside the waves.

> *He drew me out of many waters.*

The worst—and it is surely a miracle—is over.

• • •

Lucrezia and her ladies move through the palace like a flock of multicolored birds. If any of them were sick they have made a miraculous recovery. An extra day! Such a victory their mistress has achieved over the stuffy Stilts. They wheel up and down marble staircases, through dozens of elegant, connected salons. In one they sit cheek to cheek with gargoyle faces carved into stone seats. In another they sigh over portraits of female saints and martyrs, so exquisitely dressed that it makes them think of fashion rather than sacrifice. In a third they stand transfixed before a painting of a fabulous new city, perfect in its pristine architecture and proportions. What is Stilts always saying about Ferrara? How the old duke has built a whole other town in the modern style. "Imagine living in such a place, my lady duchess! We could dust the marble streets with our skirts!"

And they all laugh, for they are experts in enthusiasm. These pretty women are all that is left now of Lucrezia's life in Rome. Exiled together, they have been picked for their youth and gaiety along with their loyalty and breeding. Some have grown up with her, seeing her through times of joy as well as sorrow; others were freshly recruited to mark this new turn in her life. They are her bodyguard against homesickness, and they take their work as seriously as any armed cohort. A few rooms later, when they come upon a painting of the Virgin mother holding a Christ child, his faraway gaze older than his baby flesh, they watch her carefully. Is the shine in her eyes an appreciation of beauty or the on-slaught of memory?

"My lady, my lady. Come! Come over here. Isn't this the ugliest man you have ever seen?" Angela Borgia, distant cousin by birth, is the new-est and most mischievous of the flock. At fifteen what does she know of the vicissitudes of life? "I'd run a mile if he came anywhere near me!"

"Hush." Lucrezia smiles. She knows how alert they are to any sign of sorrow. It is why, sometimes, she chooses to be alone. "That is a painting of our host's dead father and his duchess."

"Well, whoever he is, he is still uglier than sin. See how she insists on being separated from him, even in paint."

The profiles of husband and wife stare coldly out at each other from a divided frame: her face as ordinary as countless other women of her age, his a study in hideousness: squashed and misshapen, with a jutting chin, a bulging fish eye and a viciously beaked nose, which looks as if someone has hacked a wedge out of the bridge. Since court artists are employed to flatter, the honesty of this ugliness makes it almost shocking.

"Oh, but you are right, my lady," Angela squeals. "I see the family resemblance now! Think about the present Duke Urbino. His chin would come into a room well before him if he stood upright enough to carry it. He's like . . . like a walking question mark!"

"And you know what everyone says: how that is not his only ail-ment?" another adds darkly.

"And what exactly does *everyone* say, Camilla?"

The women exchange hasty glances. They recognize their mistress's high tone, but raised in the cesspit of Rome, where gossip is as normal as breathing, they simply cannot help themselves.

"That the Duke of Urbino can't do it!" Angela jumps in with a theat-rical whisper. "He is a gelded goat. Isn't that right?" She turns to her companions eagerly; this tasty morsel is new and it is best to be sure of its veracity.

"Yes, no, it's true, my lady."

And now they all pile in.

"Though that doesn't stop him trying."

"Apparently his wife never knows when it's going to happen, and she has to fight him off, because he jumps on her like a dog."

"Sometimes he even tries to hump her leg."

"No! Drusilla, Camilla, Angela! All of you." Lucrezia struggles to keep her face stern as she puts her hands over her ears. She has been too much the victim of outrageous slander to believe every rumor that floats in the air. "Our host the duke is a fine man, and his wife, Elisabetta, an even finer woman, cultivated and modest. We are guests in their home and I will hear no more of this."

Still, once it has been said, how can she ever look at Elisabetta in the same way, her or her question mark husband? Such is the greasy slide from rumor into fact.

She detaches herself from the group and makes her way into the next chamber, where a set of elegant windows is lit by the setting sun. She pushes open an intricately leaded frame. It is high up here and the drop to the valley floor is breathtaking. The greatest marvel of the palace of Urbino is how it could have been built at all. That had been her first thought as she glimpsed it from the road: how it seemed to sprout out of sheer rock, its dazzling white façade decorated by two delicate Byzantine towers soaring up toward the heavens. Looking down, she sees the very same path they traveled, like a length of grubby cord winding through the valley floor. Anyone standing here now could spot an invading force twenty, even thirty miles away.

She thinks of Cesare and his reputation for war, how his cannons have blown apart seemingly impregnable fortresses to take half a dozen cities north of here. His military success is the only reason she is here at all. Though she might carry with her a dowry to make a sultan's eyes water, that alone would never have "persuaded" the Duke of Ferrara, head of the ancient family of Este, to marry his son and heir, Alfonso, to the twice-married and gossip-stained bastard daughter of a pope. No. It is fear of her violent brother that twisted his arm. The alliance is a triumph for the Borgias, another building block in the formation of a dynasty. What had it mattered to him if it had been bought at the price of the murder of her adored last husband?

Alfonso: it is a particular cruelty of fate that Lucrezia's new husband has the same name as her old one. Except that *her* Alfonso will never be old. She might live until she drowns in fat or shrink till her skull shows through her skin, but her Alfonso will always be young and lovely: the dancer's leg, the smooth chiseled face and those extraordinary blue eyes, like chips of polished lapis lazuli.

The drop grows vertiginous beneath her and she has to steady herself by holding on to the window ledge.

"No, Lucrezia," she murmurs under her breath. "This is not the time . . ."

But it is too late. She is back there again, hearing the howling inside her ears as she stands in front of her brother, a cohort of armed men at his back as he tells her how the death was necessary, how his own safety had been threatened by a plot against his life! Coward! Liar! At the time she had met his deceit with ice rather than fire, but standing here now she has a different image of her grief, seeing it as a raging wind, sucking him up, lifting him across the room, smashing him through the windows and hurling him into a fire-spitting vortex, one of the circles of hell made flesh by Dante's violent poetry.

Only what then? What would that mean for her? To be a woman without a husband or a brother. A shiver runs through her.

"I am fine," she says quickly, registering the touch of Angela's hand on her arm. "The view made me dizzy for a moment, that's all. Come, it is time to get ready."

And it is true. She is fine. Within a few weeks she will be duchess of one of Italy's most cultured cities, for though the old duke still lives, with his wife dead the title will be hers. She will have a court of her own filled with musicians and poets, and though she will not command an army or breach any walls, she will wage another kind of warfare: one that needs no deaths to take prisoners. As she will do tonight when she laughs and dances, watching everyone in Urbino melt under the warmth of her charm.

What? Do men like Stilts really believe that full skirts mean empty heads? He should have been with her in the Vatican when the Pope was away and she was left in charge of domestic business, or looked over her shoulder as she read petitions and court cases put before her as governor of Spoleto and Narni. If diplomacy is war without weapons, why shouldn't women play as well as men? Her father has never been so shortsighted. They both know that Urbino and the papacy have had their disagreements in the past; indeed they had discussed it before she left: how this visit would be an opportunity to show the connection between them. And now she has gained an extra day, she will do whatever she can to forward the cause.

No, brother, she says to herself as she turns from the window. *You are not the only one who can take cities.*

• • •

Cesare, who has never had any patience when it comes to waiting for divine intervention, is fighting nausea with fury. There is no time for this; in Rome there are dispatches waiting to be read: news of his sister's progress, offers of arms and men for sale, informants to squeeze for information. Yet here they are penned like pigs squealing in fear of the butcher's knife. Damn to hell this captain and his superior airs.

He glances round the cramped cabin. Like his father, he keeps only a few men close: Spaniards from old families schooled in loyalty and soldiering. They would give up their lives for him without question, though at this moment they are more worried about losing the contents of their stomachs. No time for prayers here, only the sound of retching and swearing.

Only Miguel de Corella, the duke's bodyguard, sits unperturbed. His face is an artwork of scars carved by someone who didn't live long enough to see the blood dry. Had it been five or six of them he had dispatched that day? The number grows with each retelling. Though not by him. Michelotto, as he is known, does not bother with stories. He is already a legend: a man who has disciplined himself to be free from all vanities of self, his mind and body absorbed only in the service of his master. In another life, with another God, he would have made the most impressive monk, withstanding pain, thriving on physical hardship, rejecting all temptation and holding to the commandments with the same fervor with which he now breaks them. If Cesare Borgia has any confidant, then this man is it.

He is aware of the duke's fury and frustration, knows exactly what he is thinking. The violence of the swell is calming and the thunder of the rain against the wood dying away. He catches Cesare's eye, nodding in acknowledgment of what he knows is to come.

"God's blood, I cannot be the only one who has had enough of this." Cesare's voice is strong and clear as he gets to his feet. "Are there any here who cannot swim?"

To the left of Michelotto a hand starts to rise, then sensing its isolation comes firmly down again.

"Good." The duke grins. "Then tonight we will sleep on featherbeds."

• • •

"The blue silk, I think, with the cap of pearls." Back in her room, Lucrezia runs over the two outfits laid across the chest. "The slashes in the sleeves show well on the dance floor."

Tonight, as always, the festivities will include envoys and spies from all over the country, their mission to note her every gesture and to price each piece of jewelry, every yard of cloth for their dispatches home. This outrageously rich dowry that she brings offers an easy excuse for envy and spite, and there have been moments when she has misjudged the level of ostentation necessary to impress, when the number of precious stones resting on her skin or sewn into her skirts has made it hard for people to see the sincerity in her eyes. But she has learned fast.

"I think the gold would be more fitting to the occasion, my lady."

"Perhaps, but I wore it already in Rome. Imagine the pleasure it would give my new sister-in-law to read *that* in her man's dispatch."

He is the worst of them: masquerading as a hanger-on in someone else's entourage, but in reality the ears and eyes of Isabella d'Este-Gonzaga, the Marchesa of Mantua. Everyone knows what a gorgon she is in matters of fashion and that she is outraged at this marriage of a scandal-soaked bastard daughter to her most noble brother. From the beginning, this tubby little diplomat spy of hers had attached himself to Lucrezia like a traveling burr, obsessed by every outfit, counting each jewel however big or small and noting them down in a small book he keeps chained at his side. His diligence has made him a laughingstock, but he fears his mistress more than mockery.

"You should have seen his eyes bulge when I told him the number of pearls, diamonds and rubies in your crimson cloak. He'd already gone half blind trying to count them."

Thank God for Donna Angela's youthful flashing smile. These last weeks she has gone out of her way to befriend him, flirting and gossiping and using the intimacy created to feed him inner circle information on the wealth and styles yet to come. This contest can be played both ways, and one would not want the marchesa to underestimate the sartorial challenge on offer here.

"I told him I only knew the exact figure because it was my job to count them every time you wore it to check if any had fallen off in the journey. I swear he believes every word I utter."

In return the man has let a few secrets slip himself. Somewhere in the ducal palace in Mantua a team of Illyrian women, experts in embroidery and gold threading, has been locked in for the best part of two months to ensure that the work gets done on time. What Lucrezia wouldn't give to know the styles and fabrics they have chosen. Well, that is tomorrow's battle. For now it is Urbino that must be taken.

Once she is dressed, her bedchamber servants move hand mirrors in a slow dance around her head to check her hair: a labyrinth of swirls and curls piled up under a pearled cap showing off the delicate shape of her ears. Her rib cage feels squeezed beneath the fitted bodice. She takes a few breaths to judge its pull.

"The seamstress has put in extra stitches, my lady."

Catrinella, black as night with fresh fruit lips and sharp white teeth, is newly made head of the bedchamber for this journey and is intensely proud of the promotion. How she has grown! Lucrezia thinks. She had been a child slave when she arrived in the Borgia house, purchased as a fashion accessory for Lucrezia's first marriage. She can still see the girl, wedding train in her hands, the dark of her skin against the white silk making a wondrous contrast in a sea of color. And always her fierce little face, determined to get everything right.

"You have lost weight these last weeks, my lady. Everyone says you must eat more tonight or the dancing will fatigue you," she says, clicking her tongue in motherly fashion. Fluent now in Italian and two dialects of Spanish, as well as the language of fashion, she offers loyalty that is boundless and unshakable.

"That's as may be. But I must also still be able to breathe."

Lucrezia lifts up her pale blue skirts and underpetticoats to reveal a set of well-turned ankles. Tonight she will flirt carefully with the duke, while being ever aware that she does not overwhelm the duchess. And then, because his bent back means he does not choose to dance, she will dance for him, a modest Salome with no motive other than to bring him courtly pleasure.

One last thing. Catrinella, crouched at her feet now, holds two gilt leather shoes in her hands.

"Oh, no, not another new pair," she groans. "I will wear yesterday's again."

"You can't, my lady. They had mud stains on them and are still wet from the swabbing. We have stretched these as best we can on the wooden foot."

Not far enough. Her toes sing out in protest as the leather bites.

The earnest shining face looks up at her. "After the first few passes you will barely notice them."

She laughs, because she knows it is true.

• • •

"In God's name what are they doing?"

The storm may be over, but the Pope's good humor is draining fast as through the lifting cloud he watches Cesare's galley, its sail now hoisted to catch the remaining wind, heading directly toward the coast.

"Your Holiness, you are wet to the skin. You must come inside and let us warm you."

But Alexander is not going anywhere. "Sweet Mary, look. Look! They are heading toward land! Don't they know there are reefs all along this coast? If they go too far in they risk running aground."

Smashed like a bunch of kindling twigs. That was how it had been: a brace of churchmen and courtiers sucked under the sea, their bodies spat out along a beach with their chests of costumes and silver chalices strewn around them. And all he and his fellow travelers could do was watch it happen: the same coast, the same treacherous waters. God would not deliver such a blow now, surely.

"Bring the captain! We must stop them. Don't they know how perilous it is?"

"The commander is an experienced sailor, Your Holiness." The captain has been asking himself the same question from his position at the wheel. "He must be going toward the shore in order to launch the rowing boat."

The Pope yanks his sodden cap farther down on his head. "But! But that is hardly less dangerous! What in God's name would make him do that?"

"I would suggest an order from Duke Valentine, Holy Father," the captain says evenly. "You will remember how keen the duke was to get back to Rome. If the rowing boat makes land and they find horses, Corvetto is not far away."

An order from the duke. The words have an appalling plausibility to them. The Pope grips the rails tighter and lets out a groan. What does it matter if he can help bring a ship through chaos, if he cannot get his own son to obey him?

"Can we stop them?"

"There is too much distance between us. By the time we get there the boat will already be launched."

"Just how dangerous is it?" Alexander says quietly.

"If the storm is past and the men are strong at the oars . . ."

If. Such a small word. *If* the last hour had seen them take on more water, *if* the main mast had shattered rather than splintered under the strain. The sea is a mistress fluent in ifs. . . . Yet they are still here now to count the ways.

"I am sure they will make land safely, Your Holiness."

But Alexander too is thinking about what is, against what might have been. Such a long journey it has been since he was witness to that shipwreck so many years before. Success, wealth, influence, the papacy, the foundation of a dynasty, and now the Borgia name in charge of a string of city-states with the promise of more. So much achieved. Yet so much still to do. However powerful he is, he cannot do it alone. He has already lost one son to the stupidity of vanity. This is not a time to lose another. He lets his chaplains lead him inside. After the showmanship of the storm he is in need of private prayer.

The rowing boat hits the sea with a violent splash, taking in buckets of water as it rights itself. The drop from the bulwark rail is sheer, the hull a moving cliff face on one side. The rope ladder bangs frantically against the wood. Cesare, stripped down to a shirt and jerkin with a rope around his middle, stands stock-still, waiting for the moment, two of the boat's strongest galley men poised to climb next, Michelotto and his own men behind. All signs of nausea are lost in the flood of excitement. His mind is as sharp as a blade, his senses singing. Death, when it comes, will feel this clear, this sweet and shining. He knows it. What is there to be afraid of?

He pulls himself over to the top and onto the ladder. He is barely three rungs down when the galley lurches wildly, flinging him off and slamming him back against the hull. He rights himself fast, oblivious to the pain in his ribs, then pushes off against the wood with his feet, using the rope as a lever to bounce his way down until he hits the boat beneath, falling among the oars and laughing manically.

"It's just like breaking horses," he yells triumphantly, steadying himself against the side as the next wave hits. "Come on."

On deck the captain watches as the men follow, whooping and yelling to drown out their fear. He has done what he could for the safety of his "cargo," explaining the risks, exerting what command he had left. But the alternative had been made very clear to him.

"I would see it as a promise rather than a threat." Michelotto's smile was so thin it could have been another scar across his face. "The Pope loves his son most dearly and would have no mercy with anyone who tries to oppose him."

When choice is no choice, a man must pick the one that does least damage—and what captain would want to return to his own galley shackled to the rowing bench?

"Get the duke to shore alive and you will be free men," he had said as he unshackled his two strongest oarsmen. "Fail and you might as well walk back into the sea."

As for himself, he knows he will not command another galley. If they succeed, the duke will ruin him for his intransigence, and if they don't, well, the oarsmen will have a sweeter death than his.

The devil take this Borgia pope and his godless offspring, he thinks as another thrust of lightning rips through the sky above them all.

CHAPTER 2

❖

*T*he devil take this Borgia pope and his godless offspring.

The captain's thoughts reflect a popular sentiment over much of Italy these days. Though not everywhere and not with everyone.

In years to come as the coral sediment of history builds and calcifies it will be heresy even to suggest it, but there are places here and people now for whom Borgia rule is welcome, even celebrated. In the papal cities of Imola, Forlì, Faenza, Cesena, Pesaro, Rimini, a set of urban jewels strung out along the great Roman road of Via Emilia that mark part of Lucrezia's journey, war-weary citizens have watched security grow from chaos.

Before the dark prince, no man could move a cart of produce from one village to another without losing part of it—or his own body—to brigands; now it is the robbers who are strung up as fresh food for carrion crows beside the road. The journeys do less damage to the carts and wheels because along the carriageways between the cities' potholes are being filled, broken bridges repaired and new ones planned and built. And all this without the burden of extra taxes. The cities' old rulers, having paid a tithe to the Church, had squeezed them for all they could get, but the Pope so loves his son that once he has paid for the war to win them back, he also pays for the peace to make them prosper. In the duke's chosen capital of Cesena, the cathedral, still unfinished after two hundred years, is soaring toward the sky again and each season sees another festival where the wine and food flow free courtesy of the government. A generation ago an ambitious Spanish cardinal called Rodrigo Borgia had won over the citizens of Rome with his public hospitality and largesse. Now it is his son who spreads those qualities around. Who cares if the family name is foreign, or if behind closed doors the language is Catalan and not Italian? As the people flock out to greet their new duke's lovely, gracious sister, their cheers are genuine, for they are celebrating not just her good fortune, but their own.

For her part, Lucrezia is cheerful enough; it would be churlish to be otherwise and when she is not skewered by memory she enjoys being the center of attention. She has lost count of the number of garlanded arches and choirs of young angels, hitching up their wings to keep them straight, which have welcomed her along the road.

Last night a group of children—boys as young as five or six—sang at my table. But suddenly one of them burst into tears and had to be taken away. They told me later the tailors had left a pin in his tunic and it was poking him like a little sword. Imagine that, Rodrigo!

She puts down her pen and reads back the words. She writes to him every other day, but what can you say to a child who cannot yet read? What words will he possibly understand? *Be good and listen to your nurses and your teachers, my sweetest son. This comes from your loving mother, who prays for you every day.*

But prayers will be no better at keeping her alive for him. Her son is barely two years old. What age was she when her father took her and her brothers from her mother's house? Six? Seven? Does she really remember the sound of a woman crying or did Cesare tell her that later? Just as she can't be sure, when she encounters a certain mix of frangipani perfume, if it is her mother that she smells again or some wet nurse or servant who cared for her.

Within a few years little Rodrigo will have no memory of her at all. In the end it will be better that way. She knows that. He is in the care of a family cardinal and will grow into privileged life wanting for nothing. *You're not the first nor will you be the last widow to leave a child behind in favor of a new husband,* she says to herself angrily, even though the very words themselves seem unbearable. This is how the world works and no railing and shedding of your tears will change it. What would it benefit any son to learn that his mother had died of sorrow? No, she must look to the future.

Ferrara and the wedding are only days away. Yesterday they crossed the border from her brother's cities and tomorrow they board the barge to travel through the lowland canals into the river Po. She thinks of the stories she's been told about her new home: how the land around is so rich that while others starve, the citizens of Ferrara feast on broad beans and salt cheese, and that if they have a yearning for fish all they need do is put a hand into the river and wait for the eels to slither up round their arms into the net. A living bracelet of eels! Whoever heard of such a thing?

Today they are guests of the ruling family of Bologna, who have offered their country villa to house her entourage. Last night the whole clan descended upon them, father, sons, sisters, cousins, all falling over themselves to pay tribute to the "most esteemed pope that Christendom has ever seen" and "the wondrous beauty and goodness of his daughter."

"Ha! They would like nothing better than to dance on our graves." Her father's advice before she left Rome had, as ever, been realistically sanguine. A separate briefing for every city. "Don't believe a word they say and count the rings on your fingers after they've kissed your hand. They are a tribe of lying, thieving monkeys, the lot of them."

Monkeys perhaps, though sitting at dinner watching her ladies furtively tucking their skirts under their seats to avoid the attentions of so many wandering hands, she had thought that slimy squids would be more accurate.

She pulls a new blank sheet of paper toward her. How her father will savor such a description!

Every day, my sweet child . . . he had said to her as she left. *I will have a letter from you every day with at least a few words written in your own hand to prove to me that you are well. And when that husband of yours stands in front of you for the first time, if he does not swoon with pleasure at the sight, I will send out an army straight forth to bring you back.*

And if that happens, Papà, should I ask for the monies to be returned as well?

She had kissed him sweetly on the forehead and pulled herself away from yet another last embrace, for by then there were just too many tears.

The Pope. Her father. Lucrezia is not so coddled that she does not know how others see him: this monster churchman ripe with corruption, favoring his children above God and spending his nights with a young mistress. But all she has ever known is a man so fond that his letters carry tear marks on them. Fortune may have dealt her some cruel blows, but it has also rewarded her; from birth she has been loved, no—adored—by her father and her brothers. With such a bedrock of confidence, no man can easily undermine her.

Somewhere in the palace there is the rise of women's voices, a matter of clear excitement. The babble gets closer. Outside the door she hears Angela's urgent whispering, a good deal quieter than the hushing that accompanies it. Her rest hour, when the journey allows it, is sacrosanct. Whatever this is, it can only be serious.

"I am not sleeping," she calls out. "You may come in."

The door bursts open. "Oh, madam, madam! Such news." Angela's face is a plump little heart, her eyes big as ducats. "He is here. Here right now! Standing in the hall."

"Who? Who is here?"

"Your husband! Alfonso d'Este. He has ridden all the way from Ferrara to meet you!"

"What? But . . . Why? How did he travel? Is he alone?"

"Just him and three of his men. You should see them. Like knights on a quest—covered in sweat and mud from the road. They must have ridden for hours."

"But how can I meet him? Look at me! I am not dressed. Why were we not told of this? Where is Stilts?"

"Oh, he is as amazed as we, my lady, running about like a chicken with his head off." Donna Camilla's voice thrills with the romance of it all. "It must have been the duke elect's idea and his alone. Oh, imagine how he must be longing to see you. Such things he will have heard!"

Such things; no doubt about that. But what exactly?

As they fuss over her dress and hair, she sits as calmly as she can, wondering what could possibly make him break the rules of courtship and come now. Perhaps his father has sent him to make sure that, despite an avalanche of money, the House of Este isn't being sold a pup? She may be feasted and feted across half of Italy, but she knows the viciousness of her marriage negotiations: how the naughts on the dowry had risen with each exchange of letters. At least both my eyes look in the same direction, she thinks wryly, remembering the strangeness of Giulia Farnese's wedding. The bridegroom's squint had been so bad that during the ceremony no one could be sure if he was looking at his wife or his cardinal uncle, soon to be Pope Alexander, which was a fitting confusion since everyone knew that the marriage was only a front for Giulia and Rodrigo to carry on their affair.

Lucrezia's supposed defects, however, are ones that cannot be detected from the outside. The silence as she enters a room speaks of the conversation that has just stopped. She reads the questions in the men's faces as they greet her: did she really sleep with her brother, or her father? Or poison her rivals? Or carry a child under a high-waisted dress while standing in a Church court swearing on oath that she was still a virgin? The darker the story, the more pleasure there is in imagining it. There've been moments in these last few weeks when, for the sheer mischief of it, she has wanted to bend her head and whisper that everything—*everything*—they suspect is true, just to watch their tongues hanging out. Oh yes, her new husband will have heard things about her.

She takes her seat in the receiving room close to a newly lit fire, her crocus yellow skirts spread and her hair looped inside a golden net with a few carefully careless locks falling free to her shoulders. Above a modestly scalloped bodice, she wears a single strand of milky pearls, a symbol of purity as well as wealth. How prettily their sheen shows off the paleness of her complexion.

"The next time he meets me I will be trussed up like a golden chicken," she had said as she waved away the casket of jewels. "This way at least he'll be able to see there is no defect in my neck."

She folds her hands in her lap over an open book of hours. In the end women are the harshest judges of their own beauty, and Lucrezia's hands, smooth and white as a dove's feathers, rival those of the best-painted Madonna. They would be worthy of a sonnet should her betrothed be the kind of man interested in writing one. He has come all this way to meet her. How can she not be excited?

She knows his image well enough from the painting, yet as she lifts her eyes to greet him, the difference freezes her smile. Her first thought is how large he is. The second how uncomfortable he looks. His clothes seem to have been made for someone else. No doubt they've suffered from the ride: a little straightening of his hose or brushing down the velvet nap would have helped. Such scruffiness speaks of eagerness, at least. Still, she thinks, he might have run a hand through his hair. It sits flattened to his head where the cap has been clamped on it, and while some locks flow richly over his ears, others hang lank and greasy. It's a while since a courtier has come into her presence looking so—well—so uncourtly.

Stilts and the duke's own men step backward to leave him the stage.

"Most esteemed Lady Lucrezia. You must forgive the unexpected nature of my visit. But I could wait no longer to be in your luminous presence after so many months of keen anticipation."

The contrast of frilly words spoken in a bass voice can flatter the man who delivers them as much as the woman who receives them. As long as the sentiment is sincere. Or at least spontaneous. Yet she can't help thinking that his horse might have heard this greeting before she has.

His walk is purposeful, almost athletic, and as he gets closer she registers a heavy nose and thick lips, a large square jaw, bruised with stubble. The eyes, if she could see them properly under the thicket of brows, would be brown and perhaps a little bloodshot. She knows from Stilts's enthusiastic commentary that her husband has a reputation for his achievements at the foundry, smelting metals for cannons in fires hotter than hell. Is this the remnants of soot in the pitted surface of his skin? Still her smile does not waver. There are worse-looking men in Italy. She has met a good many of them over this endless journey.

Her ladies, in fan formation behind her, sink low in curtsy. As they rise, Lucrezia motions them to withdraw into the shadows. This meeting will be as private as it is public, with a dozen witnesses who see and hear everything while appearing to note nothing. Chaperoning is a well-practiced art.

His right hand, still encased in its riding glove, is huge as it envelops hers and he bows his head toward her.

Noblewomen are early connoisseurs in the art of the courtly kiss, and over these last weeks Lucrezia has been gobbled and pecked, dribbled on and stubble-scraped, has even felt the nibble of teeth and odd teasing flash of a tongue. But this, this, she thinks, is more like a wet dog flopping down onto a hearth. As he lifts his head she takes in a lungful of sweat and leather. If perfume has been applied, it is long lost in the dust between here and Ferrara. She can feel her smile growing wider, as if unless controlled it might break into a laugh. Nerves, she thinks. But are they just her own?

"Please, my dear lord, sit and warm yourself. You must have been in the saddle for many hours."

"Not so many; five, maybe six." He sniffs a little as he lowers himself into the chair. "We left at first light and made good time."

"So fast! And they say it will take us two days by boat. How was the weather? Did you battle your way through much fog? I . . . I mean we hear that in winter—well—"

"Ferrara's famous fog, you mean," he says gruffly. "And what of Roman snow? They say it never snows in Rome, but you rode out in a blizzard."

"Indeed we did." What? He knows this? Of course, Stilts sends dispatches every day, but still she never dreamed that . . . It seems he has been following her progress. "It was . . . most strange," she says, remembering the ghostly light, as if the moon had become the sun for a day. "It was like riding through wet lace."

"Wet lace . . ." He nods. "No. We have no wet lace here. Our fog is more like cold soup. Though once you find your pace, there's nothing better than flanks of warm horseflesh between your legs."

Above his shoulder she notices Stilts's face, set unnaturally rigid as he stands pretending not to hear, and now she has to bite her tongue to stop the laugh. *Cold as a monk's gonads.* That had been her brother Juan's comment once in answer to Aunt Adriana's innocent question about the weather as he strode into the room, inducing a fit of vapors in her at his vulgarity. Which, of course, had amused him even more, for of course it was all deliberate provocation on his part. But that is surely not the case here.

"And how was my new home when you left?" she says brightly to cover up any embarrassment.

"Ferrara? In a frenzy of decoration for your arrival."

"Really. Tell me more!"

"I . . . There's not much to tell. Stages, garlands and arches everywhere . . . Anyone who stands still long enough risks being gilded and stuck on a plinth." From the edges of the room the witnesses twitter their approval at his descriptive powers, though Stilts's smile remains somewhat pained. "I am not exaggerating," he plows on, goaded by their appreciation. "There's more gilt and gold on show than in a who—" He hesitates, spotting too late the trap his enthusiasm has him galloping toward.

Lucrezia waits. What else can she do?

"—than in a—the house of a goldsmith," he finishes gallantly.

"It sounds wonderful, my lord. I am beside myself with excitement at the prospect of seeing it all at last."

"And it at seeing you," he says, with studied care this time, checking that the courtly syntax makes sense.

She looks at his huge gloved hands, the leather rough and well used. By rights, he should have taken them off by now. She clears her throat. "And my new father, the duke? He is well?"

"He was well enough last night."

"He knows that you are come?" she prompts.

He shrugs. "He will when I get back."

So it is true! This is not state business he is about. A chill runs through her. In Rome, during the protracted courtship, her father had tried to hide from her how hard the House of Este had fought against this marriage. "Over my dead body" had been the old duke's refrain. Yet his son has made this journey of his own accord. But for what? To see for himself the woman he will take to his bed?

Except that now he is here he doesn't seem that interested. Since they took their places at the fire, he has barely given her a glance.

Can he really be so oblivious to my appearance? she thinks. By now any other man would have half smothered me in compliments. She wonders briefly if she should take offense, except it doesn't feel as if any is being given. Perhaps he doesn't care, so long as she's not deformed. What is this marriage but politics? And breeding. In the end, the space between her hips will be more important than any beauty he might find in her face. . . . Still, she thinks, he will have to look at me sometimes.

She gathers herself again.

"And your sister, the Marchesa of Mantua?" she says sweetly, pulling his eyes from his lap, her brightest smile showing off a most becoming dimple in her chin. "She is arrived in the city? I am most eager to meet her too."

"Isabella? Oh, she's well settled. Along with her thirty chests of luggage," he says evenly.

"I am sure. She is famed for her wardrobe, as she is for her taste in all things," she replies, carelessly rearranging her voluminous skirts and tilting her head coquettishly to receive the return compliment. Which, amazingly, still does not come.

Oh sir, she thinks, for your own skin you would do well to take note of what I am wearing. Your sister's envoy can't get enough of each and every outfit. When she finds out where you have been today, you will be put to the inquisition.

Perhaps he is thinking the same thing, because now finally he holds the gaze.

Whatever he does or doesn't think of her, the fact is he is here of his own accord. And that is no small thing.

She gestures to a servant in the background. "I insist you take some refreshment. However fine the ride, you must be in need," she says, busying herself with the wifely business of serving him.

He grunts an assent and, carefully unbuttoning the fastenings on the gloves, strips them off, letting them fall into his lap.

As she turns with the filled goblet, it is all she can do not to cry out at the sight that greets her. Freed from the leather, his hands are still large in proportion to his body. But that is not the problem. There is something wrong with them. The fingers, thick and stubby, are covered in lacerations, like half chewed ribs of cooked flesh, while the skin from his knuckles to his wrists is equally raw. But the strangest thing is their color: a mottled purple, like the surface of rotting meat. He takes a hefty drink of the wine, then holds the goblet in his lap between his hands with no evident self-consciousness to the gesture.

She glances up at his face quickly. Whatever it is, it must be causing him pain surely? Yet there is no sign of any discomfort. Of course, she is no stranger to deformity. Even in the best-tended court there are men or women born with a finger too few or too many, or splashes of purple birthmarks crawling above collars and out of hairlines. Then there are diseases that write themselves on the flesh: scabs, boils, poxes, scars and carbuncles. Is this one of those? What else can it be? She thinks of the island in the Tiber, where the lepers of Rome are sequestered on pain of death. There is never anything to see as all the windows are kept closed for fear of contagion, yet she knows from the Bible how flesh can be eaten away until it falls off the bone.

She stares back at his hands. The heir of Ferrara a leper! No. Such a thing could never be concealed. And however much they might need this marriage, her father would never . . . never . . . So what then? A courtier who does a laborer's job in a foundry? In the Arsenale in Venice, they say most of the workers have one eye or half an arm from forging the state's cannons out of the heat of hell. Is this what happens when a duke plays with fire?

The silence stretches out awkwardly between them. A diversion is needed.

"I hear you are a master at the viola da braccio, my lord," she says, realizing too late the horror in the image.

She remembers it so clearly: *He plays like an angel*. It had been one of the first things the envoys sent to negotiate the marriage had told her. Like an angel? Not with those hands, she thinks.

"I am no master." His voice is gruff. "But do I play, yes. And you?"

"The lute. But not so well. I . . . I like to dance." She rushes in.

Has he heard? Of course. It seems everybody else has.

"Do you relish the dance, my lord?" She is wondering how it would be to have her hand in his as the music starts.

"No. I am too busy with . . . with practical matters to be much the courtier," he says, draining his goblet and putting it down on the table. "Perhaps you have heard that about me already?"

She lets out a nervous laugh. Her own courtly manner seems to have deserted her entirely. Help me, she thinks, I don't know what to say.

"Madonna Lucrezia," he says after a pause, and his voice drops low now, so that what comes next is heard by her and not the rest of the room. "I came here today because I thought we should meet before . . . before the wedding festivities begin," he says, as if the very thought of such a thing appalls him.

"Yes." She looks at him. "It was good of you to do that."

"It seemed right that we . . . knew something of each other. Where we stand, what to expect . . . When the time comes," he adds, as if this somehow explains it all.

"Something of each other," she repeats. "Yes, it does help. Thank you."

He starts to pull on his gloves. How can the action not cause him discomfort? Perhaps the skin is dead and he can feel nothing. She keeps her eyes on his face. For a while neither of them speaks.

"You and I have met before, you know," he says at last. "In Rome many years ago."

"Yes . . . well, I know they tell me we have."

It had been soon after her father's accession to the papacy and she and Giulia Farnese were playing host to the many new admirers arriving in Rome to congratulate the family. Though they all wanted something in return.

"I came to lobby for a cardinal's hat for my brother."

"I . . . I was very young, I think. Barely twelve years old."

"Yes, you were. Very young."

The polite thing to do now would be to pretend she has some memory of the meeting, to say something—well, courtly. "I'm afraid I don't remember you at all."

"It's no matter. I forgot you soon enough too," he says bluntly. "However, you are less forgettable now, and we are both old enough for what is to come, wouldn't you agree?" He glances down at his gloved hands, a lopsided smile on his face.

Sweet Mary, this is a compliment, she thinks. He is paying me a compliment but he doesn't know how to say the words. She has to suppress a sudden need to laugh out loud.

"Yes, I am sure we are," she murmurs.

"Well, I will not keep you." He is up on his feet, as if the words have embarrassed him. "The light will go soon and I must be back by nightfall."

"Of course. I . . . I am glad you came."

"It was nothing." He picks a thick scab of mud off his doublet and flicks it to the floor. "I like to ride. Perhaps we might go hunting together. Afterward."

Afterward . . .

"Hunting?" She pauses. "Riding through cold soup. Yes. There is much to be said for the feel of a warm horse on a winter's day."

He catches her eye to check the depth of sarcasm, but she is smiling roundly. As he takes her hand the aroma of leather and horse sweat is now mixed with woodsmoke: a most masculine perfume. She feels a trickle of perspiration slipping between her breasts. How many strange encounters has she had with men over these last weeks since she left Rome? Fifty? A hundred? More . . . But nothing quite like this.

As he strides to the door, a thought comes to her. That after so much flattery, so much courtly bowing and scraping—in the knowledge that she has only to turn away to feel the hiss of the poisoned darts behind her back—that what has just passed between them has been . . . well, what? An honest exchange?

Honest. It is a strange word to describe this most cynical of unions.

That night, pulling on her creamed gloves to protect her perfect white hands, Lucrezia thinks of her betrothed husband, Alfonso d'Este. For she has no other.

CHAPTER 3

❧

Fiammetta had been woken by the screech. Her bedroom overlooks the Tiber, which is witness to all kinds of mayhem on its banks. The noise comes again.

Craak-screek.

Cicero? What is the parrot doing awake at this hour? Once the salon is in darkness he never makes a sound.

She registers the clammy hand on her breast. No danger here. The archbishop is a man easily satisfied and would sleep till Judgment Day if she didn't wake him in time to return home for morning mass. She listens for his breathing, low reverberating snores. Like many of her profession, Fiammetta is an expert on postcoital relaxation. On the rare nights when she cannot sleep she amuses herself by trying to match the sleeping habits of her clients with their professions: the banker who hoards air as he hoards money, holding it so tight to his chest that you would think he will never open his lungs until, with a sudden angry explosion, he grabs for the next breath. The ambassador who mutters all night long, a running commentary even when he is unconscious. If she could understand what he was saying she might have developed a profitable sideline in espionage, but it is a stew of foreign words, as if he writes in code even when talking to himself.

Creekt. Much louder now. Sweet Jesus and all the saints, could he be ill? Or has someone been stupid enough to remove his hood and disturb him? He is the most coddled of birds, and there is indignation in the squawk that suggests disruption.

Valteeeenn.

She is wide awake now. No, it cannot be. If he were mad enough to come in the middle of the night with no warning (and of course he is), then the guards would never have let him in.

Forliii.

Except how could they stop him?

Imola. Forliiiiii.

She cannot help but smile. There is no smarter parrot in the whole of Rome. He had learned those words when he was young, coaxed by the promise of nuts plucked like kisses from her own lips as they rehearsed the praises of a returning conqueror by reciting the names of the cities he had taken. Later, she allowed the bird to forget them, for who wants to be reminded of the achievements of an absent competitor while being entertained by a courtesan? Cicero has not sung out those words in a long time now.

She disentangles herself carefully and waits while the archbishop's body settles, his mouth puckering a little in protest. It is amazing how many men seek the breast long after they have taken its nourishment. Sometimes she wonders if the allure of prostitutes comes from that first earthy smell of wet nurses rather than the perfumes of the mothers whose daughters will eventually become their wives. Ha, she could write a treatise on the way in which men move from monsters to babies once their pricks subside. But who would publish such a thing?

Forlii. She recognizes the note of excitement now. Cicero's indignation has been replaced by the pleasure of attention.

She washes herself from the basin of water, drinks a prepared flask of liquid, bitter and fat with grease, to stop conception and applies a cream that is said to guard against the French pox. Some say that the old woman who prepares such things and has the business of half of Rome's courtesans used to be pretty as a picture herself not so long ago. But that is not something she chooses to dwell on.

She checks her face and hair in her gloom of a hand mirror, then slips out of the room, to find Tremolino, the majordomo, standing in the hall poised to rouse her. With his mane of white hair and wrinkled face he looks more like a sage than a courtesan's pimp.

"There was no stopping him. I did everything I could. He refuses to leave until he sees you. He is adamant."

"I didn't think he was in Rome. Where has he been?"

Tremolino shakes his head. "All I know is he is not dressed for company. And there is something 'unpleasant' to him." He puts a finger to his nose.

"Has he come from another woman?" she asks sharply, for there are things that are not to be tolerated.

"More like a shoal of fish."

"And his man? Is Michelotto with him?"

"Like a shadow. I told him that you were not to be disturbed. But—"

She stands on tiptoe to kiss him on the forehead, as one might a father figure. It is a strange business partnership: her glorious body against his housekeeping and accounting skills. Though when needed he can be as slimy as any courtier. "Stay close to the door in case I need you."

In the receiving salon with its tapestries and painted ceiling of roses, the parrot sits uncovered on his perch, his golden tail aflame in the lamplight, rocking to and fro on his claws, chattering petulantly to himself. Having been woken and made to perform, he is now left unrewarded.

A figure is lying on his back in front of the embers of the fire. His hands are cupped underneath his head like a pillow and his eyes are closed, though it is hard to tell whether he is asleep. In a chair close by another sits, his fingers laced in front of him like the skeleton of interlocking ship timbers, his legs stretched out, watching, waiting.

"Signor Michelotto?" she says quietly.

He looks up.

"I am here now. You can wait downstairs."

Without a word he gets up and moves to the door, passing close to her. She is used to gauging the tremor of attention that her presence causes in men, not so much vanity as professional observation, but she has never felt a scintilla of interest from this man. At first she had thought he might snuff out such thoughts deliberately because she belonged to his master, but now she doubts he feels anything toward any woman. There is no one in Rome who doesn't know the stories: his prowess with a dagger or the garrote, the way the Tiber swallows the bodies when he is finished with them. Maybe that is where the thrill of coupling lies for him. There are men in the world like that; she knows because it is the business of a good courtesan to avoid them.

When his master was a regular visitor she had once wondered what he might feel if it were her neck under his wire. She, who is not frightened by many things in life, had been frightened by that.

She settles the parrot first, offering him some treats out of a leather pouch slung below the perch. He takes a peck at the skin of her palm to register his annoyance. She slips a finger inside the thick ruff of feathers under his neck and scratches him gently, murmuring soothing words, and after a while he puts his head to one side, cooing now.

"I should have bought you a female parrot. It would have been more of a challenge." The voice, behind her, is as lazy and petulant as the bird's. "The little bastard bit me," he adds sourly.

"You woke him up and did not feed him. What do you expect?" She slips the dark hood over the structure of the perch. From underneath comes a single shriek, then silence.

"Come here."

She stands where she is.

"Come here, Rome's juiciest whore."

She moves toward him and sinks down, her robe billowing out around her. She knows how lovely she will look in the fire glow. She has been two feet away from herself since she was old enough to remember, assessing what others see: in this case her flawless porcelain skin, with a riot of unruly dark curls coursing over her shoulders and down her back. A woman made for bedding; those had been the words of one of her earliest lovers. His enthusiasm had financed an elegant hunting tapestry in the hall; it was the first such household luxury she had owned rather than rented, a fact she recalls with satisfaction each time she passes it.

"Well," he says through half closed eyelids. "Aren't you going to tell me how pleased you are to see me again?"

"I would be more pleased if you had given me notice."

"I was busy."

"And so am I. It is Tuesday."

"Tuesday?" he repeats, as if the word is new to him. "Well, I daresay you have had a clash of diaries before in your long years of work."

"There is no clash," she says tartly. "You had no appointment."

"Who is the lucky man? Church or state?"

She shrugs.

"Roman or foreign? Come—give me a clue."

"He is no one you know."

"But he knows me?"

"If I were you I would not see that as a compliment," she says impatiently.

He lifts himself on an elbow and pulls her head toward him, playing with his tongue around the edges of her mouth, before probing further.

She registers the telltale snip of desire in her gut, she who in her time has slept with a dozen men in half as many days with no hint of excitement. In her profession she should be better at controlling it. She pulls away. "You smell . . . rancid, my lord."

"Blood and seawater. I am arrived from Piombino."

"You did not swim all the way, I hope."

"Only some of it. It was a small shipwreck." He waits, pleased by the alarm that crosses her face. "Don't worry. No one died." And he shivers a little, because even Cesare Borgia cannot breathe underwater, and he now knows that panic that comes when the sea grips you and somersaults you down and over and over in darkness.

"You look tired," she says, a little flattered that he has chosen her after such danger and aware yet again of that vast other world out there, good and bad, that she will never, ever, be allowed to experience. "I will call for food and have the fire rebuilt."

"No. Don't call anyone. I will do it myself."

He gets up, putting a few large logs into the grate, then squatting in front of it, like a servant, using the bellows. After a while the flames leap eagerly and he sits back, warming himself. In the brighter light she sees the cuts on his face, like the mark of a tiger's claws down one side.

"The sea has women's nails," she murmurs, putting up a finger to touch them.

"My God, it was like coupling with Medusa," he says, thinking how the reef had risen from the seabed out of nowhere, colliding with the waves to capsize the boat and tangle them in its ropes, pulling them under. Even as they struggled free, the current had raked them along the rocks, opening up fissures of flesh they weren't aware of until they had crawled their way up onto the beach and saw one another, laughing crazily, streaked and streaming with blood. "She is a jealous mistress toward anyone who tries to get away."

"I will get some salve," Fiammetta says, smiling at such unaccustomed poetry. "And then you must rest. How long have you been on the road?"

He shrugs as if the question is too difficult.

"You need to sleep."

"That's why I came: for someone to sleep with." He intertwines his fingers through hers, pulling her toward him.

"My lord," she says firmly, "you cannot do this."

"Do what?"

"Disappear from my bed for months and then walk back in expecting me to disrupt my regular clients to accommodate you."

"Yes, I can." He laughs. "That's what I have always done, remember?"

"Well, not this time. I have an archbishop in my bed."

"Ha! Then give me his name and I will get him a cardinal's hat before the end of the month. Look at me, Fiammetta. I nearly died yesterday. And I have been bereft without you."

"That's not what I hear."

"Spoils of war, that's all. Duty as much as pleasure. You know my bird would peck your fig over all others any day."

The slang of the familiar court game makes her laugh. Birds pecking figs: how coy the world is for those who can afford courtesy, children knocking at the gates of an adult world. But there is no childhood in a courtesan's life.

The first time she met him she had been warned by those who knew: cocky and insufferably arrogant, yet able to charm the seeds up out of the ground in winter when he chose. When she looked back later, it had not been his compliments, for they had been no less clichéd than a hundred others. No; it was something more unsettling: a recognition that here was a man who flirted with risk as much as she did, appreciating how fear could bring its own pleasure. She had known then some of the things he had done, and each new victory brings more tales of outrage. But whatever he does to others, he has never treated her badly. On the contrary, he has shown her favor, at times even fondness, though it lasts only as long as the encounter. Everyone knows that the only woman with a place in his heart is his sister, Lucrezia. However, now he is here she will not turn him away. They both know that.

"What shall I do?" she says, more to herself.

"Tell him that Duke Valentine, ruler of Piombino and all the cities of the Romagna, has come to sleep with his favorite whore. And he can piss off and find himself another."

She shakes her head. "I think such a speech would do neither of us any good. Don't you have enough enemies, Cesare?"

"Never." He puts his head back and closes his eyes.

And yet there is something else here now, some tremor of vulnera-bility in all the bravado. Could it be that death actually touched him out there in the middle of the sea? He, who is never afraid and will never die. The pulse of desire in her has been replaced by a quieter feeling. She is beguiled, perhaps even a little moved. Ah, she berates herself. How can a businesswoman be so stupid?

"Give me a while."

"No." He lies back on the carpet, pulling her hand with him.

"I will be back," she says firmly.

She instructs the kitchen to prepare some food and gives notice that her majordomo is to wake the archbishop if she is not returned by the time he must leave.

But when she comes back, he is fast asleep, sprawled out on the car-pet, heavy legs falling wide and head lolled to one side like some sated Adonis. She sits next to him for a few moments, marveling at the vulner-ability of his abandonment. She has a vision of Delilah with her scissors set to change the course of history. She smiles, then bends down and starts to unfasten his doublet.

If this is to be business, then business must be done.

CHAPTER 4

❖

"My dear ambassador, I still don't see what this 'complaint' has to do with us."

Inside his apartments, Alexander has been back barely long enough to dry his clothes before he is firefighting.

"With respect, Your Holiness, the man was a citizen of Venice, residing in Rome under the jurisdiction of the Roman government, which makes his treatment an offense against both cities. I am instructed to bring it to Your Holiness's attention, so that some redress may be found . . ."

The ambassador has worked himself up into a righteous frenzy waiting for the Pope's return. Alexander shifts his bulk delicately on the papal throne, sniffing loudly. His head is stuffed and he can feel the mounting pressure of a sneeze. With God's help he might calm the boiling seas, but he can't stop his nose filling up with snot. He should be enjoying a hot poultice in front of the fire, not listening to the moans of an inbred Venetian aristocrat.

". . . I must remind you, Your Holiness, of the details. Not only were this man's right hand and his tongue cut off, they were then *exhibited*, nailed to the window of the prison. His screams could be heard all over the square."

"Hmmn. That does sound quite unpleasant. And you're sure this was the work of Duke Valentine?"

The ambassador throws up his hands involuntarily. "It is common knowledge," he says, unable to keep the disbelief from his voice.

On the other side of the room, the Pope's Master of Ceremonies, Johannes Burchard, has found a spot on the brightly tiled floor and is studying it intently.

"Well, be assured we shall talk to him about it. However—" The sneeze mounts. He stops, frozen in waiting, before it subsides again. "However, Ambassador, this 'citizen' of yours is hardly blameless. From what we gather he was marching through the streets shouting out the most outrageous vitriol against the Holy See, not only the duke's name but also our own."

"But . . . !" the man splutters. How much saliva of outrage has been sprayed around this lavishly decorated room? "The contents of the letter he was reciting were known to all. Even in Venice we have heard them."

"You amaze me. I would hope the government of your great state had better things to do than to listen to foul slander."

On the table nearby, the latest dispatch from Ferrara sits newly delivered, no doubt informing him of his daughter's arrival into the city. And later he is called to say mass in Santa Maria Maggiore to celebrate its new gilded ceiling, on fire with the first shipment of gold to arrive in Rome from the new world. Evidence of God's favor is everywhere, yet here he is dealing with this sordid little "incident" from weeks before.

"Let us be clear here, Ambassador. This 'letter' as you call it, everyone knows to be an anonymous forgery, an act of sedition. I would venture that had such . . . such excrement been written about your own doge, you would have already lit a pyre under any man who repeated it publicly. It pains me even to refer to it again, but—since you insist."

His cold smile now takes in his Master of Ceremonies, who still sits blank as a new gravestone. What an asset Burchard is on such occasions; the perfect dignified witness to the drama and bad behavior of Church diplomacy. Alexander has recently thought about having him sculpted. Then he could be in two places at once, sitting here in marble stillness while busy elsewhere orchestrating a dozen different Church ceremonies, the protocol of each one remembered down to the smallest detail; the man is a miracle of memory! He would like to see Burchard's face were he to suggest such a thing, although of course it would probably show nothing. Like now, as he sorts through his papers, selecting the relevant page to offer to the Pope.

"No. No, you read it, Johannes. I cannot even bear to hold the scurrilous object in my hands. Start with the bit about the Carthaginians."

The Master of Ceremonies clears his throat.

"*The perfidy of the Scythians and Carthaginians, the bestiality and savagery of Nero and Caligula, all are surpassed in the palace of the Pope,*" he reads flatly. It is a joke among his peers that he could make the Song of Solomon sound bureaucratic. "*Rodrigo Borgia is an abyss of all vice, a subverter of all justice.*"

The Pope raises his eyes. "An abyss of vice. Nero *and* Caligula. I ask you. Is that fair? Even the emperors might have objected."

The ambassador drops his eyes. He has said what he came to say. The rest is theater. His job now is to remember everything that is said so it can be transcribed as soon as he gets out of the room.

"Leave out the next bit. It is all more of the same." Alexander gestures to Burchard. "Read the words about Cesare—Duke Valentine. That, I think, is the matter in hand."

"*His father, the Pope, favors Cesare because he has his own perversity and his own cruelty. He lives like the Turks surrounded by a flock of prostitutes, guarded by armed soldiers. At his order or decree men are despoiled of all possessions, wounded, killed, thrown into the Tiber.*"

There is a short pause. The Pope sighs. Of course when the letter had first come to his attention, he had been angered by it. Its timing—

the date of Lucrezia's betrothal to Ferrara—was vicious, but it had done nothing to spoil the celebrations of marriage and the sweet send-off of his daughter. Until Cesare decided to take revenge.

"You see, my dear ambassador, in the murky waters of Roman politics, such slander is part of life. If we were to retaliate against all those who attacked our good self, we would need to repopulate half the city. We should have had our own vice chancellor killed a number of times, for God knows he schemed against us violently," he says, warming to his subject. "And that reprobate Cardinal della Rovere, who lost the papacy to us, has never been able to open his mouth without poison issuing from it."

Burchard is still staring at the page, but blinking in a most unstatue-like way.

"But, as befits the head of the Holy Mother Church, we have cultivated a gentler disposition. However, it is true that my son, the duke, though he is a good-hearted man, cannot endure insults. Something about the way he is. You know about his remarkable escape from the storm at sea, yes? Being such a man of action, I suspect he finds the repetition of insults . . . well, rather cowardly."

What reply can the ambassador give? Should he talk about the number of bodies pulled out from the Tiber, count the stab wounds, name the names? To do so would also be to repeat the gossip. And he must be careful, because although wrong has been done, he is unsure how much the Pope knows of the provenance of the letter itself.

"So where does that leave us? You with your outrage and us with ours. I could try to do something for this dumb, left-handed citizen of yours, but I fear his future is limited. Because as you may be aware, the letter was not sent from the army camp in Naples as it claims, but—and we have this on excellent authority"—he pauses, readying himself for the climax—"from Venice, where certain members of the Orsini family now reside. With our own daughter now duchess of your close neighbor, Ferrara, and many of the cities of the Romagna ruled by our beloved duke, it pains us most deeply to think of your great state harboring enemies with such vile imaginations."

· · ·

"Well?"

The room has been empty for a while but Burchard remains silent.

The Pope blows his nose noisily. His head is stuffed with wet sand. "Come come. I know what is behind that stone face, Johannes. You think I should have told him his precious citizen is dead. Well, a man without a tongue or a hand is no use to anyone, and it's quite possible the poor soul threw *himself* into the Tiber as a measure of his despair. With luck he won't find out for a while. I haven't the stamina for another scene. Beh! Children! You cannot imagine the headaches they can cause."

"No, Your Holiness."

"You know, had the duke not been such a strong swimmer, he would have died that day at sea. Indeed for the longest time I thought he had. Such worry he causes me. It seems young men cannot be brave without being reckless. My own father used to scour the streets looking for me, and I was barely a child then. Did you ever cause your parents such distress, Johannes? No, I imagine not. Well, I had better see the boy. Send a messenger to his apartments."

"I—I believe Duke Valentine is not at home at the moment."

"Where is he? Still out celebrating, no doubt! Find out where he is and get him back here." Alexander fumbles for a fresh kerchief in his robes. "So, has anything else vital happened in my absence? And no more bodies, please."

"The Cardinal of Capua is taken ill."

"Giovanni Battista? What ails him?"

"He is sick to his stomach. He refuses to be bled or to take any medicine. It seems he does not trust his doctors."

"More likely he doesn't want to pay them. I have never known a stingier cleric." Alexander chuckles. "Still, he has served us loyally. I should visit him. Or offer him the papal physicians."

"I am not sure that is wise."

"Why not?"

"I . . . there is a rumor."

"Not another one. What? That I had him poisoned so the papacy could take his inheritance? Is that it, Johannes? Do people really think I would have made the Vatican's most profitable notary a cardinal just in order to dispatch him?"

"Not his doctors, Your Holiness. His doctors are clear that he has a fever."

"Thank God for men of science; they alone are above the superstition of rumor. Poor Giovanni. He spent so long amassing his fortune, it will pain him greatly not to be able to take it with him." Alexander drums his fingers on the wood of the chair, lost in thought. "He is at his palace near St. Peter's, yes? We should have guards ready to close it down and seal off his effects. If he does die there's bound to be a rush of creditors and it would be unseemly to have a riot on our hands. You will work with his staff to arrange the funeral, of course. I'll sanction a place close to the altar of our beloved uncle Calixtus for his interment."

Burchard sits ready for further instructions, but the Pope has fallen back into reverie. He gathers his papers to leave.

"Johannes," he says as he reaches the door. "I . . . When it comes to it, you will oversee my funeral too, yes?"

"Of course, Holy Father. That is my job."

"Good. I mean . . ." he says, as if making light of it, "I mean I would have no one else."

The sneeze he has been playing with explodes suddenly into the air, knocking him backward with its force. He waves a hand as he fumbles again for his kerchief.

"And to avoid it happening too soon, tell my chaplains to prepare an herb inhalation before I dress for church."

Once he is alone, Alexander's thoughts soon turn from death to the pleasures of mathematics. How much is Giovanni Battista Ferrari worth? Before he was elevated to the cardinalate he had spent twenty years selling papal offices with a cream off on each one. Thirty, forty thousand ducats at least. A cardinal's wealth returns to the Church after his death, which is only right and proper, for it is in the service of God that it has been amassed. And then there is the money to be made from the selling on his benefices. It could not come at a better time. Cesare's army campaigns are a bottomless pit; however much water one pours in, it never seems to rise to the top. Of course people will shout corruption. But that is hardly new. Popes have always feathered their family nests. It goes back centuries. And in his time he has done good work for the wealth of the Church. How easy it is for people to forget that! For thirty years he held the position of vice chancellor; Sweet Mary, he barely had time to worship given all the schemes he was pursuing to bring in more taxes. There was never a word against him then from all those who benefited. As any banker will tell you, it is a sign of a healthy business that income rises rather than falls.

He blows his nose again, but already he is feeling better. If Cardinal Ferrari dies he must also give some thought to who will take his place. With Cesare now outside the Church—he had always made a most unlikely cardinal—there is no direct Borgia candidate for the papacy, and so the college must be weighted up in their favor. It would be a fitting step up for the Master of Ceremonies. Alexander tries to imagine Burchard's hatchet face under a scarlet cap. Except what would he do without him, this man who sees everything and says nothing? No. No cardinal's hat for Johannes. Not yet. There will be other opportunities and there is still so much to do.

Oh, but how he loves it, this work of his. Please God, let him live forever.

He levers himself up from his chair and pads his way over to the table to the new dispatches. There it is: the fat seal of the Borgia crest. Before he has to face the intransigence of his son, there is triumph to savor. His beloved Lucrezia has arrived in Ferrara.

CHAPTER 5

❖

*I*t is a ghostly procession. To arrive in time the barges must travel through the night, compensating for the sluggish river with a dozen harnessed horses on the bank led by men with lamps on poles to light their way. At a prearranged point a flare is set off to mark their progress. Somewhere in the darkness ahead an answering plume of white smoke rises. Inside the city walls, court musicians are being shaken awake and the soldiers on the battlements change watch to make room for the artillery commanders.

Lucrezia, who has slept only fitfully, lies waiting for the day. The pipe and twitter of river birds on the edge of dawn is interrupted by a fanfare of distant trumpets. Eager for her first view of her new home, she leaves her ladies sleeping and makes her way alone out onto the deck, where she is swallowed up at once inside a clinging fog, the only relief in a sea of gray the glow of the lamps pulsing like fireflies on the bank.

"Ah, madam, madam." The top half of the tall Ferrarese envoy looms down at her out of the gloom. "Such a shame. I feared as much. She has waited for you so long that she is grown coy at showing herself," he says, his face so far above his feet that it gives the impression of a turret emerging from the mist. "Still, those of us who love her find a special beauty in these gauzy winter veils in which she wraps herself."

Lucrezia smiles at his choice of language: how men do love to see the guiles of women in everything. But there is no mistaking the feeling behind his words. "You are most fond of your city, Signor Pozzi. How long have you been here watching and waiting?"

"Since before dawn. I had hoped to show you . . . well . . . no matter. We are getting closer all the time. The fog will burn off soon enough and then you will see her for yourself."

ROOOMB. A reverberating boom coming from nowhere and everywhere at once shatters the misty silence

"There it is! The sound of your husband's cannons announcing our progress. Hear the richness of that sound. Two meters long the barrels. Designed by him and cast in his foundry. The Este guns. He will be on the battlements commanding the gunners himself this morning—all in your honor. Such a welcome is prepared for you."

She imagines her husband-to-be, tall and swarthy, wrapped in fog, holding out tapers in his gloved hands. But the tapers turn to ribs of meat in her imagination as she sees again the purple skin of his fingers. The cannon fire is followed by a further fanfare of trumpets and horns. *Tell me,* she wants to say, *what is wrong with my husband's hands?*

The horses whinny fretfully in the fog and an invisible gull screeches overhead. The boat slides along, gray river meeting gray air with little to tell between them. She feels a sudden melancholy lapping around her. A scrap of verse plays at the edge of her mind:

I come to ferry you hence across the tide
*   to endless night, fierce fires and crushing cold.*

What mad thoughts for a woman on her way to her wedding. This will not do at all.

"May I ask you a question, Signor Pozzi?" she says forcefully.

"Of course, madam, anything."

"I was wondering . . . about my husband's first wife, Anna Sforza."

"Anna Sforza?" His face is obscured by swirls of fog.

"Yes. What was she like? How did they get on?" The diplomatic tightrope between Rome and Ferrara is strung taut under their feet. "She died in childbirth, yes? Did my husband mourn her very much?"

"The whole of Ferrara mourned her. She was a fine woman. Fine." He pauses as if he too must test the tension in the rope before he takes the next step. "Though she suffered from a somewhat 'delicate' disposition. She and the duke elect . . . well, one might say that they were not natural companions."

"I see." She stares into the fog. The silence grows around them.

"Is anything wrong, madam?"

"No," she says brightly. "Nothing at all, though I have some concerns that my chosen outfit may not be suitable. Cream silk sewn with pearls on such a day: it would not do for me to disappear inside . . . this cold soup."

He laughs, manifestly relieved at the change of subject. "It will have long since burned off. You have my word as a native of Ferrara. Though even if it didn't you would shine through it. Of that I am sure. You bring your own sun with you."

"Ah, Signor Pozzi. You are a man of honeyed words, even for a diplomat."

"That does not mean they are untruthful, my lady," he says quietly.

He peers down at this slender girl with her soft blue eyes and creamy skin, the slight pout to her cupid bow lips. Not a beauty, perhaps, but pretty by anyone's standards, made prettier by the flash of her smile. It would appear that she is, after all, nervous. It barely seems possible. It has been a fraught assignment, shepherding this troupe of confident, entitled young women halfway across Italy. But it has had its compensations: not least the pleasure of watching her win over all manner of powerful men whose noses have been bent out of joint by the Borgia rampages. No, a second Anna Sforza she is certainly not. They say her brother had the same easy charisma once, before the acid of ambition burned it off like a layer of skin. In Rome now people spit on the ground when they hear his name, though only if they are in safe company. Yet this slip of a Borgia girl has had men's mouths puckering into a quite different shape. He has seen her exhausted, rigid with boredom, infuriated by insults whispered behind her back, yet her natural charm, mixed with an equal natural cunning, has never failed her. She would make an admirable diplomat. Part of him would like to tell her that, to suggest that she will find it a useful combination when she enters the bear pit of Este family politics. Well, she will find out soon enough.

The next crash of cannon fire startles with its proximity, and inside the answering trumpet fanfare there is new clarity of notes. As if it had been prearranged, the world around them begins to change. The solid air comes alive, thinning into smoke tendrils and then disintegrating, allowing a blood orange sun to break through. Soon the outline of a crenellated tower is visible, followed by one, no two spires, and then the fortress battlements of a city gate and long majestic curves of wall throwing protective arms around a jumble of emerging roofs and brick chimneys. And lacing around them, the course of the lazy, now sun-dappled river. She gasps. It seems the city has been there all the time, waiting for her mood to change so that, as promised, they might both show each other off to their best advantage.

"Ferrara, my lady," he says with a flourish. "I think cream silk set off by your smile will do very well indeed."

• • •

The choreography of the coming celebrations is elaborate and precise. And this, the first ceremony, the meeting with Duke Ercole himself, will take place outside the city.

The setting is a convent where his illegitimate daughter is a nun. A pale winter sun beckons Lucrezia off the barge. Her trumpeters, already disembarked, are in line, their horns high and ready. Behind her, her ladies and a throng of Spanish dancers and jesters jostle and laugh as they try to arrange themselves in formation. Nerves are everywhere. She hushes them with a look. The trumpeters let out their blast, and the convent doors are flung open to welcome them.

The procession makes its way in through the entrance, across two sets of cloisters and into a large open space, once a garden but now transformed into a forest glade. There are dozens of constructed arches, each one clad in such thick-cut foliage and fresh winter berries that even birds have become interested. The air is filled with the scent of crushed lavender scattered in her path, and at the end on a raised dais, flanked by tall, decorated columns, sits the duke himself. In all good myths before hero and heroine can be joined together there must be tests and trials. And before she beds the son, she must first woo his seventy-one-year-old father. She smiles. It is the kind of challenge she was made for.

She pauses under the first arch, her enchantment at the decorations around her plain for all to see. Then she starts to walk, head high, her pristine gilded shoes—the eighth pair—peeking out from a lake of silk, her eyes straight ahead.

It is clear even at this distance that Duke Ercole d'Este, like his son, is not an object of beauty. Age has shrunk him one way while expanding him the other and his chins have multiplied downward, leaving no room for his neck. He looks, she thinks, like a richly padded chair. As to his personality, the Borgia intelligence machine has already briefed her well.

This new father of hers has ruled Ferrara for over thirty years, and despite a fiery temper has been much loved, first by his people, for his name and the wars he fought when he was young, and second by the women he chose, though in his case he only ever wanted two: his wife, Eleonora of Aragon, and a mistress by whom he had a bastard daughter and son, the latter already more trouble than he is worth.

These days he sees himself as a man of peace. Or rather a man loath to spend money on things he doesn't enjoy, and recently war has become a most expensive pastime. In its place he has elevated culture, building and God. He loves theater, with its spectacle and special effects, and his court is a honeypot for musicians and actors from all over Europe. His relationship with God is fertile too. The mad monk Savonarola, who brought Florence to her knees in more ways than one, was a son of Ferrara, and the duke is a follower of his brand of fiery unforgiving piety. But his greatest passion is for nuns. Not the everyday type (Ferrara is full of convents of well-bred women with nowhere else to go) but the spiritually chosen ones, young women—and they are usually young and of humble birth—so consumed by love of Christ that they have come to live on the sacrament of His body alone, some weeping blood from miraculous stigmata in their hands and feet and visited by Him through trances and visions. In a country caught in a vortex of invasion and turmoil, their faith has become a symbol of God's grace in a graceless world and they are highly valued by the cities that house them.

Barely a year before, he had managed to extract—or more accurately steal—the sublimely holy Sister Lucia from a convent in Viterbo. In the midst of the Borgia-Este marriage negotiations, he had asked Lucrezia to intercede with the Pope to allow other nuns of the order to join her. When she wrote to tell him of her success, Ercole had been beside himself with gratitude. As she had known he would be. He is already building a whole new convent to house his prize. Expensive, of course, but how could it not be worth it? The dowry that she brings him will come in most useful. Could it be the thought of that dowry that is now warming his smile as she walks toward him?

Lucrezia, who in her time has charmed many a padded chair—the Vatican is full of old men who eat too much—lifts her skirts to climb the steps. And as she does so, half a dozen figures somersault down the leafy pillars, agile as monkeys, tossing handfuls of petals and leaves all around her. She laughs in delight, throwing her hands up in wonder to catch the rain of flowers, and her spontaneity brings a smile to everyone's face.

Covered in petals she sinks into a deep curtsy in front of the duke, who is now grinning from ear to ear.

Oh yes, he thinks, his ambassadors have done a good job. If she is half as sweet under the skin, she will do nicely. He lifts her up, embracing her, then holding her at arm's length, assessing her costume. The diamonds around her neck alone must be worth what—five hundred ducats? She will look even better wearing the Este rubies and sapphires across her chest, though they will always be only on loan: should she fail in her duty they will return to their rightful coffers.

Of course she had not been his choice. He had spent months in correspondence with the French king, telling him that he would rather die than graft this parvenu whore bastard daughter of a godless pope onto the great Este family tree. If His Majesty would only offer someone else . . . But though France might own the state of Milan, the king needed the Pope and his son's army when he came to attack Naples, and so sadly no French bride was available. Ercole had no alternative but to give in. Four hundred thousand ducats and a reduction in papal taxation in perpetuity: the greatest dowry Italy has ever seen had been the sweetener. How many nuns and musicians can he buy with that?

He embraces her again. A little more flesh would be better perhaps, for his errant son does seem to like his women uncouthly large. But she will certainly do. It is five years since his first daughter-in-law expired with a dead baby stuck between her legs, and it's time Alfonso stopped poking his rod into hot places and got on with the job of providing Ferrara with a son and future heir.

Outside the cannons roar and the acrobats twirl their way upward again.

Yes, Lucrezia Borgia will do well enough.

"Come, my dear daughter-in-law," he says, loud enough for the world to hear. "Your family is waiting to welcome you."

She takes the offered hand and drops her shoulders a little as they walk so she does not appear too tall beside him.

CHAPTER 6

❖

"You saw me standing on the shoreline! You knew I was safe. I've been busy with my own affairs."

The walls of the Pope's chamber are frescoed with vibrant images of the saints, men and women who without a murmur, even under the most unimaginable of tortures, gave themselves up to God. It is, however, a good deal noisier in here now.

"What? Drying out your clothes in front of a courtesan's fire? Don't raise your eyes to me like that. I remind you, you were the one pushing so hard to get back to Rome. The Venetian ambassador had smoke rising out of his head. You should have been here to defend yourself. Did you really have to exhibit the man's tongue and hand, so half of the city would see it?"

"The exhibition was the point, Father. You're too soft on insults."

"On the contrary—I am just keeping our enemies down to manageable proportions to make room for the next one," Alexander grumbles, but the tone is more cheerful now. Whatever the wrangling, he is, as ever, delighted to see his handsome, triumphant son.

He reaches across the table, helping himself to bread and more fish, licking his fingers gleefully before pushing the plate toward Cesare.

"Don't tell me you're full already. A warrior must keep his strength up."

"On what? Half grown fish?"

"Why not? Christ fed five thousand on a handful of them."

"I doubt they were sardines."

"Well, they should have been," the Pope says, shoving a fat raw fillet into his mouth. Taste is memory, and whenever his teeth release the juice of the flesh marinated in honey and vinegar he is back in the bishop's palace of Valencia, a hungry young man with everything to look forward to. "As I have told you many times they are the sweetest and most humble harvest of the sea. I have even initiated Burchard into their wonders. Imagine. A German eating raw sardines!"

But this is not an image Cesare cares to pursue. There are moments when his father's relish for such things seems almost indecent.

"So, let us talk business," Alexander says. "With Piombino secured, you are now the effective ruler of seven territories. If this season we add the cities of Camerino and Sinigaglia, both of which are under papal jurisdiction, then we have the firm foundations of a viable Borgia state. I have already drafted the bill of excommunication for the ruling families on the ground of nonpayment of papal dues."

Cesare shrugs. "Camerino and Sinigaglia are barely worth the time it will take to march there," he says bluntly. "I think given how far we have come we need a bigger target now. Something to show everyone that we mean business."

"Such as?"

He shrugs. "Pisa or Arezzo."

Alexander frowns. "The papacy has no direct claim on them. They are within Florence's domain and she would be apoplectic with outrage."

"Let her. She's getting used to suffering vapors. If we were to move fast we might even get inside her own walls."

"Florence? You want to take Florence now?" Alexander says, his mind now fully off the sardines. "What—you have become both Caesar and Alexander rolled into one?" And he laughs immoderately at the weakness of his own joke. "No. As long are we are allied to the French, it can't be done. The city is under their protection."

"You think King Louis gets rich on what Florence pays him? I tell you the time is ripe, Father. People need to see what we are capable of, and such a move would astonish everyone. The city's in trouble. That raving monk Savonarola sucked all the life out of her and now she's left with some feeble dream about bringing back a republic that never worked in the first place. She is up to her eyes in debt, with no standing militia to defend her and no mercenaries to call on."

"Of course not. We have all the best ones on our payroll."

"Exactly." Cesare snorts in frustration. "And a number of them would happily shaft Florence for insults delivered in the past. Vitellozzo Vitelli can't wait to turn his cannons on her walls. God knows we came close enough last year."

"Yes. And you will remember very well why you backed off. Because while you were up there on your fine white horse, I was here defending your back against the French. Sweet Mary, Cesare, you think I do nothing while you're out waving your sword around." Alexander's voice rises sharply to meet the fight. What more could a man want than to argue with his son about which glorious summit the family should scale next?

"My God, you should have heard the ambassador's language. All strut and threat about how if you took one more step into lands protected by King Louis . . ."

Oh yes . . . no, no . . . I understand what His Majesty feels. I had no idea this is what the duke would do or I would have stopped him long before. Alexander has a penchant for playing every part when the story calls for it. When he returns I will see to it he is sternly reprimanded.

He lets out a theatrical sigh. "I am diplomatically black and blue from taking beatings on your behalf."

"It is how we work, Father," Cesare says lightly. "As a strategy it hasn't failed yet."

"That may be true, but it is in danger of losing its edge of surprise," Alexander retorts firmly.

"Anyway, King Louis doesn't really care about Florence. He wants Naples back under his control. We all know that. And as long as we help him get it he'll trade bits of the north in return."

"Maybe he will and maybe he won't. But either way this is too much too soon. You will listen to me on this, Cesare. Yes, yes, I know you bridle at being lectured, but I tell you, you are too impatient. It is a disease of the young. For now we leave Florence alone and concentrate on consolidating the lands we already have."

He lets out a small fishy belch to mark the end of the matter.

"I think you're wrong, Father. I tell you—"

"And I tell you, no. No! You will show some respect! You can rattle your armor as much as you like on the battlefield, but here, inside these walls, I remain both your pope and your father, is that clear? We will hear no more of Florence."

The clash over, the two of them sit for a while in stony silence.

As ever, it is Alexander who recovers first.

How splendid this son of mine looks, he thinks, even without his mask. Out of the sunlight the scars are not so bad. Anyway, the world is full of pockmarks these days: the scabs and pustules of this new plague are almost become a mark of virility in a man. Still, he should smile more. When one is wielding so much power a little charm goes a long way.

"Come, don't sulk with me," he says, softened by his victory. "When there is a baby in Lucrezia's belly to cement our ties with Ferrara, then we will talk of such things again."

But the mention of his sister does nothing to lift Cesare's mood. He glances toward the desk where the day's dispatches are cracked open. "How is it with her?"

"She is welcomed like a daughter and a duchess." Alexander chuckles. "The duke is struggling to outdo us in feasts and festivities. And you heard of her triumph in Urbino? She had the whole court eating out of her hand. My God, but I miss her. It is a daily dagger thrust into my heart." And he puts his hand onto his chest, somewhere near the spot where indigestion begins. "What? She does not tell you all this herself?"

Cesare shrugs angrily. "Banalities, descriptions, courtesies. I get nothing of import. Nothing of *her*. It is as if we barely knew each other."

"Ah, Cesare." Of course. It is this, as much as any row about Florence, that is turning him sour. Alexander lifts his hands as if to show this spilled family milk is none of his doing. He has tried to make peace more than once, but who would blame a woman for taking offense when her husband is strangled on the orders of her own brother?

"I told you! The man was conspiring against me," Cesare says automatically, as if he is reading his father's thoughts. It is a lie he has repeated so many times he almost believes it himself. Even Alexander had been tempted by it at first, for when his daughter's grief was at its worst the alternative had been too painful. "Her life would be nothing if she were still joined to that sap. Instead she is duchess of one of the finest states in Italy. She should be licking my hand in gratitude."

The image of his daughter like one of Cesare's hunting hounds is not lost on Alexander, nor the vast dowry he himself had raised from family and papal funds to pay her passage. But there is nothing to be gained by further antagonism. It pains him greatly for there to be family discord.

"I know how much the two of you love each other," he says firmly. "She will come round. Give her time and all will be well. Meanwhile, let us make our peace too. We have enjoyed triumph these last weeks. There are other jewels ready to be plucked. What you lose here you will gain in the money you squeeze out of me for the next campaign, for I can refuse you nothing. Come, give your long-suffering father an embrace to show there is no bad feeling."

Cesare moves toward him. He knows his father is wrong. That he has grown old playing games of Church politics and he has forgotten how to seize the moment. Elba and Piombino fly the Borgia flag only because he had ordered a forced march when everyone thought his army was returning to Rome. What in the council chamber looked like a risk, on the field was no risk at all. And as long as King Louis needs the Borgias' help on a claim to Naples, he will make concessions elsewhere.

As he helps his father out of the chair, his mind is on the chessboard of central Italy, calibrating an alternative strategy to counter the blocking by what he had thought was his own queen.

He embraces the great bulk, catching a noseful of sweaty flesh and the tang of returning fish on his breath. In recent months these old man smells have grown stronger, as if something inside him is starting to rot.

They may be building an empire, but there is one question that never leaves Cesare's mind now: how much longer have they got? Whatever comes next, it must send a chill down the spine of all who might ever dare to oppose them. He thinks of his sister's triumphant passage through the golden cities of the Apennines, and by the time he reaches the door an idea is already forming in his mind. My God, now that would be something that would stun them all.

He turns, but the Pope is busy mopping up the fish juice with a chunk of bread. Well, let him wait. The surprise will be all the greater.

CHAPTER 7

❖

It is well after dark when the wedding night witnesses take their places in the bedchamber of the ducal palace in Ferrara.

Of course, there must be witnesses . . . how could there not be? Lucrezia's marriage to Alfonso is an alliance of states more binding than any diplomatic treaty, and once the dowry has been counted and the vows exchanged, it's only right that the act of consummation—the bodily bureaucracy if you like—be officially recorded. Custom demands it, because even now there are things that could go wrong. It is amazing what can be concealed beneath the sheets: men who shrivel rather than grow, brides with pathways so small that the only husband who will have them is Jesus Christ (which is as well, since once the secret is out, a convent is where they will spend the rest of their days).

Then there are the considerations of this particular union. The bridegroom's father is an old man. For the Este succession to go smoothly, his heir must himself have an heir to provide a security of lineage. Past generations have bred like rabbits so the palace is full of half brothers and cousins, slipped out from both sides of the blanket:

vigorous, ambitious young men who while they swear loyalty now, might be tempted to make a bid for power should the occasion arise. The duke may have negotiated a fortune along with this Borgia bride, but unless she can give the family what it needs, he will still be the loser. That she is fertile is beyond question. Nevertheless, a new husband needs new proof.

Equally on the Borgia side, the Pope did not lay out a fortune to have a son who does not do his duty in bed—he has played with the fire of such lunacy—and clear evidence of commitment is necessary. Then there is family pride. The Pope's daughter deserves a man who appreciates her beauty. What celebrating there had been when the report of Cesare's wedding night in France had arrived in Rome. The duke had "broken his lance" eight times! Eight! Who could ever doubt the virility of Borgia blood after that? In private, Ercole d'Este might ridicule such bragging, but in public, for it to go well tonight he will be embarrassed by—say—fewer than two. No, a number of lances must be broken here tonight for this coupling to be counted as a success.

Given so many interested parties gathered in this high-class marital bed, it is a tribute to the power of nature that any conjunction takes place at all.

We are both old enough for what is to come.

Lucrezia has thought a lot about her husband's words whispered during that first meeting, not least because they remain the most intimate exchange they have had. Over the last few days they have sworn vows and swapped rings, shared banqueting tables, danced together—he is by no means as bad a dancer as he claimed—watched concerts and plays, and sat through speeches so hyperbolic and endless that on one occasion she had pressed her elbow into his side to alert him to his snoring. But any sustained or personal conversation, even the odd secret look or smile acknowledging each other as coconspirators in this elaborate ritual—this has not happened.

She draws comfort—if *comfort* is the right word—from the fact that it is not only her he treats this way. Alfonso d'Este seems singularly ill suited to the role of courtier. There are times when, like an adolescent at an adult gathering, he appears indifferent to the point of sullen. Though his wardrobe has clearly cost a sack of money and been fitted by the best tailors, he shifts and fidgets as if a dozen fleas are biting him. It makes her think of her son, Rodrigo, so boisterous with energy that he cannot bear to be trussed up in court robes and after a while tries to keep pulling them off. How they would laugh at him.

"Oh, let him go, he is a boy," the Pope would say, waving an arm, before puffing and panting theatrically as he got down on his knees to tickle Rodrigo. And how little Rodrigo would squeal and giggle helplessly then, as if he was in danger of dying of the pleasure.

But there is no laughter between this father and son. Indeed, from what Lucrezia can see there is no affection of any kind. The two men act like strangers to each other: their greetings barely courteous, their embraces cold and soon over. If the son is indifferent, the duke himself seems furious. She has watched his face when the two men think they are not observed, seen how he can barely contain his disapproval, as if this lack of engagement on Alfonso's part is a personal insult. Coming from a family where her father's love is so fierce and public that it can feel embarrassing, she has been fascinated and distressed.

More than once she has caught her father-in-law staring at his son's hands. The tailors have done their work well, and when he is not wearing gloves, the duke elect's sleeves are cut fashionably long so that they mask his fingers when he is standing. Certainly others do not seem to notice: or perhaps they notice so much that they choose not to look. Except when the attention of the whole court had been on them: the moment when this burly, surly husband of hers had joined a group of court musicians and picked up a gleaming six-stringed viol.

She had been transfixed, almost terrified; like watching a piece of Venetian glass perched between two slabs of uncooked beef. Oh, what an awful thing to think. She had closed her eyes to dispel the image.

When she opened them again it was in awe that two such powerful senses—eye and ear—could be so utterly at war. Because Alfonso d'Este is an excellent viol player. The music he makes is joyful, intimate, witty, exuberant and charming. Everything, in short, that he isn't. When he finished, she had applauded so merrily that people couldn't help but note her enthusiasm. It had been a warm touch in an otherwise rather cold wedding.

Cold, yes, she thinks. That's the right word for it. And such hard work; all the plucking, perfuming, creaming, corseting, lacing, powdering of her body and endless crimping of her hair: in readiness for the wedding night, her scalp has been furrowed like a new field; a hundred little sections of hair wetted and curled, pinned to her head and wrapped in a succession of hot towels to accelerate the drying.

It had been worth the effort. The release of each boisterous golden ringlet had been met by gasps of approval from her ladies, and when she entered the salon, an appreciative wave had run through the waiting women of the Este court. The real triumph, though, had been written on the face of her new sister-in-law. Because in the absence of any drama between husband and wife, it has been the bare-knuckle fight of fashion that has given the chroniclers spice for their dispatches.

Lucrezia Borgia and Isabella d'Este. They have much in common. Both are intelligent, cultured, wealthy women with the innate confidence that comes from being spoiled by adoring fathers. What separates them is breeding, age and looks. The Este lineage—and her clear legitimacy— puts Isabella's nose much higher in the air. Seven years older than Lucrezia, she was betrothed at six, married at sixteen into the noble House of Mantua, and she has proved her fertility with two daughters and now, finally, a young heir while along the way she has used her own and her husband's money and influence to create a court that is famous across half of Europe.

All this Lucrezia readily admires and aspires to. But there has been another more primal comparison at stake. At nearly twenty-two, Lucre-

zia is a flower in full bloom; her pale, perfect skin lights up any jewel she
wears and the more voluminous her skirts the more gracefully she carries them. Isabella, in contrast, has little of the girl left in her. After three
children she is already stout and spreading with an upper lip that needs
tweezing weekly and a jaw that would benefit from the decoration of
soft falling curls (for a married woman the seduction of hair is no longer
appropriate).

So when Lucrezia had set out for their first public meeting, on her
wedding day, dressed from head to foot in white and gold, she had been
confident that she would be the brightest star in the firmament.

Isabella, though, had been well prepared. What could possibly
eclipse white and gold? Well, how about a sultan-style turban covered in
jewels to make her taller and a gown of midnight blue velvet, enhanced
by embroidery? And not just any old pattern of birds and flowers. No.
Instead each inch of golden thread represents a symbol of musical notation. Musical notation on a dress! A woman making music as she walks!
Who had ever heard of such a thing? Such panache! Such daring! And
also the most witty compliment to their host, the duke, a man famed for
his love of music.

The marriage ceremony has been the least of the show. What everyone was waiting for was the moment when the two women met, costume to costume. The crowd had parted like the waves of the Red Sea
to give them a stage for the encounter.

It was Lucrezia who had taken the initiative. Swallowing her fury,
she had embraced her sister fondly. And then, roundly and very loudly,
complimented her on the beauty and utter brilliance of her dress. Not
once, not twice, but many times.

Oh, but it is the most original fabric in Italy.

Please tell me, was the idea yours or your dressmaker's?

The compliments went on and on.

*I warrant there's a tune hidden in all those folds. When the dancing comes
we must stay close together, so I can try to fit my steps to it.*

After the first simpering thank-you there was little Isabella could do
but stand and listen, for Lucrezia leaves no time for answers, so that in

the end it was the Marchesa of Mantua who was the more embarrassed of the two: exposed in her strategy of upstaging this young pretty woman of such fresh and guileless spirit—despite the gossip—that she remained graceful and courteous even when faced with malicious provocation.

It hadn't taken long for Lucrezia to get her revenge. That night as her rival remained seated (Isabella's feet are a good deal flatter than her voice, and all that velvet would be a burden when one is trying to fly), she had moved onto the dance floor and been airborne within minutes; the dozen cunningly cut white silk panels that fell from each of her elbows streaming out like banners of light around her, while the jewels in her skirts caught fire under the lamps, effectively eclipsing the dark velvet of Isabella's musical night.

In the privacy of her rooms, everyone agreed that the day had gone to the Borgias. Though no doubt the opposite assessment was made in the chambers of the marchesa.

We are both old enough for what is to come.

To minimize the assault on a woman's modesty, it is customary for the bride to be undressed and prepared before the witnesses arrive. And Lucrezia is ready.

She is a veteran of two husbands. The first had puffed and fumbled through the night, too anxious about his own body to be much interested in hers; the second had been so eager for ecstasy that it had been easy to share it with him. But she has vowed not to think of him tonight.

In the room at large the candles are now snuffed out. The embers of a fire lie in the grate, their glow barely strong enough to pick out the shape of the great raised curtained bed with a chest at its foot. Not even the sharpest sight could read the morally invigorating story of Susannah and the elders painted on its front. But then, this is not a job for the eyes. Like the duke's musical performance on the viol, posterity's report here will be based almost entirely on sound.

At the back of the woodpaneled room a door creaks open, then closes again. There are footsteps followed by a rustle of heavy material and a noisy settling of wooden planks under a mattress as they accommodate a noticeable extra weight. The three witnesses strain forward and close their eyes to concentrate.

An hour or so later, including two short intervals, it is all over, the conclusion marked by a further parting of curtains and heavy footfalls as the bridegroom retraces his steps to the door and leaves the room. The witnesses gather up their robes amid surreptitious clearing of throats and make their way out of the chamber. Their reviews will be unanimous: a fluent, well-orchestrated performance in a gamut of vocal registers, with some spirited allegros building to three clear crescendos, and a few tentative harmonic moments on either side. No diplomatic audience could possibly be disappointed in such a concert.

But what of the players themselves?

For Alfonso the performance was hardly an overwhelming ordeal. After all, he is a man well known for his experience in making this kind of music. For years now he has taken part in regular concerts in less salubrious areas of town, accompanied by willing professional partners with a wide and colorful repertoire.

And Lucrezia? How was it for her?

The ducal bedroom has not been empty for long when:

"My lady?"

At night, Catrinella goes barefoot, invisible as a cat, passing through doors and across floors as if she has never been there at all. She parts the bed curtains and holds up the lamp.

The bed is a storm of crumpled linen. Lucrezia is propped up against the pillows, a halo of muzzy curls around her face and her shift halfway up her body. She holds a pad of fresh gauze between her legs. Catrinella lets out a small gasp of horror, and her expression is one of such alarm that Lucrezia, who until that moment has been unsure if she is feeling sadness or triumph, can only laugh out loud.

"It's all right. There is nothing wrong. I am not hurt. It is normal for there to be leftover liquid. Praise be to God it is all in a good cause. We are man and wife. Come, help bathe me."

Standing and slipping off her shift, she feels a prickling heat inside her in the place where he has been. Three times. Women can bruise on the inside as well as out. But there is no pain. The truth is her husband had been as courteous as the process allowed. Three times. She can still hear the thick warble of his voice as he reached for the edge of the cliff. There had been moments during the last ascent when he had felt to be almost in pain getting there. Still, it had not been terrible. She would have liked to have helped, but with his body on top of hers there had been nothing she could do but wait. As he fell back on the pillows he had seemed to be laughing. Perhaps he had felt relief as much as satisfaction. Three times. No, not so terrible at all.

They work together, Catrinella tender with the sponge, then patting her dry with a perfumed cloth before helping her slip into a new night-shift.

"What are you looking at now?"

"There are marks on your neck, my lady. Redness. And on your cheeks."

"Ah! The rubbing of skins." She thinks of those meat-slab hands, their scabby surfaces moving in rough caress over her. Sometimes it is useful to fear something too much, for it makes the real thing quite bearable. "I shall not need a pumice bath for a while," she says gaily, but Catrinella is clicking her tongue angrily. At the grand age of fourteen and a half she has already made the decision that she will remain a virgin forever, convinced that all Italian men are as hairy as monkeys and even less courteous.

"If you are finished you may leave me now. The night is not over and my husband may come back."

The young girl drops her eyes, busy with the basin of water.

"What? What is it? Come, you have no secrets from me."

"He has left the palace, my lady," she says quickly. "Angela and the other ladies saw him from the windows. He had his men waiting on horses in the back courtyard and after . . . well, after, they rode out together."

Oh! Such sharp eyes they have, my ladies, she thinks. How could she ever want for a better spy system?

Make him welcome every night but never complain when he leaves you. . . . Men are like that. She remembers her father's stumbling words as they made their last goodbyes in Rome. *Men are like that.* Of course they are.

Triumph and sadness. At times there is little to tell between them.

"Well . . . If that is so then . . . then you can bring me some hot wine and something to eat. Yes, yes, some cake or milk pudding for, now I think of it, I am quite hungry. And do not look so glum. Your mistress is the Duchess of Ferrara and there is much to celebrate."

• • •

Three times. The next day, word of the duke elect's performance is already halfway to Rome, and in the court of Ferrara there is no one who does not know it. Lucrezia sleeps late and, with conscious mischief, keeps everyone waiting awhile before she emerges into public gaze.

In her rooms across the courtyard, Isabella picks up her quill and writes to her husband in Mantua.

Last night Lord Don Alfonso slept with Lady Lucrezia, and from what we have heard he walked three miles, though I have not spoken with either of them about it. Nor did we visit them to perform the morning after songs, as is called for, because to tell you the truth, this is a most frosty wedding. Today we stayed in our rooms forever because the lady herself took such a long time to rise and get ready. . . .

To my credit, I am always the first person up and dressed, and my appearance and that of my company, I believe, has compared most favorably among all others.

SPRING
1502

The duke Valentine is truly magnificent. In war there is no enterprise so great that it does not appear small and in the pursuit of glory and lands he never rests, nor recognizes fatigue or danger.

—Letter from Machiavelli,
envoy to the Council of Ten in Florence
June 1502

If the couple make love, then that is enough.

—Cardinal of Capua and Modena,
after a visit to the court of Ferrara
April 1502

CHAPTER 8

"So, members of the council, it is agreed, yes? As long as Florence is under the protection of the French king we stand firm against any hint of Borgia aggression or pressured overture of friendship. The Pope is an old man. At his death the money and influence will disappear and Duke Valentine will fail. When that happens Florence's stalwart position will give her status in the world to come."

In his seat in the corner of the council chamber, Secretary Niccolò Machiavelli notes down the general murmur of approval. Piero Soderini, the elected leader of the republic, is an honorable and principled man, and it is impossible not to respect him. In another era, one of honor and principle, Niccolò thinks, he would make a most successful politician.

"Secretary, if you would stay behind for a moment."

High on the frescoed wall of the council chamber, St. Zenobius, the first bishop of Florence, stands with open arms, giving his blessing to good government, with a mischievous glimpse of the cathedral's famed dome peeking out from a pillar behind. It pains Niccolò every time he sees it, for this city that he so loves has changed dramatically in the years since the great Domenico Ghirlandaio stood with his brushes on the scaffold. Once respected everywhere for her wealth and stability, she now spends her diplomatic life looking nervously over her shoulder, like a young virgin on the street at night. For her to survive with her name, if not her purity intact, what is needed is a government that can temper republican honor with a more pliant pragmatism. But these are not the thoughts that he is paid to deliver. Unless directly asked.

"Do I gather you have some issue with the decision of the council, Niccolò?"

"I am its secretary, not an elected member, Gonfaloniere. It is my job to advise, not conclude." .

"Except with you one cannot always tell the difference. And since you have spent time at the court of King Louis, I would hear your thoughts."

"Your brother, Bishop Soderini, is as familiar with the French court as I."

"But he is not here now. And you are. So speak your mind."

"I think—" He takes a breath. "I think whatever King Louis's ambassadors may say publicly, privately the king does not give a fig for Florence's independence." The hawk comes in so fast the shrew would not even register the wind of its wingbeat. "In his view we are a second-rate power with no army to defend ourselves and no money to pay properly for others to do the job."

It is a conclusion born of the bone as well as the brain. The French court at Lyon had been Niccolò's first foreign assignment, and he can still feel the freezing chill of its antechambers, waiting for an audience that never came because there was always someone more important to see than a Florentine diplomat. He'd missed the death of his father and his sister while waiting, had spent so much of his own money that he could no longer afford to eat properly and his one good suit of clothes had grown shabby and behind the fashion, details that were not lost on the king and his cardinal minister, when they finally deigned to see him. As a lesson in international diplomacy the humiliation had been almost exhilarating.

My God, you look scrawny, his drinking companions had joked when he got back. *So tell us some dirty French stories and we'll buy you dinner.* They had even urged a wife upon him. *Once a man turns thirty he needs proper meals and a soft bed. You can't live in whorehouses forever.*

No, Niccolò Machiavelli has little time for French promises.

"The king needs the Pope and the Borgia army to help him beat the Spanish in Naples and he will do whatever it takes to keep them as allies. If it came to it, he would cut us adrift without a second thought."

"Anything more to add?" the gonfaloniere says mildly. "Some insight perhaps into when the Pope will die? That would be helpful."

Niccolò smiles. In Dante's hell the soothsayers walk round with their heads twisted backward to show that only God has the right to foretell the future.

"His uncle, Pope Calixtus, lived till he was seventy-nine, though he was only interested in fighting the Turks. In my opinion, Gonfaloniere—" Niccolò hesitates. "In my opinion, if the pace keeps up as it is then he will only need a few more years. Eighteen months ago Duke Valentine had to buy in French troops to help him take the cities of the Romagna. Now he could take most of them on his own. He never stops recruiting and has every local lord and mercenary in his service, which gives him the loyalty of the very men who should be most fearing his ambitions. The Borgia state they are helping him build will eat up their territories easily enough. The duke is fortunate that they are too busy weighing their purses and settling their own scores to notice."

Soderini laughs bitterly. "Indeed. The most powerful of them being Vitellozzo Vitelli and his public obsession with taking revenge on us."

He sits with his hands intertwined. Absentmindedly, he begins to crack his knuckles. Niccolò starts to count. He had a tutor once who would do the same thing, a most inspiring scholar who had opened his mind to all manner of wonders before he tried to move on to his body. When his father had dismissed him—eagle-eyed in the education of his son—the relief Niccolò felt had been tinged with sadness. Great men, he was already learning, do not always do great things.

"Well, Secretary, as ever I am grateful for the . . . clarity of your views. We will talk further on all of this tomorrow. I daresay your wife would appreciate you home occasionally to enjoy her company. Tell me, how is marriage suiting you?"

"Well enough, Gonfaloniere," he says, tasting again the layer of congealed fat on last night's pigeon stew when he returned from a later debriefing session in the tavern near the bridge. Still, better a woman with some spirit. He had worried how this new state might bore him, but the challenge she offers had kept him keen enough.

"Before you go, Niccolò, one further question. From everything that crosses your desk you still see no sign of when the duke's next campaign might start?"

Give me money to run a real intelligence service and I will give you the intelligence it finds, he thinks sourly. Oh, for the open purse of the Pope . . . Outside he hears a trill of birdsong. He no longer bothers with the clay bottle from home. Soon enough it will be too hot in here rather than too cold.

"Valentine's commanders haven't been paid since December. I would say something will happen soon enough."

• • •

"How long are we meant to sit around here waiting for his scar-face lieutenant, Michelotto?"

"Oooh, the new ruler of Fermo is feeling the power of his title! How does it feel, Oliverotto, being 'the duke'? Makes your beard grow faster, does it?"

The young man scowls. He might have known that his fellow mercenaries would be the last to congratulate him. "Valentine should have come himself," he says, ignoring the sarcasm. "Professional commanders deserve more respect."

"What? Like the respect of a nephew knifing his loving uncle in the back?"

The story has been all over Italy for weeks: how on the excuse of returning to his home city of Fermo for Christmas Oliverotto had in-

vited his uncle and his advisers to a celebration banquet, then slaughtered them all to snatch the government and the title.

"Fuck off, Baglioni," he says petulantly. "I looked him straight in the
eye and he fought me like a lion."

"With what? A candlestick?"

The mockery reverberates around the room.

"All right, all right. . . . Save the insults for our enemies."

The room falls quiet. Even among hired hands there is a hierarchy,
and everyone listens when Vitellozzo Vitelli speaks. He was born into
the saddle, and without his soldiering they would all be counting more
dead men, for his expertise is artillery: lightweight cannons that move as
fast as foot soldiers, blasting holes in fortresses and sending a rain of
death onto the civilian population inside.

He shifts his position in his chair to try to calm the burning poker
stab that is running through his legs. He needs his wits about him now.
He glances round the room. There are six of them altogether: soldiers
of fortune, condottieri, as they are known. It's no longer the honorable
career it once was, but then times are hard and Italy is full of sons of
powerful families for whom there's no room in the Church or government so instead they have developed their natural talents for brawling
into the profession of war. They are chancers, all of them, he thinks.
Ambitious young thugs like Oliverotto, the quarrelsome Baglioni brothers from Perugia or hangers-on from the Orsini family, men with insuf-
ficient inheritance to finance their lifestyle. There is not a natural ally of
the Borgias among them. In the past they've all spat snake venom at the
sound of their name, calling them dagos and poxy foreigners. But right
now, until the tide turns, the Pope and his warrior son are too powerful
to be ignored. Especially when there is such good money to be made
out of them. "We'll know what is coming soon enough."

"Our newly elevated duke is right though," Gian Paolo Baglioni
growls. "Duke Valentine treats everyone like shit. When the wedding
circus came through Perugia, we laid out a fortune entertaining his precious sister and her entourage."

"How were they, all those lovely ladies?" another chimes in.

"Ripe as summer melons," he replies with a grin. "Especially the bride."

"Wooah! You weren't tempted to have a taste?"

"You know me—I don't do leftovers."

The room erupts into crude laughter. Everyone knows the rumors about the Borgias: father and daughter, brother and sister. Well, why not? She wouldn't be the first young woman to keep the family bed warm. There are men here who with a little wine in their bellies would testify to the succulence of sisters with no hint of shame on their faces.

"Still, I'd be careful who you boast to, Baglioni," Vitelli's voice comes in quietly. "That ripe melon you talk about is now the Duchess of Ferrara."

"Ah, don't deny us our pleasure of a little imagination, Vitelli. Your trouble is you don't have enough fun off the battlefield."

It is the first mention anyone has made of it, how during the break a vigorous middle-aged man seems to have turned into a crippled old one. These past months, Vitelli has felt as if death itself has been making a play for him. The pain wakes him most nights and by day sings through every limb. He doesn't know when or where he caught the French pox—no busy soldier has time to keep a record of his whoring—nor why he has got it so much worse than others. But what he does know is that with each new attack of the pustules and cankers the damage bites deeper inside him.

He has taken the advice of a dozen quacks, slathering himself with ointments and poultices laced with mercury, but the numbing always gives way to even worse burning so that his temper has grown as raw as his skin. His teeth are loose in his gums, and his joints—or is it his very bones?—are so constantly on fire that he finds it easier to be in the saddle than standing on the ground. War will be a relief, and this next campaign may bring him something even sweeter.

"I thank you for your concern, Baglioni. But I'm looking for something more than fun."

Revenge. For Vitellozzo Vitelli it is, like everything else in Italy, a family affair. He had been apprenticed in the craft of war through his elder brother, Francesco. But a few years before, when Florence still had the money for it, Francesco had gone solo, selling his military services to the city. When the expedition to quell a revolt in Pisa had gone awry, the government had accused him of treachery. A gross insult against the family name. On the day of his brother's public execution Vitellozzo had sworn undying vengeance on the whole city. He has always known that backing the Borgias would be his best chance of getting it. These days it is what keeps him loyal, as well as what keeps him going.

"You should be praying that it happens, my friend," he retorts sharply. "As long as the duke is hungry for Florence's territories he won't be interested in Perugia."

"Ha. He wouldn't dare!"

"You're sure about that?"

They fall silent. It is their job to talk big—modest mercenaries don't get much work these days—but the reality is the Borgia war machine has impressed even those who fight for it: the merciless speed and strategy of a man who has no code but winning and always seems two steps ahead of whoever is in his way. As long as it is directed toward others there is only profit to be had. But who can be sure? Perugia, Città di Castello, Anghiari, Fermo, even Bologna. No one in this room needs to look at a map to know that any of their own cities would fit nicely into the expanding Borgia state.

"Well, for now we are all safe," Vitelli says evenly. "Every one of us has done better from fighting with him than against him. If and when that changes we can talk again. I for one am still in, for this season at least. Anyone disagree?"

In the silence that gives him his answer, they hear a commotion of men and horses in the courtyard below. It seems their orders have arrived.

. . .

Michelotto has ridden from Rome stopping only to change horses and with a single servant at his side. Two days' wind in his face have painted his scars livid, and his pulled left eye is running with cold tears.

He enters the room, shakes each man by the hand and then settles himself without a word. He brings no sealed instructions and he carries no notes. He speaks only for a few moments, and when he has finished he pushes six thick purses across the table.

"Any questions, gentlemen?"

Oliverotto da Fermo glances round at his fellow soldiers. Well, he is a duke himself now and his thoughts deserve to be listened to.

"I don't understand. You're telling us that Vitelli's job is to stir up Arezzo. Which means Duke Valentine is going for Florence. Yet the orders to the rest of us are to be heading the opposite way? It's a blind, right? So when do we make the move back?"

For a moment it seems that Michelotto will not even bother with a reply. He is already up from the table, fastening his cloak.

"I wouldn't worry about such things now, my Lord of Fermo," he says, larding the title with exaggerated courtesy. "Just keep that sword arm of yours loose and ready. Your next great battle may be against men who are armed."

Oliverotto scowls but swallows the insult in silence.

In his seat at the end of the table, Vitelli can feel the stabbing in his leg subsiding a little. He stretches it out and rubs his fingers over his thigh.

Arezzo. And then Florence! It is amazing what good news can do for an ailing man.

CHAPTER 9

❖

S pring comes fast to Ferrara that year. The fogs disperse and behind dozens of convent and palace walls orchards are in blossom, so that when the wind rises, the streets are showered with a confetti of petals. In the medieval quarter of the city, where the tradesmen and laborers live stacked like bales in a warehouse, braver souls are unstitching themselves from layers of winter serge and kicking out livestock from under tables and hearths to clear out the winter stink. Pigs, goats, chickens, geese tumble out of doors, rooting their way in search of fresh rubbish, fighting for space with horses and loaded carts in the narrow streets, which fan out from the wharfs that line the riverbanks. The trade may not be as rich as that of Venice, but there is enough to sustain a thriving economy, and with Duke Ercole's expansion of the city, there is a demand for everything from bricks to braising pots. The stages and celebratory arches that marked the flamboyance of her marriage have long since been scavenged or dismantled, but when the sun comes out Ferrara can still put on a show to impress its new duchess.

It is a mutual seduction. Having settled herself, Lucrezia is eager to escape from the confines of the great palace and fortress. Duke Ercole and the main court are housed in the palace, but she and her husband have the privacy of their own apartments in the adjoining castle, its towers and battlements stark reminders of how the Este family had clawed its way to dominance by subduing any and all who opposed it. It still boasts the protection of a moat, in one direction stretching halfway to the city walls, in another bordering on the grandest of gardens with orchards, fountains and summerhouses, reached by a flotilla of little boats. The old duke stages naval pageants on this inner-city sea, with monsters rising from the deep and pirates jumping from the rigging of one galley to the next with firebrands in their teeth. Such violent pleasures there are to be had in peacetime.

Lucrezia's and Alfonso's suites are in separate towers, the refurbishment and decoration of her own directed by Ercole himself. There is a small garden overlooking the moat with potted orange trees and a most luxurious bath chamber, with a freestanding tub and marble seats for her ladies to rest on. The colors in all of the rooms are fierce: crocus yellows, wildest blues and fiery ocher reds. Her taste is for something more peaceful to the eye, but it would only offend to change the décor too fast.

As the weather grows warmer she uses it as an excuse to move outside. In Rome she was closeted within the Vatican district, the rest of the city too sprawling, too dirty, too dangerous to frequent without an armed guard. She had been barely seventeen when her brother Juan had been pulled from his horse at night and butchered like a market animal before his body was thrown into the Tiber. No, the streets of Rome had been no place for the daughter of the Pope.

But here everything is on her doorstep. For her first forays she and her ladies take her carriage. They follow a new route every day, and the Ferrara they discover is not one but many cities: to the south a labyrinth of alleys and timber warehouses blackened by centuries of trade, to the north the duke's famed new town. Though not as perfect as the panel painting they had marveled at in Urbino, the buildings are finely proportioned with brightly painted façades that catch the sun, and in between them thoroughfares wide enough to waft away the smell of horse dung offer open views to the sky. If this is the future, how generous, how clean it is.

But she likes the old center best. On the journey from Rome, Stilts had often talked of how Ferrara was a city of music, and he was right. The main piazza in front of the cathedral is so close that from her terrace she can hear the voices of the blind troubadours, singing epic tales of courtly love leavened with rough humor. The best of them—they seem almost a fraternity—accompany themselves on viols, with boys on pipe and drum to emphasize the more dramatic moments. The boys also provide the eyes of the act, since with so much going on it is hard for a blind man to hear whether the clinking records coins going into the hat or being taken out.

Then there are the markets. Few traders ever found their way into the Vatican enclave, but here in Ferrara, God and commerce go hand in hand. An arcade of shops runs along the whole side of the cathedral: drapers, metal merchants, bookbinders, silversmiths, apothecaries, their presence as old as the church itself. In the mornings they are joined by dozens of carts and stalls. The first time Lucrezia and her ladies venture out they are in the company of her majordomo and a few guards, their heads covered and baskets on their arms, rich young women playing at shopping. Stilts is dubious, but she cajoles: what harm can it do? And they have been closeted for so long. There is a whole section of the square reserved for fishmongers, rows of wooden barrels, the water churning and spitting with silvered bodies: pike, lampreys, trench, carp and of course river eels swarming like snakes. The sellers thrust hands as tough as barnacled hulls into the frenzy, pulling out two or three at a time, slapping them down on the block and chopping off their heads with a single *thwack*, which sends sprays of bloody water everywhere. The ladies squeal with delighted disgust, and soon a crowd gathers. It is fun only until the crush starts to panic the guards.

Next day Lucrezia has to send out a purse to compensate those with spoiled produce or broken noses. But the story is everywhere within hours and the gifts flood in: a duchess who is in love with her city is rewarded by a city that wants even more to fall in love with her. It is not only sentiment. This pretty lady may arrive caked in scandal, but her very bastard status means Ferrara is now favored by the Pope. In the violent chaos of Italy, that fact alone means citizens can hold their heads a little higher.

She attends court evenings in the loveliest of the old palaces, Schifanoia, the word itself a play on the expulsion of boredom. Inside the great salon, the seasons of the year unfold through a dazzling set of frescoes, the dead Duke Borso d'Este sitting in state surrounded by admiring women, a benign presence despite the fleshy nose and double chins. She will need such painters of her own now, but the men who created this wondrous world are all dead, and when she asks it is clear there are no rising stars in the city. She must look elsewhere. Meanwhile, she is invited to visit the university. Ferrara boasts one of the oldest medical schools in Europe, and a few weeks before, when the weather was still bone-crushingly cold, there had been a dissection of an executed criminal in one of the churches. Her own physician had asked leave to attend. He keeps the secrets of the corpse to himself but returns filled with wonder at the school's botanical garden, where they are growing hundreds of medicinal plants, including a few brought back from the new world. It would, of course, be their honor to show her around.

"Here, my lady, crush these flowers, good for digestion . . ."

"Put this to your nose: it is a well-known remedy for headaches . . ."

"Taste the sweetness in these seeds, their oil is excellent for troubled nerves."

Before she leaves they present her with a leather wallet, each pouch filled with a different concoction, including, one says with a quiet blush, "something to aid conception and ease the pain of partum."

Conception. The business of a male heir is on everyone's mind. Certainly she and Alfonso are hard at work on it. The rhythm of their coupling reflects the wedding night. On the chosen evenings—not all, but at least three, sometimes four times a week—Alfonso sends his servant a few hours before to make his intention clear, and Lucrezia, after being sure to take the herbs mixed in warm wine, retires to bed, curtains drawn and candles extinguished.

When he comes in he may mumble a greeting, or simply take off his clothes and start. His usual way is to bury his face in her neck, then move his scaly hands over her breasts and down her body until, when he is ready, he climbs on top of her. At times it is fast, at others it takes longer, and during these moments he will moan and shout, so it is unclear if he is in the throes of desire or just impatient. Once or twice she has found her own voice catching in her throat as an unexpected pulse of pleasure starts to build inside her, and at such moments she holds on to him tightly to encourage him to take her with him as he climbs. Everyone knows that children are more readily conceived when both voices sing out together. But not all men know how to listen at the same time as they perform, and if husbands and wives do not talk to each other, then how can such things be promoted? Still, there have been a few instances, when there is a touch of pleasure in the duty, that she has almost been sorry their music does not last longer.

Afterward, they lie together while he catches his breath, and occasionally they may fumble their way toward a little conversation.

"How do you find your apartments?" he had asked after the fifth or was it the sixth visit, as if they were strangers swapping courtesies in a crowded room. "The orange trees for the terrace were grown in a hot room in the botanical gardens."

She too has done her best. "You have been away from court for over a week, my lord. Your contribution on the viol is much missed."

"I am busy with engineers from Bologna."

Once, she asked him outright if he would like to stay longer, maybe partake of some refreshment.

"I am sorry. I have work to do."

"It's very late."

"When we are smelting, the furnace burns whatever the hour."

It is true. His workshop, set far in the back of the gardens on the other side of the castle moat, is often lit long into the night. But when he leaves her that evening he makes a strange little noise with his tongue and says, "Good night, Lucrezia. I hope you rest well."

If there is no passion there is also no cruelty. Indeed, he can be almost solicitous. A couple of mornings they have gone hunting together in the forest around the country villa of Belriguardo, accompanied by the duke's prized leopards, animals of sinewy majesty brought from the Indies that slide through the undergrowth oblivious to their lack of camouflage, moving faster, when they sense their prey, than the fastest of the hounds. Alfonso is a fine huntsman, fearless and strong, and she is a good rider. On the first occasion they had traveled for miles inside a gray lake of mist, which rose above the horses' flanks, and he had asked if she was dressed warmly enough, for the Ferrarese fog could get into your bones, he said in a way that made it feel as if he genuinely cared that she should be well. She had ridden like a courtly Diana that morning, out in front of him at least twice, and when he caught up she could see from his face that he was impressed, though of course he said nothing.

Sometimes she wonders if it is shyness that besets him. Or something arising from his blatant antagonism toward the duke. As a much-loved sister and daughter, she is an expert at making peace between father and errant sons, but the one time she intervenes, suggesting he might attend a certain ceremony to please Ercole, his scowl makes him look just like his father.

She knows it is not just the duke or the pull of his precious foundry that keeps her husband away from court. There are also the women. He could have his pick of court ladies—everyone knows his father's mistress had been his wife's lady-in-waiting—but even in this he goes out of his way to do what the duke does not, and takes his custom to the whorehouses in the old part of the town. They say he likes his women round and loud, like his cannons, though with tighter holes, and that he comes and goes as he pleases with no affectations or commitment. And that such lack of courtesy suits him.

But though the images are crude, the reality is not so bad.

"These *puttane* are nobodies." Angela, who is a duck to water in the murky seas of court gossip, has become the spokeswoman of her ladies. "Gross whores with no power or status, while the whole court knows that he regularly comes to your bed."

Angela is eager to put a good gloss on it, yet in essence Lucrezia knows she is right. No woman, be she duchess or dressmaker, can expect a husband to be faithful, and when it comes to marriages of power, who would want the daily shame of sharing the banquet table or the concert chamber with some gloating rival from the court? Whatever his appetite, Alfonso shows her more consideration, if not more honor, than other men might.

How she loves her ladies. Along with her confessor they are her greatest confidantes. They are also her responsibility. On the journey from Rome these starling chatterboxes, each and every one unmarried, had tasted the excitement of young men sniffing around them, and they are blossoming under the attention of new admirers.

When they all sit together in the afternoons, sewing and discussing the business of fashion—as necessary to the vibrancy of court as music or poetry—the drama of flirtations is the chief entertainment. Angela, in particular, tasting life and love together for the first time, is dizzy with it all. One afternoon a few weeks before, Lucrezia had come upon her and the duke's illegitimate son, Don Giulio, nibbling at each other in a secluded corner. It had sent a shiver through her, recalling a moment many years before when she had found her brother Cesare with his hands up her sister-in-law Sancia's skirts. She had been such an innocent then. Still, her ladies are in her care and she must look to their moral welfare. Don Giulio is not the only bee buzzing round the honey. The old duke, when he hears of the dalliance, is most displeased and orders him not to visit so often. Angela pines and whines. "Don't worry." Lucrezia laughs. "If his intentions are honorable . . ." But everyone knows they are not. That is what makes them so exciting. A good court needs dalliances to give it spice, and the women's chatter and exuberance are everywhere.

But their meetings are not always so joyful.

Because the fact is that not all her ladies are still with her. Some have been sent back to Rome.

No. While she may not be unhappy, Lucrezia's life is not without conflict.

Her problem is her father-in-law.

CHAPTER 10

✦

*T*he doctor opens the door of the great hinged barrel and Cesare staggers out in a cloud of pungent-smelling steam, his naked body shiny with sweat. He sits heavily on the seat, taking gulps of fresh air. Torella, his priest's collar rising from his black robes, takes a cloth and dries his patient's upper torso, carefully studying the muscled forearms and the solid chest: alongside old ridges of dagger wounds are dozens of scarlet notches incised into the skin, like badly healed burn marks.

"Well?"

"Very good, my lord. Very good. There is no discharge and the skin is firm. Is there any sensitivity to the touch?" He presses his finger on a notch near the duke's nipple. The duke lets out a bloodcurdling scream.

The door bursts open and half a dozen men fall into the room, naked blades already out.

"I am tortured by a mad surgeon," he yells, then bursts out laughing as he waves them out. "You should see yourself, Torella. You're as white as the Madonna's breast. No, it doesn't hurt." He pushes down onto his own skin, turning the blotches pale, then watching as the color seeps back again. "In fact I think I could do with a little more feeling," he says, thinking of Fiammetta's fingers running over him.

"You have had no further outbreaks of pustules?" Torella is regaining his composure.

"No," he says, reaching for his clothes.

"Excellent. That shows the toxic humors have been driven out by the steam."

"I still sweat like a pig at night sometimes. I wake up swimming in my own lake."

"I believe that is a good sign. If there *should* be any further buildup of malicious humors, they are finding their own way to expel themselves," he says, mumbling a little with the last words to gloss over what might be construed as a contradiction of reasoning.

"Hmm. What about my face?"

"The scars are no longer angry, my lord," Torella says, staring hard at the rash of pockmarks across Cesare's cheeks and forehead. "And . . . and the beard is a most healthy growth, which is not always the case on damaged skin."

"Is that it, man?"

What more can he say? Before the pox, Cesare Borgia's beauty had been almost unbearable: the splendor of fine bones under the soft kid leather of boyish skin. No women—or men—could take their eyes off him. The illegitimate son of a pope: what wonder that corruption should look so lovely. It had almost been a relief when he opened his mouth and a brash, ambitious young man was revealed, too self-absorbed to appreciate what he had been given. As a priest, Gaspare Torella has sometimes worried about the poison of vanity, but among the sack of sins this young man will take to his grave, that one weighs less now. "You are a soldier, my lord. You need to see these as wounds from another kind of war. One that has been fought within your own body. There are many who do not survive it."

"Don't worry." Cesare smiles. His teeth are unexpectedly white. When he chooses to wear his black velvet mask for public appearances, the contrast is dramatic. Exactly as he would have it. "You have done a good job. You may leave us now. Michelotto and I have business."

"My lord." Torella hesitates. "I . . . I have a favor to beg of you." He takes a breath. "I have written a short treatise on my work on this new plague, which I hope to distribute around the universities of Europe. I would like to dedicate it to you, as my employer and patron. I believe that it will be of import in the future of medicine."

"What? To Cesare Borgia, the man you cured of the French pox." He roars with laughter, and this time Michelotto joins in. Their humor is always strangely without mirth. "I had a more prestigious epitaph in mind, Torella."

"Oh, I do not mean that you are referred to as a patient. No, no. Of course I have learned from your treatment, but in the treatise I call you by another name."

"Who am I?"

"A young man called Tomaso who contracted the disease in Naples. As you did. Rest assured, no one will recognize you. And it will be medical history, my lord."

"I shall think about it."

But before the door closes on the priest, the request is forgotten.

"So?" Cesare turns to Michelotto, who has sat waiting patiently all this time.

"They are all instructed and waiting on the word."

"Good. And Vitelli?"

"He is eaten up with pain as well as anger."

"He should find a better doctor. Still, he will feel pleasure soon enough, until it turns to bile. We're ready then. All that remains is to tie up the loose ends in Rome. Unless you need to rest from your journey?"

But Michelotto is already on his feet, the dust of the road rising off his clothes. "You do not need to be involved in this, my lord," he says as he straps on his sword. "This is work I can do on my own."

"Of course it is. But when you give a man your word, Michelotto, it is only fair to be there when you break it, wouldn't you say?"

• • •

Privilege and despair. Like wealth and poverty, they live close together in Rome. But the contrast is at its fiercest inside Castel Sant'Angelo on the bank of the river Tiber.

When the Pope is tired of his rooms in the Vatican, it is here that he comes, padding unobserved along the raised corridor to this fortified mausoleum. The upper floors are luxurious now, newly restored and decorated with a garden on the roof, glass in the windows, frescoes and tapestries on the walls and pomades of burning herbs to sweeten the air and keep the insects away.

In the bowels of the building, the dungeons too have been renovated, dug deeper and darker, a few chambers with water pits in the middle so that the rats can flourish and any guests must cling to a narrow platform for fear of falling in. This building knows a thing or two about rotting bodies since it was once the tomb of Emperor Hadrian. But then he had been dead when he came in.

The cells where the Manfredi brothers are kept are mercifully dry, with thin light from a slanting window, enough to differentiate day from night. There is one room for sleeping and another for living, and these two young men have done what they can to carve out an existence here, in the hope that fortune has not deserted them entirely. Not all prisoners die in their cells, and their only crime is owning something that Cesare Borgia wanted more: the town of Faenza.

In the year they have been incarcerated, their jailers have grown almost fond of them. They have a lute and a few books and keep a manservant, who tastes every meal before they eat it, though not to judge how edible it is. At the beginning they had hopes that they would be released. At the age of sixteen, Astorre Manfredi had surrendered his title as Duke of Faenza on the promise of their lives and an offer to join the Borgia army. His own citizens had advised him against it, but the cannons were roaring and there were no more dogs in the city to be eaten.

No sooner had the Borgia duke shaken hands on the deal than both brothers were in chains.

In recent months the younger one—just twelve—has succumbed to melancholy. He cries often and talks wildly in his sleep. Astorre Manfredi is more resilient. He exercises, walking to and fro between the walls, prays regularly and until they took his writing instruments away, wrote daily to the Pope: not sniveling letters, but simple eloquent ones, pledging loyalty and love of God and asking that they might be allowed to leave the country and live quietly somewhere else.

The Pope, who held no personal grudge against him, found these letters painful to read and so asked that he receive no more. Manfredi now scratches poems on the wall. He has heard of men who beat their heads against the floor as a way of getting out, and he fears that his brother may do that. But he, so far, has resisted despair.

When the door opens on Cesare Borgia that afternoon, Astorre wishes he might have had some way to trim his beard.

"My brother and I are at your command, Duke Valentine," he says.

He knows, of course, what is coming, but it will be a small victory not to show it.

"We are ready to march with you in unswerving loyalty in the terms of the treaty negotiated between us in good faith fifteen months ago."

"And I wish I could honor it," Cesare says carefully. "Really I do. But I can't. And it is better that I tell you directly. I have waited as long as I can to put this off, but as you of all people will understand, the security of Faenza demands that it have only one ruler."

"I mount no challenge to you," Astorre says, gesturing to the prison walls around him.

"But you remain alive."

Michelotto now enters the room, kicking the thick wooden door closed behind him. In the corner the boy, who had been watching open-mouthed, starts to moan, sliding down the wall, his arms clasped around his chest.

"Don't be afraid, Brother," Astorre says loudly, never taking his eyes off Cesare. "I will be with you every step of the way. Duke Valentine,

Faenza is your city. There is nothing more I can do to save her. Or myself. I have only one request. For the love of God and family."

He takes a step toward the duke. At the back of the cell, Michelotto lets out a growl, but Cesare silences him with a wave.

Astorre is close now, head down, speaking fast under his breath so that only Cesare can hear him. When he stops he looks up directly at Cesare and boldly puts out his hand. After a moment's hesitation, Cesare unsheathes his dagger and hands it to him. Michelotto swears softly behind him but does not move.

Astorre turns, concealing the blade at his side, and moves toward his brother, curled and moaning in the corner.

"Come, Brother, look at me." He squats down in front of him. "No. Look at me. Good. They will not hurt you, do you understand? I would never let that happen. Come now, stand up. We must get you ready. See, it is just as I promised. You are going to be free from all this. So get up. Good. Good, now, stand straight so we may show these enemies of ours what the Manfredi family is made of."

The boy does as he is told, pulling his shoulders back, his eyes locked on his brother's face. Astorre pulls him into a fierce embrace, ramming the blade in fast, up and under the left ribs, straight toward the heart. The boy lets out a constricted scream. Astorre holds him tighter, talking all the time, a litany of whispered words of praise and affection, taking his weight as the boy collapses onto the knife.

Michelotto growls again. This is not his way.

It does not take long. They slide together to the ground, and Astorre cradles his brother in his arms as his gasping agony subsides, the more serious business of dying taking over.

When it is finished the cell is silent, as if they are all equally caught in the gravity of the going. Then Astorre's voice starts again, words not of consolation but of prayer.

"That's enough." Cesare is suddenly angry. "It's done. You had your wish. If you want God's forgiveness then you'll have to die in order to get it."

It is amazing how a man who was once a cardinal should be so averse to prayer.

All three of them now move at once. Astorre—dagger out proud like a bayonet in front of him—is flinging himself at Cesare, who is already out of range. He never would have reached him anyway, for Michelotto, faster than any of them, is behind him, the wire garrote up and over his neck.

He yanks his head back, kicking feet repeatedly from under him at the same time, straining backward to lift him off the ground. The dagger skitters across the stones. As the young man jerks and gurgles, hands groping desperately for the wire, Cesare picks up the knife and turns toward him. He stands in front of the flailing body, watching, a half smile on his face.

The garrote breaks the skin as Michelotto yanks again, yelling his own war cry as a necklace of crimson leaks out from under the wire. Manfredi's head is already falling strangely to the side as Cesare moves in and finishes the job. As befits the end of a dynasty, there is a lot of blood.

"That was too much risk," Michelotto says, breathing heavily from the exertion as he pulls the bodies into a pile. "What if he had moved faster? Or used the blade on you and not his brother?"

"You have no faith in human nature, Miguel. I could have predicted what he would do from the minute I shook hands with him on the battlefield," Cesare says, eyes shining, for it is a while since he has been so intimately involved in killing and he has forgotten the heart-thumping exhilaration to be found within it. "If the sea could not kill me, what chance has a boy with a knife? I am cured of the incurable pox, remember. With every step I take I make history." And he rocks to and fro on his feet fast like a boxer, throwing a fast punch at Michelotto as his laughter echoes round the cell.

◆ ◆ ◆

In his study Gaspare Torella inscribes the frontispiece of his manuscript in a long looping hand. Pride may be a deadly sin, but there are moments when even a man of God must excuse himself. Eight years it has taken him to finish it: eight years since this flesh-eating plague first erupted out of the city of Naples, leaving the world bewildered and stunned by its violence and speed of transmission.

At first there had been so many theories. A conjunction of the stars with Venus and Saturn in strident opposition. A mad clash of humors—heat and moisture in a city of prostitution invaded by soldiers during a spring of too much rain. Then there were those who saw it as a new disease altogether, brought back from the new world in the loins of soldiers who had copulated with barbarian women. But most majestic of all was the idea that God, angered by the cesspit of man's corruption, had decided to expose and punish the sins of the flesh by covering men's skin with weeping itching pustules. As a man of science Torella has studied them all, coming in the end to favor a collision of a number of them: God's hand played out in fatal coupling in a Neapolitan brothel—like a gross inversion of Adam and Eve; lust, like fire spreading as far as Northern Europe and the coast of Africa within a few years.

He had been one of the first physicians to experiment with mercury as a possible treatment. He had used it with some success on other afflictions of the skin, but the secret was the mix and the quantity. Get it wrong and it could kill with as much agony as the disease. He was trying out various salves (the Vatican had its fair share of sufferers) when the duke had become infected. It was now his life's work to save him. The idea of fumigation had come to him in France, where a second attack of facial pustules was wreaking havoc with Cesare's marriage negotiations. Having experimented on himself, Torella had built the fumigation barrel, a traveling hospital for the afflicted. The healing properties of infused steam: it will surely make him famous throughout the medical world.

The effect had been remarkable. After the second treatment the boils had stopped oozing, and when the scabs had formed, the pits they left had been smaller than those of untreated ones. He knows this because his desk is littered with other doctors' records and their measurements of the wounds. Those same records also recount the agonies men feel, how what starts on the surface soaks inward, penetrating even to their bones. At the University of Ferrara a few years ago, they had dissected the corpse of a sufferer and found that a number of his internal organs had been eaten away. Torella could only pray that the man had received last rites before he died, for if not he must have gone screaming into hell.

Praise be to God it has been otherwise with Duke Valentine.

After three outbreaks of pustules and pain he has been free for over a year.

It is true certain "symptoms" remain. Cesare's moods have grown noticeably unstable, his impatience too often blurring into fury, his energy ricocheting between mania and strange lethargy. Torella has read of a few other cases where the mind seems to have been equally corrupted, but there is too little information to be sure. And this dark prince of his was always a man of unquiet temperament.

What is indisputable is that five years after being infected, Cesare Borgia is alive and in no pain. Therefore he must be cured. It is how he sees himself, and as both a doctor and a priest, Torella knows how important that is: for the patient who believes in his recovery will profit more than one who remains in terror of death. In this wondrous partnership of healing, where man and God hold hands, the spirit is as important as the body. And though Torella has never seen this arrogant young man pray, there is no doubt that his spirit is very strong indeed.

Yes, he thinks. Cesare Borgia is cured.

Who would want to be his doctor if he was not?

"You should have changed your clothes."

"I did."

"Then you should have washed better," the Pope growls. "There's still blood on you. Today is the ceremony of dowry giving to young women in La Minerva, as you should remember well enough. It will not do for me to arrive as if from the slaughterhouse. What will Burchard think?"

"Whatever he always thinks. He never talks to anyone except his precious diary. The Manfredi deaths need to be news anyway. They tell the world that we are on the move."

"Still, one cannot help feeling pity for them. He wrote such pretty letters, the elder one, filled with poetry and loyalty. I will remember them both in my prayers. It is a burden, being born into a great family." Alexander says this rather cheerfully, though it's not clear whether he means theirs or his own. "So, we are ready then?"

Cesare nods.

"What about your man Vitelli?"

"He will do exactly as he is told. His hands are itching anyway."

"Riddled with the pox, I hear. A most despicable fellow. As are they all. My God, it turns my stomach sometimes that we should be allies with such vermin. Especially the Orsini, murderous snakes with their hands dripping in blood," the Pope says, unaware it seems of the irony of the comment. "Sweet Mary, Cesare, when I think of Juan's body—"

"Not now, Father," Cesare answers quietly; five years on and his brother's death can still have the Pope crying like a baby. "We will deal with the Orsini in the future. For now we need them, and they wouldn't dare cross us. Not yet anyway. How is it with Camerino?"

"The Varano family are shouting like deflowered virgins at their treatment. But they are excommunicated anyway and the state is ours for the taking. When the fate of the Manfredi brothers reaches them, they will be falling over themselves to get out of the city before you arrive."

"And Urbino?" Cesare is prowling the room. Half of him is still in the cell, nerves on fire and blood splattering the flagstones. "None of this will work unless—"

"Yes, yes. It is done. The duke will give you safe passage. Our families are too well connected now for there to be any question, and our dear Lucrezia was such a gracious emissary. Ha! I must say, Cesare, it is a most elegant plan. Masterly. How long will it take?"

"By the end of the month Vitelli's agents will be in Arezzo fomenting trouble. When the moment is right they will open the doors to his army and Florence will have a full-blown rebellion on her hands. The government will be shitting itself to get ambassadors into my presence to negotiate. We will have a treaty in our favor soon enough."

"Yes! And I will have the French yelling treachery in my ear again," Alexander says, grinning broadly, the ceremony of virgins and their dowries slipping away in the exhilaration of the moment. "Ha. I can see the ambassador's face when he stands in front of me. *My dear man, we are as distraught as King Louis over this. Vitelli is a poxy maverick and this is his bilious ambition at play, not ours. The duke would never countenance such action, and if it is discovered otherwise, then I tell you plainly he is no son of mine.*" He waves his arms theatrically. "Louis won't believe a word of it, of course, but he can be mollified later. I will send a special diplomatic mission across the Alps to meet him."

"You won't need to. The king will be in Milan by midsummer. I will see him myself."

"Oh no, you won't. If this works, half of Italy will be lining up in Milan to vilify you. You would be walking into a lion's cage. You will stay where you are and I will defend you, remind Louis of our papal solidarity when it comes to his designs on Naples."

Cesare shrugs. He has it all planned anyway. He could try to tell his father, describe to him the bond that exists between him and the King of France; how if this plan works the lion will welcome him and together they will share the kill. A year ago he might have fought the point, confident that Alexander would see the step beyond the step, note what others regularly miss. But these days he is not so sure.

"Just as long as you are convincing in your outrage, Father," he replies.

"You doubt me? The beauty of it is that I don't even have to lie. My God, you have had me running every which way with this new madness. I have a church to govern as well, you know."

"If you'd let me go for Florence, we wouldn't be doing this at all."

"But oh, this is a far, far better plan," Alexander says gleefully. "I tell you, when we work together no one can beat us. People will be stunned. In awe! I can't wait to see their faces. I only wish I could go with you. A warrior pope—what a wonder that would be. Ha. Well, another time. And when the dust is settled it would be good for you to see your sister. I still wonder if we should—"

"No," he breaks in harshly "No one can know. No one. It is the only way it will work."

"It will cause waves in Ferrara when it happens."

Cesare gives a bitter laugh. "On the contrary, it will make them treasure her all the more. How else could they be sure of their own safety? How is she?"

The Pope flaps a hand to bat away the question.

"Is something wrong?"

"Diplomatic peccadilloes, that's all. Nothing a pregnancy wouldn't sort out. I wait for news every day. Everyone says that Alfonso is a most attentive husband."

But this doesn't please Cesare any better. Such thunder there is in his face. The boy has always been too prone to anger when it comes to his sister's husbands.

"I think that concludes our business, Cesare," Alexander says loudly, switching into Italian. At the door stands Burchard, two chamberlains behind him carrying the heavy white ermine stole decorated with pearls that the Pope must wear for the afternoon's ceremony.

"Yes, yes, I know, we are late for the ceremony," Alexander tells him. "The duke is just leaving. Though he used to love this ceremony when he was a cardinal, isn't that right, my son?" he says, dismissing him carefully without the usual familial embrace.

Burchard drops his eyes as Cesare marches out. It would not do to note the smears of dried blood on his chin, or the ill-concealed anger in his eyes. Even when the Pope's son had been a cardinal there had been only the barest ceremonial politeness between them, and that is long since gone. Burchard knows how much the duke dislikes him. How much he dislikes anyone who he thinks might be privy to his father's intimacy. There had been moments when for all his uprightness, this master of papal ceremonies had not been beneath listening at keyholes. But experience taught him fast that even when a German could follow the rapid fire of vernacular Catalan, it was better not to know what he might learn.

It is Johannes Burchard's great fortune to have been born with a phlegmatic disposition, further honed by being a penniless choir scholar in the great church of Niederhaslach, where climbing the ladder of ecclesiastical politics was a study in survival. A man could have no better apprenticeship for Rome.

"So, let us get ready, Johannes." The Pope beams. "You will have organized the procession down to the last detail, I am sure. Not too many soldiers, I hope. You know how I like to greet the crowd."

"There are guards at each stopping post, Holy Father, as protocol demands."

The Master of Ceremonies does not add that in recent months he has felt the need to use more of them. Since the circulation of the slanderous anonymous letter a few months before, there has been an undercurrent of disgust in certain elements of the citizenry, and it would not do to have the Pope heckled on his way.

"And tell me again, what is the dowry purse for the young virgins? Fifty or seventy-five florins? I can never quite remember. Seventy-five? My goodness. They are lucky to be under the care of Our Lady's friars. We shall add some gold ducats of our own, and make sure all the cardinals open their purses equally widely. The Church will have to find good husbands for these gentle young women to do them justice."

That afternoon, eighteen young women, veiled in virgin white and weak with nerves, wait inside the gilded nave of Santa Maria sopra Minerva, flanked by chaperones and Dominican friars, with cardinals and dignitaries filling the pews in front. At first Alexander's mind moves waywardly over the momentous events to come, but after a while he finds himself sinking into the richness of the ceremony. The Vatican is full of churchmen who snore their way through worship, but that has never been his way.

He still remembers the first great church he entered. Recently all manner of childhood memories in Spain are growing clearer, like a fog burning off a once familiar landscape. He had been nine years old; his father had died that winter and his mother had brought the family from the village of Xàtiva to Valencia under the protection of her brother the bishop, soon to be appointed cardinal in Rome.

The city's cathedral was famous, built on the ruins of a mosque, a symbol of Christ's eternal victory over the heathens and shining with a brand-new bell tower. Such theater it had offered after his local church: soaring Gothic arches like the ribs of a vast upturned boat, the wonder of a new double dome rising high above the altar with creamy daylight filtering through its thin alabaster windows, and below the heady smell of incense and the stark misery of Christ's tortured flesh on the cross, flowing with painted rivers of blood. But it was not Christ who had captured his heart that day. Nor even the great relic of the Holy Grail that brought daily crowds in pilgrimage. That honor had gone to a particular statue of the Virgin. The church was dedicated to her, and there she was: dressed as the Queen of Heaven enthroned in a sea of freshly gilded wood—he had never seen so much gold—while under her crown the sweetest face shone out, pale, lovely and loving. He could not take his eyes off her. Oh, how he yearned to climb up and sit wrapped inside her robes, looking out at the world with that gentle face above him. Such a safe place to be—in a woman's arms. It is a feeling that has never left him. When, a few years later, he was told that he, like his uncle before him, was to enter the Church, all he could think of was the Virgin's beauty. And all that gold.

No surprise then that Santa Maria sopra Minerva is his favorite church in Rome. It too was once a heathen site, a temple for Minerva, goddess of war and wisdom; it holds the body of Catherine of Siena, who died from an excess of ecstasy in a convent nearby. Then there is Mary herself, to whom it is dedicated. He has only to turn his head to the right to see a luminous annunciation in the chapel commissioned by Cardinal Carafa. The fresco had barely been dry on the wall when he became Pope, and every time he sees it, it makes his heart beat faster. These Florentine artists are alchemists; their color palette makes the walls sing. He has never seen a more radiant painted Virgin. What man could help but worship a woman who moves with such grace from fear and incredulity to the quiet acceptance of everything that God is asking of her? On the odd occasion when his mind strays fretfully to the gates of heaven, his entrance is always bathed in the serene light of the Virgin's smile.

The mass ended, Alexander welcomes the virgins, who kneel and kiss his feet, charming him all over again with their youth and modesty. As he gives each her purse, he makes sure to say a few words before she rises, making this the most important moment in her life and leaving any husband found for her forever in the shadow of God's most favored man on earth.

Before he leaves he passes by the image of Filippino Lippi's Virgin again. Could it be that she so enchants because her willowy beauty and unruly fair hair also remind him a little of the women in his own life: the lovely Giulia Farnese and his own, dearest Lucrezia? Yes, now she has grown into womanhood there is surely more than a touch of Lucrezia here. Well, once the armies have been paid and the map of Italy rewritten, there will be time to put her face all over the walls of Rome. Perhaps that way he will come to miss her less. God help that old miser Duke Ercole if he does not treat her like the priceless jewel that she is.

CHAPTER 11

❖

*L*ucrezia's troubles had started not long after the festivities officially ended. Ferrara had been under the gaze of much of Europe, and of course it had all been monstrously expensive: the ever-rising
bill for housing, feeding and entertaining envoys, ambassadors and their
retinues painful for a duke who likes to keep the string on his purse
double-knotted.

The foreigners soon drifted away. The French took longer, but they
are well known for enjoying others' hospitality, and as long as they rule
Milan no one would dare to criticize their manners. That left the entourage of Spaniards who had accompanied Lucrezia from Rome, and they
were in no hurry to go home. Free beds, a fine kitchen and an almost
nightly concert or play in the great hall of the palace; it was a sweeter
life than the occasional comforts of the Borgia Vatican. The duke's smile
had become frozen on his face. Ferrara already had a court and did not
need another. He made it known that these "guests" were no longer
welcome.

Reluctantly the courtiers took their leave. Which left Lucrezia's own household. Of course his daughter-in-law must have her ladies and her servants around her, but it's obvious to Ercole that there are just too many of them. The castle apartments echo to the sound of a foreign language. This is Italy, not Spain! It is insupportable. Something must be done.

When he raises the subject directly, Lucrezia, mindful of her need to fit in, is careful with her response. She studies the lists of her household and gives way over some lesser members. But the sticking point is her ladies. She goes to Stilts, who has become an unofficial go-between for both of them.

"I cannot, will not, part with a single one of them. They are my dearest companions."

He is understanding, but not encouraging.

"Clearly you must keep the very closest, but . . . I think the duke's fear is that with so many of them it leaves no room for any young Ferrarese women of good breeding who would give anything—anything—to serve their new duchess. You have already been so graceful and generous to the ordinary citizens in the street. Perhaps now you might see your way to extending that generosity to the families of the court."

Lucrezia listens, trying to work out if the tears she feels pricking at her eyes are fury or sorrow.

Her last stop is the papal envoy.

"It will pain His Holiness greatly to hear this," the man says gravely. "However . . . the makeup of your ladies is, well, rather a domestic matter, and I am not sure . . ."

He gives the smallest shrug. The silence is eloquent. Her dowry is paid and Ferrara is ruled by her father-in-law.

On the last day of March, Girolama, Drusilla, and two others of her inner circle ride out with the rest of the Spanish courtiers, and a small part of her heart goes with them.

But the real battle is yet to come.

To make a home here, she must also make a court. Ferrara has not had a first lady of any cultural force since Duchess Eleonora of Aragon, dead years before. Her father-in-law is now seventy-one years old, and if her husband is too busy or too surly to invest in his own court, then she, Ferrara's new duchess, must lay the foundations for both of them. It's the work she has been waiting for, and the prospect excites her deeply.

She takes her cue from Ercole himself. Though he may be famously miserly paying for others, he is profligate with himself. It is not just half the town that is new; the ducal palace is in a constant of state of rebuilding. His courtiers seem to think nothing of walking around with a permanent coating of brick dust on their clothes. The tennis court is being refurbished, more angled walls to enrich the game, and the old (though it is hardly that old) chapel has been pulled down in favor of a new one. There are plans for a bigger, grander theater space. When Lucrezia expresses surprise at such largesse she's met with compassionate smiles. She should have been here three years ago, when a whole group of courtiers arrived home from the summer progress to discover their quarters had been demolished while they were away!

Then there are the artists he keeps on the payroll: writers, actors, composers, singers, musicians. Barely an evening goes by without some spectacle. True, not every one is successful; the duke has a penchant for unwieldy classical plays that go on half the night and stupefy everyone except him and the performers. But no one sleeps when music is playing. The orchestra has near on sixty players and singers. Sixty! Many of them wooed away from someone else's court. Then there is Bartolomeo Tromboncino—a man with a voice to stir the gods, recently arrived from Mantua under a storm cloud of scandal for having murdered his own wife. Luckily for him, the lady had been in bed with another man at the time, so the duke finds it easier to pardon him. Lucrezia's enjoyment of his glorious baritone fades a little when she hears this, not least because it dovetails with whispers of how in the Este family history, if a wife is found in any other arms death is considered a light punishment.

She invites him to visit her. Many of the songs he sings are his own compositions, and their brilliance is beyond doubt. Would he consider writing a piece for her new court? She would be happy to supplement her small troupe with further players if he needs them. Perhaps he could suggest some names?

"I am afraid good musicians are at a premium in this part of the country, your lady. Duke Ercole has already snaffled up all the best ones."

"Then we shall pay whatever it takes to find others," she says with a smile. For money is no problem. Her huge dowry includes an annual income of ten thousand ducats. More than enough.

But a week later the head of her household comes to her with notices of bills to be settled and the revelation that there is no money to pay them. No money. What about her promised allowance? It seems it has not been released.

The meeting with her father-in-law begins with flowing compliments and smiles on both sides.

"Of course, of course, my dear daughter, you have only to ask and it shall be given. Eight thousand ducats will be in your purse by the end of the month."

"Thank you. And when might I expect the rest?"

"The rest? Oh no, my dear, I think you will find eight will be more than enough."

"But it was agreed that I would have ten," she says quietly. "And I will certainly need the whole amount."

"Yes, it has been a most costly time! For myself more than anyone. But now the wedding is over we can all make adjustments. Ferrara is not Rome, my dear, and ten thousand is excessive. Which is why I have decided on eight."

Lucrezia stares at him. While she has had troubles in her life, she has never, ever, had to worry about money. Her father's largesse has flowed like water in a new fountain: clothes, favors, titles, lands, income . . . To be fighting over two thousand ducats seems . . . well, embarrassing.

But if that is the only way to get what is her due . . .

"I'm sorry," she says brightly. "But I cannot live on that sum. I need the whole allowance."

"It's difficult, I know. I suspect that in your young life you have never had to think about such things, but in your position it is important. You must make an inventory of all your staff and their salaries and your outgoings in terms of food and clothing and entertainment. See—here, I have had my accountant do some calculations for you and . . ."

She sits in horror as he follows the numbers on the paper in front of him, stunned not simply by the patronizing tone but by how much he seems to be enjoying himself. What were the words her father had been heard yelling from his rooms as the negotiations over her dowry had become ever more acrimonious: *The man bargains like a common trades-man!* But is he also a liar?

"No." She cannot keep the anger out of her voice. "I cannot . . . I will not do that." She stops and tries again. *Dear Duke and honored father . . .* that is what she should say. Charm, Lucrezia. . . . Remember how men react. But the words stick in her throat. "My lord, when I left Rome it was made clear to me that my allowance would be ten thousand ducats a year. And ten thousand a year is what I need."

He says nothing, but his mouth is moving angrily.

"A duchess's court has standards, as you know well: musicians and scribes, envoys, stables, kitchens, my wardrobe—"

"My goodness, you cannot want for more clothes!" he says briskly. "Well, of course women do. And there are marvelous fabric merchants here in Ferrara. Most reasonable prices."

"I am sure." She smiles tightly. "But the best fabrics come from Venice. And it is to Venice that I send to clothe myself and my ladies—"

"Ah! Your ladies!"

"—Are a paltry expense," she throws back hurriedly, realizing her mistake. "It is *my* wardrobe first and foremost. You would not want me to look drab."

"You would never look drab, my dear." But the compliment falls flat. His voice is sour now. "I know you women are much concerned about such things. But I am not without experience. I may be a widower, but I have children who understand the price of fashion, and I must tell you I have taken advice on this."

Not my husband, she thinks. Alfonso would never do such a thing to me.

"My own dear daughter, the Marchesa of Mantua, has helped me. We spoke of it when she was here for the wedding, and since then I have been in correspondence with her. She has made an assessment of her own household to guide me. And she assured me that she conducts herself on eight thousand ducats most adequately."

For a moment Lucrezia is speechless. The poisonous toad! Eight thousand! Enough for Isabella d'Este? A woman famous for outbidding anyone and everyone when she wants something: statues, paintings and antiques? Isabella d'Este, who has a palace full of musicians and poets and keeps a stable of dressmakers and designers? The Marchesa of Mantua would have to go around in pleated sackcloth with a bag over her head to survive on such a sum. What a vicious meddler! She should have kept her waiting till doomsday on those mornings after the wedding.

She can sense a sweat on her skin now, and she feels suddenly sick to her stomach. No, no, this won't do. She did not fight her way out of Rome into a loveless marriage to be denied a court of her own.

She sits for a second, trying to regain her composure.

"I have to tell you that my father, the Pope, would be most unhappy to hear of this conversation," she says, keeping her hands carefully folded in her lap to stop them trembling. "The *considerable* dowry that was negotiated in good faith between our two families"—she does not add *the biggest in all of Italy*—"made it quite clear that my allowance was to be set at ten thousand."

Oh, but he doesn't like hearing about good faith or the Pope. Not at all.

No. It is his face that goes darker, and he makes a gruff grumbling noise as he shrugs his shoulders. There is a heavy silence. In the standoff they are both clearly thinking the same thing. The Pope may feel anything he likes, but Rome is a long way away and there is too much riding on this marriage for it to be broken over a sum of two thousand ducats.

. . .

She had left the audience barely able to hold back hot tears. She, who doesn't often give in to anger, had stomped around her rooms.

"How could he! *Tradesman* is too good a word. He is . . . well, he is a thief!"

Her ladies had gathered around her in a kind of awe.

But her sense of shame and fury is half directed at herself. From the moment this union with Ferrara was first suggested, Lucrezia had used every ounce of energy in pushing it through—the grief at her husband's murder, the fury at her brother, her aching pain of leaving her own son—all of it soaked up in her determination to get away. For what? A husband with a stable of prostitutes and a miserly father-in-law?

"It is all right when it is about his pleasure. New buildings, choirs, convents for stolen nuns; he vomits up the money easily enough then." She is weeping with rage now, spitting the words in half gasped breaths. "It comes pouring out of every hole. Oh, don't look at me like that! I have heard half of you use worse language when you think I am not listening. And he deserves it. The man has broken every promise. How dare he deny me what is rightly mine? As for the duplicity of his vile, vain daughter . . ."

It is just as well there are no Ferrarese young women yet employed in her entourage to hear all this. The famous Borgia temper, Angela mutters, as they stand and watch. One should not cross it. But of course they all rather admire it. They have never seen their mistress like this.

Fortunately, the same afternoon, a young nobleman had called to visit, Ercole Strozzi, a poet, a superior gossip and every inch the courtier despite a birth defect that makes him drag his left leg behind him, for it is one of the best dressed legs in Ferrara. He has a natural eye for fashion, women's even more than men's, and has become an instant favorite with Lucrezia's ladies. He is leaving for Venice and is happy to take any orders that the duchess might have. A cargo of first-rate embroidered silks is docking next week from India, their dyes as rich as peacock feathers. How they would suit her!

She welcomes him with flirtatious courtesy, giving him a full list of exactly what she requires. Payment is not mentioned. It would please him mightily to help see her clad in a new dress every day, and when the merchants find out that it is for the Borgia-Este duchess, credit will be automatic. The idea pleases her too. That night she sleeps soundly. It seems battle suits her after all.

Three weeks later and neither side shows any sign of giving in. She pawns a few of her less precious jewels in the knowledge that she will always be able to redeem them later. The price is good. The city, if not her father-in-law, is most eager to help. She tries not to let her bitterness spoil the sunshine of these spring days, but there are times when she finds herself tearful or short-tempered, or too tired to bother with much. Where has the fight in her gone? She attempts to settle herself through prayer, hearing mass every morning in her private chapel and sitting for hours over her rosary. She doesn't possess many objects from her previous marriage, but this is one of them, Spanish silverwork at its best, each bead a filigreed hollow ball filled with musk-soaked padding, so that as her warm fingers move over them the very act of praying releases the scent more strongly. Perfume and memory.

"Hail Mary, full of grace, the Lord is with thee. Blessed art thou amongst women and blessed is the fruit of thy womb . . ." she whispers, but the words tease themselves into different thoughts: of Rome and her other Alfonso, playful and attentive, as the spark in his eyes moves toward desire, which in turn makes her own insides twist and sing. Such a sweet feeling! The sensation moves from her stomach toward her throat, and she realizes suddenly she is closer to nausea, as if something in the very life she is living is disagreeing with her; that or the sickly potency of the musk.

"Get me another rosary," she calls to her ladies. "This one smells too much of sorrow."

She makes excuses to miss the duke's concerts and retires to bed. She is too tired to dance, but her absence works also as a punishment, for she knows how much he likes to show her off. Still, he does not relent.

She wonders about asking her husband to intercede on her behalf. Such an attack on her status is surely also an attack on his. When he tells her that he will be leaving for a diplomatic mission to France within the next few weeks, and will be away for some months, she knows that she must do it before he goes. It would be the kind of conversation best brought up inside the privacy of a curtained bed. She fashions her argument, but when it comes to it, it doesn't happen; it seems their bodies converse better than their tongues.

A few days before his departure, she and her ladies spend the afternoon in the sprawling gardens on the other side of the castle moat. They picnic close to the fountain under a bower of roses, their scent so powerful it almost overwhelms her. How sensitive she seems to such things these days. The mood is sleepy, and a few of the ladies doze off on beds of cushions, but Lucrezia for once is wide awake. She leaves the group and takes herself on a walk along an orchard path and then through a layout of topiary box trees in the direction of the western perimeter of the estate. She can see plumes of smoke rising out of the complex of foundry buildings situated by the walls. While the sight is familiar enough—from her rooms in the castle she often watches such clouds spreading and dispersing, their centers shifting from ruby red to soot black—she has never been this close. Her husband spends half his life tending his precious fires, yet even after all these months she still knows nothing of what goes on inside; he has never offered and she has never asked. It is not what women do.

Oh my lady, it is no place at all for a duchess.

Imagine the filth.

And the heat. Worse than hell.

The men strip off all their clothes to handle it.

Her ladies, like a flock of disapproving hens, had long since pecked any life out of the idea of visiting. *Any lady would have her dress go up in flames from the sparks.*

If she has not died first from the stink alone.

No, not a place for a duchess.

Still, today she keeps on walking.

As she gets closer, she sees that it is not one but two buildings, or at least an outer casement of another. Ferrarese bricks are famed through the Veneto for their regularity and color, warm ocher, which lights up under the summer sun, making even the highest run of convent walls look welcoming. As these do now, in contrast to the rising noise and smell. The huge gates that mark the entrance are closed, but when she pushes them they fall open easily. Does she want to go any farther? How awful can it be?

Inside, she is on the edge of a large courtyard, piles of timber everywhere along with carts staked with ingots of metal and pieces of scrap, including maybe half a dozen large church bells. A memory returns to her, of a moment in yet another ceremonial mass in yet another church during their wedding festivities: how as the bells had rung Alfonso, by her side, had lifted his head eagerly, all semblance of prayer forgotten.

"Cracked," he had whispered as she looked up at him in question. "Can't you hear it?" His smile was perhaps the most spontaneous display of pleasure she had ever seen from him. Is that one of the bells here now, waiting to be transformed?

In front of her, the foundry itself is a long double-storied building with doors thrown open and large windows everywhere, smoke billowing from them all. The noise now is overwhelming; hammering, yells, the clanging of metal, voices straining, even snatches of song. She can feel the heat from here; going farther would be like walking into an oven. Or the mouth of an inferno.

She thinks of her predecessor, holed up in her rooms with only her servant for company. If a wife shrivels from neglect, doesn't she bear some responsibility for the process? I want my rightful dowry, she thinks. Even if I have to dirty my dresses to get it.

She crosses the courtyard and goes in.

For a moment she can see nothing, the air is so thick with smoke. At last she makes out the shape of a furnace in one corner, a gaping open mouth of fire inside a structure of bricks built like a large anthill and narrowing to a chimney up into the roof. But that is not where the action is now. There must be a score or more men, not naked, but most of them stripped to the waist, some gathered around a steaming crucible tilted dangerously over hot coals into a pouring position and some close to an open pit, like the entrance to a big grave, with a funnel sticking out from the packed earth. The rest stand between the two, monitoring the flow of molten metal that courses along a fat clay channel suspended on a gradually descending platform of bricks between the cauldron and the funnel. They are chanting loudly, more grunt than song, for every ounce of concentration is directed to this lava red river, their sweat-drenched bodies painted a rich caramel color in its glow. Vulcan's workforce, forging a new world out of fire, as shocking in its beauty as it is in its power.

And her husband? He is standing in a sleeveless jerkin with his back to her, next to the half submerged funnel, bent, head down, checking the speed of the flow as it plunges into the ground. But where is it going from there? It makes no sense. She feels her breath catch, and the world begins to spin around her. The smell, the heat and the smoke are suddenly unbearable.

It is not clear who sees her first. There is the odd fast glance from the laborers, clearly amazed, but their heads are soon down again, intent on the task in hand. Alfonso though is now turning, squinting in the daylight that frames the open door. She makes out a look of horror on his face, and for a moment he seems torn between his wife and his work. Then he is striding toward her, his hands encased in great leather gloves, waving her angrily out of the building, his mouth moving but any words lost in the roar of the fire.

She backs hurriedly into the open courtyard. As he looms in front of her, he seems to have grown, the black fuss of chest hair crawling up his neck from his open jerkin and his face devil dark with soot and grime. She feels a hot wave of shame in her cheeks. They are right; this is not a place for a woman.

"What? What are you doing here?" With the roar of the workshop still ringing in his head, he is yelling like a madman.

"I—we were in the gardens . . . and . . . I was interested . . ."

Oh, Lucrezia, she thinks. Don't grovel to him. His precious weapons will defend a city that is yours as much as his now.

"I . . . had the urge to see you at work. You spend half your life here—why not? Oh, but it's so hot. Was that the metal for the cannon you were pouring?"

"What?" he says as if he cannot quite believe his ears.

"That flaming liquid, is that the bronze? Did it come from the bells?"

"Some of it. If they crack, they don't have the right mix of copper and tin, so it has to be remixed."

"But where is the cannon?"

"In the casting pit. Underground. Sweet Jesus, Lucrezia . . . you should not be here. This is no place—"

"—for a woman, yes, I know, I know. Don't shout at me. But—but there is something I need to say to you, Alfonso."

He stares, then glances back over his shoulder. His molten river is calling him. "Can't it wait?"

"No. No, it can't."

But neither can she tell him. She sees it suddenly with perfect clarity: he couldn't care less about an annual dowry; all that matters to him is to stay as far away from his father as he can. To help her fight him would be too demeaning. And anyway, what woman could come between him and his molten pleasures? Is this what happened to his first wife? she thinks. She came in strong only to be made feeble by this cursed family.

He is staring at her now. "Well, what is it?"

She looks down at her feet, and the ground shifts underneath her again. Only this time she cannot hold herself upright. She feels the taste of bile in her throat. I am going to be sick, she thinks. She forces herself to gulp it back. He catches her under the elbow to steady her.

"Are you ill? What is wrong with you?"

She straightens up and attempts a smile. How fierce he looks, this husband of hers, caked beard, heavy eyelids, and the thick body smell of him. She imagines him on top of her, the way his eyes close tight, throwing his head back, straining and panting, then grabbing on to her suddenly as the climax comes upon him.

The coupling of husband and wife. Another wave of nausea hits her. Dear Mary and all the saints, how could she be so stupid? This business with her father-in-law has curdled her brain. But . . . but how? She is a few days late with her menses, but that is not unusual, and she had bled last time—God knows, her cycle is public knowledge inside her court. The flow had been light, though, much lighter than usual. Catrinella had remarked on it as she carried out the spotted rags. So little blood in comparison to the usual flood. So little blood. Tears and tantrums, too tired to dance. She pulls her arms up tight against the bodice of her dress, squeezing her breasts hard. Ah, there it is: an answering sharp pulse of soreness. She laughs out loud.

"What's wrong?" he says again, her strange actions and mirth now alarming him further.

"Nothing. Except, as you are leaving so soon, I thought it right to tell you . . . I believe that I am with child."

"With child?"

Alfonso stares at her, clearly dumbfounded. It is not how such news should be delivered, the two of them, standing together in the middle of a woodpile with a foundry spewing out hellfire behind them. He clearly has no idea what to do.

He gives a rough and awkward laugh. "With child," he repeats. "So soon."

She feels suddenly light now, as if her body is blown up with color and air. She realizes that she is happy.

She puts her head to one side. "It seems we both were old enough," she says with a touch of the coquette.

But he does not respond; perhaps he no longer remembers the words.

"What about the duke?" he says. "Does my father know?"

She shakes her head. "No one knows but you, my lord. I wanted you to be the first to hear it."

After all, that is the truth, she thinks as the smile on his face trumps that caused by the sound of the greatest cracked bell.

• • •

It is done, Father, she thinks as she presses the seal down on the folded parchment, ready for the dispatch rider. I have done it. Just as you said.

She can almost hear his voice booming out to Burchard and anyone else who might listen. *What did I tell you? Married barely three months and the duchess is carrying an heir.* For, of course, everyone will know that it will be a boy. Why else would fortune smile on them so quickly and openly?

The heir to the heir of the Este dynasty.

If this isn't enough to squeeze an extra two thousand ducats out of her skinflint father-in-law, then what is?

CHAPTER 12

❧

*I*t is early June when the bodies of the Manfredi brothers, bloated and fish blown, are pulled from the Tiber somewhere downstream from the Ponte Sisto. As the news spreads out around Italy, the Borgia campaign begins in earnest.

In the city of Arezzo sudden insurgent activity erupts, brawls and civic unrest everywhere. The authorities do their best to keep the peace, but a week later in the middle of the night the rebels mount an attack on the main gate and open the doors to let in Vitelli's men, conveniently camped near the walls. On the Tuscan coast, in Pisa, which also chafes under the yoke of Florentine rule, rebel elements take their cue, marching through the streets shouting the name of Cesare Borgia.

As predicted, the government of Florence tumbles into diplomatic panic. Such actions are clearly precursors to a full-scale invasion. Inside the Palazzo della Signoria, the town hall of Florence, Gonfaloniere Piero Soderini and the Council for Liberty and Peace meet in emergency session. They send appeals to King Louis and furious complaints to the Pope. But they must also confront the man himself. Except Cesare Borgia is nowhere to be found. It seems he has already slipped out of Rome, and by the time there is any news of him he is marching the opposite way, toward the city of Imola in the Romagna, where the rest of his mercenary forces are gathering, ready to join him for an attack on Camerino. But why Camerino if Florence is his goal?

Then comes news of a communication from the duke to his general Vitellozzo Vitelli. A leaked letter telling him that his occupation of Arezzo is against the duke's orders and that he must leave the city.

A second urgent meeting takes place, and two envoys are picked to go to Imola immediately and seek the duke out.

When the call comes, Machiavelli, who has been at his desk for the best part of two days, is cleaning his teeth with a rag soaked in rosemary and vinegar. In his excitement he swallows when he should spit and is taken with a fit of coughing. The honor is commensurate with the responsibility. His fellow envoy, the gonfaloniere's own brother, Bishop Soderini, will be the chief negotiator, but it will be he, Niccolò, who will write all the dispatches home. Having watched the duke's comet scorch its way across the sky for the last three years, at last, he will meet him face-to-face.

"So, make sense of this if you can, Secretary." Soderini's knuckles have cracked so often these last few days that his fingers look longer. "Who is playing whom in this game?"

How many answers has he reached for and discarded? As the reports have flown across his desk, he has traced the trajectories of all the main players, matching character with action, pushing each possible scenario to its best and worst conclusion. In the end he is left as much with the feeling in his gut as with the logic in his head.

"However desperate he is for revenge against us, Vitelli would never have acted alone. He doesn't have the manpower to see it through, and for him to even attempt it without the duke's approval would be signing his own death warrant from both sides."

"In which case all this denial is a smoke screen and the duke *is* coming for Florence."

"I am not sure, Gonfaloniere."

"You are not sure? What does that mean? It was your opinion that Valentine would soon be ready to fly in the face of France."

"Yes, but if this was the moment and if Florence was the target, he would never have played his hand so openly. His strength has always been speed and surprise. And he has neither of those if his army is on the other side of the country."

"Exactly. So what is happening?"

"I think the smoke screen may be going the other way."

"What? You think he is heading for Camerino after all?"

"No, no. It is too small to waste so many troops on."

"Even though the Pope had excommunicated the Varano family?"

"Camerino is doomed. Now or later, it doesn't matter."

"So where, in God's name, is he going?" Soderini growls.

Niccolò drops his eyes to the floor. He knows how effective deceit can be in battle. His head is full of Livy's stories of great generals: Hannibal as he goaded the Romans into defeat at Cannae, Scipio Africanus when he turned the tables on him. But hindsight, he is learning, is a powerful thing, and the mind of Cesare Borgia remains closed to him.

"I am still not sure," he repeats quietly.

The gonfaloniere throws up his hands in frustration. It was this same level of external threat and insecurity that had triggered the fall of the Medici from government ten years before. The republic is fragile enough as it is.

"Is there anything, Secretary, that you are sure about?" he asks with little sign of humor.

"Only that Duke Valentine never does what anyone expects."

• • •

"Oh, but I should have known sooner. How can I get everything ready so fast?"

"You knew as soon as I did, Marietta. There is nothing to upset yourself over. I will not be away long."

"What do you mean? You may never come back!"

Outside the house on Via Guicciardini, there is the muted rumble of carts as the city closes up for the night.

"What if this Borgia monster kills you or takes you hostage?"

"Wife, you have no understanding of such things. Nothing will happen to us. My fellow diplomat is Bishop Soderini."

"A bishop? That won't stop him. They say that the Pope poisons bishops and cardinals every day to get his hands on their money."

"You listen to too much street talk," he says, laughing.

"Well, what else is there to do? My husband is never here, and when he is he never tells me anything," she mutters with a touch of petulance in her voice; their marriage is young enough to accommodate a little sparring.

"The city is in crisis. I have been working."

"Where? In the alehouse?"

"It is your own vinegar and rosemary that you smell on my breath."

"Yes, that's what I mean."

While she is no great beauty, when her spirit is up her eyes glint and her cheeks flush. Some weeks before, an early pregnancy had been washed away in a blood tide, and though she had coped well enough—a woman's life, she had informed him, is full of such wounds, which men can never comprehend—it is clear that this news of his has upset her more than she would choose to show. He should be more solicitous, but the prospect of his journey has wiped such matters from his mind.

"Well, I have done my best with your shirts," she says, looking up from the bundle of clothes on the table. "See—these two have new collars and there is a change of doublets, both clean and pressed. Of course it is not enough. But at least this way if this godless duke sticks a knife in your back it is only old velvet he'll be ruining—and before you say again that nothing will happen to you, what about those brothers that were fished out of the river in Rome? That wasn't street gossip. They were the rulers of . . . well . . . wherever it was—"

"Faenza. But they no longer ruled. The city was in Borgia hands. Their deaths were inevitable."

"Niccolò!"

"No duke can afford to have rival families left for opposition to graft itself onto. What? You want me to talk to you about what is happening. I am telling you how men are, Marietta, not how you might like them to be."

"Then you all are equally godless, and if only women kept their legs closed there would be fewer of you," she says, primly committed in her disapproval. "Sometimes I think I should have married that apothecary from Impruneta. He had a very good business, you know. And I could have been of use to him."

"What, making rat poisons and poultices for old men's gout? You would have shriveled up with boredom."

She grunts. The truth is that Marietta Machiavelli is not sure how far her husband's unorthodox views offend her, for just as he seems to enjoy voicing what others might think but never say, so she has found a role being the foil for them. It is better to have him talking than always living in his head. And not just in his own. There have been dinners where the table felt crowded and there was no one but the two of them sitting there.

She pushes the last of his clothes down into the small traveling bag, ties a leather belt over and drops the bag onto the floor, where it hits a metal cooking pan, waking the dog, whose bark then disturbs the goose so that the house is suddenly full of yapping and honking.

He laughs. He would give odds against any robber who tried his luck while he was away. The farmyard welcome would be followed by a madwoman wielding a copper pan. If she had her own troops, Cesare Borgia would probably be buying his wife into his service. Marriage. When he has the time to think about it, he would probably say that he could have done worse. God knows he could not have borne a stupid or docile wife.

"Here," she says, holding out something in her hand. "Perhaps you will do me the favor, husband to wife, of wearing this?"

"What is it?"

"The badge of St. Anthony. Attach it prominently to your hat when you are on the road."

"Marietta! I am not a pilgrim—"

"Would that you were! Then the saint will protect you."

"What? Even from a godless prince?"

• • •

They leave at first light, through the east gate of Porta San Piero, follow-ing the course of the river to Pontassieve, from where they start their climb into the hills. The road is well traveled and the day is soon warm—summer heat has risen fast this year—with dust and flies everywhere. But a few miles into the climb, one of the horses picks up a stone and they have to return to the village to have it pried out. It is late afternoon when, leaving the forge and heading out on the main road, they encoun-ter a dispatch rider coming the other way. He is almost past them in a cloud of dust when the bishop calls out to halt him.

"You ride as if the devil is pursuing you, sir. We come from the gov-ernment of Florence. If your news is so vital, we should know it too."

The man shields his eyes and stares back at them, his mind still tum-bling with the gallop of his horse. "I have an urgent dispatch from the Romagna. But it is for the Council of Ten and Gonfaloniere Soderini alone."

"If you opened your eyes wider you would see you are addressing his brother, Bishop Soderini. I assume you know something of what it says?"

The messenger nods.

"Then you will not need to break its seal to tell us."

"Last night Cesare Borgia took the state of Urbino without a fight. Duke Montefeltro was outside the city and has fled his lands, leaving the Borgia troops in control of the whole area."

The bishop's expression is one of stone. At his side, Machiavelli is having trouble stopping a smile from breaking out on his face. Urbino! One of the jewels of Italy, secure, admired by all and ruled by a long-term ally of the Borgias. How could he dare? And yet, given that it is the last place anyone would have thought of, how could he not?

The pieces tumble instantly into place. Only days before, news had come that the Pope had asked for—and been given—safe passage for part of Cesare Borgia's army to march through Duke Montefeltro's territory to shorten its journey en route to Camerino. Meanwhile, he had other soldiers still garrisoned in the Romagna waiting for orders. Once inside its borders, all the duke had to do was force-march his men north to join the troops coming south and within a day he would have had— what? Over two thousand soldiers outside the gates of a city so confident in its own safety that its ruler was not even inside. The oldest papal state in the country, ruled by a family recently woven by marriage into their own, now absorbed into the Borgia state without the loss of a single man! And while it will have the French king worried (he did not invade Italy to have to share with the Borgias), he still needs their help to take Naples, and unlike an attack on Florence, it does not challenge his power directly.

The very impossibility of it now makes it obvious. You should have predicted it, Niccolò, he thinks sharply, but the chastisement is spiced with exhilaration. How he is looking forward to sitting in the same room as the man behind this.

CHAPTER 13

*I*t is not possible for a man of Alexander's age and bulk to jump, even if the reason is joy, but he does his best. He marches around the Hall of Mysteries waving his fists in the air and calling on the Madonna and all the saints in gratitude. What a triumph. What a family. His beloved daughter is pregnant with an heir to the state of Ferrara and his son now sits in the ducal palace of Urbino. It has worked! Worked every step of the way. While everyone's eyes were on Arezzo and Florence and the escalating public row between the Pope, his son and his lieutenant Vitelli, Cesare had joined two forces and, with free rein to march through the duke's land, taken the prize. And no one, not even Duke Montefeltro himself, had an inkling of what was coming.

What a time he now has ahead of him. The Vatican waiting rooms will be heaving with diplomats desperate to express . . . what? Anger? Outrage? Indignation? Panic? Of course. Well, he will handle it all. Because under the language of protest there is already another at work.

"Your Holiness, there is amazement everywhere in the city."

Burchard: not a man prone to exaggeration. Of course there is amazement. When the Borgias put their mind to it, they can achieve the unachievable.

How he wishes he could have been there.

"Very well." Alexander settles himself on the throne, purses his lips and lets his jowls fall so that his pose is more somber. "Show the first one in."

It doesn't take long for the triumph to creep back: even as the Venetian envoy rises up from kissing the ring and opens his mouth to protest vehemently against this act of unmitigated aggression, it is impossible for him to completely conceal the admiration in his eyes.

• • •

In his quarters in Arezzo, they cast lots to determine who will tell Vitellozzo Vitelli. For days he has been in excruciating pain, matched only by the fury when the news came through that Cesare Borgia had joined the Pope in a public denunciation of his occupation of the city. *The commander, Vitelli, was in our employ, but these were never our orders and he has notice to withdraw immediately if he does not want to incur my further displeasure.*

The pus-filled scorpion. *Never orders!* It had been agreed. That broken-faced thug Michelotto had stood in front of him and given the message himself. Get yourself into Arezzo and stir the rebellion. You will have reinforcements within the month. He roars with the pain. They have helped create a monster that will devour them all. Revenge. There is even more need for it now. Florence can wait.

• • •

In Ferrara that morning, it is not the effects of her pregnancy that make Lucrezia sick to her stomach.

Her brother has taken Urbino! The third side of the great triangle with Ferrara and Mantua, bound fast in a web of marriage and recognized by history as a haven of stability and culture in a world of increasing barbarity. The city where the duke and duchess had vacated their palace to house her on her travels, where they had treated her like family and where she had worked so hard to celebrate the binding of their houses. How could he?

The news gets worse as the day progresses, dispatch riders colliding at the gates with their tales of woe: not only is the city taken but Duke Montefeltro is missing, pursued through his own lands by Borgia soldiers. His duchess—the modest, generous Elisabetta, in Mantua visiting her brother and her Este sister-in-law, is frantic, with no idea whether he will ever reach her safely.

How could Cesare do such a thing, and how could her father let him? Was this already in their minds when they married her off? Or had they waited till there was the promise of a child to secure her place? But that news can only have reached them just a few weeks before. This was surely an older plan.

She should have been told! Yet what would she have done if she had been?

She rushes through the corridors of the palace to find her father-in-law, courtiers moving aside to let her pass, heads bowed so they won't have to look her in the eye. The shock is everywhere, shock and fury against the name Borgia.

"My dear father Ercole, I cannot believe the news," she says, sinking into a low curtsy, the distress written on her face for all to see. "Though I am born a Borgia, I am now Lucrezia d'Este, Duchess of Ferrara, and I tell you from the bottom of my heart I feel this outrage as acutely as you."

He grunts. It was always a risk taking a Borgia viper into the nest. How peaky she looks, he thinks, not at all the plump little partridge that danced off the boat four months ago. Does she have the stamina to carry this child to term? Maybe she will die with it stuck inside her, like the other one. Except that would be no good either, for it is only while she is alive that Ferrara is safe. As for this murdering papal bastard, be it fortune or a pact with the devil, destiny is favoring him.

"Of course you do, dear daughter. You must not upset yourself with things that you cannot mend."

He lifts her up and embraces her.

"We shall meet this with forbearance and strength. Your job is to look to yourself, for you will be mother to a duke of Ferrara, and that makes you precious to us above all things."

Urbino. Heavenly Father, he thinks, this thug brother of hers must have iron balls in his codpiece. While he may hate the Borgias with a vengeance, a ruler should always think of the blood he is mixing for the generations to come.

Back in her rooms, Lucrezia breaks dry biscuits into morsels and chews them carefully to make sure she can keep them down. Her ladies sit watching, subdued; even Angela can think of nothing to say. After a while, Lucrezia sets about the business of the letters she must write: words of condolence to Elisabetta waiting anxiously in Mantua, to her father and of course to one other: to congratulate the new Duke of Urbino. Perhaps she will leave that to another day.

Her feelings toward her brother have grown so confused over these last years that she cannot separate out the colors. Love, fear, pity, fury, flashes of hatred. As a child he had been as constant as the sun in the sky, always able to make her laugh, chase away bad dreams, shield her from the careless spite of their brother Juan. But as she had grown into womanhood, something changed. What had once been a protective love became fiercer, more possessive. On the dance floor there had been times when he prowled more like a lover than a brother or held her in an embrace that left her breathless. But the worst had been his barely veiled aggression toward any man who came near her.

He had openly threatened to kill her first husband for not making her happy, and then ordered the murder of her second for doing just that. Of course, it had been couched in the language of politics, but they both knew it was more than that. After the death of Alfonso she had vowed she would never trust him again, had believed that she would hate him forever. Yet almost against her will, he has found his way back into her thoughts, so that there have been moments these last months when she realizes that she is missing him: his diamond-sharp energy, his certainty and confidence about everything, and his raw, absolute, undying love.

And now he is ruler of Urbino. Though she might wish it were otherwise, there is triumph as well as horror in this news. He is making history, and as long as his star rises, so does her own. She sees again the soaring façade of those delicate white towers, that glorious man-made eagle's nest looking down on the valley below. She remembers her eager rush through the palace rooms, each one of them filled with works of beauty and elegance: ideal cities, melting Madonnas, exuberant cherubs, ancient statues, a treasure-house of culture, the work of one of Italy's greatest courts.

Except the only court in residence now will be an army of victorious soldiers, with Cesare in the center, his murderous henchman behind him, the scars on his face like the stains on his soul.

That night she keeps Catrinella and a few of her ladies with her until she falls asleep. She is free from nausea now, and says that she is of good cheer, but when they come to cover her before they slip away, her skin is clammy to the touch. Perhaps she is sweating out the shame of her family.

CHAPTER 14

❖

*L*ucrezia is wrong about one thing. There are no victorious soldiers billeted in the ducal palace of Urbino. The building is eerily
empty save for Cesare himself, Michelotto and a few servants to cater to
their needs. Outside, the city is equally quiet, every window and door
shut and bolted. Less than two days on from its invasion, Urbino is in
lockdown, or at least that is the impression gained by Niccolò Machiavelli and Francesco Soderini as they arrive on that evening in June 1502.

They have ridden hard all day, and it is coming on to sunset as they
reach the northwest city gate, the summer sky a pageant of color around
them. The great wooden doors are barricaded, and they would never
have been allowed entrance had the guards not had express notice of
their arrival. Once inside, they are given an escort through the town.
Their horses' hooves echo brightly on the deserted cobbled streets. A
military victor with no army plundering allowed. Impressive in another
way, Niccolò thinks.

He strikes up a conversation with the guards who accompany them, expressing wonder at the brilliance of the operation and the calm mood of the city itself. They are only too happy to talk; the triumph is jangling new still and there has been no one to boast to.

It was, as they put it—"a fucking masterstroke." As part of the duke's own command, they had been in wait near Camerino when the orders suddenly changed. Thirty-five miles they had covered that day, in a forced march back northeast under a summer sun without a single stop to eat or drink. By evening they were at Cagli, inside the boundaries of Urbino. There, under the eyes of a fortress that could have blocked their passage for weeks if it chose, they had joined the mercenary troops of Oliverotto da Fermo and Paolo Orsini, all given free passage through Montefeltro lands by express agreement with the Pope. Duke Montefeltro was so lulled into security he wasn't even in the city.

"He never knew what hit him." The relived excitement comes off the guards like steam. "He and his men were at dinner in some monastery in the country when he found out. Barely had time to pack a bag and start running."

When it comes to their own leader, there is nothing but the fiercest loyalty. "Duke Valentine's a proper soldier. He does everything we do, and more. If we don't eat or drink or piss, then neither does he. He's as fast in the saddle as any man, and he never sleeps."

How often has Niccolò read those same sentiments in Livy's voice, extolling the virtues of those Roman generals who led by example.

"What about the rewards?" he asks, as the silence of a city hangs heavy around them.

They shrug. "He pays well and regular. So you don't always fill your pockets with booty—half the time you lose your share fighting some other fucker for it anyway. Though more women wouldn't go amiss. You tell him that when you see him, right? But don't mention any names."

When at last they reach the palace, its forecourt, framed on one side by the cathedral, is filled with empty carts with dozens of mules standing tethered, makeshift mangers and water troughs in front of them.

Are they bringing in provisions or getting ready to take things away? Some prize ducal souvenirs for the victor perhaps? Niccolò will be painting pictures in words soon enough, and no detail is too small for his eye.

Inside, they are given elegant rooms with a covered terrace that looks out onto an inner courtyard garden, so that air circulates even in the heat of the summer, like now. Niccolò sits enjoying the splendor, stretching his limbs to compensate for the ache from days in the saddle; his small wiry body has never been as well trained as his mind.

Still, the time had not been wasted; he and the bishop had spent the journey analyzing the state of Italy, describing, pondering, diagnosing, like doctors standing over the body of a patient on the table in front of them. Except the more they look, the bleaker the prognosis. That much they agree on. As long as France has her sights on retaking Naples, the future will be foreign wars on Italian soil, pulling everyone else into orbits of allegiances. The wild card, though, is the Borgias. Cesare's money and muscle may come from the Pope, but his own appetite for power is now matched by military skill. All around him sit dozens of little states at the whim of corrupt families dedicated to their own interests, which shift with the prevailing wind. What, or who, could forge something bigger and more stable from this chaos? Niccolò might have wished the journey had lasted longer, for it is a conversation he never tires of, as nutritious to his personality as the prospect of the next sexual conquest or twist of his racy humor. The bishop, a man more rooted in Church and family, sees the world through a narrower lens. But for this moment in Urbino, at this juncture of history, they are soldered together in the same fire: their love for their beleaguered republic and the need to uphold its interests, whatever conditions are about to be presented to them.

The summons comes long after midnight. Of course, Niccolò thinks as he checks his doublet and runs a hand over his cropped hair; this is a

duke who never sleeps. A single servant guides them up staircases
through a network of darkened rooms where once the voices of sophisticated men and women rang out, debating the skills of the perfect
courtier: the balance of scholar against athlete, musician against dancer,
the wit of men against the modesty of women. The very silence seems
to mourn their passing.

Cesare has taken up residence in the duke's own suite, with a fine
view overlooking the drop to the valley below.

There is a wash of cold moonlight through the open windows, with
strategic candles elsewhere illuminating a portrait of the old duke and
his son propped against a wall and a life-size carving of a naked, sleeping
Cupid, his winged body sunk luxuriously into a bed of stone.

Cesare sits in the middle of the room, wide awake, still in soldier's
clothes, his body sprawled across the arms of a wooden chair, masked
head in one corner, booted legs hanging over the other side. For a commander who has just pulled off the greatest military coup of his career,
it is a deliberately casual, even insolent, stance. He doesn't move when
they enter, motioning them instead to two chairs that have been placed
in front of him. Behind him stands a figure with a ruined face who they
know to be his bodyguard.

The servant brings wine, pouring the duke's first, then theirs. The
door closes quietly behind him. In the three years since he became a
diplomat Niccolò Machiavelli has sat in rooms with many men—and
even one woman—whose decisions have sent countless others to their
deaths, but none of them have wielded the knife or the garrote themselves. Cesare Borgia and Miguel de Corella are both murderers. Is the
churning in his stomach anticipation or fear?

The duke lifts his goblet, watching as they do the same.

"It's not poison, gentlemen," he says at last, when it becomes clear
they are waiting for him to drink. "More likely one of the best wines in
Italy. The Duke of Urbino was saving it for something special. Which I
think we can agree this is. Welcome to my new state."

His voice breaks the spell. The bishop pours out good wishes and
congratulations on his military brilliance, along with hopes for a fruitful

exchange: the usual dog-sniffing-dog stuff. Niccolò knows his confident boss well enough to detect an edge of nerves. Perhaps they should have brought gifts. But then what could this man, whose sword is engraved with Julius Caesar's own motto, possibly want? In the half-light he catches a glint in Cesare's eye.

"You are privileged to be the first to visit me, but I did not let you in to hear your compliments. I wished you to know why I am here and how the future will be for us." His right foot sways rhythmically, responding to some unheard drumbeat. "I have taken Duke Montefeltro's state from him because as I was traveling toward Camerino I heard that he was planning treachery against us. In this way I will deal with all those who tell me one thing and do another."

Gravel mixed with honey: the perfect tone for delivering lies and ultimatums. The two diplomats ready themselves for the attack.

"Florence has not behaved well toward me. When I stood with an army on your borders a year ago, you were full of protestations of alliances and promises. Yet all I hear is how you run to the French king to complain like jilted suitors. It does not sit well with me, and if we cannot agree to friendship—which is all I want—then we must decide on the opposite."

"My lord, I must protest," Soderini says, reaching for dignity. "You speak of friendship, but the signs are all of war. Arezzo is Florentine territory. Yet your condottieri invaded and stirred rebellion up against us. If you desire friendship you should—"

"I have no sympathy for your city's plight, Bishop, for I think she deserved it. Still, I tell you Vitellozzo Vitelli is no longer a man of mine. I quote you the letter I wrote to my own father barely a week ago. *He was in our employ, but these were never our orders and I have written to him insisting he withdraw if he does not want to incur my great displeasure.* You smile? No, you, sir—in the shadows."

"If you saw a smile it was in the candlelight, not my face, Duke Valentine."

"And you are again?"

"Niccolò Machiavelli, Secretary to the Council for Liberty and Peace," he says clearly, as he tries to rearrange his face; he is thinking that such a private letter is made public only if it was written precisely for that purpose.

"Aha. Which means you are paid a salary by Florence, yes, so your role will not change every—what is it? six months?—as this damned republic of yours changes with each newly elected pack of inexperienced merchants. It is one of the reasons your government is anathema to me. No consistency or vision."

"My lord!"

"With respect—"

"Ha—now I have upset you both. Good. Spare me the defense of your ancient republic. Because in truth, what has it brought you: Medici dictators and a stark mad monk? And so precarious a standing that you must go hiding in French skirts every time someone says boo to you, while you shout value and virtue as if they were weapons rather than dreams. It's all in vain. I understand King Louis better than any man in Italy. We are like brothers, and as brothers we help each other in every way."

Niccolò is having trouble not smiling again. He is remembering the moment when he had finally come face-to-face with the French king, and how, after some desultory foreplay, he had watched the fist of power emerge from the diplomatic glove, the knuckles bared white underneath. He had felt a palpable physical excitement. As he does now. He has never met the Pope, but even his enemies say the man has a natural grasp of strategy, playing politics like a winning hand of cards. A talent passed through the blood or a lesson well learned? Either way it is impossible not to be impressed by it.

"I say again, I want Florence's friendship. But if I cannot have it, I will do what is necessary to live without it, and that will be the worse for you." The duke leans back in his chair, making an impatient clicking noise with his tongue.

Theater, Niccolò thinks. This is theater, all of it! The mask, the lapping candles, the moonlight, the palace with the silent cowed town at his feet. His eyes slide toward the door of a small room behind, where

the candlelight offers a glimpse into the old duke's studio: an entire vi-
sual world created in marquetry from a thousand slivers of different
types of wood. It is famous all over Europe, this artistic wonder of Urbino. Will it too become the spoils of war, the panels hewn off the walls
and put onto carts to be transported to wherever the duke sees fit? It will
outrage the world, such plundering. But then outrage is this man's spe-
cialty. Does anyone ever challenge him? Niccolò wonders. In the background, Michelotto stands statue still. Theater, yes, but backed up by
threat.

"Am I boring you, Secretary?"

"No, my lord duke, not at all." He brings his eyes back swiftly.

"I still see you smiling when you tell me I do not. Move your chair
toward me so I can see you better."

Niccolò does as he is told, and now the eyes behind the mask meet
and hold his own.

"No, it's not the light. It is the shape of your face. Quite a weasel set
of features you have. So, tell me, what is the 'secretary of Florence'
thinking now he is out of the shadow?"

"He is . . . he is filled with admiration." Niccolò pauses, calculating
the risk and judging it worth taking. "Both at your achievements and at
the way fortune so favors a man who seizes the moment as you have
done."

The bishop clears his throat noisily, as if to disassociate himself from
the implied insult, but instead Cesare's huge laugh engulfs the room.

"Fortuna! Ha, indeed, yes, she is a magnificent strumpet. And as you
say, she cannot get enough of me these days. But then as with all women,
playing the courtier with her only gets you so far. You need to risk putting your hand up her skirts if you really want her to come through."
He is clearly savoring the crudeness of his language. "It is a lesson Florence with all her frills and principles could learn from. Look around
you."

He gestures to the portrait of the first Duke Federigo and his son
leaning against the wall, ready for transportation. The old man, nose

like a broken jetty, sits in full armor reading a book, while the boy, fair haired and chubby faced, stands by the throne like an uncomfortable, overdressed cherub.

"The grand Montefeltro family! Everything you need to know about Italy is there: the warrior father and his puny son, the present duke—or rather no longer the duke—since he has just lost it all. And why? Because he was too taken up with the trappings of art and culture to be looking at the sky as the weather changes. No wonder Fortuna deserted him. Just as she deserts a city that is paying some broken-nosed sculptor to carve a marble David to trumpet her purity while at the same time turning down the offer of an alliance with the only man who can secure her future."

Intelligence, Niccolò thinks. It is one thing having the resources to get it, another to know how and when to use it. He can feel the bishop shifting uncomfortably on his chair.

"You see how carefully I follow your intimate civic business, gentlemen. So. Which one of us will go down in history? I wonder." The voice now is almost seductive. "Your statue or my state? Because I promise you this: while there are those who see me as a thug, I am not a gadfly, here today and gone tomorrow. No, I am here for the future. Stability, order, law, strength, justice. I will rid Italy of this swarm of insect tyrants who sit in every other town thinking only of their own wealth and pleasure. Because as you say, Secretary, I have Fortuna on my side. So." He pauses. "It is your decision how you move into that future. But make it speedily, for I don't have much time. And remember, between myself and Florence there can be no middle way; either you are my friend or you are my enemy."

A silence falls. Nothing has moved in the argument, but it seems as if he no longer cares, as if, rather, he is almost enjoying their company. Or perhaps it is the sound of his own voice, because dialogue has largely given way to soliloquy. Niccolò finds himself wondering what that face would look like without the mask. Is it really so deformed by the pox that it has to be hidden? Or does this too fit the theater of threat? If his soldiers are still nervy with the iron taste of action, then their commander will surely be even more in its thrall. Sleep must seem tame to such a man, even if Fortuna is waiting in his bed.

"You look weary, gentlemen of Florence," he says after a while.

"We have been on horseback for some days." The bishop's voice is subdued.

"A long journey for old bones, I can see that," the duke says, mockingly. "Yet, the Pope, my father, would still choose a good horse on the open road had he the time. But then he is an exceedingly healthy man for his age. I wouldn't be surprised if he outlived us all." The information is delivered almost as an encore, since every military commander, especially those who pay their troops well, must be sure of the longevity of the patron who foots the bills.

They leave him lounging in the chair, wine in hand, the Urbino night bleaching toward day through the windows behind him.

After they have gone, Cesare sits for a while, his right foot twitching still. In the shadows Michelotto's breathing pattern starts to change, a grasping half snore giving away a man now dozing on his feet. How long have the two of them been awake? Two and a half days, maybe more. It is one of the attractions of war, how it breaks the rules of time and nature, he thinks, blocking out the first agonies of a wound, stealing future energy to fuel what feels like an endless today. But even the best soldiers have to give in to sleep, eventually.

But not him. He is already busy with the future. The taking of Urbino has changed the game, doubling his fame and his enemies in a stroke. With Florence no longer the immediate target, he needs her at least to be neutral. What will her diplomats say? At least she had not sent him sheep. The bishop is almost certainly too connected to his brother in government to grasp the nettle (would a cardinal's hat help?), but that sly secretary might fashion a dispatch that captures both the urgency and the essence.

He pulls himself out of the chair and moves to the open windows.

The sky is a wash of violet with the dawn, the air crisp and pure still. He can feel the thud of a pulse marking time inside his head. It will not be long before it becomes a hammer blow that will make sleep impossible, however much his body may start to crave it. When he can stand it no longer he will call for Torella, whose calming drafts have become an occasional medicine since his cure of the pox.

More light brings the deep drop view beneath him into focus. He can see for miles. What if he were to open his arms now and jump? Would he fall like a stone, or find himself lifted up by currents of air, a man swooping like a bird across the valley on the rising winds of Fortuna? He stands grinning broadly, imagining the disbelief of those on the ground gawping up at him.

• • •

In his room, Niccolò rolls the conversation over and over in his mind, retracing each shift and nuance. He wishes he could have stayed longer, asked more questions, probed deeper, casting aside the veil of diplomacy to discuss the wounded body of Italy with another kind of doctor, one who has had his hands deep in the patient's innards.

He picks up his quill and starts to write; any dispatch must leave immediately if they are to get a fast enough response from Florence. He transcribes large gobbets of the duke's words verbatim, for he has a formidable memory in such things. *Stability, order, law, strength, justice.* Noble words disguising what others might see as thuggish acts. But since when did the acquisition of power have anything to do with goodness? No, if Fortuna is at work here, then so is *virtù,* that shimmering slippery word that mixes strength, vitality and skill in equal measures. However black his mask, Cesare Borgia is a living example of it.

He is still writing when the light grows and the city starts to wake. Florence may not want to hear it, but it is his duty to tell them what he sees.

This lord is truly splendid and magnificent. In war there is no enterprise so great that it does not appear small, and in the pursuit of glory

and lands he never rests, nor recognizes fatigue or danger. He arrives in
one place before it is known that he left another. He alone decides, only
at the moment of action, so that his purpose cannot be known before-
hand. He is popular with his soldiers and he has collected the best men
in Italy; these things make him victorious and formidable, particularly
when added to perpetual good fortune.

Niccolò hears gates and doors opening, the rumble of carts rolling
into the central courtyard, the thud and drag of large objects, the
mournful complaint of mules as panniers are strapped to their backs
with men's voices shouting out around them. The great plunder has
begun.

He goes back to his dispatch, the words now pouring from his quill.
And at the end of it all, what to say about the man himself? This enemy
who so wants Florence's allegiance. Given all that he has seen, Niccolò
cannot keep the admiration from his voice.

• • •

A few days later, an exhausted, bedraggled figure in peasant dress accompanied by two similarly disguised servants reaches the main gates
of the city of Mantua. His arrival at the Gonzaga court causes jubilation
and consternation in equal measures. Until a week ago, Guidobaldo da
Montefeltro was the Duke of Urbino. Now he owns nothing but the
clothes he stands up in and they are not even his. He has barely slept for
the danger around him, on the run like a common criminal through his
own lands, dodging bands of Cesare Borgia's troops sent out to catch
him.

That evening—after the most sad and joyful reunion with Elisabetta,
his wife; her brother Francesco and her sister-in-law, Isabella d'Este—all
sat at the banqueting table listening in mute horror to his stories. Fury
and fear are everywhere, a rain of insults against the Pope and his
barbarian son. And his daughter, Lucrezia, of course, is not left out. Isabella has the most to say on that subject, for the rivalry she feels toward

this upstart woman who has already taken her mother's title, and will soon take her full place, has grown darker since the news of her pregnancy.

"My poor father and brother! That they should suffer the shame of living with that woman in their midst."

Later that night, when their guests, now permanent visitors in exile, have retired to bed, she and her husband relive the outrage.

"You never met her, Francesco, she is like a serpent in the garden. As for Guidobaldo, it's better that he doesn't know the worst of it, though we will have to tell him soon enough: the way that monster is plundering the ducal palace. Imagine, all that wondrous art, those priceless items stuffed on the backs of mules, hauled up hills and sunk in bogs only to be stored in some fortress cellar in Imola or Cesena. Or even worse, sold on across Europe to raise money to further his murderous campaigns. For none of them gives a fig for art."

"Don't worry about it. He'll die skewered on a sword soon enough and God willing, it will be mine. Guidobaldo and I will go to Milan to await the arrival of King Louis. However much he needs papal support, he cannot let this go on."

"Francesco, you must be careful," she urges; years of marriage have taught her that her pugnacious husband is not built for diplomacy. "Promise me you will conceal your fury until you see which way the wind blows. As long as the Pope lives we may have to swallow our hatred or Mantua could be his next victim."

That night, the marchesa rushes through her prayers. So many different things she longs for; she will have to leave it to God to sort out the right order of importance. But afterward, as she lies awake, she walks mentally through the palace of Urbino, cataloging all those artistic treasures, a number of which she has admired, at times coveted for her own collection.

Next morning, she sits down and writes to her brother Cardinal Ippolito d'Este in Rome, a letter filled with the scandals of the moment, but coming to rest on a specific matter.

It would be a crime if all this great art were to disappear, never to be seen again. Given that, I wonder if you would intercede with the Pope and his son, the Duke Valentine, on my behalf, with regard to two of them, both works of the highest beauty and standard. . . . I cannot think this will be an inconvenient request, since I know that His Excellency, the duke, does not take much pleasure in antiques.

• • •

"Listen to this. The fat gorgon is interested in *a small statue of Venus and a stone carving of a naked Cupid asleep on a bed, his wings laid out behind him.*"

In such a volatile climate it doesn't take long for the request to reach the ears of Cesare Borgia himself via the intercession of Cardinal Ippolito. The letter causes him such delight that he has to stop every few sentences to savor the victory.

"Do you remember these objects, Michelotto? My brother-in-law cardinal says here that *they are unimportant works, worth very little, but that my sister has taken a quaint fancy to them, and as we are all one family these days . . .*"

He gives a mock frown. "Of course, being a bastard marauding philistine, how would I know a priceless ancient treasure from a worthless fraud?"

What tales he could tell about that naked stone Cupid.

"Well, if she wants them, she shall have them. Crate them up and dispatch them while I write a few pretty words to her. I'd like to see Montefeltro's and his wife's faces when they find their stolen treasures on show in their sister-in-law's palace! God's blood! And behind our backs they bitch about how we have no decency."

He pulls a piece of paper toward him.

"The lady will be paying for her statues soon enough."

SUMMER
1502

God preserve the duchess elect, because it would not be to anybody's purposes that she should die now.

—Bernardino di Prosperi,
Ferrarese noble and correspondent,
writing to Isabella d'Este
August 1502

CHAPTER 15

❖

*T*he loaded carts are still rolling out from Urbino when news comes of the surrender of Camerino. The event is more an inevitability than a military wonder, but in Rome, Alexander celebrates extravagantly with feasts and cannon salutes pounding out from Castel Sant'Angelo. With every acquisition the Borgia belt of power pulls tighter around the middle of Italy.

In public, he cannot get enough of his son's exploits, retelling his triumphs to every envoy and cardinal who comes into his presence. And yet . . . and yet, he is not always so effervescent; when he is alone, or sometimes with his chamberlains or Burchard, his manner is more muted. Perhaps it is the weather, for it is already uncomfortably hot. It is not usually a problem; he has memories of summers when he sat up half the night watching his daughter and her ladies dancing, before padding his way through the Vatican to the neighboring palace where Giulia Farnese would be waiting for him, powdered skin under cool silk.

Perhaps a visit would soothe him now. The journey will be longer, as this summer she has moved out of Rome to Subiaco, to a house he has

given her and their children, Laura and Romano. There will be a third
baby early next year. The idea rather tires him. The world will no doubt
see it as further proof of his rutting corruption, but in truth he finds
himself less driven by demands of the flesh these days and this conception was the result of a meeting he barely remembers. Not that Giulia
isn't lovely. And available. She is a widow after all now, poor woman. Or
rather, poor husband. For just at the time Alexander might not have
minded him getting his wife back, the man had had a ceiling fall on his
head. For years he had been Rome's most famous cuckold, yet he found
no dignity even in death: the wooden beam that might have jolted his
eyes back into alignment—he suffered the most terrible squint—had
stove his head in instead.

"Your Holiness, we are honored that you could find the time to visit
us."

As ever, Giulia welcomes him with open arms, though her belly is a
little too swollen for an easy embrace. They lunch under a vine-clad loggia. His four-year-old son runs among the trees chased by servants while
Laura, now a gawky nine-year-old who does not see him regularly
enough to be comfortable in his presence, sits pretending a grace she
does not feel. Papal business and empire building have left him little
time to enjoy his latest family. When Lucrezia was this girl's age her
welcoming smile could turn his worst moods to sunshine. He glances
back at Laura. How she has grown. He can see traces of the budding
young woman in her face; alas, she will be nowhere near as pretty as her
mother. A marriage must be arranged soon and a convent found to take
her till she is ready. Dear me, he thinks, is it really nine years since her
birth?

That evening he sits alone with Giulia, cupping his hand over the
gentle hillock of her skirts. There was a time when a woman's fertility
only sharpened his desire; Vannozza, Cesare and Lucrezia's mother,
used to tease him about how his appetite grew at the same rate as her
belly. But she liked it too. No question of that. My God, they could not
get enough of each other in those days; no man could have had a more
satisfying mistress. Still, Giulia is most lovely. He pulls her head toward

him and kisses her on the lips, testing out the sweetness of her mouth with his tongue. Perhaps if her sleeping chamber is not too hot . . .

She returns the kiss affectionately, but with no great enthusiasm. She has no wish to go to bed with this great walrus. At twenty-seven, she has lost some of that peach bloom of youth, which drives men mad to reach the juice underneath, and she finds the respite almost relaxing. Her body has already made the Farnese fortune, earning the family a cardinal and money and houses enough to see her—and others—into old age. In time perhaps she might take another husband. For now, though, it is a pleasure to have herself to herself for a while. Not many women of her age can boast such a thing. It is a gift that will be hers for as long as the Pope lives.

He knows, of course, that the whole world is busy whispering those same words. In a few months he will be seventy-two years old. Ha! It is nothing. Nothing. His uncle, Calixtus, the first Borgia pope, had lived to be nearly eighty, and though he governed the Church from his bed, his mind stayed sharp as a pilgrim's pin. Alexander will do the same. Cesare's conquests are not over, and more important, he must outlive Giuliano della Rovere, his oldest and most bitter cardinal rival, who sits in self-imposed exile in his palace in Ostia, growing meaner on his own bile with each passing year. Everyone knows the man has the French pox. God willing he will be one of those who die in agony from it.

That night he shares Giulia's bed and they indulge in a little wet fondling, which is sufficient for both of them, and when, in the night, he is taken with a bout of cramp in his left leg, she rises and goes in search of some ointment. He lies on his back as her fingers work to release the knotted muscles. Where once she gave him pleasure, now she brings relief from pain. The irony does not escape him. She is indeed a lovely woman.

• • •

Back in Rome, the fever has arrived. He is not worried for himself—he has the constitution of a bull when it comes to illness—but the deaths of other men give him pause for thought. In particular, Cardinal

Giovanni Ferrari. The hardened old Church administrator had survived his bout of sickness back in March, but now his refusal to allow a doctor near him proves fatal within days.

Alexander is ready and waiting to seize his assets—but the manner of his death and its aftermath affects him more than he expects.

It is Burchard who brings the news, the nearest the taciturn secretary gets to gossip. It seems that even on his deathbed the cardinal was still ranting about unpaid loans and had to be brought to his senses by two monks wielding the crucifix like a stick in front of his face, insisting that he favor God over money at such a moment. At the funeral, inside St. Peter's Basilica, a member of his household had pushed in and grabbed the gloves out of the dead man's hands, yelling how the old miser had stolen them from him, and later someone had carved images of a gallows and gibbet into the coffin lid, with an inscription about how God had accounts to be squared too, and those owing would be tormented with eternal punishment.

The outrage soon breeds an even better story: how when the cardinal reaches the gates of heaven and tells them his name, St. Peter asks him for an entrance fee of 100,000 ducats. When he says all his wealth has been taken by the Pope, Peter keeps lowering the price, then finally sends him packing to the other place, where hell's janitor takes one look at his empty purse and banishes him to the lowest circle of infernal torment. The day before the joke spreads the Pope had sold on one of his benefices to the dead man's nephew, the cash already destined for Cesare's war chest. Perhaps that is the reason he can't get the cardinal's death out of his mind.

"He should have been more generous when he was alive. No one likes a miser and he had more than enough money," he says as he and Burchard sit together going through the day's events. When he gets no response he plows on. "The fact is, Burchard, this business of selling off so many offices predates our papacy. You of all people know that. Pope Innocent tripled the number of posts in the curia with a single stroke. You were lucky to get in before the inflation started. What did you pay to become Master of Ceremonies back then—a couple of hundred ducats?"

"Four hundred and fifty, Your Holiness," Burchard says quietly; it is not a sum that a man from a humble background forgets in a hurry.

"Bah! It would be five or six times that now. Anyway, men have always complained about it. When I arrived from Spain—Sweet Virgin Mary, it must be fifty years ago now—they were arguing about such things then. How the Church was going to the devil and reform was essential. I remember the debates, treatises being written about how priests showed more reverence for gold and silver than they did for Christ. What were you doing then, Burchard? Learning your catechism probably."

The Master of Ceremonies gives a small shrug. He has come a long way from the noise and stink of the alleyways of Niederhaslach and does not go back there willingly. "I was honored enough to be given a place in the College of St. Florentius," he says, choosing instead to see the great façade of the Gothic church, and the secret places of its library, where he drank in words as if they were the water of life.

"Ah yes. That prodigious memory of yours marked you out early. Did you always want to go into the Church?"

Burchard frowns. He is not used to such personal questions, though since Donna Lucrezia's leaving he has noticed that the Pope likes to salt business with more chatter. "I . . . There was little else for a family like mine . . ."

"Indeed. Indeed. And that is surely part of the argument, Johannes. What chance would men like you have in a poor Church? It's what the others said—new thinkers, theologians, who turned the question on its head: what good is a poor Church? Poverty doesn't bring men dignity. On the contrary it encourages envy and crime. In which case, those with enough money to buy their offices are the only ones able to avoid corruption rather than to foster it."

He is laughing now, invigorated by memories of being a young man fresh off the boat ready to engage with elevated discussions. Valencia had been the biggest city in Spain, rich and sophisticated by its own standards, yes, but from the moment he became a churchman there had always been the promise of Rome, the thrill of being at the center of things, the closeness of power, the wonder of possibility.

"And then of course there is the argument that the Church must have majesty as well as doctrine. How could it hold its own with kings and princes if its officials arrived on foot with begging bowls?" He stops to draw breath. "So, what is your opinion on this, Burchard? After all these years we have never really talked of such things."

"I . . . I think for the Church to be honored, there must be authority in her ceremonies and the upholding of her traditions."

"Undoubtedly. And corruption?"

"It is not within my remit to have an opinion on such things," he says stiffly.

"Still, I am sure that doesn't stop you," Alexander retorts brightly, for when he has the time it can be a pleasure of sorts, goading this most proper of proper men. "Perhaps you keep such thoughts for your own writing."

Burchard stays quiet. He has no idea where the rumor about his diary came from, but he will never forget Cesare's dark mutterings about it after the death of the Pope's son Juan. He had begun it soon after his appointment as a way of recording the complexities of Church ceremonies and the challenges of keeping men's personalities in line with the protocol of their offices, a modest kind of history certainly, but one that might, in time, be of some use to the Church. On occasion he has slipped into more personal recollections: a visit to volcanic wilds around Naples, or the insistent drama of world events, the coronations and marriages of kings, the French occupation of Rome. But as the political temperature inside the Vatican rose, he had grown more circumspect. It is one thing to record an unexpected death, another to write down the name of the man who might have caused it. Recently, he began keeping the pages in a strongbox under his bed. You cannot be too careful in Borgia Rome. Men have ended up in the Tiber for less.

"My goodness, Johannes, you look queasy. Don't worry; I have no interest in whatever you wish to keep private. How long is it we have known each other now? Twenty years? And ten years of those we have worked together closely. We have things in common, you know. We are both foreigners, both from somewhat humble backgrounds—though yours is more humble than mine—and both masters in our own way: I of the Church in its time of trouble, and you of its rituals and traditions. I always knew we would get on well. You are an exemplary Master of Ceremonies, and I would be lost without you," he says, grinning.

Reassured, Burchard feels the muscles in his face start the slow, unfamiliar journey toward a smile.

Yes, indeed, lost without you, the Pope thinks, which means I cannot offer you elevation to the College of Cardinals yet, even though there is a place free and you would surely have the money to pay for it.

"Thank you for your kind words, Your Holiness."

Alexander stares at him. He used to wish the man smiled more, but seeing him now he thinks perhaps it is best as it is; he looks as if he is about to cry.

He signs a set of documents, enjoying the scratch and flourish of his pen, such a secure feeling, the sight of a man's name flowing out across the page. How many documents had the dead Cardinal Ferrari signed in his lifetime?

"When it comes to *my* funeral, Johannes, you will make sure it goes off without any problems, won't you?" he says. "I mean it would not be good for the standing of the papacy for there to be—unseemly behavior. The city can turn nasty on a pope's death."

Burchard stares at him. In all their partnership he has never heard Rodrigo Borgia talk of his own dying, yet now he has asked the same question twice in only a few months. Has he really forgotten so soon?

"I assure you, Holy Father, as Master of Ceremonies I will take personal charge of everything."

"Of course you will. I have asked you that already, yes?" he says, shaking his head. "Well, my, my—it is hot here, and we have been at the desk for hours. Let us take a rest. The daily dispatches must be arriving now. And I am eager to hear from Ferrara. I would not want Lucrezia exposed to any summer contagion. The ambassador assures me she is safe in one of the duke's villas, but I would prefer to hear it from her own lips."

CHAPTER 16

❖

When did this pregnancy turn from natural sickness into something darker? She can no longer quite remember.

After the capture of Urbino she had set out to embrace gaiety, holding soirees and unpacking the latest trunks from Venice, including the loveliest—and most expensive—engraved silver crib by a master craftsman from the city. She has commissioned a piece from Tromboncino for the festival of the Assumption of Our Lady with her own musicians as core players, and at night, while she does not have energy for the dance floor (her famous twirls make her nauseous now), she dances with her hands and the tap of her feet as she sits watching others.

The dowry standoff between her and the duke continues. Still, the promise of an heir has softened him a little. He sends presents—prayer books and bolts of the best Ferrarese cloth—and before he leaves for Milan to see the French king, he asks her to accompany him on a visit to his visionary, Sister Lucia.

"I take no journey without her blessing, and with Alfonso away, her prayers will intercede to keep you safe," he tells his daughter-in-law.

Lucrezia accepts gladly. She has sweet memories of time spent as a child in a convent: the abbess and her teachers all kind women, motherly in their way. But she's never been in the presence of a truly visionary nun. How wonderful if Sister Lucia's intercession would protect the baby, perhaps help put an end to this stage of retching bile on an empty stomach. A pregnant woman growing thinner is not a happy sight. And, oh, how she longs to blossom.

Until her own new building is finished, Sister Lucia is housed in one of the city's older convents. It already has its own saint, the corpse of a nun that leaks miraculous liquid on the anniversary of her death, and while the abbess entertains them royally, it's clear to Lucrezia that she is less gracious when it comes to her "guest." Sister Lucia is of such humble origins that she can neither read nor write, and her "condition" is such that she cannot work nor go to chapel without sometimes being carried, so that she is always served rather than serving. As for the visions, well, the abbess herself has not witnessed any. The duke, oblivious to all the sarcasm, gobbles down the cakes and best convent wine. Lucrezia has never seen him so excited.

They are guided to a cell in the corner of the cloister where a young nun stands guard. She bows her head and opens the door for them.

Long before the sight of her there is the smell. How to describe it? Rich, heady, sickly sweet, like fresh flowers mixed with rotting lilies, overwhelming despite the generous bunches of hanging herbs. Lucrezia feels her stomach rising, but the duke is gulping down lungfuls.

"You smell it, yes?" he whispers noisily. "It is the odor of sanctity, proof of God's grace. There is nothing like it in the world."

As the gloom recedes Lucrezia sees a pallet raised on wood to the height of a bed, with a figure lying in a shift, a threadbare blanket over her, the shape barely registering under the cover. Her first thought is it is a child, for no woman could be so small and thin. But the face is not childlike at all; instead it is almost shrunken, closed eyes deep in their sockets, chin and cheekbones pushing against stretched skin the pallor of overrolled dough.

"How old is she?" Lucrezia asks softly, trying not to stare.

"She was born in Narni in 1476," the duke replies, instantly becoming a Church historian.

Which would make her what? Twenty-six. Only four years older than herself. Impossible. She looks more like sixty.

"She no longer needs earthly food. I told you that, yes? God sustains her through the host alone. That is how holy she is. Sister Lucia? It is Duke Ercole here."

The eyes flick open, huge in the semidarkness, and it seems her lips are moving too, maybe they always are—for there is no sound, just a silent stream of rapid prayer. Does she really exist on nothing but the body of Christ? Is that why she looks both alive and dead at the same time?

"Ah! Yes, see—she knows we are here! Sister Lucia," he says loudly. "I have come to gain your blessing for my journey to Milan." His eyes are shining. It's like he has turned into a little boy, Lucrezia thinks, all the belligerence and pomp washed out of him. "And—and I have brought our new duchess to see you."

Ignoring the chairs put out for them, he moves closer, beckoning Lucrezia to follow, and as she does so, the nun's face changes, her mouth stretching into a smile that swallows her lips, and the mumbling is now audible, a warbling singsong like water running over rocks. Then, suddenly and with no apparent effort, she sits bolt upright, as if her torso is hinged, her back straight and thin as a plank of wood and her arms shooting out in front of her, as if to welcome them, or something invisible—because her eyes, as yet, have not blinked—in the air in front of her.

"God bless you," she cries out, a big booming sound coming out of nowhere. "God bless your journey to the north, my lord, and blessed be the fruit of thy womb, my lady."

Why do the words send such a shiver through her? This pregnancy of hers must be known about inside the convent.

"Ah, ah. Hear that." The duke is beside himself. "She can see the child inside you. Sweet Jesus and all the saints, say something. Talk to her."

Say something. But what?

"Dear Sister Lucia." Lucrezia edges closer until she might even put out a hand and touch the visionary. "How is it with you?"

And at the sound of her voice, the little nun's face snaps round in her direction, her mouth falling open into a wide grin, exposing a graveyard of rotting teeth and a blast of fetid air.

"Blessed. Blessed, be the fruit." She repeats the words, nodding furiously. "Blessed . . ." Then, equally suddenly, her face changes again, the smile collapsing and a series of little gasps and pants coming out of her, like an animal in pain. Her body, under the shift, starts to tremble, and as Lucrezia stands transfixed, a gob of saliva seeps out of her mouth and dribbles down her chin.

"She is being taken by a vision." The duke's voice is full of awe. "It happens sometimes while we are here. See how she shakes. God is inside her. We will get little more from her now. Come, come, we must pray."

But Lucrezia is still staring. Is she in pain? Should they try to help her? Behind them the door opens and the young nun moves quickly up to the pallet, putting her arms around the rigid figure, gently urging, helping her to lie down. There is such tenderness in the young nun's face. It would seem the two of them have done this many times before. Lucrezia lowers herself onto the cushions provided, the duke, beside her, already in fervent prayer.

Blessed is the fruit . . . The womb in the prayer is Mary's, but here surely it is also hers. Oh, holy Sister Lucia, intercede for me. Take this sickness from me and care for this child as he grows inside me. Please, please . . . How she pours her soul into the words, but in the heat the stench is ever stronger so that soon she is fighting not to be spewing out her own river of saliva onto the flagstones. And when she opens her eyes and sees the thin face and gaping mouth, she cannot stop a shudder of revulsion.

. . .

"It is to the eternal glory of Ferrara that she has chosen to live here with us." In the carriage back, Ercole is on fire with civic pride. "There is not a holier nun in the whole of Italy."

But all Lucrezia can think is that, far from having chosen, this little woman has been abducted, brought here against her will by the duke. She remembers all the grinding, winding roads between Narni and Ferrara; they must have wrapped her in feather pillows to withstand the juddering, for those brittle bones would surely have shattered into a hundred pieces otherwise. God must love her a great deal to give her the strength to deal with such suffering.

As her ladies had rushed around her to ask her how it was, she was lost to know whether she should be describing wonder or horror.

Was she very holy?

Did she rise into the air?

Did you see her eat the host?

And the smell? Everyone says there is a smell. Was it the odor of sanctity?

That question alone she can answer. "It was more like decay."

• • •

The following week, after the duke and his entourage ride out, Lucrezia moves her household to the summer residence of Belfiore, now within the newly extended city walls. Here, for a while, she finds some relief. The building is splendid and spacious, more a palace than a country house, with as many rooms as there are days of the year, and airy loggias and gardens perfect for long summer days, and the history of the Este family singing out from frescoed walls. The duke's dead wife becomes her silent companion, for her image is everywhere, sitting at concerts, dancing to pipe and drum, glorious and gracious in her wedding procession into the city. In the future perhaps she too will sit staring at a celebration of herself: this miserly duke has a bottomless purse when it comes to glorifying his family.

But Lucrezia is no longer thinking of her allowance. The birth of an heir is of much more importance, and while she is no longer sick daily—

praise be to Sister Lucia—there is precious little blooming going on. Stilts, promoted from the post of Ferrarese envoy to head of the duke's household in his absence, now takes up residence in the palace to watch over her.

"You must not exert yourself, my lady."

While he has nothing but admiration for her spirit, he is beginning to feel anxious for the flesh.

"And on no account can you receive visitors from the town without telling me. These are dangerous months for the fever."

She would like to laugh at his worry. She has lived through years of seasonal illness in Rome, dancing and dozing in a dozen country villas while summer fever stalked the city, its febrile fingers occasionally stretching outside the walls as far as farm hovels or servants' quarters. But, as Stilts reminds her gently, she has never lived in Ferrara, where the network of rivers and waterways seems to delight in trapping fogs in winter and, in the summer, spreading contagion. In the diplomatic circles of Italy, envoys are known to fear a posting to Ferrara when the fever is abroad.

Angela is the first to fall: one afternoon she is bright as a songbird, out with the other ladies spearing carp in the fishpond—there are so many fish and they are so well fed that they are too lazy to swim out of the way—the next she is sweating and groaning in her bed. Lucrezia is denied access to her. Messages concerning her welfare pass along a chain of command; she is on fire, thrashing and then babbling like a madwoman. But the delirium is mercifully short, and within a few days, during which she claims she would have taken death over life so wretched did she feel, she is up and dancing again. It is into August now, and half the city is sweating or shivering, but the good news is that what comes fast goes fast and the only deaths so far are old men and sickly children. It has been much worse.

When, as it must, the contagion reaches Lucrezia, its nature seems to change. What starts as a fever disappears within a day. A few nights later, after supper, she is seized by a violent fit of vomiting and on the order of her doctor spends two further days in bed, after which she is better again, light-headed almost with the pleasure of her fast recovery. Her ladies look on anxiously as she sits in the evening breeze, listening to the charming, dazzlingly dressed Strozzi deliver a cycle of poems on the bucolic beauty of summer, "like a woman in high blossom with the carrying of new life."

She is so determined to be that woman that ten days later, when she falls ill again, she is almost angry with herself for what feels like a failure of character.

Blessed, blessed be the fruit of thy womb, she says to herself, awake and feverish in the night, Catrinella waving a fan over her and mopping her forehead. "I am protected by the holy sister. I cannot be ill. This is simply the heat and I know how to carry a child through summer, I have done it before." She thinks of those balmy months when she and Alfonso, her first Alfonso, rode out through the territories of Spoleto, where she was governor, and the people flocked to see them, barren women especially eager for her blessing, for they were such a handsome couple and she was indeed radiant with a boy child riding high and healthy in her womb. The joy of the memory is unbearable.

"What is it, my lady? Are you in pain?" Catrinella says softly as she leans over to wipe away the traces of tears.

"No, no, I am in heaven," she murmurs. Then frowns. "I must get up tomorrow. There is so much to do."

She puts her hands on her stomach, a noticeable growth now under the soft weave of cotton.

"Do you feel him?" Catrinella asks.

"Yes, yes, though he is a small fish as yet. But they are sly, you know. They often wait till you are trying to sleep. Boys are like that. If you never have a husband, Catrinella, you will never know such things. And that would be a shame, for there is great joy in this."

But Catrinella sees no joy in the worn, anxious face and swelling body of the woman whom she worships. If she was not so dedicated and if there were convents that took black nuns, she might choose to go now; she does not need to grow any older to know that God is a better bet than any man that she has ever come across.

"Except . . ."

"Except what, my lady?"

"Except, I wonder if that is true. Perhaps he is so quiet because I rest too much? We would not want an Este boy who sleeps all the time. No cannons would get made that way." And she laughs, fever lacing the humor.

Next morning her ladies meet in conference with Stilts. That night he writes to the duke, who dispatches his own personal physician back to the city to take over her care.

Lucrezia too is busy with her correspondence, dictating jaunty little messages to both of her fathers. *If anything could give me swift relief from my present condition it is your welcome letter,* she writes sweetly to Ercole. And to Alexander in Rome: *It is a passing summer fever. I will be up and well by the time this arrives.*

But the word *fever* sends a blade into Alexander's heart. And when he summons the Ferrarese ambassador, the man's face tells him everything he needs to know.

"I tell you plainly, sir, the well-being of our daughter is more important to us than our own and this news shakes us deeply."

Rome is full of diplomats who have felt the lash of Alexander's tongue, and everyone knows that his famous rages contain an element of theater. But not this time. This time there is an icy honesty to his delivery.

"The duchess's distress over her inadequate allowance has been made clear to us more than once, and it would not surprise us if this illness arises partly from melancholy at her bad treatment. We warrant a swift end to this business would help bring her back to health. Because it would not do, no, it would not do at all, for this 'condition' of hers to become more serious. The duke should look to his house, for he holds the most precious thing in his kingdom within it. I trust we understand each other. We will have fresh news from you every day."

He orders masses to be said in his favorite churches and sits in vigil in the little chapel of St. Nicholas, its architecture more conducive to private prayer than the echoing majesty of the Sistine. But even a pope's voice is not always steady or humble enough for intercession to be guaranteed, and next morning he orders his own physician, the Bishop of Venosa, to pack and leave for Ferrara.

The man rides for three days, his saddle sores soothed by dreams of curing the lovely lady Lucrezia and basking in the Pope's gratitude. But when he arrives at the villa, he is just one of half a dozen doctors and the house is in crisis. The duchess has suffered a violent nosebleed. She is lying on the bed, her head pushed backward with a thick distillation of coriander and borage dripping slowly into her nostrils to staunch the blood flow, her ladies gathered round her like a chorus from one of Duke Ercole's translated ancient plays.

The bleeding stops, she rallies and everyone lets go of the breath they were holding. Next day she is well enough to have her hair dressed and sit up in bed with the windows open so she can hear birdsong. This "illness" is making up its own rules as it goes along, taunting the doctors as much as the patient.

Outside the bedroom, her two fathers conduct a power struggle through their physicians. Having spent years keeping powerful old men aloof from death, both doctors are certain of their own abilities, and though one of them treats a pope, they have both had experience of pregnant women.

After a week of cautious surveillance, during which she gets no worse, but no better, they differ wildly in their judgments. The bishop notes a certain instability in mood as much as body; the lady Lucrezia is not just ill, she is anxious, even distraught; if her humors could be rebalanced then perhaps her body would be soothed. In contrast, Ercole's man, Francesco Castello, who has survived decades of Ferrarese fevers and considers himself an expert in such things, is not convinced. He studies samples of her urine and lays his ear close to the hillock of her stomach as if to hear any complaint that the baby might have. He prescribes a poultice and foul-tasting drink whose ingredients he refuses to divulge, and they both agree on a small amount of bloodletting.

In a week it will be the Feast of the Assumption, when Our Lady is lifted up by all the angels into heaven. Statues of her will be paraded through the city, and Tromboncino's composition will be performed with a dinner later to celebrate this, the first musical commission of Lucrezia's court.

"What do the doctors say when they are with me?" she asks Angela, who sits with her that afternoon. "Will I be better by then?"

"Yes. Yes. They say you will be completely recovered," she answers with a big smile. But Angela, everyone knows, is a terrible liar, and the greater the deceit the more energy she pours into it.

The assumption passes, and in respect to Ferrara's other lady the premiere does not take place.

Meanwhile, the healers keep on coming. The latest is Gaspare Torella, sent on the express orders of Cesare Borgia himself. Exactly where Duke Valentine himself is, no one quite knows, though half of Italy is looking over their shoulders to make sure his shadow is not falling across their path. Gaspare brings with him a letter for Lucrezia from his master that makes it clear that unless he has news of her immediate recovery any pleasure at his own good fortune will be meaningless. *For what wonder can there be in the world if my beloved sister is not well?* It is signed *from your brother who loves you more dearly than he loves himself.*

After she reads it, she asks to be left alone for a while. She runs her fingers over the ink on the parchment. She is trying to hear his voice in the words, to imagine his face, but it seems she can no longer remember what he looks like. Does he still wear the mask? She must ask Torella about his health. No more attacks of the pustules and pain? Yes, she will talk to Torella. She knew him once, in Rome, remembers him as a good man. But there are so many doctors now: when she sees them all, huddled together in their black robes and cornered black caps over solemn, nodding faces, it is hard to tell one from another. They gather daily in the antechamber like a flock of crows, cawing and chattering over some new theory or remedy.

Madam, you must . . . My lady, you should . . . Perhaps if the duchess might . . .

I am trying to get better, she thinks angrily. What more do you all want from me?

"I am sorry to cause you such concern, gentlemen," she announces when they gather at the foot of her bed. "This is an intermittent bout of fever and a baby, that is all, and I am sure that with your knowledge and help, nature will take her course."

But the next time her temperature soars and she is forced back to bed, the fever does not pass, so that by the third day she burns so hot that she goes into convulsions and all they can do is wrap her in damp sheets and hold her down.

One does not need to be a doctor to know that the lady Lucrezia d'Este-Borgia is now very ill. News comes that her husband, Alfonso, has already crossed into Italy on his way back from France to be at his wife's bedside. That night, Duke Ercole's doctor, Francesco Castello, sits down and writes to his employer.

It is my considered opinion that the lady Lucrezia will only be freed from her distress by the birth of the baby.

But any birth is still months away.

CHAPTER 17

❖

"They were Duke Valentine's actual words, along with certain observations formed from the visit."

"However the bishop, my brother, says that you alone composed the dispatch."

"Nothing was sent without his approval."

Despite the closed shutters and a ceiling three times a man's height, the air inside the fleur-de-lis room of the Palazzo della Signoria in Florence is stiff with heat. Anyone with the wherewithal to leave has gone to the country. Those who govern the city, however, must remain.

"You don't need to defend yourself." The gonfaloniere waves Machiavelli to a chair. "Florence is beholden to you. You did a fine job."

Hold this man dear, his fidelity, zeal and prudence leave nothing to wish for in him: those had been the bishop's words when he had finally got back from Urbino, punch-drunk from further meetings with the bullying Borgia.

Niccolò nods gravely. Following his encounter with the duke, he is cultivating a more opaque manner; a diplomat's face must be as unreadable as his mind. "Yet the council remains opposed to any treaty with him," he says evenly.

"The decision was not a rejection of your views. We were simply not convinced that after this act of—of daylight robbery, the Duke Valentine will still have King Louis's support."

How often has he played this same question back in his mind since he left Urbino? *I tell you now, I understand King Louis better than any man in Italy. We are like brothers and help each other in every way.* The duke's boast had been backed by two of his own condottieri, who had gone out of their way the next morning to tell him the same thing. But then that is exactly what they would have done if there had been any doubt. Had both he and the bishop been so mesmerized by the duke's charisma that they had not dug deep enough behind the words?

"There is no question you are right about the danger," Soderini continues. "As you yourself said to the council—the man is like a fox in a chicken run with a moonless night on his side." His mouth puckers at the memory of the discussion the image had caused: the good burghers of Florence had not warmed to the image of themselves as chickens. "And our no could still become a yes. We have only asked for time to consider. Meanwhile, we will not let him out of our sight." He pauses. "Though right now, of course, no one has any idea where he is. Urbino? Rome? Cesena? There are rumors but nothing more." He looks expectantly at Machiavelli.

"I think he may be on his way to the king." For, of course, he has thought about it a great deal.

"Milan is full of his enemies. Why would he do that?"

"Because once again it is what no one expects. And because . . ." He pauses, tasting again the insolent confidence of the man. How effective would it be if the purpose were charm rather than intimidation? "If he has any doubt as to Louis's support it would be better to meet him face-to-face."

"And if that happens, do you think he will prevail?"

"Yes, I think he will."

"Hmmn. And what else do you think, Niccolò?" Such a delicate thing a republic, yet a crushing weight on the shoulders of the men who support it. There have been times over these last years when Soderini has feared he is losing the zest for the job. But never when he is in conversation with this man.

"I think if fortune remains with him, she will guide him to look to his back. The cost of Urbino was the humiliation of Vitelli, and he is a man who knows how to hold a grudge. Up until this moment all of his condottieri have been busy settling their own scores. But they'd need to be deaf and blind not to realize that from now on they are as likely to be the prey as the huntsmen."

Soderini nods thoughtfully. If he were to press him further, would the adviser back up his soothsaying with an example from the ancients? As well as enjoying Roman history, it seems this clever young diplomat likes women and wine as much as politics; that he can turn the air blue with his jokes and that while recent marriage has given him a wife with spirit, she fights a losing battle. A serious man then, but with a capacity for fun. How Soderini wishes he had such a talent.

"We will know soon enough if you are right. Which brings me to my news. Today, the council appointed you permanent envoy to the court of Duke Valentine. When he appears you are to join him. From now on you will be the ears and eyes of Florence, never moving from his side." He leaves a suitable pause for the news to sink in. "It is an honor. You need not thank me."

Envoy, not ambassador. Niccolò holds the half smile on his face. He is not surprised. The Machiavelli name is not good enough to qualify for the higher rank. Permanent envoy. Of course there is nothing he would like more than to be the shadow of the duke, watch his every political and military footfall, but this is a poisoned chalice, since such a post is a guarantee of bankruptcy to any man without a private income. He is a veteran of the abuse that the state can deliver: expenses that never arrive, dispatches you end up paying for yourself, clothes that became food for moths, as no tailor will carry on working on bad credit. It is not just the man who suffers. At the French court, both he and his puny republic had become a laughingstock.

He pushes his smile wider. "Indeed, I am honored. But . . . but I have a house and wife to support and . . ." How ironic, he thinks. Fortuna opens her legs to me and I am adding up household accounts. What would Cesare Borgia do in my place?

"You will be paid your salary every month, and there will be full expenses. I shall see to that. For now you are given leave to spend some time with your wife. She is in the country for August, yes?"

There is no point in arguing. He sees an image of a green sloping vineyard where the Machiavelli family has produced its own wine and produce, the roots going deep in the earth, for a century and a half. The grapes will be growing fat, the barrels being cleaned out ready.

"Go and breathe some fresh air, Niccolò. It is a luxury one does not get often in government."

• • •

It is certainly his intention to go home that night. Indeed he has already sent a message to his wife to expect him. But a little relaxation would not go amiss, and he has debts to settle. Drinks for colleagues who have defended his back while he has been away, because internal politicking doesn't stop when a man leaves his desk, and though he has made his mark these last few years, there are men inside the Palazzo della Signoria with better family names and lesser careers who would enjoy seeing him taken down a peg or two.

"You're a lucky man, Il Macchia. The council is most taken with your style."

His fuzz of black hair, for all the world like an inkblot covering his head, had got him his nickname early. He'd tried to grow it once, but at the first opportunity it writhed and corkscrewed out in all directions, making him more like a jester than a diplomat.

"Always straight to the point with no fancy language, though the more oblique references to Roman history throw them a bit. And a few more jokes wouldn't go amiss as we wilt under the sea of work you give us."

Biagio Buonaccorsi is his greatest defender: smart enough to know he will never be as smart as his boss and not interested in letting the venom of ambition get in the way of living life. Inside the vipers' nest of government, Niccolò has found no better friend. And no more resilient drinking companion. By midway through the second jug he is feeling sweetly at home.

"Jokes, Biagio? You wanted jokes from a meeting with a bishop and two murderers?"

"Pockmarks and scars, one and the other, you said, yes? You must have seemed quite handsome in comparison. Did you have that secret little smile on your face? The one that happens when your brain is overheating?"

Niccolò winces.

"What? Did the dark duke think you were laughing at him? Come on, Il Macchia, you're not with the gonfaloniere now. Let's get on to the real stuff."

It's not only Biagio. They all want to hear it firsthand: the Borgia duke is a legend, and not many men have sat in the same room as him and lived to tell the tale. The third and fourth jugs are on them. And then of course there is the celebration for his new post—because it is known in the tavern as quickly as if the town crier had shouted it from the bell tower of the town hall: Niccolò Machiavelli, permanent envoy to the court of Duke Valentine.

One tavern leads to another, and once they have exhausted the subjects of war and plunder, the only thing left is women. Everyone "knows" this Borgia stud keeps a harem of prostitutes wherever he goes. Niccolò must have had his eyes sewn shut not to have noticed. Maybe if he cozies up enough to him in the future the duke will pass on a couple when he is finished. It isn't long before some of Florence's professional women find their way to the table, offering their services at a discount to a man who has come so close to glory. Between his travels, an occasional mistress and this new wife of his, they haven't seen enough of him lately. How better to welcome a diplomatic warrior than to offer him a further conquest in bed?

All things considered it is a fine Florentine celebration. When he wakes up in Biagio's house, his head thumping like a blacksmith's hammer, it is already halfway through the next day. Marietta will be fretting. He will go straight home. Only then Biagio returns, and by the time Niccolò finally rides out of the southern gate of Porto Romana, the sun is setting and the world is lit up around him. Such beauty to behold.

Night falls as he gets closer to Sant'Andrea in Percussina. The farmhouse is not far from the post station where dispatch riders from Rome to Florence sometimes change horses. Of course he must stop to check for the new traffic, but the stables are shut up and the place is dark. He turns his horse toward home. A farm rises and sleeps with the sun. Just as well, for he would not want to walk in on a combative Marietta. Better to get reacquainted between the sheets. No one could call Niccolò Machiavelli a coward, simply a pragmatist.

Blunted by pleasure, he does not have his wits entirely about him as he crawls into his wife's bed. *Shush now,* he says quietly to himself, *don't wake her.* She is curled to one side of the bed, her hair unbound and spreading over the pillow. There is a sweet smell of chamomile. She has washed it ready for his return. From the stories he hears from his married friends, not all wives are so fond. Sentimental with success and wine, he rolls himself closer to her and slips a hand over her body.

She responds sleepily and is halfway into his arms before she realizes. But as she does he feels her stiffen. He waits. She is clearly awake now. He closes his eyes and would be asleep within minutes were it not for a distinct sniffling, followed by a few little theatrical sobs.

"Marietta."

"Yes?" A small voice, sewn up tightly.

"I have been busy. There were last-minute dispatches to be sent."

Silence, like a held breath. Well, diplomacy is his job . . . "Your hair smells good."

Still nothing. My God, Cesare Borgia would not stand for this.

"Are you there, Wife?"

"I do not answer to that term anymore." The sobs have gone as quickly as they came. "I have decided to go into a convent."

He laughs out loud, for though he might want to be cross, he is suffused with the good humor of life: promotion, praise and the warmth of a woman's scented flesh. Ha. Ah well, a few more jousts. If she were a conquest yet to be bedded, he would find such talk an aphrodisiac. "Good. Then you can pray for me."

"You are beyond prayer!"

"Oh, I cannot believe I am that bad."

"Niccolò! I have waited patiently for over two weeks. Your message said yesterday, without fail. I thought you had been murdered on the road."

"Then how happy you must be that I was not. I told you—"

"More dispatches at work, yes." She sniffs. "You dip your pen in beer these days?"

She regrets it as soon as it is out of her mouth. She has given it thought over the time he has been away, how to handle this young marriage of hers. She knows that complaint is not the way. But here she is complaining. How do other wives do it? Of course, gossip has trickled through to her—how could it not?—about the life this big-brained husband of hers leads. One night, when she was missing him, she had made the mistake of going through the papers in his desk. No snoop ever read well of themself. But she had read nothing. Amid pages of notes she does not understand about everything in nature living, dying and being reborn without the need of any God, she finds a poem written in her husband's hand celebrating love like a bolt of lightning, passionate yearning words addressed it seems to every woman rather than his wife. She who shares his bed and will mother his children is left outside when he steps inside his mind. She is angry with herself for expecting more. Such is the punishment for a woman who falls in love with her own husband. Her mother should have warned her.

"So what name will you give yourself?" he says. "I might suggest Sister Long-Suffering."

"I would start as a novice," she says, her voice still small, but warmer. She hesitates. "Perhaps Sister Who-Should-Hold-Her-Tongue would be better."

He laughs. "I think even with God's help, Wife, you wouldn't manage that."

Outside, an owl hoots like a mournful ghost. Soon enough he will be packing his bag again and heading back into the maelstrom of politics. In his own way he will miss her.

"How was he then?" she says after a while.

"Who?"

"The Borgia devil."

"Ah. Black and clever."

"Though not as clever as you."

Her faith is touching. "And the farm?"

"There was talk of flies in the grapes a few days ago, but they seem better now. Pietro says if the weather holds we will harvest in late September. Will you be here?"

"I don't know." He tells her of the new post.

"Permanent envoy. How long will you be away?"

"Oh, not that long," he lies smoothly, for why find trouble before it finds him? "It is a great honor for the family."

"You don't have to tell me that, Niccolò. I am not a child."

"You could go and stay with your mother."

"Oh no! A convent would be better than that. I will be quite well alone." She tries to keep the disappointment from her voice. She turns to him now, opening her shift to let her breasts spill out. While there are prettier, certainly easier women in his life, with one's eyes closed their breasts are no fuller or smoother than hers.

"So," she says softly. "Give me something to remember you with. With a little Fortuna"—and she smiles at herself for the use of the word; snooping has its uses—"it will be a boy, as ugly as you with the same moleskin of hair. That way when I stroke his head I will miss you less."

Niccolò Machiavelli, permanent envoy and valued and honored servant of the republic. He thinks of his father, how proud it would have made him, and how much he would have relished holding a grandson in his arms, and his prick rises effortlessly to meet the softness of a wife who smells almost as good as a mistress in bed.

CHAPTER 18

❖

*I*nside Belfiore, heat, heavy as poppy syrup, moves through the summer palace, lulling, culling everyone into rest. The very air now seems infected, sliding up stairs, under doors or under windows, to each and every room. Once medicine has done all it can, living or dying becomes God's concern, and sleep is a fine cover for the work of angels, be it killing or curing.

They are busy over the next few nights. Lucrezia is not the only one struck down. Two more of her ladies and one of the older doctors lie heaving and sweating on their beds in their rooms above. When the palace wakes he is stiff on his pallet, eyes glassy and staring, mouth wide open as if to let his soul slip out more easily. The servants shroud him up hurriedly and carry him away.

The ladies who are left take turns to be at the duchess's bedside. But the nights are still reserved for Catrinella. She perches on the high bed, a cloth in each hand and a basin of water at her feet. With one she bathes her mistress's face, with the other she dribbles water between her lips when they grow too dry. If she sleeps she seems to do so with her eyes open. They marvel at her, these doctors, her endurance and her ruddy health. The more empirical of them would like to see if she resists other common plagues, the measles or the skin pox, in the same way she resists the fever. If they could take the essence of this ferocious little negress and bottle it up, how they might cure the world, or at least those in it whom it is their job to heal. For they are not doing well with their patient.

Lucrezia seems to have taken her leave of Ferrara now. Occasionally she might return to smile at Catrinella or recognize one of the men in their black robes and exchange a word here or there, but mostly she is traveling beyond them, in time and in place. Though it is delirium brought on by the fever, it is not as mad as they have seen in others. Indeed often she is quiet; she lies staring at the wooden embossed ceiling, eyes open but seeing nothing, talking to a child, only not the one in her womb. She uses his name—Rodrigo—only once, but her ladies know him well enough: the way she talks of him running across the grass, or throwing himself down on the cushions in a room, waiting for her to catch him.

"My sweet boy . . . My handsome little Spaniard," she calls. And then she laughs, oh, how she laughs, a full-throated sound, gurgling up from within her. It unsettles all those who hear it, for there is something about a fevered woman laughing in such a way that is more chilling than moans.

At other times, she keeps her eyes tightly closed as she tosses and turns, addressing dozens of people, none of whom are in the room. She talks about Lancelot and Guinevere and asks forgiveness over and over for something, while never saying what. There are urgent conversations with her father that no one can understand, bar a few words about a marriage bed and how she must tell the truth before God, and once she cries out: "Sancia, we must not leave him. Not for a moment!" And then she says the name Alfonso. Again and again and again.

"Hush, hush, dear duchess, calm yourself."

Her ladies who have been with her from the beginning, Camilla and

Nicola, know only too well where she is. And because so much of her life has been common gossip, Stilts and a few of the doctors know it too. But no one speaks of it. How can one chastise a woman for an infidelity of memory?

Halfway through the next night she stops talking altogether and falls into a heavy sleep. Catrinella is so worried that she welcomes the sudden hoarse labored breaths, for at least they show that she is alive. She has no intention of letting her die, though she has no idea how she will prevent it.

• • •

"Lucrezia. Lucrezia."

Such a gentle sound. Like a breeze through summer leaves, or sprinkling of cool water onto hot sand.

"Lucrezia."

Comforting. Inviting.

"Lucrezia Borgia! Speak to me."

But so insistent. Not now. She does not have time now. Better not to listen.

"I know you can hear me. Come, open your eyes, Crezia. You remember how much darkness used to frighten you."

She knows this voice. Or does she? It is all so far away. She sees a night lamp spitting as the oil runs low, shadows leaping like claws across the walls and floor, clutching at her bedclothes. She pulls a hand back to save herself from them.

"No. That won't help. You must open your eyes. Come, welcome me."

Dim, charcoal air, thick and hot. Somewhere between day and night. She turns her head and there he is, lying next to her on the bed, his black eyes looking straight into hers.

"*Cesare?*"

"Who else spent his childhood slaying dragons for you?"

Cesare? Can it really be him? Of course. Everyone else has been here. Crowding round to meet her. "And Papà? Where is Papà? And Juan. Have you brought Juan? Oh, I would like to see Juan."

"No, no, don't close your eyes again. Keep looking at me. Feel my hand in yours, yes, yes. Do I squeeze you too tight? Then open your eyes and I will stop. Come—speak to me again. Say it. Say my name."

So much anger and cruelty, so many bodies. Who would believe the tenderness in this voice? "Cesare," she whispers.

She looks beyond him to see the room, her room, empty. No crows, no ladies, not even Catrinella. She focuses on his face again: Cesare? How strange he looks, with his wild hair splayed out on the pillow and on his chest a great white cross embroidered on a black doublet. She puts out her hand to touch it. Cesare, a man of God again? How can that be?

"How long have you been here?" she asks, marveling at the sound of her own voice.

"I have just arrived," he lies, smiling. "They said not to disturb you, but I could not wait. You looked so lovely. So how are you, sweet sister? Are you ready to dance with me?"

"I am . . . I am thirsty."

He sits and reaches for the goblet, pulling her up, putting his hand behind her neck to support her head. Such a firm grip, as if he will never let go. She sips, and then leans back. Too much effort. "I have to sleep again."

"No. No. You have slept long enough. You must talk to me. I have come a long way to see you."

"All right," she says, but her eyes are already closing.

"Lucrezia Borgia!" He has her in his arms and he is shaking her now. "No more sleeping, do you hear me?" There is urgency, even anger, now in his voice. "Come—sit up with me."

There is shuffling behind the door. Their ears must be pressed hard against the wood. It cracks open. The Bishop of Venosa, the Pope's own doctor, clears his throat noisily. "Your Excellency?"

"What?" he says, never taking his eyes off her.

"The lady Lucrezia is very weak. We must—"

"The lady Lucrezia is alive and talking," he says icily. "Which is more than all you have achieved with your bleedings and potions. Look at her. She is skin and bones. Bring some food."

The men behind the door exchange glances. Amid the bickering and medical negotiations, there has been acknowledgment of the problems that come with doctoring powerful patients: when to insist, when to give way.

"If I may—"

"No. You may not!" Cesare yells. "Leave us alone. Though someone can open the poxy shutters and let in some fresh air. It is a charnel house in here."

Catrinella, who has stood sentinel outside for hours, slips in between the doctors' robes, a dancing step and a grin on her face.

An early evening light floods in, fat with apricot and gold. Its flattery does little to disguise the gray tinge of Lucrezia's skin and the sunken eyes. But they are open now.

She puts out a hand to touch his caked beard. "It is really you. But . . . where have you come from?"

"Ha! Urbino, via Rome, via Milan." He laughs. "You could cut steaks off my flanks they are so roasted from weeks in the saddle. But it is worth it to see your face. Always. Always." He cups a hand to her cheek, and then brings it up to her forehead. Her skin is hot but not burning. "Everything, everything I have ever done has been to bring you security and happiness, Lucrezia," he whispers.

"I . . . I have the fever, Cesare," she says weakly.

"Not anymore. I sucked the contagion from your lips while you were sleeping."

She lets out a little moan. Little sister. Big brother. Always. However old they grow. From the beginning, from her earliest night terrors and his proud strutting protection, something in this most natural of affections has alchemically fused to make them both, in the end, its victim. He, in the intensity and jealousy it engenders, she in her inability to hate him, even when the damage done should allow no forgiveness. Always, always, this consuming connection. What chance does she stand now, when she is crawling her way back from the dead?

"If you took it from my lips then you will suffer it now." She smiles.

"No. I am protected. See?" And he leans back to show her the fat white cross across his black chest. "It was a bribe, a pact with God. I agreed to join the Knights of St. John if He would make you well."

• • •

Afterward, when her ladies talk about it, they can barely contain their excitement, for it is a most chivalric tale: how he and his men disguised as knights of God have crisscrossed half of Italy to reach her bedside. And when they arrived they were covered in filth and stinking to high heaven, ordering and threatening the guards at the city gates, then trampling in and pushing aside any who tried to stop them. If the duke's own doctor, Torella, hadn't recognized them, it might have ended at sword point. Instead, Duke Valentine had ordered everyone from her room and thrown himself onto the bed—by any standards a man who has not slept for forty-eight hours must be a little crazy—taking her semiconscious body in his arms and crushing her to him, calling her name, over and over again.

"He was crying, crying!" Angela would interject at this point. Though the others would be scornful. In such stories a hero like Cesare Borgia does not cry, or if he does the tears are made of blood. The fact that the door had been closed by now makes no difference to their imaginations. The violence of romance: it quickens the hearts of all who encounter it, rousing any self-respecting duchess from fever and restoring her to life.

Except later, when Lucrezia is a little recovered, and he has eaten and washed—though still not slept—his own story is equally extravagant in its detail.

• • •

A certain subterfuge had been imperative. Unless he travels with an army, the most hated man in Italy must disguise himself in some way. He and his men had slid into Rome dressed as tradesmen and left again as warriors of God. Who would dare to question half a dozen Knights of the Cross on a vital assignment sanctioned by the Pope himself? Their costume and the legends of their exploits had been their own guarantee of safe passage; even the slashed canvas of Michelotto's face now spoke of glory, each scar gained in the service of the Lord. The pace had been that of the hunt: first as far as the court in Milan, and then, when the news of her worsening illness arrived, thundering down to Ferrara. There is no gang of brigands they cannot outrun, no tavern or staging post that does not welcome their trade. Except that when they do stop, God's warriors swear like sailors, piss in the fireplace and grope the women who serve them. If further proof was needed that Italy is going to hell in a handbasket, this is it. The size of the purses they leave when they ride out before dawn covers the costs but not their reputations. Later, when their real identity is revealed, it will simply add to the legend of Borgia outrage.

He is in too much of a hurry to let such things concern him. This is who he is, who he has always been, pressing onward, thinking on his feet, delighting in being three steps ahead of the next man. If there is any other way of living, then Cesare Borgia does not know it. In Milan he had secured the ear of the French king, and having hammered out an audacious deal under the noses of his enemies, he is now come to save his sister.

The next morning finds her propped up against bolstered pillows, hair brushed, sweet scent behind her ears, eyes watery with the leftover fever, but no further delirium; the very force of his will appears to have pulled her back from the edge.

"Milan? You are really come from Milan?" she says as he coaxes her to take another spoonful of broth. "Duke Ercole and the Marquis of Mantua are there. I hope they did not speak ill of you to the king."

"It wouldn't matter if they had. King Louis and I have an understanding. I will help him take Naples, he will give me free rein elsewhere. So . . . it seems my little sister does care about what happens to me, after all." He laughs. "No, we will never speak of it again. There has never been anything between us but love."

She frowns. These are things she has tried so hard not to think about. Not now, not ever. "How long will you stay?"

He shakes his head. "I must go within a day. There will be trouble now and I need to be in the Romagna as it unfolds. What is it?"

"When such things happen . . . I mean like Urbino, I should know," she says quietly.

"No one knew. That was how it had to be. But you have nothing to fear. You are the Borgia-born Duchess of Ferrara; your power is boundless on both sides."

She gives a weak smile. "It is not that easy, you know, being a Borgia in the House of Este."

"What—do they treat you badly? Alfonso—?"

"No . . . no. Alfonso . . . my husband, is an honest man. He does me no harm."

He has been gone almost two months now, she thinks. He will not appreciate this change in her, he who enjoys his women big as dairy cows.

"What about the pious old miser?"

She gives a little shrug.

"And his viper daughter in Mantua?"

"Isabella! Ah, yes, she is the one who really cannot abide me. At the wedding I think she would have stuck a knife in me herself if she could."

"Of course!" He laughs, a big and guffawing laugh that reminds her of their father. "She is a jealous cow and your beauty will have driven her mad. But you are revenged. The only knife being wielded now is mine, and she will smile through the pain. She is already groveling with gratitude toward me."

And he tells the story of the statues asked for from the palace at Urbino.

"But the duchess Elisabetta is her greatest friend!" Ah, the tonic of gossip and revenge. Lucrezia is almost ashamed of the pleasure it brings her. "How could she do such a thing?"

"The gorgon prefers stone to living flesh. Ask her husband, he is in every bed but her own," Cesare adds coarsely. "This time though she has got herself a fake. You remember it, yes? The stone Cupid lying asleep on the bed. It was in my house in Rome. You were most impressed, till I told you it had been carved in Florence the year before, then dirtied up and buried in the ruins of Rome to fool some gullible collector. I bought it for a song, and then sold it on to Urbino later. Made a handsome profit on the deal."

Yes, yes she does remember. Their father was newly Pope and Cesare called back from university. She was thirteen, growing up fast, already being groomed for marriage. He had teased her about her womanly wardrobe, this sophisticated brother of hers, and she had been a little embarrassed by the statue, with its beautiful, boyish nakedness. So lifelike . . .

"But I have even better news for you, Sister. For I am taking a purer revenge on Isabella for you." He stops, noting a slight glaze in her eyes. "This doesn't tire you too much? No?"

"Oh no . . . no," she says, though she is indeed tired. "It is an elixir having you here. Tell me."

"Mantua and the Gonzaga-Este family will make a marriage alliance with me."

"Marriage? Between whom?"

"Their son and my daughter."

"But . . . but they are still babies."

"They will grow up."

Isabella's only son, Federico, the guarantee of the Gonzaga lineage, and Cesare's daughter, who has never seen her father, since he had left France before she was born, now betrothed in the crib as substitutes for armies. How long before there is a wife for the heir she carries? Lucrezia slips her hands over her stomach. She has felt so little movement since the fever deepened. Perhaps now the worst is past . . . "But—Isabella and Francesco will never agree."

"They already have. Though the marauding Duke Valentine may have no respect for in-laws of in-laws, he would not attack cities with direct family inside. You are the proof of that. Look at you! See how this news brings color to your cheeks."

The door opens and Castello, Duke Ercole's doctor, pads in and stands square in front of them. He is a touch deaf and thus able to withstand Cesare's shouts when the couple are disturbed. This time, however, he is met with better humor.

"You do not need to tend to her now. I will be gone in a few hours and you may have the patient back. Though there had better be no relapse or I will have you all strangled with your own guts."

Lucrezia hushes him slightly, and the doctor gives a tight smile. He still has his own ideas concerning the journey of this "illness," but no one gainsays the new ruler of Italy.

"My lady duchess," he says stiffly. "Your husband, Don Alfonso, has returned."

CHAPTER 19

❖

*D*uring long hours in the saddle Alfonso has found himself thinking about his life and what might await him when he arrives home, for this second marriage of his has affected him in ways he does not fully understand.

Such thoughts, however, always move to the one person he would prefer to ignore: his father. Ercole d'Este may have been a great ruler, but in Alfonso's eyes he was a miserable father. His childhood memories are of an irascible distant figure, who was somehow always disappointed in him, as if whatever he did, he could never be as clever or as charming as his older sisters. In return, he had grown up surly, better at brawling than at study. He might have moved on to other things faster if his father had had the decency to die at the right time. At twenty-six he knows that he is in his prime: athletic, virile—the pox had only slowed him for a while—and eager for glory. Yet Ferrara is still ruled by this skinflint old man in love with convents and concerts.

He, himself, enjoys music well enough; indeed, to everyone's surprise—but his own—he has become a most skillful viol player. But

not to please his father. Performing frees him from the worst of the frip-
peries of court life. He finds such behavior—no feels it, feels it deep in
his gut like the weight of constipation—to be a painful waste of time.
Give him the sweat of the crucible and the casting pit anytime, the al-
chemical mix of copper and tin, the swirl and color inside the cauldron,
the flow of molten metal into the funnel, and the camaraderie of men
committed to dirty honest work.

*These . . . these uncouth pastimes of yours are not worthy of a man of our
blood. You only pursue them to thwart me,* his father had said once in a moment of unbridled rage. Of course he had been referring as much to the
women, another obsession that had come early. Alfonso even knows the
moment it started: a certain fresco on the walls of the Palazzo Schifanoia, celebrating the arrival of spring where a couple of courtiers had
their hands dug deep into women's bodices. Twenty years on and he can
still remember the strange stirrings it had caused in his body.

He, like many young noblemen, had done his apprenticeship with
professionals. Such a relief it had been to be in their company: women
with no airs or graces, just wide smiles and big welcoming bodies, handfuls of warm flesh spilling out of clothes, inviting him on voyages of
discovery into secret passages, forgiving any roughness or overenthusi-
asm on his part. No courtesy necessary; nothing polite or breakable
here.

His first marriage had been a disaster. It still pains him to think about
it. Both of them had been barely fifteen, but the similarities had ended
there. She had been a scrawny delicate thing, Anna Sforza, despite the
weight of her family name. The wedding night had been excruciating,
and from there things had gone from bad to worse. Eventually, after
three years doing his unpleasant, increasingly sporadic duty she had got
pregnant and given birth. She and the baby had been dead within days.
As the court went into mourning he had been hard-pressed to feel anything at all, save a little pity at the waste of it all.

There was always going to be another wife, and he hadn't cared
much who it was. The scandals that whirled around Lucrezia Borgia did

not interest him. There was even a certain satisfaction in watching his father being outmaneuvered. Meanwhile the ever-rising dowry suited him too. Not even his father could live forever, and Alfonso's vision for the city's new fortifications would cost money. In the end, he had decided that this one would do as well as any other. At least she was no shrinking virgin and would not suffer a fit of the vapors in the marriage bed.

As the wedding grew closer, he had ridden out to meet her because, despite himself, he had become curious about the "most evil woman in Italy." Expecting little, he had been surprised. He had known early that he felt no great physical attraction toward her, but he had been struck by her confidence. Anna Sforza had taken years just to look him in the eye. This woman sat up straight and answered back. And not just with him. When Isabella had sailed into town like a warship in full rigging, her guns loaded with sarcasm and snobbery, Lucrezia had held her own. It was something he had never mastered.

The bedding had gone well, and aware of the eyes of the world upon them, he had been rigorous in his attentions. Nor had it been any hardship; at times he had actually enjoyed himself. At this rate an heir would be easy.

What impressed him most was how she took on his father. It still brings a smile to his face as he remembers it. When the business of her allowance had come up, he had steered well clear; he could think of nothing more distasteful than a row over money with his father. But instead of giving up, she had fought him on her own. And with such tenacity. On one occasion she had held a dinner for the whole court, an excuse to show off her status. Every piece of gold plate, or majolica, every silver fork and spoon, every goblet and wine decanter had been given to her by a pope, a king or a cardinal. I am not a nobody, the table said, and you would be ill advised to treat me as such. Of course his father had not given way; the more attacked, the more stubborn he became. But you could see the display had shaken him a little. Alfonso had almost congratulated her.

And then there was the afternoon when she had come to the foundry to tell him her news. My God, he had felt such triumph. *See! I am as potent as you,* he had wanted to spit in his father's face. *Why don't you let go now and leave it to me?* In his exhilaration he had not taken account of her indisposition. A woman sick in early pregnancy was normal enough and she had made light of it, writing regularly, dutiful news from court with a touch of wifely affection. His replies—poetry has never been his forte—were short and crisp. Still, their correspondence has made him feel like a married man. Not such an uncomfortable state after all.

The news that she was seriously ill disturbed him enough to cut short his journey and head homeward. He knows the rapaciousness of Ferrara's summer fever, has seen it scythe down women sturdier than she. As the miles pass, he finds himself worrying about what he will find. He, who lives almost entirely in the practical present, has started playing with ideas of a future, when he is a player in the politics of Italy with a wife who knows how to manage a court and a brother-in-law with whom he can talk guns rather than gallantry. No, he may not have wanted her in the first place, but by God, he does not want her to die now.

• • •

"Lady Lucrezia's brother, the Duke Valentine, is here," they tell him as soon as he arrives; first the guards, then the servants, then the doctors, their black robes flapping like wings.

"We could not stop him, Your Excellency. He was most insistent."

"And my wife?"

"She is . . . she seems a little better."

He hears their laughter before he enters the room. Lucrezia is sitting up, big eyes in a ghostly face, the duke lying, lounging, at the foot of the bed. It is a scene of such intimacy that he cannot tell if he feels outrage or envy. Such affection between himself and his imperious sister Isabella is impossible to imagine.

Her smile grows wider at the sight of him. To have another man arrive still dusty from his journey shows a level of concern that is warming after so much loneliness and conflict. She extends her hand in welcome, and he kisses it, holding it for longer than simple courtesy. Cesare, who at first does not move, now gets up, and the two men face each other.

With no time to prepare for the moment, it must go according to instinct.

In private, there is no man Alfonso's father reviles more than Cesare Borgia: *this unscrupulous, ungodly, uncouth, whoring, warring bastard son of a Spanish interloper who uses Church money, defying even his own father in his ambitions.*

Whoring, warring, blasting guns, defying his own father; there have been moments listening to such rants when Alfonso has felt a secret affinity with Cesare Borgia. After the taking of Urbino, the shock had been tempered with thrill and, yes, admiration.

And Cesare? Well, he is so heady with sleeplessness and swollen with the success of saving his sister that he behaves exactly as the mood takes him; civil, even relaxed toward this florid-faced fellow who, rumor has it, has built one of the best cannon foundries in Italy.

The handshake is firm. From palm to palm it moves to wrists and then into a slapping bodily embrace. They are, after all, family, and there will be a Borgia-Este dynasty before long.

A few awkward moments follow; stilted inquiries about her health and small talk about their comparative journeys and the state of the roads. Lucrezia doesn't seem to mind; she sits back against her pillows, quiet, almost dreamy.

"Gentlemen," she says after a while. "I am tired now and think I would do better to rest. Alfonso, perhaps you might show our dear brother something of the city. He must leave us soon and I am sure he would enjoy the battlements and your foundry, for I think you have interests in common."

And because no one can gainsay her, these two fierce men meekly take their leave and go.

In their wake, her ladies flock in, followed by her doctors.

She leans back exhausted, then lays her hands on her stomach.

Now, she thinks. Just a small kick now. Please.

Eventually she falls asleep, so deeply that she does not even register the cannon fire.

CHAPTER 20

❖

Cesare has not long ridden out of Ferrara when Duke Ercole arrives back from Milan, bursting with indignation at the latest Borgia diplomatic coup, so beside himself that as he launches into it no one—not even Alfonso—has the courage to tell him that his city has just played host to the monster who caused it all. Old men's humor, like their bones, reacts badly to too many hours in the saddle, and he must talk it out first.

Half of Italy had been gathered at the Castle of Pavia near Milan, all lobbying King Louis to take a stern line with this naked Borgia aggression, when without word or warning, His Majesty had absented himself from the gathering, returning three days later with the Borgia devil pup on his arm, the two of them laughing and joking together like long-lost brothers!

As his father explodes with fury, Alfonso is reliving Cesare Borgia's contagious energy as they stood together over a simmering stew of copper and tin, his foundry workers eager spectators on the moment.

Meanwhile, in Pavia there had been consternation everywhere.

When had he arrived? Whom had he traveled with? Where had he come from? All they knew was that he was made manifestly welcome. And suddenly everyone was falling over themselves to congratulate him on his victories. What else could they do? It was clear that behind closed doors a deal had already been done. The ousted Duke of Urbino, Guido-baldo da Montefeltro, was summoned and slunk out from the meeting ashen faced. Of course it leaked out soon enough: how in exchange for his dukedom, the Pope has offered to annul his marriage and make him a cardinal. A cardinal! Was the duke's impotence really such common knowledge! The magnificence of the insult had taken everyone's breath away. Meanwhile, Isabella's husband, whose state had been harboring the poor man and who everyone knows is itching to stick a sword up the Borgia backside, was soon backslapping him in welcome and announc-ing the betrothal of his baby son, Federico, to the Borgia French baby daughter, Louisa.

"I tell you, there is no limit to this monster's audacity, Alfonso. He is without manners or conscience, ungodly, unscrupulous, uncouth, war-ring . . ."

But Ercole is finally running out of steam.

"He embraced me so hard I could barely breathe, calling me his most beloved father-in-law, and then proceeding to grill me about the condi-tion of his sister, as if I was personally responsible for her illness." He splutters to a halt. "How is she now? Recovering, I hope."

Alfonso sees her pale face against a mound of pillows. "The fever had peaked by the time I got back. The doctors say she is past the worst. Though there is something you should know, Father . . ."

"How dare he? How dare he? The devil take his insolence! Ha! We should have skewered him at the gates."

Alfonso sits impassively as Ercole absorbs the news.

"How could he have got here so fast? He must have ridden with a witches' wind behind him. I tell you, Satan himself is at home in that family."

Alfonso has learned over the years that the angrier his father gets, the better it is if he distances himself from it. Still, if an old man could expire from an excess of outrage, this surely might be the moment. The thought shocks him less than it should, but one of the pleasures of being immune from court foibles is that you can feel a thing honestly without having to pretend that you don't.

"And so then what happened? After he forced his way in? Don't tell me you fraternized with him."

"He is my wife's brother. What else could I do?"

"And?" Ercole roars.

"He was most accommodating," Alfonso answers calmly. "I gave him a tour of the battlements. He has a keen eye for matters of warfare."

"We should pray he never has occasion to use the knowledge against us! At least you didn't go whoring together," Ercole says sourly. "Thank the Lord for the breaking of the fever. I am hoarse from the prayers I have uttered for her recovery. I tell you, my son, I have looked into the eye of the devil these last weeks, and Ferrara will be a lost cause if she dies on us. Why are you staring at me like that?"

Alfonso has no idea that he is staring. But he knows what he is thinking: it is something that Cesare Borgia had said to him later as they were walking the battlements together, assessing the range of the guns and discussing new turning mechanisms to make them more effective against the power of light artillery. How the two of them, he and Alfonso, were men of young blood filled with the heat of action and how when death came to their fathers, as it must soon for they were both old, they would be the ones to lead their states into a glorious future.

It would be best not to mention that now. It seems there is a bit of the courtier in Alfonso d'Este after all.

Outside, there is a sudden commotion. The door opens after urgent knocks that do not wait for a response and a servant stands red faced and stammering.

"I am . . . I am sent by the duke's physician, Signor Castello. The lady Lucrezia has gone into labor."

• • •

When she had woken that morning, her skin had been cool to the touch. No fever at all. "I am cured," she said to herself, slipping her hands over her stomach, and as if her thought had been spoken out loud, Catrinella was already by her bedside, smiling, eager to welcome her back into the world.

"I shall get up today. Tell them to make ready a chair for me," she announced, but as she pulled herself up onto the pillows, she had felt a throbbing inside her head and deep into her back. Her ladies brought warm water to wash away the sweat of so much sleep, and when they uncovered her, Catrinella noticed with alarm that her joints were swollen: wrists and ankles thickened as if they were pumped with water.

She had closed her eyes, but almost immediately the throbbing in her back returned, intensified, pressing down on her bowels.

"I have to get up. Let me up!" she shouted, throwing off the bedclothes, pushing everyone away from her as she rose, for she knew that if she didn't she would soil herself. But as soon as her feet touched the floor, she was falling, both hands clutching at the base of her spine as if someone had stuck a dagger into the back of her pelvis.

Angela was already screaming her way out of the room, colliding with the doctors, roused from the daybeds that had been installed downstairs for them to rest when they were not wanted.

Ferrara's own man, Francesco Castello, is not sprightly enough to run, but it doesn't matter. He knew better than anyone what was happening now and that nothing good could come of it. All one could hope was that it did not take too long.

He was almost relieved when he found her clutching at a blood-soaked shift around her legs. As he helped her back onto the bed, she held on to him, eyes wide with terror. "I cannot lose the baby. Don't let him die, you hear me. Don't let him die."

"You are not to worry, madam," he said gently. "God will take care of everything. You must look to yourself now, we have work to do here."

Work. Sweat. Effort. Endurance. Labor: women's business, the plea-sures of the flesh wiped out by the pain. However many times he wit-nesses it, Castello remains in awe of the cruel poetry of the punishment of Eve. The former duchess Eleonora, in other ways the perfect lady, had been such a screamer that half the palace had gone about their busi-ness with their fingers in their ears. But this young woman has a differ-ent kind of grit in her. The terror and importance of the work she must do now give her an energy of will that her body doesn't have. She has delivered one live child already and retains a subterranean memory of her own muscle power. This thing inside her—for it is no longer her son—will be expelled, and she must help as best she can.

It takes from early afternoon to the coming of the night, the pulsing snake band of pain squeezing ever tighter, leaving less time to recover or even to breathe properly between contractions. And then finally, on an endless groan and tearing push, it is all over. The doctors, who have computed the pregnancy insofar as it is possible, estimate the lady Lu-crezia is twenty-five or twenty-six weeks with child. Quite how long the baby has been dead they do not know, but inside the pulpy mess that they gather up and swiftly carry away so that she is saved the sight, there is a fetus developed enough for a doctor to divine its sex. It falls to Cas-tello to do the job. The duchess elect has given birth to an ill-formed baby girl.

She does not ask and they do not tell her. It does not matter. When a baby is expelled too soon, the risk of childbed fever is high. The only thing that matters is that she stay alive. Given how weak she is, her life or death is not a wager many people would take willingly.

They clean her up as best they can so that Alfonso, who has been waiting a few rooms away, can come to her bedside.

The swelling is fading, and her face though pale is serene, almost virginal; her agony has washed away Eve's sin. Or perhaps it is simply exhaustion.

"I am sorry," she whispers.

His huge scaly hand envelops her small one. "It is nothing," he says gruffly. Uncomfortable with such closeness, he finds it hard to know how to behave. "As soon as you are well we will get on with making more, an army of boys."

It is the most intimate thing he has ever said to her. But her eyes are already closed.

"Did she hear me?"

Behind him the doctors murmur reassuringly.

"Everything is all right, yes? I mean she will get better now," he says as they usher him out of the room.

Castello makes a gentle wave of his hand, open to whatever interpretation the watcher might chose to give it.

"She must not die. If she dies . . ."

He does not finish the sentence.

"If she dies . . ." In Rome, the Pope sits in his bedroom, the dispatch still in his hands, tears dropping onto the page and smudging the ink. The Ferrarese ambassador, pulled early from his bed, stands nearby, his mouth twitching with the effort of appearing confident. The air is thick with old man's sweat, which has soaked into the folds of sheets. The herb pomades dangling from the ceiling do little to disguise it.

"I tell you if my daughter dies . . ."

"That will not happen, Your Holiness. Five doctors are at her bedside constantly. Every church and convent in the city is saying prayers for her recovery. The well-being of the lady Lucrezia is as dear to our duke's heart as was his own wife, Eleonora."

"Then he has strange ways of showing it," Alexander growls. "I should never have let her go so far away from me. A man is nothing without his family. My dear sweet daughter, how could I . . ." And he waves the ambassador away, as if this pain is too much to be witnessed by another.

When Burchard enters a little later, he finds the Pope bowed over, sobbing unashamedly.

"Your Holiness, can I be of any assistance?"

"Ah, but we are undone. She is delivered of a dead baby months before time. Sweet Mother of God, at least it was not a boy. And now she lies in the arms of death. What have we done to deserve this? How have we so offended God that He brings such sorrow upon us?" He moans as the sobs engulf him again.

It is not a question that looks for an answer. Burchard watches silently, remembering the period of crazed grief that had followed the death of Juan. The Pope's cry had been the same then. Why? How? What had he done to deserve this?

The world outside this room is filled with men who would gladly cite chapter and verse on that, laying myriad crimes and corruptions at his door, but he does not see it like that. For Alexander, this thing is only between him and God, always somehow a personal battle between equals.

• • •

For Lucrezia now it is simpler.

There had been moments following the birth when the spasms in her belly felt like the start of a second labor and she had known that the fever had returned. But all that has faded. Time and pain are as meaningless as any of the faces that hover in and out of her vision. It is as if this body of hers, which has caused her such distress for so long, belongs now to someone else.

She is dimly aware of consternation around her—hushed voices, the sound of weeping—but it does not bother her. She has fought as hard as she can and there is a relief in knowing that there is no more she can do. It is quiet where she is. There are no companions populating her delirium, no insistent memory loops to remind her of the past, or what she is leaving. Instead the pull is toward sleep, deep and dark, lapping like rising warm water around her; no threat of drowning, just the promise of gentle buoyancy. She has an image of herself floating, her shift lifting her, filled with pockets of air, her hair like plant tendrils waving about her head. Then as the water rises higher, she returns to her body. She can hear a rushing sound in her ears like the sea and the rhythmic pulse of what she knows to be her own heartbeat—*thud thump, thud thump, thud thump*—as if she is alive inside herself. There is still no fear, only the same sensation of weightlessness, warm and secure. Is this what the baby felt as it rolled and settled itself inside her? *Thud thump.* Such a close, safe place. Dying in here would be a gentle leaving. God will understand. She will be forgiven. She has done her best. She feels the touch of warm liquid on her forehead and her feet. Curling around the heartbeat she hears the drone of something, in the distance, voices in prayer helping her on her way. It is all so easy . . .

She opens her eyes onto darkness. A single creased face looms over her, and a hand is feeling for hers, running its fingers over the inside of her wrist, probing, searching. She recognizes the features of Torella, her brother's doctor. How strange that he should be here at such a moment, but then of course he is also a priest.

"Don't worry. There is no pulse," she says quite clearly. "I am dead."

And she falls asleep again.

Oh, how they will talk about those words later, moving them through a chain of whispers and letters that will crisscross the country, bringing painful smiles even to those who consider themselves her enemies. Few people come so close to dying twice, and graveyards are full of women buried with their stillborn babies. The Lord is merciful. That is the mantra that travels with the news. Her doctors, who would dearly like to take the credit, for it has been a long thankless summer of risked reputations, are the first to acknowledge it: childbed fever is a killer. The Pope's physician, the Bishop of Venosa, had made a final plea for bloodletting, but soon enough he and Torella had swapped their physicians' caps for priests' robes, leading the prayers of last rites and the ceremony of extreme unction, anointing her forehead, hands and feet with warm oil, as they called for the forgiveness of her sins in preparation for her journey to God's side.

It is, everyone agrees, a miracle.

In her temporary cell, it is said that the holy sister Lucia lifted off her pallet and floated in the air at the very moment the doctors were saying last prayers, in her own magnificent intercession for God's grace. Sadly, by the time the duke got there she had already descended back to earth, but the heady smell of sanctity that flowed out through her gap-toothed smile left him in no doubt about Ferrara's special relationship with the Almighty.

When the duchess is well enough for the news to be made public, the whole city erupts: the musical thunder of church bells as people flock to mass and take to the streets to give thanks for their duchess's survival. It is only nine months since they were celebrating her wedding, and memories of her energy and good humor are fresh in people's minds. Her recovery secures Ferrara's safety from the Borgia menace and marks the end of the worst of the summer fever; the angel of death is moving on for another year. As for the baby: well, where there has been one, there will be another. If the world wailed over every loss of a child, no one would ever stop crying.

"Oh, madam, you should have seen Torella's face when he came out of the room!"

"He said he found your pulse only after you told him there wasn't one."

As soon as she is well enough to sit with her ladies, their joy at her return is spiced with the stories they can weave from it.

"He went straight to the chapel and stayed there for hours. We think he was asking God to help him in his doctoring skills."

Lucrezia watches them talking, so chirrupy and sunny.

I am dead. The words are the saddest she has ever heard.

"Do you remember it, my lady?" Camilla asks gently.

"No," she says, "not at all."

All she remembers is the sensation of floating, warm and weightless, no body, no pain, no fear. How close was she before she was pulled back? Sitting here now in the sunshine, she feels as if she has yet to fully return.

Everyone agrees it will take time: before she returns to court there must be a prolonged period of convalescence. A convent would be ideal. Ercole is delighted; she can live close to his beloved holy Lucia. Her first sign of recovery comes in her refusal. Bone-thin women and bad breath are not what she needs now. Instead she chooses the gentler Clarissan convent of Corpus Domini, tucked away in the heart of the old town, intimate shady cloisters, the perfumes of flowers and herbs and nuns who like to laugh as well as pray.

She is not the only one absenting herself from court. Alfonso d'Este now reveals that when he had feared she was dying, he had made a secret vow that he would make a pilgrimage on foot to the shrine of Our Lady of Loreto if she was saved.

"You on pilgrimage? On foot?"

When he announces it to his father, things do not go well.

"You amaze me! Well, I suppose it will do you no harm. Though Loreto is a long way away. You should go by horse or you'll be gone for half a year, and we need another pregnancy sooner rather than later. Or are you planning to use the trip to study cannons and fortresses along the way?"

Alfonso, who had been toying with the same thoughts—both the horses and the cannons—feels the fury rising. These last weeks have seen his dislike of his father turn to something more fiery.

"And, Father?" he says bluntly. "What will you do to show your appreciation for my wife's recovery?"

"Me? I shall press ahead with the building of Sister Lucia's convent. It is her we thank for this intervention. You know that she actually levitat——"

"That's not enough," Alfonso cuts in.

"What?"

"It's not enough. The Duchess of Ferrara deserves more."

"What do you mean?"

"You should pay her what you owe her. Honor the dowry agreement that was made with the Pope and give her her full allowance."

"I really don't—" The duke hesitates. For years he has despaired of his surly uncommunicative son. But this is not what he was looking for. "I don't see what this has to do with anything, Alfonso."

"The Borgias are too powerful for us to hold our noses in the air any longer. Lucrezia brought a fortune with her, and you have treated her badly for long enough."

"Ha! Now I understand. This is that bastard brother of hers talking. What did he say?"

"I don't need anyone to say anything to me. This is what I think."

"Then how dare you!" Ercole croaks, puffing himself up like an offended toad. "Questions of state are my business and I will do as I see fit."

"No, Father, you won't."

Alfonso takes a step forward. Such a powerful man he is grown into, those ham-hock hands on arms strong as a wrestler's, and tall now, at least head and shoulders above the shrinking old man in front of him. He could knock him down with one blow. "If you want the House of Este to survive, you will treat my wife with the status she deserves."

Ercole's mouth has fallen open. As he struggles to find the right words, Alfonso is already walking out of the room.

Whoring, warring, blasting guns and defying his own father. These are momentous times in Italy, and men of hot young blood have to stick together.

AUTUMN-WINTER
1502

*The Lord [Duke Valentine] is very secretive and I do not
believe that what he is going to do is known to anyone but
himself. . . . Hence I beg Your Lordships not to impute it to
negligence if I do not satisfy you with more information,
because most of the time I do not even satisfy myself.*

—Niccolò Machiavelli,
dispatch to Florence from the city of Imola
November 1502

CHAPTER 21

❖

"Every one of you in this room knows why we are here."

Vitellozzo Vitelli sits hunched in his chair, his face shiny with sweat. A pox on this pox. Each new attack digs deeper into his bones. He'd started out that morning on horseback, but within a few miles it had felt as if his legs were breaking and he'd done the rest of the journey to the Orsini castle propped up in a blanket slung between two poles, swearing at every pothole. But his pride wouldn't let him be carried into their presence, and so he has crawled, crablike, up the low-tread stairs into the gloomy chamber. The company of men around the table have waited on his arrival. Of course. For there is no one in Italy who has more to say about this pus-filled treacherous monster of a papal bastard.

"We are staring at our own destruction. Valentine's attack on Urbino, his treachery toward his own men and this new deal he's made with the French are a declaration of war. King Louis will not lift a finger as he chews and spits out each and every one of us. The only chance we have is to hit him before he hits us."

He pauses—turning to look each man in the eye. Some he already knows well: his fellow condottieri, Gian Paolo Baglioni from Perugia, the two Orsini cousins Paolo and Francesco, and Oliverotto da Fermo, who less than a year ago knifed his way to power in a room not unlike the one in which he sits now. Then there are the newcomers: an envoy from the deposed Duke of Urbino, a representative from Siena, and another from Bologna. The latest rumor is that the Pope has signed a bill of excommunication for the ruling family in anticipation of an invasion. If Bologna is to be next, there can be no clearer signal of what is to come.

And finally there is Cardinal Giovanni Battista Orsini, the head of one of Rome's oldest families. He is not wearing his scarlet robes today, but then he is not about God's business here. If indeed he ever was, Vitelli thinks sourly. The carving of the family's crest stands sharp on the fireplace behind the old man's seat. The castle had been a gift from the Pope in return for the cardinal's support in the conclave that had elected him ten years before. But the two families had always been more enemies than allies, and two years later, during the first French invasion, the Orsini had spectacularly changed sides, stilling the guns on fortresses north of Rome and giving the invaders safe passage into the city. The scale of the treachery had taken even Vitelli by surprise. In retaliation the Pope had had the head of the family. Four months later, he'd been fishing his own son Juan out of the Tiber, his body riddled with stab wounds.

Vitelli can still remember the fury and panic rolling out of Rome in the days that followed. Juan had been an arrogant little prick, and the Orsini weren't the only ones with cause to rip his guts out, but their names came top of the list. It was always only a question of time till the Borgias meted out suitable punishment. Vengeance. He is not alone in being sustained on its promise; it runs like a blood-colored thread through centuries of Roman history. Nevertheless, if the Orsini are going to make the first move, they will need to be convinced they can win.

"Everything you say is correct, Signor Vitelli. We all know the threat." He has a thin whiny voice, the cardinal, as if his nostrils don't take in enough air to fill his lungs. Certainly there have been tougher, more charismatic heads of the family, but his political instincts, honed on decades of Vatican backbiting, are sharp as ever. "However, as long as the Pope and his bastard son have France behind them, it would be better if we had others on our side."

"There are no others, Cardinal," Vitelli answers firmly. "If there were they would be here already. Ferrara and Mantua are tied up by blood and Florence is a state of craven fools."

"It is also, as you know, protected by the king. In name at least," the cardinal says mildly. "It's a shame that Venice cannot be persuaded to go openly against them. She would be happy enough to pick up the pieces."

"God's blood, there'll be no pickings for Venice here!" Gian Paolo Baglioni from Perugia is up on his feet, his hands balled into fighter's fists in front of him. If the Baglioni family had managed to squeeze a pope out of their loins, everyone knows it would be him out there now terrorizing half of Italy. "If you're not in on the risk, you're not in on the spoils. That's what this is about. Once we've taken Valentine's states they'll be divided up among us all."

There is a small silence as they all digest the wonder of that prospect, and the infighting that will ensue. "Go on, Vitelli," Baglioni urges. "Tell them how we do it."

Vitelli pulls himself up in his chair; the throbbing in his bones could be the drumbeat an army might march to. Since the humiliation of his retreat from Arezzo he has been caught in a depression as black as the devil. The only thing to rouse him is the thought of coming face-to-face with the man who betrayed him, for both of them to die with each other's daggers buried deep in their guts. "We launch a twofold attack. Use local discontent to stir a rebellion inside one of the fortresses near Urbino, then, while the duke is busy protecting the jewel in his crown, a separate force from Bologna marches to attack him in Imola. With artillery and surprise on our side we can blast our way in."

He knows, *knows* that if they move fast enough they can do it.

"What about da Vinci's fortifications? He's been on the duke's payroll for months." The envoy from Bologna has a growth on his nose the size of a ripe grape. Vitelli imagines himself opening it up with a stiletto.

"Da Vinci's a clever engineer. But he's been in Imola only a few weeks. Even he can't rebuild a fortress in so short a time. Which is all the more reason to move fast."

"Exactly!" Baglioni jumps in. "The longer we piss into the wind the more time he gains. I tell you, it's started already. Two days ago my men intercepted a courier from the Pope to Valentine with a message instructing him to invite all his condottieri to a meeting in Imola and seize them all."

His words have the desired effect, everyone yelling curses and descriptions of what they would likely do to intimate parts of the Borgia body. Vitelli throws him a furious look. In a league of equals this intelligence should have been shared earlier—if indeed it is true at all. Being in partnership with the Baglioni is like being tied in a sack with scorpions.

"And if he finds out what we're doing?"

Scorpions and cowards, Vitelli thinks. Lady Paolo, that's what they call the pudgy young condottiere Paolo Orsini, because he's always the one in need of a little seduction.

The room falls silent. Spies. How do they feel about everyone else at the table?

"God damn it! Look at you all. Like a sewing circle of women!" Baglioni can barely contain himself. "I know this Borgia bastard better than any of you, remember. My brothers and I wrestled with him in the mud when we were children at school in Perugia. Any chance he got he would bite chunks out of you. He was a bully, a liar and a cheat then and he is the same now. The only thing that stopped him was hitting him hard when he wasn't looking."

The idea of a young Cesare and the Baglioni brothers rolling in the mud with their teeth in each other's flesh is a dish too rich for many imaginations. The cardinal and Vitelli lock eyes. All this is wind and fury, not enough to tip the balance. Something more is needed.

"What if we had someone of our own?" Vitelli says slowly. "Someone working from inside his camp?"

"You have someone in mind?" the cardinal says quietly.

"Valentine's governor in Cesena, the Spaniard, Ramiro de Lorqua. He's a vicious fucker, but I hear he's been creaming off the profits from grain supplies to line his own pockets. If Borgia were to learn about that, he'd cut his legs off. I know the man, I've ridden with him. I believe we could use that as leverage to bring him over to us." He pauses to let the information sink in. He can feel the cardinal's attention on him. "His nose is out of joint now too because the Duke has him out running all round the Romagna recruiting new troops. I could be at his side within a few days. It won't be hard to stir up trouble in Urbino. And once that starts . . ."

He leaves the words trailing.

"Very well." The cardinal speaks for all of them. Whatever his doubts, it would be ten times worse to leave without a plan. "With that plan in mind I am ready to put my name here and now on a pact of allegiance."

There is a rolling murmur of agreement around the table.

"Don't worry about ink," Baglioni shouts, gleefully jumping to his feet and pushing his sleeve up to expose his arm. "We'll sign in blood."

The cardinal suppresses a small sigh. This is not the moment for second thoughts.

CHAPTER 22

❦

From grief to rage: such weather-vane energy the Pope has.

First he is prostrate, drowning in tears for the lost baby and his daughter's illness, now he is stomping along the corridor that connects the different rooms of the Borgia apartments, cardinals and chaplains dancing after him as he vents his fury. His secretaries could fill a dozen papal bulls with the tortures, on earth and in hell, that he will unleash against the poxy Vitelli, the Baglioni trash and the Orsini traitors.

But most of all the Orsini. Five years, five whole years since Juan's body was dragged out of the Tiber, knifed by their hired thugs. Sweet Jesus, how he had loved that boy! Every anniversary of the death has been marked by a mass in case his appetite for revenge should be allowed to wane. It had always been only a matter of time. The greater Cesare's victories, the sooner they can cut loose their ties from men they need but do not trust, bottom-feeders like Vitelli and da Fermo and the lesser puny twigs from the Orsini family tree. Once they are gone, he can move in for the kill, take down the rest of the house, finish the job they had started long ago. And now this: the head of the family, a cardinal no less, launching a revolt against them.

"What? They thought we wouldn't find out? All of them on the move at the same time, leaving slime trails like snails in their wake. My God, they must be more stupid than they think we are."

Burchard spends the first days putting out excuses: His Holiness cannot see anyone right now for he has eaten something that disagreed with him. But as the diplomats fill up the papal receiving room, it's impossible to miss the stream of sweat-soaked dispatch riders being given immediate access. Even without the tentacles of Borgia intelligence strung across Italy, the meeting in the Orsini castle at La Magione was bound to leak out. The size of the egos involved was proof of that.

The world's eyes will be on Duke Valentine, for he is the target. But it is Alexander who will foot the bills.

"How much is that?"

"Sixteen thousand ducats, Your Holiness."

As ever Burchard is on hand for the more delicate matters of massaging funds out of the papal treasury.

"Not enough. The duke needs eighteen to pay for new recruits. Find the extra two from somewhere and an armed guard to take it. What? Does this offend you in some way?"

Burchard as usual has remained stone silent, but the Pope's belligerence is overflowing.

"This is not profligacy, Johannes, this is war. A member of the College of Cardinals rising up against his pope is treachery against the Holy Mother Church herself. I tell you we will have the Orsini lands and benefices to pay back twice what he makes us spend now."

Eighteen thousand. He knows that will not be the end of it either. With their enemies united, they'll need French troops to supply artillery. Eighteen thousand. It is almost as much as he spends annually on the whole of the Vatican court, wages, ceremonies, provisions, everything. Though his enemies never stop whining about Church corruption, half of them would refuse an invitation to dinner because the food isn't lavish enough. Two courses and a jug of simple Corsican wine is his favored fare. You could endow a convent on what he saves here. *I know monks who eat better,* he wants to shout in Burchard's face. But it isn't Burchard he is fighting. Faced with Cesare's endless demands for cash over these last years, Alexander himself has felt if not conscience, then a certain foreboding about how he is plundering the Church for money. If he were to add it all together . . . But he will not do that now. Whatever the price it will be worth it to see this rebellious scum crushed. How much is Cardinal Orsini worth? When he has trouble falling asleep that night he does the sums to keep him happy.

⋅ ⋅ ⋅

In the city of Imola, barely thirty miles from what is now the enemy territory of Bologna, Cesare lives in a single room, plans of fortresses and battlements stuck to the walls and a floor caked in mud from the boots of riders. There is a bed in one corner, but he hardly uses it, for who could sleep at such a time? When the news of the meeting at La Magione had reached him—always in every conspiracy there is a weak link, a man as frightened of his friends as he is of his enemy—he had been elated rather than alarmed. Ever since he first saw the eyes of his condottieri grow wide at the purses he threw across the table to them two years ago, he had known that eventually it would come to this. He might wish he was more ready, another few months would have made him invincible, but he will fight with what he's got. He likes it that way.

"Who's there?"

He hears the footsteps before the knock on the door. The less he sleeps the sharper his senses.

"The envoy from Florence has arrived, my lord. He begs leave to make an appointment to call when you are ready to receive him."

"Florence? Show him in now."

With so many enemies he could do with a few friends.

Niccolò had never expected immediate access. He had already been kept waiting at the western gate as a stream of dispatch riders took precedence over all traffic. The arrow-straight Roman road that runs from Bologna to the coast stretched out behind him. Three years ago Duke Valentine had traveled this same road, his army swelled by the very men who would now bring him down. More than once in his journey Niccolò had looked over his shoulder in case he might make out a dust storm of rolling guns and foot soldiers, for these last days he had heard nothing but rumor: the rebels are on the move; they will besiege Imola; they are massing outside Urbino; they are fighting among themselves; they are everywhere and nowhere at once, though with each retelling the size of their force gets bigger.

Once inside the gates, he passes the great four-turreted fortress that stands on the southwest corner of the city. He notes gangs of soldiers digging trenches farther out from the moat, presumably to hamper any offensive artillery positions. What happens if they are not enough? Could it be that Lady Fortune has slipped out of the duke's arms so soon after becoming his faithful mistress?

He follows the guard upstairs to the small room, wiping his hands over his face to get rid of the grime, lifting his arms to gauge the stink in his cloth. What do they say in the drinking holes of Florence? That diplomacy is the art of covering bad smells with sweet words. However tired he is, his anticipation will trump it. History is being made in this little town, and short of sitting with Titus Lucretius in ancient Rome as he composed his treatise *De rerum natura*, there is nowhere else that he would rather be at this moment.

"Ah! The man whose face smiles even when he claims it does not. You left as secretary and return as permanent envoy. Congratulations are in order."

From an indolent, insolent conqueror, the man who greets him now is eager, almost boyish in his good humor. And this time he wears no mask, a handsome face still, Niccolò notes, despite the shower of pockmarks. Energy, like a bright halo, pulses out around him. "Florence must have valued your advice, Signor Smile. Though whatever it is you wrote it did me no good."

Having practiced a dozen opening gambits for this moment, Niccolò now discards them all. "I told them what I thought, my lord. That you were a man to be reckoned with, loved by your men and much favored by fortune."

"Which would explain your promotion, for all that is true. Though no fortune was needed to secure the support of King Louis, I told you that I had that already. So how is the eminent bishop Soderini and his most civic brother?"

"Well, my lord. They both send you warm greetings."

"Hm. I cannot help thinking how the bishop would suit scarlet robes. I shall talk to my father when I am next in Rome."

Niccolò drops his eyes in case his astonishment might show. The change is extraordinary. Cesare waves him toward a seat, but he lifts his hands to show that he is content to stand.

"Too many hours in the saddle, eh? You should be a soldier—that would toughen your rump fast enough. You came in through the southwest gate, yes?" he asks as he sees the little diplomat's eyes ranging over the maps on the walls. "What do you think of the fortifications?"

"I . . . I think that if the lady Caterina Sforza had done as much she would have held your army up for much longer," Niccolò says, trying hard to keep his face impenetrable.

"Caterina Sforza, eh? Is it the woman or her fortresses that interest you?"

"I was on diplomatic mission to the lady once."

"Ah! And? What did you make of the virago?"

What can he say? It had been his first solo mission as a diplomat and he'd been nervous as a young racehorse. Such a reputation she came with: a woman as lusty and bloodthirsty as any of her enemies, she had once exposed herself on the battlements to show her attackers how she could make more sons if they killed the ones they were holding hostage. Before their first meeting he had had a dream of her coming out of the forest like an Amazon warrior, her naked breasts leading the way. She had got the better of him in the negotiations, giving in to everything, only to change her mind at the last minute. It was a Pyrrhic victory; the Pope had already excommunicated her and her destiny was written inside the mouths of Cesare's cannons. The gossip about what took place between them the night after her capture had scorched the tavern walls: two scorpions in a ring of fire, strutting around each other before the final sting. Alas, there is no diplomatic language to pursue that subject.

"In battle I think she would have been as brave as any man. Maybe braver."

"You are right there." Cesare gives a bitter little laugh. "Though once she started squealing you couldn't mistake the woman in her. So, Florence sends me a military strategist as well as a diplomat!"

"Simply a student of history, my lord," he says with studied modesty.

"Then you will be good company, since history is my business too," Cesare grunts. Though he had feigned surprise, he had known whom Florence had appointed, had made it his business to find out more about the wily little diplomat who had danced so skillfully in the shadows of their last meeting. "You will know the Rubicon flows close to here, and that greatness awaits the right man who crosses it. I have his words on my sword."

"*Alea jacta est*," Niccolò smoothly picks up the cue. *The die is cast.* Caesar, he thinks. Always Julius Caesar. Rome's history overflows with greatness, yet it is the general who destroyed the republic rather than saved it that ambitious men measure themselves by.

"Indeed. And we shall find much to speak of, I am sure, for whatever the past, there is no bad feeling between Florence and myself. How could there be? With or without a treaty, we are joined in natural friendship, for we share the same vision of a secure and stable Italy, able to defend herself against a storm of thugs and traitors."

Ah! At last he has the scent, as pungent as if the dog has cocked his leg and pissed on him. He jumps in fast. "The council is most sorry to hear of this trouble with your erstwhile allies."

"What? You mean the vermin Vitelli and Baglioni joining with the cockroach Orsini and others? Ha! A congress of losers, every one of them. Which Florence should be grateful for, since this rebellion is more dangerous to you than it will ever be to me. I would remind you that two years ago when I stood on your borders I had Vitellozzo Vitelli on his knees, begging me to let him take Florence. Ha! My refusal just fueled his fury. If he and the Orsini get their way, you'll have no precious republic left to write aphorisms about."

Every word he speaks is true, Niccolò thinks. But adversity cuts both ways: if Florence needs the duke more than she did, then at this moment he also needs Florence.

"Nevertheless, they claim a great number of soldiers, my lord. You don't fear at all for the safety of Urbino?" he asks casually, alighting on one of the many rumors swirling in the air.

"I thought you said you had just arrived from the road," Cesare snaps back.

Niccolò's face does not move a muscle. My God, he is thinking, the duke is going to lose Urbino. This is news indeed.

"Whatever they *claim* is horseshit. Remember, I know these men and what they can and cannot do. The Orsini are dribbling girls in soldiers' clothing and Vitelli has never done a worthwhile thing in his life. As for Urbino, it is even less than nothing: an uprising of a few disgruntled men in a fort near the city; nothing to do with these traitors, though I daresay they will try to take advantage of it. It is already being dealt with."

"Your commander, de Corella?" Niccolò says, since Michelotto, whom everyone knows to be the duke's shadow, is nowhere to be seen.

"Who is not important," he retorts brusquely. "But since your business is information, Signor Smile, I tell you this for free. As we talk, seven hundred new recruits are already marching toward Imola, and I could show you now a letter of promise from King Louis for a thousand artillery and Swiss pikemen. These traitors do me a favor. They cannot show themselves at a time when it will damage me less, because I know now who are my enemies and who my friends. Write that to your earnest council. Unless they have sent me an envoy who they are still disposed not to listen to. Ah! Now at last we have a smile, or is it just the way your face behaves?"

• • •

Who would not smile, Niccolò thinks as he makes his way down to the courtyard. He has mined nothing but gold today: Urbino on the edge and promises of troops who have yet to arrive. All the facts point to a commander who should be frantic, yet it is impossible not to be impressed by his confidence and vigor. Mounting his horse, Niccolò counts more dispatch riders, heads down, mouths muffled against the dust. Add those to the ones at the gate earlier. The Borgia intelligence network is legendary; some liken it to a great spider's web strung across Italy, catching everything that wanders into its path. But watching this restless activity, he is reminded more of bees, always in the air, always moving from one flower to another, bringing the pollen of information back to the hive. Does the duke really know the minds of his enemies enough to predict their moves and therefore their downfall, or is it all just braggadocio, the credo of a man who believes he still has Fortuna in his bed?

The next day news arrives that a force under the command of Michelotto—for it was indeed him—has crushed the uprising and retaken the fort near Urbino. Niccolò now sends his first dispatch, striving to keep the words as close as he remembers them and also adding a few of his own, because one thing is already clear to him: though the duke may be isolated, it is his very aloneness that allows him to act fast and decisively. If this were a betting game, he still would have his money on the Borgia prince.

The assessment proves premature. Having plowed their own troops into the area, five days later his old condottieri, Vitelli, da Fermo and the Orsini cousins, join forces to retake the city of Urbino itself.

CHAPTER 23

❖

*T*he news has the duke's antechamber overflowing.

Experienced in the art of waiting, Niccolò digs out his sweetly worn copy of Livy from his pocket, but he barely has time to open it before he is plucked out and given precedence over all others.

Inside the room a fire is burning—there is a chill to the air now—with the remnants of a half eaten meal on the table. Standing at the back is the familiar figure of Michelotto.

"Signor Smile." Cesare holds out his hand. He looks like a man who hasn't slept, though it seems to have done nothing to dampen his energy. "You know my man, yes?"

Niccolò can see him better in daylight, that face as violent as any story of his deeds.

"I congratulate you on your retaking of Fossombrone, sir." Niccolò addresses him brightly. "It was a brilliant stroke of soldiering." He knows it will sound like arse-licking, but he means every word of it. In the drinking holes of Imola the newly returned men are full of it: how their commander had used plans of the fortress to unearth an old tunnel running from outside the walls into the inner keep, crawling through it with a dozen men in the night to break heads and slit throats. Not a single casualty on the duke's side.

Michelotto's silence suggests that he is not interested in praise.

"When he is tired, he never talks much," Cesare says after he has dismissed his man with a wave.

The door now closed, he beckons Niccolò toward the back of the room. "Come, come, I have something to show you."

On the back wall is a map, its corners oily with the sealing wax that fixes it to the stone. It is exquisitely drawn; a man with art on his mind would find it worthy of another kind of study, but the purpose here is practical. It takes Niccolò a moment to place it. He is looking at the city of Imola as it might be seen by a bird flying overhead, its walls and defenses all rendered in seemingly perfect proportions, down to turrets in the fortress and the gradients of the land and roads all around.

"You recognize the hand perhaps?" the duke asks casually. "He is one of yours."

"Da Vinci," Niccolò says, because everyone knows the duke has him on his payroll.

"Indeed. He has spent the last three months in my employ traveling through the Romagna assessing each of my fortresses and fortifications for improved defense systems."

"It was his map of Fossombrone that gave away the underground passage?"

"Who else's?" Cesare nods. "He is worth three times what I pay him, and he doesn't come cheap. You know him?"

"By reputation only." The gossip in government is that da Vinci and Buonarotti have such a dislike of each other they have made it their business not to be in the same town at the same time. Florence's loss has become everyone else's gain.

"I would introduce you, but he is already on his way to Piombino, claims he has had enough of war. Such mad artists you Florentines breed. From the neck up he looks like an unwashed hermit, yet he goes everywhere dressed in velvet with his pouty young catamite trailing behind him." The duke stares at Machiavelli. "I hear Florence is a city that specializes in sodomy."

Niccolò offers a small shrug. Almost every man he knows could tell tales; it is a rite of passage as much as a predilection, but they are not here for tavern talk.

"Well, we've all played on the other side of the street in our time, eh?" Cesare says with a crude laugh. "I couldn't care less where a man likes to put it. It's his brain I'm interested in. And your da Vinci has so many ideas that he needs ten hands to draw them all. He's got a scheme to connect the city of Cesena to the sea, and if it doesn't fall to bits like his giant horse in Milan, he says he will build me a cannon that can fire more than one ball at a time. You're lucky though. He remains a patriot. I asked him once what he would do if I set him the job of taking Florence. Know what he said? That the walls of his city were made of more than stone. Quoted some bit of poetry in the town square."

"'Kingdoms fall through luxury. Cities rise through virtue,'" Niccolò says quietly. He has no idea what is going on here, but he has little option except to follow. "It is engraved around Donatello's statue of Judith slaying Holofernes. When it was taken from the Medici palace, they changed part of the wording to reflect the power of the people."

"Is that so?" Cesare says, manifestly unimpressed by the information. "You Florentines do so like your art. Tell me, how goes the work on your giant *David*? Buonarroti still showering the city with marble dust, is he?"

Engineers, sculptors, poets, catamites. Every subject but the one that is everywhere.

Niccolò clears his throat. "My lord duke, I am sorry to hear the news of—"

"Urbino? Yes, yes. For a few days it will be on everyone's lips, though there is nothing that could hurt me less. Like magpies, they have gone for the shiniest thing in sight. Yet all they have got is an empty palace on a hill. I had thought they might be cleverer than that." He stops. "You don't believe me? You think I am playing you, reeling you in because, faced with trouble, I need Florence more now?"

Such diamond-hard eyes he has, no hint of emotion behind them. "An alliance would help you, yes." Niccolò pauses. No diplomat worth his salt should say everything that he is thinking. Yet he is dealing with a man who never does what anyone expects. "Nevertheless, my lord, I don't doubt you in this. I think that to have damaged you, they should have gathered every man, horse and cannon that they had, to attack you here in Imola."

"You don't trust your own countryman's new defense system?" the duke says lightly.

"I am sure it will be admirably strong, should it be finished in time. But they are only walls. And until more troops arrive . . ." He trails off with a small shrug of his shoulders.

"Ha! Signor Smile, you are wasted in the council chamber." Cesare throws his head back and gives a hearty laugh. It is the first unguarded gesture Niccolò has ever seen him make. "So," he goes on, "it seems we are looking through the same eyes. Tell me then, what would you do to take the sting out of these vipers' tails?"

Niccolò says nothing.

"You carry a volume of Roman history in your pocket, which they say you read all the time. Doesn't that help?"

"Not in this, my lord." The definition of treachery is as loose as a poisoned man's bowels, and advising the enemy would fall easily within it, though of course he has thought about it. "Your story has no parallels that I can see."

The duke grunts. "Very well. Then answer me another question, if you have the balls. If I were to guarantee you that within ten, twelve days this city will be swarming with soldiers, would you tell your beloved Florence now to make a treaty with me?"

"My lord, your job is war, mine is diplomacy. I cannot 'tell' Florence anything," he says, hoping his face does not give him away more than it already has. "I simply describe what is and make suggestions."

"Hmm. Somehow I doubt very much that is all you do," the duke says softly, decorating the compliment with a sly smile.

Politics and the art of seduction. If I were a woman, I would no doubt be at his feet now, Niccolò thinks, as he consciously straightens his back.

The moment passes.

"Ha! I believe you have grown taller since we first met," Cesare says lightly. "It must be the company you keep. Well." He waves his hand, as if to show it was all only fluff and banter. "Your honesty will do me well enough. Now if you will excuse me, I have a conspiracy to deal with."

For another night the tapers burn till dawn in the war room. Though he has taken a few liberties with the speed at which soldiers can march, Cesare has not lied about Urbino. In his mind it is indeed simply a shiny bauble. He has taken it once and he can take it again. But the worry is that it will give this ragbag rabble a sense of victory, and they cannot be allowed to build on that.

He writes a series of dispatches. The longest one is to his father. It will not please him. But battles are not always won by fighting. And it is clear how they must proceed.

CHAPTER 24

❖

*T*he slow sweet healing of Lucrezia. Later it will bring her equal sorrow and pleasure, remembering her journey from death to life.

She has chosen well. Though Corpus Domini may not have its own levitating nun, there is no finer convent in all Ferrara: noblewomen with generous dowries fusing worship and life inside a marriage to Jesus Christ, in His own way a more tolerant husband than many a violent, bullying flesh-and-blood one who might have been their fate in the world outside.

When they are not at prayer, the nuns spend their time embroidering collars and altar cloths, tending gardens, teaching young girls in their care or being taught themselves by a choirmistress who trains songbird voices out of the most unlikely mouths. At court, women can only sing at private functions; professional performance belongs to men. Yet here they make up a choir whose beauty—and reputation—has its church filled on every feast day and festival.

And now they have been awarded the highest accolade of all: nursing their new duchess back to health.

The day Lucrezia and her ladies arrive, the nuns form a cordon of welcome, their voices arching like garlands of flowers in the air above her. If they are shocked by how thin she is, how gray her skin, how dull and dead her eyes, it doesn't affect the verve of their greeting. Among them, senior nuns who hold posts of special responsibility in the kitchen, the choir and the infirmary are already honing their strategies of recovery.

Mouthful by mouthful . . .

The first weeks are filled with the repair of her body.

She is almost despairing when the first serving plates are set in front of her: poached calves' kidneys, dove breasts in white wine and pears baked in sweet liquor. The kitchen mistress has permission to order in special produce to tempt a half starved duchess back into health.

"But it is too much. I cannot eat it." Lucrezia groans, tired by the very sight of it.

At table with her, her ladies say nothing, sitting with their unused spoons by their loaded plates.

"What?" She looks up at them. "Why are you waiting? I will have something later."

But they will have none of it. They are bringing their own skills to bear on their beloved mistress's care: most notably cunning. If their duchess does not eat, then neither will they.

The first meal goes back untouched.

By the second day they are close to salivating from the smells rising from the veal in sweet sauce and the slow-baked river eels with capers glistening in their own juice.

The standoff continues.

"Oh, I cannot bear this," the duchess says at last with a petulant sigh. She stabs her silver fork into a piece of veal, puts it in her mouth and chews stubbornly, like a child forced into obedience. Just for a second her eyes close as she registers the release of the juniper berries within the sauce. She reopens them onto four faces, smiling broadly. The fast is over.

The next flank of attack comes from the dispensary. Two days in and a small wiry woman of uncertain age, skin worn and crinkled like parchment left out in a storm, arrives in her guest cell.

"Lady Duchess, I am Sister Bonaventura, and I have charge of the convent dispensary. I have made up some remedies which may be of help to you. Though I have no experience of labor and stillbirth, I have treated the attrition of summer fever, and I know the vagaries of women's monthly flow and the irritations and tenderness that can affect the secret passage to the womb."

Her penetrating pale blue eyes are as disconcerting as the directness of her speech.

"You are most kind," Lucrezia says coolly. "But I have been cared for by the best of doctors before I arrived here."

"That may be so. But you are not healed yet," the nun says bluntly.

"I think I am the best judge of that," Lucrezia retorts, taking refuge in haughtiness. "I am simply tired."

"Food will help. But you need to sleep better. You suffer from nightmares, yes?"

"What do you know of my dreams?" Her sharpness is laced with fear, because it is true; her nightmares are terrible. The worst is the one when she wakes unable to breathe, struggling to give birth to a monster, half animal, half human, whose small, snarling body breaks into bloody bits as it falls to the floor at her feet.

The nun remains unmoved by her tone. "It is my task to care for all manner of distress, and God aids me to see things that others may not." She is not without her own cunning, this seasoned healer. Processing to chapel in the middle of the night for the service of Matins, she has heard the duchess's voice crying out from the guesthouse cloisters.

She slips her hands into the voluminous folds of her habit and, like some market sorceress, extracts first one, then two glass vials of liquid and a majolica pot, sealed tight with a wooden lid.

"The paler fluid is tonic for the body and best taken before food in the morning. The dark color is for the night. Eight drops in a little wine, half an hourglass before you lie down. And the ointment is for application to the inside of your vaginal passage—to help heal any fissures or tenderness that might have come with the force of the labor."

Lucrezia stares at her. None of the doctor crows have ever talked to her so directly about such things. But after the nun leaves, the light of those pale washed blue eyes and an aura of kindness remain. She finds herself wondering how many young women enter Corpus Domini against their will, and how they might need more than the rhythm of convent life to help them adjust. She picks up the sleeping draft and holds it to the light. The liquid is a deep amber color, rich like well-fermented ale. Distillation. Not a skill many noblewomen might aspire to in the world outside.

There is no pulse. I am dead.

How these words have haunted Lucrezia these last weeks. There have been moments, often at the worst times in the night, when they have felt more real than the world around her. As if she has been unable to summon up the will or the energy to move beyond them.

But here, now, it might be possible to let them go. On her desk sits a finely worked silver crucifix, brought from her own chapel. She knows this body well: ribbed chest and sinewed arms straining off the nails; a man who understands suffering, who has sacrificed himself for mankind. If she did not die, then it can only be because God wanted her alive. And how can anyone gainsay His will?

That night, after prayers that last longer than the words, she swallows the amber liquid, growing drowsy as the evening service of Compline sends out tender shoots of song into the cloisters and beyond. The sleep that follows is long, deep and undisturbed by terror.

The guest quarters of Corpus Domini are grouped around a lacy stone cloister. The scale is intimate, almost tender, and the young stone pine tree in the middle of the courtyard offers a canopy of shade and, at this time of year, gives off a heady aroma of resin. In the silence of the long afternoons while the nuns work and attend services, Lucrezia and her ladies sit with their needlework for company. She has set herself the task of embroidering a surplice for her brother-in-law Cardinal Ippolito, a deliberately challenging design of a silver chalice formed from looping long stitch, with the host rising up from it, sending out showers of dense cross-stitched red and gold stars. She has always been a most accomplished needlewoman and has forgotten the peace that grows from the simple repetition of needle and thread moving in and out of the embroidery hoop. As the afternoon sun moves slanting golden strips across the flagstones, there are moments when she thinks that she would never like to leave.

Meanwhile, she is also experimenting with the tapestry of song. The beauty and complexity of the way the nuns weave their voices together fascinates her, and she asks permission for the choirmistress to give lessons to her ladies. She is also being instructed herself. Court gossip flows easily through the parlor; visiting hours are generous; mothers, sisters, cousins, nieces, all bring nasty tidbits in exchange for convent biscuits and lace collars that the nuns produce and send out with pride. Everyone knows the stories of the wedding festivities: how the duchess's dancing eclipsed all, but how it was Isabella d'Este who took the palm for her skill with lute and voice. Of course, they love their duke's own daughter. But she has lived in Mantua for over a decade and is busy endowing convents of her own there. Their new duchess has resoundingly won their hearts and loyalty (the waiting list for new novices has doubled since she arrived). When she has daughters of her own, what everlasting honor it would bring Corpus Domini if one of them might enter its cloisters rather than any other.

The abbess gives the choirmistress dispensation to overlay sacred words onto some of the court's popular music, along with the Psalms, which she has already set so prettily to her own compositions. The two women work together each afternoon, and Lucrezia starts to appreciate the freedom that comes when a woman is encouraged to fill her lungs and open her mouth, finding a voice richer than she ever dreamed she might own.

Note by note, stitch by stitch, day by day, a stronger, more vibrant Duchess of Ferrara is emerging.

CHAPTER 25

❖

*A*lexander has heard morning mass and is in relatively good humor when Cesare's letter arrives.

I know this will go against the grain, Father, but . . .

It reads as if his son is standing next to him, hectoring.

This conspiracy is like a badly patched roof in winter. All it needs is a few slates ripped off and the whole thing will collapse in on itself. You must approach Cardinal Orsini and make your peace with him. Tell him our quarrel is not with him, but the rebels in our pay and that already they are squirming on the hook. Tell him that Bologna is already in secret negotiations with me based on a promise of nonaggression between us, and that as soon as this is made public the others will come crawling. Flatter, dissemble, lie, promise whatever you need to convince him. Swallow your pride and do this thing, Father, and I promise you

will have his and every other one of their heads on pikes later. But say
nothing to anyone. Nothing at all.

The Pope reads the letter a number of times, becoming more and
more agitated. In recent weeks the tone of their dispatches has been
changing; things told as much discussed, less asking and more demanding. Sweet Mother of God, who does his son think he is talking to? He,
who was already a veteran of politics when the boy was still peeing in
his bathwater.

He slams the paper down on his lap.

"Not bad news I hope, Holy Father?" Burchard asks politely.

Alexander stares at him. How he would like to tell him what he feels.
For as long as he can remember he has had family around him with
whom he could talk freely. Age as well as habit have made him a man
used to having license to say what he thinks.

He reads one last time. It is the tone that annoys him most. But if he
puts that aside, then the assessment of the conspiracy is solid enough.
He has thought as much himself over the last few weeks. As for taking
revenge? Well, he has waited long enough to skewer the Orsini. A little
longer will not spoil the pleasure. He throws the pages into the fire,
watching their edges catch, running a comb of flame through the parchment until it crumbles. Posterity will not hear the disrespect inside the
words. When they are celebrating it will matter less who wrote what to
whom.

He calls for his secretary.

"It is a letter to the Cardinal of Santa Maria in Dominica. Are you
ready?"

Two days later, Cardinal Giovanni Battista Orsini is ushered into the
Hall of the Saints, where two empty chairs are set by the fire and a
flagon of wine is warming. He sits, his eye drawn to a clever trompe
l'oeil on the left-hand wall, a painted fake shelf on which a painted fake
papal crown, sumptuous and jeweled, sits precariously balanced, wait-

ing to be picked up by anyone whose fingers itch enough for power. Pinturicchio is a confident artist, but he would not take such liberties unless directly instructed. The Borgias are a jumped-up band of foreign interlopers with little breeding or history behind them. But they are far from stupid. He would do well to remember that now.

He too has done his fair share of raging at impotence these last weeks: this "secret" alliance on which he has risked so much has been leaking like a sieve from the moment the ink was dry on the paper. And their trump card—the speed of an attack—is already compromised. No sooner had Vitelli and his men left for Urbino than the squabbling had begun. The latest from Bologna is that Baglioni is refusing to cede or share command with anyone, so that the force that is gathered has yet to move, consuming its way through the goodwill of the district where it is billeted. The incompetence, perversely, has given the Pope a greater admiration for the very men he would like to see dead at his feet.

"My dear, dear cardinal, how good of you to come."

The Pope waddles in in full ceremonial robes, arms open and face wreathed in smiles. The two aging enemies embrace, scarlet encased by shining white.

"I will not insult you with wasted words or pleasantries, Giovanni," he says as soon as they are settled. "This is as difficult for me as it is for you. Bitterness is a familiar taste in both our mouths, and I freely admit that over these last years I have wished you ill for the wrongs of the past. As you have me." He is sitting forward now, serious, intent, the gold fisherman's ring prominent on his clasped fingers. "But whatever our differences, neither of us has anything to gain from unleashing madness. To protect yourself from me you have got into bed with a rabble of thugs, diseased dogs with no respect for authority of any kind who would take down all order if it is in their interests. And when they run riot we will all be the losers. I asked you here today to offer you my hand, as your pope and as a father, to try to find a way to end this discord between us. To talk frankly about what we want from each other, and how we might make amends for the past before this flailing conspiracy brings chaos on both our houses."

The wine is poured, and Giovanni, hesitating only to watch Alexander take a swig before him, raises his own goblet. In among the egregious lies, there are nuggets of truth that cannot be ignored. He thinks of da Fermo's uncle butchered like a farm animal, and Baglioni using his own blood for ink. These days a man has scant choice between allies and enemies. He offers up a thin smile and carries on listening.

Such pleasure it brings Alexander as his words flow, warm and soothing as the oil of extreme unction. He may be irritated with his son, but there is still no better politician inside the Church when it comes to the art of dissembling.

• • •

In the coming weeks Niccolò is not the only one to notice the change in security arrangements in Imola. The number of guards on the towers that overlook the Via Emilia westward toward Bologna is reduced, and he and other diplomats are given ringside seats in the piazza to welcome the arrival of the duke's new recruits. The whole city is invited, and men feast on their own fattened pigs bought at generously inflated prices by the duke himself. If the citizens had their choice they would live under Borgia rule forever, for it is sweeter than any they have had before.

There has been no time to put the seven hundred new soldiers in uniform, and they have yet to master the art of walking in step, but their very roughness gives off a sense of threat. Niccolò watches them intently. These are men of the Romagna employed now to protect their own lands, in embryo a citizen militia the like of which he has dreamed of for Florence ever since he entered government. When they are joined by the French infantry and a cohort of Swiss pikemen, both on forced march from Milan, the duke will, as promised, have clear military superiority over his enemies. Enemies who were once his paid friends. Also, and in his mind this is almost as important, though the rebels still hold Urbino, not a single other town has risen up and joined them. The Borgia power base remains firm.

Finally there are the swirling rumors of rapprochement. It is impos-

sible not to be impressed, even admiring. He already has a letter out to
Biagio in Florence, requesting a copy of Plutarch's *Parallel Lives*, com-
paring the great generals of Greece and Rome. Now he sits down to
compose his formal dispatch to the government, struggling to make the
language of diplomacy sing.

> *In my opinion these rebels have taken a dose of slow-acting poison.
> The duke is a man accustomed to winning, and with the king and the
> Pope behind him, he has both the means and the will to triumph again.
> Whatever the reservations about his final intentions, it would be in Flor-
> ence's interest to make a formal treaty now.*

He uses the days of waiting to pay another visit to Imola's best
brothel, only to find that the arrival of the troops has inflated the prices.
His mood is not improved by the delivery of Biagio's letter.

Sorry, Il Macchia. His friend's cheerful voice slides into the room. *There's
not a copy of your Plutarch to be found anywhere in the city. You'll have to go
to Venice for that. It wouldn't help you anyway. The word from on high is that
while you do a fine job supping with the devil, they need less "opinion" and
more facts. And I have to tell you frankly you are an asshole if you think they
will make a treaty with His Lordship. Getting into bed with your duke is not the
way the wind blows here.*

His duke? Less opinion more facts! What? They send him to get close to
a man and then accuse him of not being able to tell seduction from sub-
stance! And yes, he has opinions! They have barely scratched the surface. He thinks again of the soldiers in the square and how much
stronger Florence would be if she had her own militia, rather than paying through the nose for professionals who shaft as easily as they support. My God, there will be much to talk about when he returns; he and
Biagio will need to take rooms in the tavern . . .

In Imola, however, satisfying conversation is becoming increasingly
hard to find.

. . .

By the time Florence's formal rejection arrives, the duke has no need of a treaty anyway, for the conspiracy is collapsing on itself. Cardinal Orsini is publicly received back into the arms of the Pope, and the head of the Bentivoglio family from Bologna comes in person to Imola to be welcomed by the duke. It seems there is no quarrel between them now at all, and Bologna's freedom is guaranteed. To his chagrin, Niccolò hears about this visit only thirdhand.

On his way to deliver Florence's answer, he can barely gain passage along the street for the press of soldiers. Outside the chamber he is kept waiting for the first time. Cesare Borgia clearly has more important people to see. After a while the doors open and a grubbily clad Paolo Orsini comes skulking out. Paolo Orsini! One of his own condottieri! Is he really so feeble of mind—or so desperate—that he thinks the duke will ever forgive his betrayal? Niccolò remembers the words of his own dispatch: *A dose of slow-acting poison.* It is just a question of where and when the bodies fall. What would he give now for an invitation to dinner at the Borgia table?

But when he is finally admitted, the duke remains busy at his desk, not even looking up to acknowledge his arrival, so that he must stand in the entrance like the supplicant he has again become.

"Good morning, Signor Smile," Cesare says at last, his eyes still on the page. "What can I do for you?"

"I have come to offer congratulations. Your commanders take back fortresses using underground passages, but here you welcome your enemies in through the main gate."

"What? Bologna and the simpering lady Paolo Orsini, you mean?" Cesare says with studied casualness as he looks up. "Yes, they have been pestering me for weeks. You see how they govern themselves, the whole cowardly bunch: write friendly letters, negotiate agreements behind each other's back, even pay me courteous visits. It falls out, I think, exactly as I told you."

Niccolò shifts on his feet. There is no offer of a chair this time. "And you believe their goodwill after so much treachery?"

Cesare looks at him sharply. "What I 'believe' is that men play games with each other. Such is the business of diplomacy, is it not?" And just for a moment it seems as if he might be tempted to talk further. But instead he smiles coldly as he pulls some papers toward him.

"As you see I have much to do and we have unfinished business between us. The last time we spoke you were waiting on a dispatch from the dozen committees that run your wondrous republic. I hear that you entertained a rider from Florence yesterday evening. So, tell me: has your command of history finally convinced them or have they grown used to the feeling of spokes up their arse from so long spent sitting on the fence?"

CHAPTER 26

❖

In Corpus Domini, Lucrezia has reinstated the hand mirror hidden at the bottom of her chest.

"Welcome back, Duchess of Ferrara." She tries out her smile. The face that stares back at her is that of a healthy young woman with full cheeks and a glow to her skin. It is time to think of going home. She is ready. Convent life, for so long a balm, has begun to feel tedious in its repetition. Winter light is draining the warmth from the brickwork, and as the nights grow longer, the mornings bring in fog, rolling through the cloisters, swallowing huddled figures of nuns inside a sea of gray. There are days when it barely lifts at all, as if the whole convent is going into hibernation, while she is in the full bloom of spring.

Over these long weeks messengers had kept her abreast of news at home and abroad, following the tightrope journey of the Borgia fortunes. Cesare's letters are short, loving but guarded, while her father, as ever, lets his feelings flow, careening among misery, fury and triumph as the worst of the threat drains away. Meanwhile, her husband's brief bulletins from his pilgrimage down the eastern coast of Italy (the shrine at

Loreto seems to have played only a minor part in the journey) now report that his travels will soon be drawing to a close. He should be back before Christmas. And she must be there to welcome him.

She visits the abbess, who feigns more sadness than she feels at the news of the duchess's departure. If the honor has been unprecedented, so has the length of the visit, and it has had its effect on convent behavior, especially that of the novices living in proximity to a group of women who pay more attention to preening than to prayer.

It isn't their fault. Ladies-in-waiting are singled out early as the daughters who will *not* be nuns, and the novelty of playacting has long ago worn thin. It has been hard for women so creative with color to be dressed in black mourning a baby they never knew, or to wake to a day that is the same as every yesterday; no male flirtation to lighten the mood, no spice of intrigue of any kind save the most petty sort that breaks out among cooped-up women whose menstrual flows have fused together into the cycle of the moon. Young Angela, in particular, missing the excitement of her illicit courtship with the duke's bastard son, has become most unhappy, picking fault with others, who in turn have started bickering among themselves.

"Oh, but we are all turning into nuns!" Angela shrieked one morning, eyes wide with horror at the thought, hanging her head in apology when she turned to see Lucrezia in the doorway.

Their leaving date is set by a message from the duke himself.

"Who would believe it?" Lucrezia looks up from the letter delivered that morning from the ducal palace.

"My father-in-law Ercole—in his own hand—tells me he remains in deepest purgatory without my smile and begs us—begs no less!—to return to court in time for a performance of a new translation of a Plautus comedy he has planned for the end of December."

There is, of course, an ulterior motive.

The wind from Imola brings daily news of Cesare's diplomatic triumph over the conspiracy. Whatever comes next, it seems certain now that the Borgia flag will be flying ever higher, and it is in Ferrara's interest for Ercole to show how much he values his beloved daughter-in-law.

Yet it isn't simply politics. Surrounded once again by the same old courtiers, he has missed the sparkle that she and her ladies brought to his gatherings. What is the point of another spectacle with no sense of occasion, no discerning audience to show it off to? He has also missed her dancing. An old man cannot pray all the time, and recently he has found himself growing misty-eyed at the thought of a pretty woman who dances with the same vibrancy as his own dear Eleonora. Strange how the longer she is dead, the more fond of her he becomes.

"And!—Oh—" Lucrezia breaks off from the letter, as if she can't quite believe the words.

"What? What?" Her ladies urge her on. This is more excitement than they have had for weeks.

"After thought and guidance from God, it is his pleasure to offer me my full annual dowry income. I shall be paid half in cash—five thousand ducats—and for the rest, all of my household allowances will be absorbed into his. Well, who would believe it?"

And the ladies are on their feet, whooping, dancing for joy, already seeing the bolts of silks and damasks unfurling their colorful way from Venice to Ferrara.

"He must have been humbled by how nearly he lost you," Camilla says when they get their breaths back.

"More likely he is in 'purgatory' because that was where his levitating nun told him old misers go," Angela chips in. "What?" she says as the others hush her. "I am simply saying what we feel. Anyway, ten thousand is only fair payment for having to sit through another of his excruciating plays."

But Lucrezia is laughing too. "You must ask God for a little more patience, Angela. Or do what I do sometimes in chapel here. Close your eyes as if you are praying and think of something else."

Their laughter has a tingle of shock to it. "You, my lady! Pretending to pray!"

"Why not? We are not become nuns yet."

Oh yes, the Duchess of Ferrara is recovered.

The trunks are packed, and a final farewell service is being planned for Vespers, when Lucrezia uses the excuse of work hour to seek out the infirmary mistress in her dispensary.

It is the first time she has visited Sister Bonaventura's workplace. The small room is made smaller by walls of shelves, on which sit dozens of bottles and jars, identified in a minuscule script as if a trail of methodical ants had walked through ink onto the labels. How many years' work is there here? How much knowledge?

She finds the nun crouched over a desk, making notes.

"I have come to thank you, Sister Bonaventura. I would not be so well without your help."

The nun raises a hand in a flutter of dismissal. "I am grateful that with God's grace I have been of some use, Lady Duchess."

Lucrezia is glancing around at the regiment of cures that stand in line on the shelves. "You have built a world in this room. How long have you been here?"

"Me? Here? Let me see—I came before Duchess Eleonora arrived from Naples to marry the duke. Which would make it . . . thirty-three, no thirty-four years."

"I see." Those eyes, even in the gloom of the room, remain arresting. Had she been pretty when she was young? Of course she had. "Did you choose to be a nun?"

"I was fourteen," she says evenly in answer.

"Fourteen? Ha! My first marriage had taken place when I was that age."

Giovanni Sforza. She has not thought of him for so long. A saggy, sad man, terrified of his own shadow. Or rather the shadow of her family. Not such a foolish fear given how the marriage turned out. Fourteen. What could one possibly know?

"I am sure God chose wisely for us both."

How much she has grown to admire this woman: her plain speaking and her calm demeanor. Lucrezia hesitates. She would not like to discover that the aura of peace disguises too much pain.

"I suspect the difference between us, Sister, is that you must always have been a little wise."

The elder woman drops her eyes. While she is at ease speaking her mind, she doesn't spend much time on herself, either in diagnosis or in remedies.

"Still, you have no regrets. I mean, given your life here?"

"Regrets. None at all." One does not need to be wise to know what little point there would be in that. At the wooden bench a small box is waiting, filled with bottles and jars. "I have prepared some drafts and further ointment for you, my lady. In case you should need them."

"Have you bottled up some of your peace in one of them?" She laughs slightly. "Court life can be so noisy and distracting."

The blue eyes hold hers for a moment. When a question is asked more than once, it deserves some answer.

"It is not my business, my lady, but over the years I have nursed a few women who have come as close to death as you. I am not sure if it has brought them peace, but I see in them a kind of resilience, in spirit perhaps even more than in body."

"Then I shall happily be one of those," Lucrezia says gaily, fearing suddenly that if she stays any longer she might start to cry.

"Tell me." She turns at the door. Is this mischief or resilience? "I don't suppose you have the wherewithal to mix up an aphrodisiac."

For once she has the pleasure of watching those eyes blink slowly in evident surprise.

"No, of course you don't." She smiles. "See—it is just as well that I married young, for I would not have made a very good nun."

After she has gone the dispensary mistress stands for a while in front of her wall of remedies, cataloging their properties and their provenance. Sleep, peace, aphrodisiacs. Such a treasure-house God had locked up in nature. And what havoc a dissatisfied dispensary nun might wreak if she were in the mood.

CHAPTER 27

❖

*T*he conspiracy is dead. From Perugia the Baglioni brothers send fawning greetings while Vitelli and Oliverotto da Fermo negotiate the return of Urbino, claiming they have been grossly misunderstood. They renew their pledge of service to the Borgia cause and await the duke's instructions. He graciously accepts and guarantees them further employment and the independence of their own cities. Niccolò watches it all as it unfolds, his admiration matched only by his incredulity. How could any of them be telling the truth?

Winter descends on the city, bringing wind and icy rain. But it is the drop in diplomatic temperature that makes his life particularly inhospitable. The duke's feelings and, more important, any hint of action are now shrouded in cold clouds of secrecy. He has no use for Florence anymore; its clever envoy has failed to bring him the one thing he wanted, and so he is cast adrift. In Cesare's place, Niccolò knows he would have done the same thing.

But it is not just Florence that is ignored. The duke seems to have turned his back on the diplomatic game altogether. Instead he has returned to his old habit of inverting night and day, so that the only time to see him is when everyone else is in bed. There are rumors of alternating lethargy and tantrums, even a reoccurrence of the agonies of the pox. But all is conjecture.

You must remember that we deal with a prince who governs by himself, he writes, not without a certain bitterness toward his masters. *So do not impute it to negligence if I do not satisfy you with more information, because for most of the time I do not even satisfy myself.*

There is no satisfaction to be had anywhere else either. The Borgia rule may have eased the burdens of taxation, but war is war and two months of a billeted army have eaten the city and its neighboring farmland down to stalks and scrag ends. There is barely a cask of decent wine to be found, and a clean woman now would demand more money than he could raise, and even then she would probably be lying. He finds himself missing Marietta more than he might like to admit. But there is no solace to be gained there: from loving letters through impatient ones—*you promise a few weeks and already you are gone for months*—she has lapsed now into petulant silence, though it seems she is shouting loud enough to anyone else who will listen.

She misses you, Niccolò, that much is clear, though she has a strange way of showing it, Biagio writes. He can almost see his friend blowing on his fingers to show the heat of her anger. *I've done what I can. For God's sake send her funds or a gift of some kind to keep her sweet.*

Except he has nothing to send. He has eaten up each month's wages and expenses before they arrive, and his requests for more money are ignored. Who would be a diplomat from a modest family in Italy? Influenza stalks the city, and he shivers under thin blankets as water dribbles down the insides of the walls. He finds himself thinking about his life up until now. Remembering youthful conversations with his father about the importance of a man serving the city he loves. And he had been educated to do just that. But instead, Florence had fallen under the sway of a zealot who believed that God had sent him to create the kingdom of heaven on earth. No dancing, no gambling, no fornication and worst of all, no words worth reading but the words of God. Niccolò had sinned enough during those years for a lifetime of penances, and he wasn't the only one. By the time a new government needed new faces, he was something of an expert in human nature, both in the past and in the present. But he was no longer a young man. At twenty-nine, he had had some catching up to do. And now, at thirty-three, he feels it even more intensely.

In late November, with no more intelligence to be gleaned, and even if there were, no money to buy it, he asks to be recalled. The council has made its decision, and he can do no more. *If it goes on like this you will be bringing me back in a casket.*

He can almost see the smile on the gonfaloniere's face as he reads the words. It does no good. His request is refused. Despite his "opinions," Niccolò Machiavelli is far too good at his job to be allowed home. That night he takes himself to a tavern where he knows that other, richer envoys like to congregate to bitch about the hardships of diplomatic living. Next morning he wakes to a blinding headache and the satisfaction of knowing that no one but the duke has a clue what his next move will be.

• • •

Meanwhile, outside Cesare's chambers, men walk on their eyelashes in case their footsteps might disturb him. This night existence has changed his character entirely. Or perhaps it is the other way around: with fortune so powerfully on his side again, there is no need to charm anyone anymore.

Dispatches arrive daily from Rome, demanding to know what he is doing, what he is thinking. With the conspiracy defeated, their enemies are ripe for the taking. How and when will he crush the gutter rats that have betrayed them?

If Alexander cannot bear not knowing, Cesare cannot bear to be pushed. It is not simply resistance. The old man is becoming a liability, his tongue growing as slack as his judgment, so that what he is told must be rationed until the moment when the information can do no harm.

No, Cesare and Cesare alone knows what he is doing, how and when and where it will be played out. They are all dead men, not worthy of thought or feeling. In his mind he has already taken their cities and is master of much of Tuscany. All this he keeps to himself. If not his father, then whom could he possibly share it with? Not the smart, febrile Florentine, who makes him think of a hunting dog, nose always to the scent. Not even the solid Michelotto, with a silence as deep as the grave. He is above, below and beyond them all now, a man trapped inside the grandeur of his own head. Where before he was fueled by anger, now he can barely summon up contempt. Where once he was exhilarated, now he is bored. It seems there is a price to be paid for outthinking everyone else.

At first he sleeps; a man who has been fighting the world deserves a little rest. He lies unconscious for twelve or more hours at a stretch, and when he wakes, rather than pulsing with energy he is enervated, easily distracted, consumed by dark moods. He sits for hours staring into the grate as if the answer to anything and everything is to be found inside the lava of its flames. If disturbed during this time, he will rage and shout like a man possessed. Torella, not long back from the most testing of missions caring for the duke's sister, notes each and every mood swing with a sense of mounting apprehension. He has seen such mental tempests before and now has the temerity to suggest that the duke may be in some way indisposed. Cesare throws him out in a storm of curses, but later calls him back.

"It is in my head." He groans, putting a hand to his forehead but never taking his eyes off the fire. "The hammer blows are back."

"Can you tell me more, my lord? When did it start?"

"Yesterday, the day before, I don't know. It smashes against my forehead as if something is trying to break out of my skull."

"Is it worse than the last time?"

"Christ Almighty, Torella. So many questions! Yes, no. I don't know. All I know is that it hurts and, more than that, it stops me thinking. Get rid of it!"

Torella stares at him. Over the years, he has patched up this reckless young man from a dozen stab or sword wounds, prodding and pulling at open flesh, with not a moan or a blasphemy to cover what must have been agony. Though his desk is littered with notes from all over Italy on the strange passage of this pox, the world is still full of other vicious diseases. This new distress may be a result of inflammation from the damp that is everywhere in the city. In his time he has seen men ready to butt their heads against walls to get rid of such pain. Or . . . or could it be that the inside of the duke's skull has grown infected in the same way as his legs and arms once were? His brain even? The doctor suggests an inhalation with a weak solution of mercury along with herbs known to soothe headaches. Cesare, who has been incandescent with anger during the conversation, agrees meekly. It occurs to Torella that underneath his fury he might even be a little frightened.

He sits every night through the falling sands of an hourglass, swathed in towels over bowls of steaming water, growling, either from temper or from pain, while Michelotto sits outside the door as constant bodyguard. After days of sweating and sleeping, he declares himself cured and sends Torella a purse.

It smashes against my forehead as if something is trying to break out of my skull.

At private prayer that evening Torella remembers the words. It is a relief that it is not his job to be the Borgia's confessor. Even so, he knows his patient has done deeds that will have the devil laying claim to his soul when the time comes. Unless, in some way, it is happening already.

CHAPTER 28

❖

"What? This is it?"

In Rome, Alexander is so starved for information that he has taken to cross-questioning the exhausted dispatch riders who stand shivering in front of the papal fire while he despairs over the single piece of paper they have brought him.

He looks up, incredulous. "You are three days in the saddle to bring me news that the duke has left Imola and taken his court to Cesena."

"It was what I was given, Your Holiness." The man is in an agony of embarrassment. He had not even been given time to relieve himself before he was pulled off his horse and delivered into the Pope's presence.

"By whom? Who put it into your hands? The duke himself?"

"No, Miguel de Corella."

"And what did he say?"

"Nothing. Your Holiness," he adds helplessly.

"What about Sinigaglia? You delivered my dispatch, yes?"

"Yes, yes, Your Holiness."

There are moments when Alexander wonders how much of his life he has squandered listening to the words *Your Holiness*. The title used to make him feel like a man elevated. Recently it seems like an excuse for prevarication.

"Yet this is no reply. Where are all the troops? What is the duke doing? You must have seen something."

The man lifts his hands desperately. "Your Holiness," he says helplessly. "I am a dispatch rider."

The set of Spanish expletives that now explodes from the Pope's mouth shows no respect for either man or God. The man stares in horror and tries again. "I believe . . . well, it seems the duke is getting ready to celebrate Christmas."

"Christmas! Did you hear what the man said, Burchard? While his enemies lick his boots pretending friendship and I bleed money to keep the biggest army in Italy at his beck and call, the duke celebrates Christmas. Sweet Mary, if Christmas is what he wanted, he should have stayed a cardinal in the Church!"

Burchard, who has taken to molding small balls of candle wax and sticking them in his ears to mute the worst of the yelling, stands patiently by. The Pope's temper has grown noticeably worse since he was forced to reconcile with Cardinal Orsini. He has embraced his enemies before, but he was not acting on someone else's instructions then. Deception is second nature to him. Impotence is something new. Meanwhile, the annual miracle repeats itself: Our Lady, weary from the road and the weight of her precious burden, is once again reaching Bethlehem, only to find there is no room at any inn, so that she must settle in a stable as the moment comes for the birth of Our Savior. Inside the Vatican, Burchard is run off his feet overseeing the necessary ceremonies and finds it hard to hide his impatience: the head of the Catholic Church should be celebrating the wonder of the holy family, not fretting about problems of his own.

• • •

The dispatch rider's assessment is accurate. The duke and his immediate court have ridden the thirty-five-mile journey from Imola to Cesena, where they are settling in for Christmas. Niccolò Machiavelli, now living on debt, has to finance yet another set of lodgings in the castle that dominates the main piazza.

The city is under the control of Ramiro de Lorqua, a stocky Spaniard with a bulbous nose and a beard as black as his temper. He had ridden out to meet them, his oily smile and fulsome welcome reserved for his employer, while he turned his back on everyone else. Niccolò has made it his business to know all he can about the men who surround the duke, and de Lorqua comes with ugly stories attached. He has been in the Borgia entourage since adolescence and over the last few years has brought a lawless countryside to order fast, but with a cruel streak that would turn most men's stomachs. The worst example comes from gossip exchanged on the journey: how when he was served by a nervous young page who dropped the tray in his presence, de Lorqua grabbed the boy and threw him headfirst into the open fire, stamping his foot down onto his back and holding it there, continuing the conversation with his men over the thrashing and screams until the chamber started to reek with the smell of burnt hair and flesh.

As he sits staring into the struggling fire in his drafty rooms, the image returns to haunt him. He knows enough about history and power to appreciate that there must be a balance between being feared and being loved, and that when a state changes hands by force, no ruler can afford to be queasy about how he imposes control. Examples must be made and cruelty is not confined to villains. But a servant boy burned alive for clumsiness by a man who clearly relishes the agony he inflicts? What can such an act achieve but outrage and more enemies? It smells of bad government as much as burning flesh. Is a duke who leads his army by example unaware of these things about his lieutenant? How could he be? In which case, does he not care? From everything Niccolò knows—or thinks he knows—of Cesare Borgia, it does not make sense.

On the other hand, with Cesare Borgia now returned to public life all the signs are that he cares only for his own amusement. There is one final conquest to look forward to. The city of Sinigaglia, farther down the east coast, will complete his control of the Papal States within the Romagna. The Pope has already excommunicated its ruling family, and they seem set to give in without a fight. It is at this point that Cesare announces that his condottieri, Oliverotto da Fermo and Vitellozzo Vitelli aided by Paolo and Francesco Orsini, will oversee its surrender on his behalf, citing their employment as proof of their renewed loyalty. Such astonishing magnanimity!

With all his enemies friends again, there is no need for the great army that his father has emptied his treasury to sustain, and that he is still paying for. Niccolò has barely articulated the thought when, suddenly, with just days to go before Christmas, the duke summarily dismisses the French artillery. It goes down badly with their commanders, and the castle echoes with raised voices. *Ten days of forced march to get here, and now we are dispatched back to Milan in the worst weather of the year!* Niccolò, who gets on well with them and uses drinking bouts as a cheap way to get information, hears it firsthand: *Why? Because according to His Lordship he has "an embarrassment of soldiers" and can no longer afford his wages bill! Ha! The king—and everyone else—will hear of it.*

When it comes to the cost of running a war with no fighting, Niccolò has already done the sums. As well as the artillery and men-at-arms, there are several hundred soldiers left in Imola and a thousand Swiss pikemen billeted in the nearby city of Faenza. A king's ransom. Or a pope's purse. Except looked at that way, it makes even less sense. Since when did Cesare Borgia ever worry about money? Behind this smoke screen something else is going on. But what and when?

Starved of funds himself, Niccolò gives in to daydreams of home: crisp Florentine nights full of stars, roaring tavern fires and jugs of spiced wines and the company of men whose conversation ricochets between politics and profanity. Biagio's letters are his only comfort: the story of a card game that ended in blows, the delivery of an outfit specially ordered from Niccolò's tailor to supplement his meager wardrobe, shabby after two months of constant wear. With luck it might arrive in time for the Christmas celebrations, for its high collar and long length give him immediate dignity, not to mention the illusion of a little extra height, which he is much in need of right now. The style had been Marietta's idea: "You wore one like it the first day we met and it was most becoming. It never hurts a man to look a little taller than he is."

Her loving mockery takes him back to last Christmas, the first of their married life. She had overseen a feast of a meal, inviting friends and colleagues. His father and sister had both died barely a year before, and as a new wife, she had been mindful that he might feel their absence. She had been right. That night he had buried his head between her breasts and she had cooed and coaxed him into love. He finds himself unexpectedly sentimental at the memory. What he wouldn't give for a night in his wife's bed and that volume of Plutarch now.

Two days before Christmas the city's most prominent families throw a dinner, their wives and daughters brought out to swell the throng. The threat lifted, they need to show how fond they are of their ruler. Hungry himself for a little female company, Niccolò brushes off his old velvet and smooths down his hair. The new outfit would not have made much difference anyway, for he and every other man in the room are immediately eclipsed by the duke. From darkness, Cesare now blazes with light: a strutting peacock in an embroidered and jeweled doublet and silk hose, all eyes drawn to his shapely calves and long, muscular thighs. They say there is not a horse that the duke cannot tame once he gets on its back. It's the kind of story that appeals to the ladies even more than to the men. In Florence, Niccolò knows an apothecary shop where if you are familiar enough with the owner he will sell you a draft guaranteed to make any woman easy, though the correct dose is crucial or it will loosen her senses along with her clothing and the challenge will dribble away. But here the ladies seem to relish the progress of their own damnation. It makes for a charged evening, especially for the husband of the lovely young wife whom the duke finally chooses, the two of them now partnered in dance, leaping and prowling around each other as if they are already halfway between the sheets.

Niccolò is considering the lesser charms of an empty bed when, sometime close to midnight, Michelotto, absent till now from the evening's revels, enters and approaches the duke. Whatever he tells him, it is enough for Cesare to take immediate leave of his dancing partner and the whole gathering. After he is gone, the lady sits, flushed and smiling, her breasts still heaving from the exertion, caught between disappointment and relief.

What business could be important enough to stop a man from slipping under the skirts of a willing beauty? It has to be fighting. Has Ramiro de Lorqua returned? The last of his purse had bought Niccolò the information that the governor was sent out two days before to meet the commanders, now camped outside Sinigaglia, to discuss plans for the surrender of the city. What has he discovered? Please God it is not something that will have them all thundering across the country once again before he manages to squeeze more money out of the skinflint council.

An answer of sorts comes the day after Christmas.

Niccolò wakes soon after dawn. A frost has set in overnight and the light through the vellum window is a sickly white glow. The snow must have come in early, and is still falling heavily, coating his eyelashes and hair, as he walks down to the edge of the battlements, which hang high over Cesena's main piazza.

His first impression is the beauty of it all: a pristine white tablecloth, the surrounding roofs and towers lifting up behind it like a snowcapped mountain range. In the middle, next to the fountain, sits a large white block, a longer flatter shape on the ground nearby, a darker patch at one end. They—whatever they are—must have been put there before the worst of the snow because there are no visible footprints.

He makes his way down the spiral stairs from the castle battlements and out through the door that leads onto the piazza. The air is as frozen as the ground and his boots crunch into virgin snow, the only sound in a ghostly silent world. As he gets closer to the center, an extraordinary tableau emerges. The large shape becomes a butcher's block, with a cleaving knife embedded in it, a ribbon of snow balanced like piped icing along its edge. And the object on the ground is revealed to be a man's body, a nimbus of dark blood spreading out from where his head has been severed from his trunk. But it is not only the neck that has bled; the whole torso is an open wound, cloven from collarbone to groin and prized apart to resemble the splayed carcass of a cow. And beside it sits the head, black hair and beard coated in whirling flakes but still recognizable. Ramiro de Lorqua, the soldier who liked to grind boys' bodies into fires, has been butchered like an animal and left on public display.

People are gathering now: men and a few women wrapped in mangy furs and blankets, their faces hardened by more than years. One or two nod or shake their heads, and someone spits into the snow, but no one says a word. The white silence sits heavy on them all. Whatever the sins of a man's life, this public, barbaric death on a Christmas morning is a shock. As it is meant to be, Niccolò thinks. Hot blood on frozen snow: a theater of justice to balance a theater of cruelty, and a show of absolute authority. Once again he finds himself in reluctant admiration of this enemy prince.

Later that day, almost as an afterthought, a proclamation is nailed to the door of the town hall accusing the ex-governor of extortion in the sale of the city's grain supplies. But Niccolò is more interested in the talk of the screaming that some now say they heard rising from the duke's quarters nearby, as if an altogether darker confession was being pulled out of him.

A congress of losers, all of them, and I know most of what they do before they do it.

He is composing a dispatch in his mind when he arrives back at his lodging to find a messenger waiting: Duke Valentine and his men are to ride out tomorrow en route to Sinigaglia, where the city has formally surrendered to his troops. Florence's envoy is offered an escort of his own and invited to join them.

He feels a hot knot of excitement rise inside him. Whatever it is, it has already begun.

CHAPTER 29

❖

"*I*t'll never work."

"In which case, Vitelli, you come up with something better. Because fuck knows, no one else will."

Oliverotto da Fermo turns furiously toward two other men sitting huddled over the fire, their eyes fixed on the flames. As the soft skin of the conspiracy has peeled away with promises of pardons and profit, its hard core—those men who having rebelled and lost have nothing left to sell—is exposed. The Baglioni have scuttled back to Perugia, locking the city gates behind them, leaving Vitelli, da Fermo and the dregs of the Orsini family, Paolo and Francesco, deserted by their cardinal and cringing in the background. For weeks they and their troops have been camped outside Sinigaglia in the dead of winter negotiating the terms of the surrender. Soldiers of fortune are used to hardship in the field, but this is punishment, not work: guilty men reduced to blunt choices and blunter feelings; scalding fires, frozen nights, stomachs rolling from fear as much as hunger, while they curse and scratch at the lice that have found sanctuary in their filth. At least inside the city they have access to hot water and decent food. No wonder no one wants to leave.

"Valentine's dispatch says he needs room only for his personal staff." Da Fermo presses on. "Less than a hundred men."

"He's lying," Vitelli growls again, his hands kneading away at his thighs in what has become an automatic gesture toward the pain that never leaves him. "He'd never come unarmed. The bastard is hiding an army somewhere."

"Where?" da Fermo snaps back furiously. "For Christ's sake, you heard the words coming out of de Lorqua's mouth as clearly as I did: the new troops were left in Imola and de Lorqua himself watched the French march out a week ago. There is no 'army' anymore. He is coming to pick up the keys of his final conquest. He thinks he's won."

Vitelli laughs grimly. "What? And you think he hasn't?"

"All I know is that we're not dead yet. However much you act as if you might like to be. God's bollocks, if you haven't got the appetite for it anymore, stick the knife in yourself and give me control of your troops. I've still got a life to live."

At another time they would have made a good father and son, these two, for the gap in age and experience between them is enough. But it is the younger soldier who is setting the pace now. It is exactly a year since he had carved up his own uncle like an apprentice butcher. How fast it moves, this wheel of fortune. From being poised at the top looking down over all others, he is now scrabbling along the ground to squirm free from the approaching weight.

"I tell you it could work. I keep a small force inside the castle, then, when he and his men are in, I open the gates to the rest of you. There are a dozen places in the town or inside the fortress where we might take him out."

It is a feeble, whining little plan, reaching only as far as a mangled Borgia body felled by a dagger or a sniper's crossbow and an ally in Ramiro de Lorqua, who had been alive and well when he left them before Christmas.

"What if it doesn't work?" Paolo Orsini's voice, like his face, is raw with cold and misery.

Da Fermo turns on him, but Vitelli gets in first.

"Then you'll be too dead to care," he snaps. Jesus Christ, if there is anyone he hates more than Cesare Borgia it's this fawning lady boy who was the first to go crawling home as the wind changed. They should have slit his throat the moment he came back with the offer. Having been closest to the center of Borgia power, Vitelli knows better than all of them that what has been done will never be forgiven; that whatever double cross they might try, it will be trumped as surely as in a card game where your opponent holds more aces than there are in the pack. But however it ends, it could not be worse than the blunt blades that saw through his legs and stomach day and night. There had been a time when his hatred and need for revenge had given him at least momentary relief, but not anymore. Now all he looks forward to is death. Da Fermo is right. Better to go out fighting.

"So, we are agreed then?" he says, shifting his leg and letting out a satisfying growl. In the silence that follows all four men move a little closer to the fire.

• • •

December 30, 1502, and across the center of Italy the day brings a peerless pale blue sky and a thick coating of frost.

In Rome, Alexander wakes to a dispatch sent three days before, as Cesare and his personal guard marched out of Cesena. Once he has read it, the pontiff's current bad humor dissolves as fast as early morning fog. His chaplains and his Master of Ceremonies can barely believe their eyes and ears when he arrives at the Sistine Chapel for morning mass with a beatific smile on his face, embracing his fellow cardinals, singing at the top of his voice, then staying on afterward for an hour of private prayer.

"There is nothing as special as these days following Our Savior's birth, do you not agree, Johannes?" he says as he settles himself down to a frugal breakfast of leftover fish and red wine, ready to welcome the ambassadors who are, as ever, already lining up to see him. "You know when I was a boy in Xàtiva—sweet little place in the middle of the countryside, I have told you about it before—I stayed up one Christmas in the church after midnight mass, hid myself behind the altar and held vigil in front of the tableau of the nativity. It was a dreadful winter, I remember, the worst for years, but I never felt the cold. The Virgin's gaze and the candle star warmed me all through the night. When they found me in the morning they were amazed. 'Rodrigo has the makings of a great churchman' is what my father and mother said. And how right they were, eh? The world is full of small miracles, don't you think?"

Burchard, who has heard this before, as he has heard most of the sentimental stories that the Pope chooses to tell these days, says nothing. These weeks have been a nightmare, and he lacks his employer's capacity to move so effortlessly from storm to sunshine.

"Ah, Burchard, I am sorry if my ill humor has made your job difficult," the Pope says. "As you know I have been most worried about my family. But Lucrezia's health is returned, my son is saved from conspiracy and now it seems his old enemies have made their peace by securing the surrender of Sinigaglia. Sinigaglia. Sinigaglia . . ." He sings the word excitedly, as if on the edge of saying more. "Yes, yes, well . . . there is much to tell. But for now there is also much to do. We must set up new staging posts between the two cities to make sure the news flows freely. And with the danger passed, it behooves us to be generous to those around us. Cardinal Orsini, for instance. He has proved himself a most honorable fellow and we do not feel we have properly welcomed him back into the fold.

"We shall celebrate the fall of Sinigaglia together, for he has kinsmen in my son's employ who have shown themselves faithful again. A dinner, I think, in our families' honor, here in our apartment tomorrow night: some good friends and perhaps a few of Rome's 'ladies' to aid our digestion. Oh, don't worry, Burchard, you do not need to attend. I would not want the rise of your nose spoiling harmless old men's fun. Now. Let us have our first ambassador. Venice today, I think. It will annoy them especially to hear of this triumph."

• • •

Dawn has yet to break when the duke and his men leave the little town of Fano to start the fifteen-mile journey down the coast to Sinigaglia. They travel for a while in darkness, the only evidence of their presence a few burning torches, the jangling of harnesses and the crunch of hooves breaking the ice on thin puddles.

A few miles out of town they stop. To their left a watery sun is rising over the Adriatic, giving way to a landscape of flat scrubland on both sides, moving gradually into rolling hills to the west. The dull light reveals the company of men: sixty-odd horsemen, twenty of them soldiers, the personal bodyguard dressed in heavy leathers with swords at their waists, the rest members of the household, better equipped for cooking than for fighting.

There is one man, however, dressed for conquest: Cesare Borgia rides in full armor. Soon the sun will start to play with all that polished steel, the smooth curved breastplate, the reptile joints of the leg coverings and the burnished dome of the helmet with a plume of black feathers sprouting from the top. All in all, a most unnecessary vanity for such a small army. But then not everyone has arrived yet.

The horses, grown tired of waiting, are pawing at the ground, sending clouds of steam snorting into the air, while the riders stuff their hands under their armpits against the bitter cold. Only Cesare sits impassive, his visor up, eyes trained out into the distance watching. These last nights, since leaving Cesena, he has slept long and soundly, at peace with himself and the rest of the world. For a man fueled by impatience and jags of energy, it is a new experience, and he has savored every minute of it. An ocean of time stretches out in front of him, as long and open as the road ahead. What starts here now will have reverberations deep into the future. My God, if only every day could be like this one.

• • •

The meeting between the duke and his condottieri has been arranged for midday at a wide bend in the road half a mile outside the walls of Sinigaglia.

Vitelli and the Orsini arrive with good time to spare, da Fermo remaining with a small force inside the city, as agreed. The sun has burned off the frost and the air is bright and clear, still not a cloud in the sky. A perfect winter's day. The best kind of weather to kill or be killed, Vitelli thinks as he holds his half crippled body up on the broad back of his mule—no longer able to sustain the harshness of a horse saddle beneath him.

He pulls at the mule's head, to stop it from grazing, and as he does so he notices how the horses around him are becoming skittish, their heads tossing to and fro against the bit. Over the years he has learned to listen to such animals, for they always pick it up first: the tremor that seems to move for miles under the earth itself, the drumbeat that human ears only hear now as wind mixed with the noise of the sea.

He scours the distance. Nothing. Nothing. Then something. Yes, definitely something: a few random glints of light, sun glinting off metal, like coded signals across enemy lines. He lifts himself up as best he can to watch it unfold. The long bend of the road ahead allows him to read each element as it comes into view.

The cavalry comes first: four or five abreast in full armor and a figure on a white horse out in front, the standard-bearer next to him, the red and yellow color clash of the Borgia crest and the Duchy of Valentinois spread out in the breeze. After, come the men-at-arms, too many to count. They must have marched from Imola days ago, camped out somewhere waiting for the moment to reunite.

What happened? Did de Lorqua change sides yet again, bringing them false information, or is his silence a more sinister sign? Well, cruel men meet cruel ends; there is no point in second-guessing the game now. Vitelli glances toward the Orsini, both of them ashen faced, their mouths open in awe. When he turns his eyes back, it is in time to see a single horseman and a section of cavalry break off at a gallop. At first he thinks it is a charge, feels his nerves singing in response, but it soon becomes clear they are wheeling around them on their way toward the town. In front, it has to be Michelotto; there are not many men of his modest stature who ride as confidently as they kill.

And still the army keeps on coming. Finally he makes out Swiss pikemen from King Louis's army, the bearded giants of the battlefield. My God, he had almost forgotten them. Where were they? Faenza? Forlì? Wherever it was, they will have marched from there, as they do now, in perfect measured unison to the sound of the roll of drums, their steel-tipped staves held out like a mobile stockade in front of them. If a man didn't know better, he might think he was watching a crusading force making its way to the coast to set sail for the Holy Land. All this to crush a miserable little band of rebels.

When the front line is maybe fifty yards away from them, the duke raises his arm to halt the horses, and little by little the metal orchestra falls silent behind him.

For a long time the two sides just watch each other. What are they waiting for? Vitelli thinks. He puts his hand on his sword hilt. What would he give for a good battle now? A death in glorious bloody cuts, given as well as received. Except he knows that is not how it is going to end.

Then, as the duke and his guard start to move forward again, Vitelli sees da Fermo and his men riding in from the side with Michelotto behind them. What excuse had he given to draw them out from the town? What the hell is going on here?

Cesare, agile even in full armor, is already pulling off his gauntlets as he reaches them, his face wreathed in smiles, grabbing hands and clasping arms with everyone around, shouting welcome. But Vitelli first and foremost.

"Ah, Comrade Vitelli, we've not kept you waiting long in this ball-biting cold, I hope. It can't be good for your condition." He turns. "And da Fermo? How are you, man? Yes, yes—I know what you are thinking. I bring a big force for a small town. But it's not for Sinigaglia. Oh no. This is the start of the next campaign, and we are here to pick up you and your men. For what is the Borgia army without my faithful condottieri, eh? Now we are reunited, let us get ourselves inside the town and celebrate."

And as Vitelli turns his mule and rides off next to the duke—for what else can he do?—he glances about to see the others, similarly smothered in greetings, corralled back along from where they came.

The walls of the city come into view: the main gate open, the bridge that leads to it flanked by two lines of Cesare's cavalry, a guard of his own escort to welcome the conquering hero into town. So slyly and smoothly done, oiled by warm words and comradely smiles. As they disappear in through the gates, the horsemen fall in line behind them, freeing the way for the rest of the army to follow, irrevocably separating the rebel leaders from their own men. What soldier could not applaud the choreography?

The farce of friendship need last only a little longer. As far as the fortress courtyard, where once they are dismounted, Cesare's men hustle the four of them upstairs, arms tight around them like the best of comrades, the grip so firm that no one can reach his sword.

Behind him, Vitelli hears Paolo Orsini's squeaky voice, begging to be let go. Followed by Cesare's booming laughter. "Oh, no, but you are needed now, Lady Paolo. How could we sit in front of the map of Italy and plan our route of triumph without you?"

When they are finally inside the room and the door closed, the soldiers fall away, to join a line of others waiting, their swords already unsheathed.

"Gentlemen," Cesare says casually, glancing first at Michelotto, then back to them. "It is good to see you all again. You will forgive me if I leave you for a little while. Six hours in the saddle have taken their toll on my bladder."

My God, you bastard, Vitelli thinks, you are not even interested in watching us die.

"Go piss yourself," he yells as they drag him and da Fermo toward two chairs. "You don't even have the balls to do the job yourself."

Cesare stops for a second, turning on his heel, the casual smile rigid on his face.

"You're right, Vitelli. I only have 'balls' when it comes to killing men. Cockroaches I leave to others."

"Fuck you. Fuck every one of you Borgias," Vitelli screams, straining against the cords, kicking wildly. "I'll see you all in hell."

And for one glorious moment before the garrote bites, he feels no pain at all.

• • •

It is growing dark by the time Niccolò and his appointed escort reach the gates of Sinigaglia. For a moment it seems they may not let him in at all, for it is clearly more than the soldiers' lives are worth to act without authority. But his name is on the list, as promised, and there is even a sequestered lodging ready for him.

Inside, the city is reduced to one of the circles of hell. There is smoke and screaming everywhere, rioting, howling soldiers—some as big as giants—careering up and down streets. Piles of furniture and chests are being hauled into carts while bodies dangle from first-story window frames or lie half trampled in the gutters. It is not the Borgia way to encourage such behavior, but the smell of revenge is in the air, and who can blame soldiers who have camped out through freezing nights if they choose a little violence to warm their blood? It is his first experience of the madness of looting, and it leaves him shaken.

Once barricaded inside the safe house, he finds a laid grate, with wine on the table. When he has coaxed a fire into life, he pours himself a drink and from his saddlebag pulls out paper, ink and quill. What else can a diplomat do as a city burns?

There is little chance I will dispatch this tonight for want of finding anyone in Sinigaglia to carry it, he writes hurriedly, as the screams curl up from the streets below. *The rebels are taken, along with the city, and it is my* "opinion"—he pauses for that last word gives him a certain pleasure— *that the prisoners will not be alive tomorrow.*

• • •

It would take even the fastest dispatch rider two and a half days to move such news from one side of Italy to the other.

Toward evening on the first of January in Rome, Cardinal Orsini is enjoying the attention of his barber, who, having shaved him perfume smooth, is now trimming his tonsure when the mad banging comes at the doors of his palace. Any churchman of worth who has spent his life in the sewer of Roman politics knows the tremor of fear that comes with unexpected guests announcing themselves so roughly at his private house. He dismisses the barber and pulls on his robes: newly cleaned for the occasion, bright scarlet against the white trim. As a uniform it can be too warm in summer, but it makes perfect evening dress for a January night in the Vatican.

He takes his stick with its finely carved bone handle and makes his way to the landing, which affords him a fine view of the curling stone staircase and the open courtyard down below. The hammering has got worse. Eventually the wood will splinter against the force of pikes and axes. He wonders how many men he might meet outside were he to try to reach the back door.

He sees again the room in his castle at La Magione, all those faces around the table distorted with fury and revenge. Once released, it is a plague that leaves no one untouched.

Well, a supper with the Pope has never been something to look forward to. Better to start thinking about the bribes that will be needed to have his own cook deliver food to his new home in Castel Sant'Angelo.

WINTER-SPRING
1503

Inside the Vatican it is believed that the Pope has grown afraid of his own son.

—Venetian ambassador
1503

Were I an angel I would be consumed with pity for any man who loved as much as I do.

—An unsigned letter addressed to FF
(nom de plume for Lucrezia Borgia), Ferrara
1503

CHAPTER 30

❖

*T*he events of Sinigaglia reverberate through the country like the aftershocks of an earthquake. For months Italy has been in thrall to the drama of this conspiracy, and its denouement could not have unfolded better: plots and counterplots, layer upon layer of deception, lurid tales of traitors hewn in half or tied back-to-back to chairs, blaming each other and sobbing for mercy as the garrote tightens around their throats. No one feels sorry for them. Treachery is a disease of the age, and there is not a ruler who doesn't dream of taking vengeance on those who have shafted him in the past. He may be a Borgia bastard, but he is a cunning, brilliant one, and his charmed destiny is capturing everyone's imagination.

Within days of his coup the dark prince and his army are halfway across Italy, the dead rebels' towns throwing open their gates to him. Fermo, Anghiari, Monterchi, Città di Castello, they are all Borgia lands now. The Baglioni brothers have fled Perugia and even the Duke of Siena ("I never agreed to their plan. My representative had no right to sign on my behalf!") is fighting for his political life. While in Rome, Cardinal Giovanni Battista Orsini, head of one of the Church's most powerful families, sits in a dank cell in Castel Sant'Angelo. The Borgias are now the most powerful family in Italy.

From Mantua, Isabella d'Este blows extravagant kisses in Cesare's direction, sending him a public gift of a hundred carnival masks, *because even the greatest leader must enjoy a little free time.* Carnival masks for a man who has many faces but never shows his own! In between the cannon salutes and festivities in Ferrara, Duke Ercole cannot stop talking about it all: his daughter's wit, his son-in-law's military brilliance and, of course, most of all, his own precious Borgia daughter, blooming with health and nightly exhausting her dance partners as she skips and smiles her way through yet another celebration.

When she sits to catch her breath, one cannot mistake the power of her beauty: the sheen of her skin, the shine in her eyes. Not only has the Duchess of Ferrara left death behind but she has embraced life with a particular vibrancy. Or perhaps it has embraced her, for there are those who believe that is what love does to a woman. Such a homecoming Lucrezia Borgia has had.

• • •

In the first days the calm of the convent sat like an aura around her. In the castle there had been fires in the grates and morning mists swirled like the steam from witches' brew over the surface of the castle moat. She had sat through court evenings, a spectator at a parade of fashion; two seasons had come and gone since the fever struck, and everywhere she spots signs of sartorial change: a different cut of the neck with stitching to show off the contrast, a new plaiting of the hair around the ears with a pendant of pearls hanging from the center. How strange, she had thought, such innovations do not necessarily make the wearer any prettier; they were striking only because they were new. But she knew even then that this was convent wisdom speaking and of little use to her here. The fact was she and her ladies would need new fabrics for new styles. And at last she had the money to pay for them.

Her chief fashion buyer, Ercole Strozzi, whose dandified ways do not go down well with the duke, had taken himself to Venice but promised to return immediately with everything the duchess could possibly want. He also promised a more particular present for which no payment would be enough, and anyway he will accept none. *For it will be your gift to me to allow me to give it.* She had had to read the sentence twice. It seemed that even courtly language had changed with the passing of a season.

As good as his word, he was back within a week with loaded mules and an invitation to a supper party at his country villa. The ladies had ransacked their wardrobes for suitable attire. How they were in need of him. The duke's great performance was scheduled in ten days' time, and everyone must be at his or her best.

Strozzi had greeted them in the courtyard, his crooked body startling in a suit and cloak of matched apple green velvets. She couldn't help but stare. Sweet heaven, she thought, if this is the color of Venice this winter, then it certainly doesn't suit everyone.

The panniers were thrown open in one of the receiving rooms, and the ladies descended like vultures. Strozzi looked on benignly, then took Lucrezia to one side and from a silk covering unwrapped a finely carved and painted wooden bird on a perch, a string hanging beneath. Holding it aloft with one hand, he pulled the string with the other, and the bird's wings flapped up and down as its beak turned from side to side, opening and closing in silent song.

"Its voice is so exquisite that only the gods can hear it. Though perhaps you caught a little of it yourself. I thought of you immediately. I could see it hanging from one of the trees in your terrace garden."

"Oh, it is quite lovely." She had laughed in genuine delight. "This must be the gift you spoke of."

"Oh no, my lady duchess. No, no, no, the gift I brought you is much more valuable."

He smiled in a conspiratorial manner, while at the same moment looking over her shoulder, raising his hands in what felt very like mock surprise.

"Ah, ah! Bembo! I speak of the devil and here you are in person. Your poet's ear must have heard the bird's call. My lady, I offer you Pietro Bembo, the son of one of Venice's finest families and the city's foremost poet and scholar of the new learning. He is come to visit your father the duke, who appreciates him dearly, and to pay homage to the sweetest duchess Ferrara has ever had, a woman who lights up the city as the sun does the earth. Thank God for her return, for the world has been a desert without her."

Caught between his ludicrous hyperbole and the bizarreness of such a "gift," Lucrezia found herself lost for a reply.

"I must apologize for my reprobate friend." He was in front of her now, a tall well-dressed figure rising from an elegantly executed bow. "I fear Signor Strozzi has been too long in Venice and grown fevered in his speech. It's a familiar malady among visitors. We Venetians believe it comes from the smell of too many foreign spices. A few dishes of Ferrarese eels marinated in vinegar should do the trick."

Pietro Bembo. Of course she had heard of him. But the only poets she has ever met have paid dearly for their talent with their looks. Here, he instead was a singularly handsome man: high forehead, clear gray eyes, patrician nose and sculptured, smooth chin, in contrast to so many men who hide the lack of one under a bush of hair.

The room had grown quiet. Behind her she made out the rustle of skirts as her ladies fanned closer. The very air was growing sticky with female admiration. But not Lucrezia's. Forced with this peacock male perfection, she had a sudden image of wrinkled old Sister Bonaventura bent low and humble over books and potions, and the contrast made her unexpectedly angry.

"Signor Bembo, you are welcome to Ferrara," she greeted him coolly. "Duke Ercole will be pleased to see you. You are invited no doubt to see his latest spectacle."

"I have been awarded that honor, yes. I look forward to it greatly. It is a long time since I have seen a new translation of Plautus."

"Then you must hope it doesn't feel even longer when you do."

Now it was his turn to stare. "You are not fond of Roman comedy, my lady duchess?"

"I would be if I had ever seen one that made me laugh."

Behind her, Angela let out a loud nervous titter.

Lucrezia turned her head to silence Angela, only to be met with a row of faces, eyes wide with apprehension.

Yes, yes, she thought impatiently, I know, such sourness is uncalled for.

But in front of her, Bembo was smiling broadly. *Forget the stories you have heard.* Strozzi had done a good job of preparing him. *She is pretty as the dawn with a siren smile to warm the coldest heart.* Yet here was something even more interesting. A challenge.

"You must forgive me. I have not been well recently," she added carefully. "It is possible I have lost my appetite for entertainment."

"Then I will pray for its return as fervently as the whole of Venice prayed for your recovery. And it does seem, my lady duchess"—he hesitated as if he did not yet have the right words—"that you are . . . splendidly recovered."

"Thanks to the nuns of Corpus Domini, yes."

"In which case I shall add them to my prayers this very night. For their care has preserved a radiance and wit without which any city would be bereft."

The compliment was offered up like a garland of flowers. To her distress she felt a slight blush rising in her face. If this was the resilience that comes from surviving death, then she would be better off without it.

"Ah," he said quickly. "Now I am the one who must ask forgiveness. It seems even a Venetian can be affected by foreign spices."

"Ha!" She laughed. "I thought you were just being a poet!"

"Oh no, my lady." And his tone was sharp. "No. Upon my honor my poetry is a good deal better than that."

Behind them, Strozzi stood amazed. He had expected this "gift" of his to be a triumph and was at a loss as to how to save the situation. Nevertheless, when the call came for dinner, Bembo offered his arm, and Lucrezia, with barely a second's hesitation, took it.

"Is it true what they say: that in Venice there are as many printing presses as there are days of the year?" her ladies heard her ask as they gathered behind them.

Venice: lacy stone palaces, sunlight on water, ships covered in gold, any and every luxury from the far-flung corners of the world. How perfect that he had come from there. And how perfect he was! A patrician poet, who could turn a compliment into verse, had little interest in cannons or whores and was surely an expert on the rules of court dalliance with a woman married to someone else. It was just what was needed to restore their mistress to her former radiance and bring some joy to her life. Clever old Strozzi! The ladies flocked around their lame, over-dressed green parrot, fussing and complimenting him on his taste in all things. Oh, the joy of men's company again, how they had missed it. Especially court dandies with an appetite for gossip.

"You know he is considered the best writer of his age," Strozzi whispered as they moved toward the salon, prettily bathed in candlelight. "Dozens of women in Venice are in love with him. Indeed he is busy composing an epic work on the very nature of that feeling. I tell you it will alter the future of Italian poetry. Ferrara is the ideal place for him to continue writing it. I am sure he would be most happy to let the lady duchess read it."

And so a poetic affair had begun.

CHAPTER 31

❖

"*I* would like to ask you to image this: the courtiers are settled in the gardens at twilight by the cool of the fountain. The subject of their discourse is the three aspects of love: its torments, its joys and the greatest love of all, which passeth all human understanding. One man makes the argument for each case, though the ladies are vociferous in their interruptions. The summer air in Asolo is sweet and the talking goes on long into the night . . ."

Bembo pauses to let his evocation of the scene sink in. Around him, his audience is entranced.

"The courtier Perottino goes first, and delivers a diatribe against human love as the embodiment of all degradation and evil."

"Wait!" Lucrezia injects eagerly. "His name is Perottino, yes? Which, if one says it very fast, sounds very like Pietrobembo, don't you think? Certainly more so than—who is it?—Gismondo, to whom you give the defense of love. So, you are putting yourself in your poem, Signor Bembo? In which case you too must have suffered these torments that he talks of."

The ladies cry out in joyful agreement. They have identified entirely with the women in the poem and are lounging in summer twilight, even as they sit by the well-stacked fire in the villa where Bembo has made his writing retreat. He would be well received at court, but he is serious about his work, and in better weather Strozzi's house, with its forests and gardens, has been perfect for his poem's bucolic setting. With winter biting deeply now, he should be thinking of returning home.

"A poet draws on his own life, as of course he must. But I would say—or rather I would hope—that Perottino's arguments go deeper than that. He links *amore*—love—with *amara*—bitterness, with each growing from the other, and he goes on to show how the fires of love destroy and corrupt, fueling hatred, jealousies, feuds and despair."

"Still, in my opinion he's at his most passionate when he talks of his personal suffering," Lucrezia says mischievously. "His words burn us much as they do him. That surely comes from the man as well as the poet."

"Yes! Yes! She hits you there, Bembo," Strozzi cries out as the women applaud. "You'd better move your work from Asolo to Ferrara. The name of the place is nowhere near as lovely on the tongue, and hardly anyone knows where it is anyway."

Everyone laughs. This is the third meeting of the unofficial Ferrara poetry society, and Lucrezia's ladies, though not natural scholars, are showing a hunger to learn equal to the pleasure it gives them to see their duchess so enjoying herself.

"I have a question now, Signor Bembo." Nicola waves her hand, eager and smiling. "If love is as evil as you say it is, then why did the ancients have a god of love? How can a god be evil?"

"Ladies—but this isn't fair." Bembo puts up his hands in mock defeat. "You have read the work already."

"No, I swear, the pages have been in my hands only," Lucrezia protests. "I have talked of it, of course, but I never mentioned Cupid. Ah, except I have now!"

His sigh is full of mock drama. "Then I am superseded in all ways. In which case I leave it to the duchess to offer my argument. I am sure she will do it better than I."

"Very well." She lifts herself up into a declamatory position. "Our poet—what shall we call him?—Perottino Pietro Bembo—sees Cupid as the perfect symbol for all that is wrong with love. First he is a child, which is what he reduces men to. Then he is shamefully naked, as he strips naked all who fall prey to him. He has wings, just as lovers foolishly feel they can fly, and he carries a bow and arrow, which speaks of the wounds love will inflict."

"Bravo," he says quietly. "I can say no more."

"Indeed you can't." Strozzi is already pulling himself off his chair. "Though next time we would all appreciate a little more in love's favor. Now, I for one would like to stretch my poor crooked legs. Perhaps some of the ladies might like to join me. I have had refreshments laid out in the salon."

They make such a handsome couple, sitting in the glow of the firelight. In the weeks since they met some courteous letters have been exchanged, along with a sheaf of manuscript paper, which has kept her up late into the night. Poetry. No great court should be without its practitioners, and while she is still waiting for her husband to return, it is good to have things to pass the time. Or so Lucrezia had been telling herself.

In fact, she has not slept well before this meeting, and now they are alone, it is hard to know what they should say, unless it is to talk more of love. So when he offers to show her the library he has brought with him from Venice, she accepts quickly.

"Aaagh!" As they enter the room something streaks across the tiled floor, running over her skirts before disappearing into the wainscot. She puts out a sudden hand toward him, then withdraws it equally fast.

"God's blood . . . infernal mice! They are everywhere. Vandals!" He shakes his head. "They've already made a banquet of my copy of Aristotle's *Zoology*, gnawed right through the leather into the index."

"What? Mice eating a book on zoology? How fitting. Signor Bembo, your library needs a cat."

"I am waiting on one from Venice. An Egyptian breed. Every print-ing press keeps them."

"Which means there must be almost half as many Egyptian cats as there are days of the year," she says, reminding him of that first meet-ing. "One hundred and fifty. Isn't that what you told me? *A man may collect an entire library simply by walking from the Rialto to San Marco.*" And her voice deepens in slight mockery.

"Was I really so pompous?"

"Not at all. Only proud of a city that has the best of everything."

"No," he says, looking directly at her. "Not everything."

She drops her eyes, and he busies himself with laying out some of his more precious volumes. A cloud of leather particles rides out from the half devoured spine as he opens the pages of *Zoology.*

"Think of me as your student," she says earnestly. "For I know noth-ing about such things."

"Ah, with these books you are always the pupil, however much you know. And Aristotle is the first and greatest teacher, in everything. Shells, fish, plants, animals, man; there is nothing that doesn't interest him. A lifetime would not be enough to know him properly."

How Lucrezia loves his enthusiasm. A scholar of the new learning, that was how Strozzi described him. Yet when he talks she's struck by how all that is new these days seems to grow effortlessly from the old. This is how my court will be, she thinks, finding ways to encourage the marriage of old learning and new art.

"And then there is Dante."

He is lost now in poetry. He could talk through sunset to sunrise on the beauty of the Tuscan vernacular; as a sculptor of words, he has cho-sen it as his material, malleable as molten metal, delicate as blown glass.

"There is simply no other way forward. Splintered into so many states and dialects, how else can Italy find the poetic voice she needs to talk to herself and the rest of the world? Yet two hundred years after Dante we are still . . . ah." He stops himself laughing. "I am a victim of Venetian spices again. I have a reputation as a bore on this subject.

Strozzi says if I talk for longer than twenty minutes without interruption I must be shackled to my bed and doused in cold water."

"Well, I would not nurse you. I like the illness too much."

How would she put them into words, the feelings she has when they are together? The way time jolts and stops; how everything seems brighter and she feels clever and kind, nervous and peaceful all at the same time.

"My lady." He drops his head in almost coy gratitude.

"I mean it," she says fiercely. "What is the point of being alive if it is not to make some difference in the world? If I were a man . . . oh." She throws up her hands, covering her embarrassment by turning to another book, a bright leather cover and a silver lock shining with polish. "So, tell me, what is this?"

"Ah, this is the newest of them all. Petrarch's sonnets. Straight from Aldus Manutius's great press in Venice."

The tang of leather and fresh ink rises into the air as he opens the volume to its title page. "Oh!" she says. "Oh, but your name is here too."

"As Petrarch's editor, no more," he says with not entirely convincing modesty.

She turns the pages carefully, studying the lines, running her fingers along the print, as fine—finer perhaps—than the best calligraphy.

"Ah, Signor Bembo," she whispers, "but this is too rich, even for the mice."

Love. She has read the commentaries, knows the ways that doctors as well as poets chart the progress of this most exquisite disease: how it enters first as a dart through the eye, then moves into and through the blood, so that when the afflicted come too close to each other it can cause hot blushes and a rushing of the pulse, as if the beating heart is trying to break through the surface of the skin. In all of life there is no intoxication of sweetness to compare with it. Is that what is happening to me now? she thinks, as the two of them stand studying the words, his left hand splayed facedown next to hers on the pretext of holding the pages open.

As for Bembo, he knows its progress only too well, for he has lived as well as described every stage of it. After the sweetness comes the pain, as it travels from the heart into the gut and the entrails, taking up home like a parasite, destroying any peace in favor of lust and jealousy. Back in Venice he has a box full of letters—copies of his as well as hers—from a lover who barely a year ago had been suffering as much as he. His poetry had got richer with each step of the dance. Still, it is one thing to coax a young widow into leaving a ladder against a canal wall at night and quite another to even think of a married duchess's bed, especially one belonging to the Este family. He will not turn Italy's poetic destiny around if his taste for adventure destroys him. Yet how can he resist?

"You know, the first time I saw you, I couldn't stop thinking about the fact you had nearly died. And that our meeting might never have taken place." He pauses. "It seemed inconceivable. But then I found myself wondering if it was that very closeness to death that made you so luminous. Ah, if I could put such an understanding into poetry . . ."

She closes her eyes. "I think you already have."

"I should go home soon," he says after a while. "I mean, between the mice and the cold, I would probably compose better there."

"Yes, yes, I see that."

"Unless . . . unless I came to court. Strozzi's townhouse, he assures me, is most comfortable."

"Yes, and Duke Ercole, I know, would be pleased to see you."

"And you, Lady Duchess?" he says softly. "Would it please you?"

"Me?" She laughs. "Oh, how can you ask? I would have you stay."

And her answer is so honest that his hand cannot help but inch toward hers, and just for a second, she does not move away.

CHAPTER 32

*I*n Rome, revenge is the fashion of the season.

Who would be an Orsini now? As well as the cardinal, half a dozen other archbishops and Church bureaucrats from the family have been visited by the Papal Guards. So much plunder is taken from their houses that Burchard has to assign special rooms in Borgia Tower to store it all.

Alexander cannot hide his exuberance. How long has he waited for this moment? This is not simply the punishment for leading a conspiracy against the Holy See, though God knows that alone would deserve it. This is the settling of a lifetime of scores: the opening of the passes of Rome to an invading army; the writing of poisoned letters about the Pope and his family; and the cruelest blow of all, the frenzy of stab wounds in the body of his favorite son. Exactly which one of the Orsini family had been holding the dagger doesn't matter. They are all guilty as hell, and he will shed no tears for any of them. Christendom will be a safer place without them.

But not everybody is celebrating so openly.

There are those, even a few of the Pope's more faithful followers, for whom this bloodletting inside the Church is an uncomfortable state of affairs.

"What? You believe that we are overjoyed to have a cardinal of our Holy Mother Church sitting inside a prison cell?" he says when a few brave colleagues pluck up the courage to plead for clemency on Orsini's behalf. "Would we prefer it not to be the case? Of course we would. But before your soft hearts melt your brains, we would remind you that this man and his family rose in open rebellion against the papacy. What is taking place here is justice; no more, no less."

"One would think I had taken an ax and chopped the man's head off myself," he says tetchily to Burchard later. "He is a traitor, pure and simple, and deserves to be in prison."

"I think the fear, Your Holiness, is that he will die there, given his weakened lungs and the fetid air."

"What? That air that comes from a river filled with animal carcasses, you mean? The same river where they dumped the body of my son, as if he too were a dead dog. When the cardinal breathes in let him remember that."

Burchard does not pursue the matter. He of all people remembers the days after Juan's death, when the Pope was so stricken with grief that all who heard him had feared for his sanity.

Nevertheless, he too is affected by the shame this infighting brings upon the Church. It is not every day a cardinal rots away in the Pope's own jail. In the antechambers of the Borgia apartments the envoys and ambassadors cannot keep the smiles off their faces. Their diplomatic profiles rise and fall with the levels of scandal their dispatches contain.

The weather remains brutal, and inside Castel Sant'Angelo, Cardinal Orsini's condition deteriorates.

Burchard makes a further attempt. "Your Holiness, if I may?"

"Well, you always do even if I would prefer you wouldn't," Alexander says good-naturedly.

"The cardinal's mother has asked me to intercede on her behalf, that she be allowed to send provisions to her son. She is concerned that what he is being given to eat—"

"Is what? Poisoning him? I would not waste the cost of the venom on such a man. Talk to the jailers. He is fed what everyone else is fed."

"Still, Your Holiness, it is not what he is used to. She has asked leave to pay—"

"How much?"

"Two thousand ducats to deliver meals to the jail."

"Hmmn. We shall certainly consider it."

"And . . ."

"And?"

"There is a further member of the Orsini household. Another woman."

"What—you mean his mistress?"

Burchard shrugs. It seems impossible that he doesn't know about these things, but it is his life's work to pretend thus.

"What does she want?"

"An audience with Your Holiness." He pauses. "She has been waiting for some hours."

"Well, send her in."

She stands in front of him: raven haired with a full figure and a face that would once have had men drooling. Nowhere near as lovely as his own Vannozza or the delicate Giulia Farnese, he thinks, but then everyone has grown older and she and Cardinal Orsini have had a comfortable arrangement for years now.

She sinks to her knees in front of him. Was she a courtesan once? He cannot remember. If I was a less scrupulous man . . . he thinks.

He lifts her up and shows her to a chair close to the papal throne.

"My dear." He pats her knee. "What can I do for you?"

Her eyes are brimming with tears. "I have brought you a present, Holy Father."

"A present?"

From between her cleavage she withdraws a bunched velvet cloth, which, unwrapped, reveals a single pearl the size of a quail's egg, alive with luster and light.

"Ah, what a remarkable jewel."

"Priceless," she says huskily.

"You know what they say about pearls, my dear? That they grow from dewdrops which fall when the shell opens to God's early morning majesty. The purer the dew, the purer the pearl. In heaven, each of the twelve gates is carved from a single one."

He studies it again, the view of her breasts in the background. Nature has so many ways to make a lovely woman lovelier. "I am sure it looks most beautiful when you wear it. I believe the cardinal bought this for you a few years ago, yes?"

She nods modestly.

"I remember now. I was interested in it too, for its size is prodigious. But he sneaked in on the negotiations and made a better offer." Any other man would have stepped back or delivered it later as a gift; God's blood, how many ways has this family delighted in undermining him? "He must be most fond of you, my dear."

"I have kept it close to my heart for many years, Your Holiness."

How he is enjoying himself. And why not? What time does he have for pleasure anymore? Giulia, now the size of an unmilked cow, has been sequestered for months, awaiting a birth that is not officially happening, for she does not have a husband, while he has been fighting all manner of vermin. A little flirtation will do him the world of good.

"Close to your heart," he repeats. "Then it can only have grown more precious from its placing."

"Your Holiness, please, it is yours now. Please take it."

"Oh, no, I couldn't possibly—"

"Please, please."

His smile does nothing to help her. She grabs hold of his right hand. "Your displeasure with the cardinal has his whole household in despair.

I fear his mother will not survive the shame. We pray daily that you might find a way to be reconciled. Until then if . . . well, if we could care for him a little. Visit him perhaps, with salves for his chest, warm clothes, blankets."

"My dear, if the man needs blankets he only has to say."

But she is crying openly now, hot tears falling on his hand, which is pulled halfway to her breast. It seems as if her heart will break. Everyone in Rome knows how much the Pope hates to see a woman cry.

"Of course you may send him blankets. Though . . . though I think your own presence would excite him more than is good for an ailing man."

Her skin is moist, soft. She is a pearl in herself. No doubt she would do anything that he desires. But at such a moment a man must abjure temptation. In fact he finds himself unexpectedly irritated just thinking about it, as if this might be a ruse to somehow undermine his enjoyment of victory. He retrieves his hand, pushing the pearl back into her own and closes her fingers over it.

I may be growing old, he thinks as he dismisses her, but I shall still outlive this wretched traitor.

The blankets and the food do little to counteract the damp, and in late February the cardinal himself makes a last desperate attempt.

"Ha! He offers us twenty-five thousand ducats to be freed from prison." Alexander glances up from the letter. "My, but his writing has got very spindly. Perhaps it is the lack of natural light. It's bribery, of course. Tell me, what would you do, Burchard?"

The Master of Ceremonies stands silent. *What would you do, Burchard?* In the past months the Pope has grown fond of this flourish of rhetoric, as if with his family gone, he needs someone with whom to discuss his decisions. Or rather to approve them. To his surprise, Burchard hears himself say,

"Clemency is a sacred quality in any man, Your Holiness."

"Indeed." Alexander nods sagely. He pulls forward a pen and paper, writes quickly, then lifts it up to waft the ink dry before reading it back.

"*Be of good spirits and just look to your own health, my dear cardinal. All other matters we can address when you are well again.* There! I think that will revive his spirit, don't you?"

Two days later, Giovanni Battista Orsini is dead.

"In all honesty I cannot say I am sorry. But I did not cause this. God has shown Himself as displeased as I was. We have closed up his palazzo already, yes? Good. Then you had better attend to the funeral. It must be correctly orchestrated as befits his status."

The Pope scans Burchard's face and is surprised to note an unmistakable tremor passing over it. Is he upset? Or is it even a flash of anger that he sees?

"You seem disturbed, Johannes? Did you harbor some secret fondness for this man?"

But Burchard has regained control of his face now and says nothing.

"Well, one way or another someone must oversee the funeral. He was a cardinal after all. But—perhaps—since you are so busy with other matters . . . I will relieve you of that burden."

He turns his attention back to his papers. Burchard, perceiving himself dismissed, backs out.

"Johannes." The Pope's voice stops him in his tracks. "I do nothing here that they would not have done to me. Indeed that they have not done already. I did not start these family wars, any more than I started the selling of papal offices. These things existed before me and will remain long after."

Burchard stays silent. He is not yet dismissed.

"I understand that I am sometimes a challenge to you." Death seems to have put the Pope in a reflective mood. "But would you rather have some grim straitlaced cleric who never moved out of line? I tell you, Johannes, if it had been Giuliano della Rovere in this chair, you would have had to endure his bad breath and cold fury. Would you really have preferred that? Better someone who smiles as well as rages, eh?"

That night Burchard leaves his rooms in the Vatican and goes out into Rome across the Ponte Sant'Angelo to his own modest house near the church of San Giuliano dei Fiamminghi. Sitting at his desk, he does not take long to write the diary entry:

> *Today Cardinal Giovanni Battista Orsini died in the Castel Sant'Angelo. May his soul rest in peace. The Pope commissioned my colleague Don Gutteri to look after the arrangements for the dead man's funeral. And since I did not want to know more about the affair than I need, I did not attend the service or take part in any way in the proceedings.*

He reads it back, then closes the book, fastens its locks and places it in the strongbox under his bed. Such is the climate of violence in Rome now that it would be better, for a while at least, to keep his thoughts off the page.

CHAPTER 33

❧

"I think you're missing it."

"What? Bedbugs, saddle sores and a government that ignored everything I was telling it. How could a man miss such delights, Biagio?"

Spring is on its way in Florence, and in the Palazzo della Signoria the secretaries and scribes have slipped the catches and opened the windows.

Niccolò has been back at his desk for months. The weeks following the taking of Sinigaglia had seen him wedged in a saddle scribbling dispatches as the army thundered across the Apennines into Tuscany, the remaining Orsini traitors garroted en route. It had taken till the end of January before he was granted permission to return, Florence finally convinced that a treaty with the duke was preferable to being next on the list of Cesare's conquests. They had replaced him with a more senior diplomat (better name, better clothes, though less perceptive) to negotiate the details. But by then he had been so eager to get home that he had chosen not to mind. Four months and twenty-one days he had been away. His wife was breathing dragon smoke, the council wanted a

full written report by yesterday and there was an army of friends waiting to buy him a jug if they could be first to hear the stories of bloody
carcasses and meat cleavers in the snow.

But Biagio now, as then, is up for the deeper conversation.

"And you were right. The council should have listened to you earlier.
But you know how they are. Everything has to be discussed and weighed
up ten times. Also there was a feeling that you were . . . well—"

"Unreliable. Or to quote your letter, *You are an asshole if you think
they will make a treaty with your Valentine.*"

"And an asshole you were if that's what you thought!" Biagio laughs.
"I was just keeping you informed, defending your back! Anyway, you
have to admit that you did occasionally sound rather . . . partial."

"Partial? What is the point of having an envoy on the ground if not
to gauge what's really going on? If Rome had had someone across the
Alps, the senate might have known that Hannibal was more than another barbarian with a few elephants at his back. I wrote what I thought.
I still think it. We have not seen a man like him in our time."

"Well, no one is arguing with you on that anymore. So, what happens next?"

"We talk over food. I gave Marietta my word we wouldn't be late."

"I meant politics, not supper!" Biagio roars, enjoying the unusual
sensation of being faster than someone who is always ahead. "You know
what they're really saying about you, Il Macchia? That the man with the
busiest prick in the Palazzo della Signoria has fallen in love with his own
wife and God help every other husband in the city."

Niccolò puts up hands as if to ward off such a contagious disease.

"Though in this, as in everything else, I am your defender." He continues the conversation as they cross the bridge to the south side of the
city. "I tell them: Cesare Borgia was no tougher an adversary than Marietta Machiavelli when her temper is up. My God, remember the day you
returned and I saw you off with the bolt of silk and the hair comb that
you'd made me buy so you had something to give her? If you want my
opinion, you should forget history. Write a tract on how to handle angry
wives instead. You could make a fortune from that."

Niccolò is laughing now too. She'd been storing up her fury like one of Florence's flash summer storms, all lightning and deafening thunder. He had even thought of dropping in on an old mistress off the Ponte alle Grazie, except she too would expect a gift after so long. In the end he had gone home, because however violent the weather there, he had missed his wife and had felt a powerful need to sleep in his own bed.

It had taken a while to get into the house.

"The reason you say you don't recognize your own husband's voice is that he's been in the saddle for three days running and has a river of dust down his throat," he had yelled back. "Open the door, woman, or I'll break it down."

Yet once he was in, stepping over the chests of books that were waiting by the front door, presumably to try to evict him, he had found her sitting with a sprig of winter blossom in her curled hair and enough perfume newly applied that he could smell it from the door. A woman who has taken such care to look her best as she gets ready to throw her husband out of his own house? My God, what is the point of being a diplomat if one can't read mixed messages and make sense of them? It was all he could do not to smile.

He had thrown his pack on the ground and without a word, walked up to her chair and kissed her. And when she had opened her mouth to start talking, he had put his hand over it and said, fiercely (for to laugh now would have been the end of his career as a politician):

"Before you say a word, I have been supping with the devil for four months. I've seen men sliced in half, others with faces like purple bursting figs from the garrote, and I've had my fill of anger and violence. I am safe. I am home and I am tired. And if that's not good enough for you then I will walk out and find someone who will offer me a sweeter greeting. And I will give to them the bolt of red silk and the tortoiseshell hair comb that I have carried over half of Italy in my saddlebag for you."

. . .

Three months on and she is pregnant and singing her way to the sick bowl. Following a marauding duke had its uses.

That night, he and Biagio eat fresh broad beans with seasoned pecorino cheese and new red wine—Tuscan fare marking the coming of spring. Then, when the servant has cleared the food away, Marietta settles herself quietly near the empty grate, her sewing in her lap, while the two men talk business over honey cakes and lemon liquor. These first weeks of pregnancy have left her tired and she will almost certainly fall asleep, but she likes the sound of their voices, the feeling of a house open to her husband's friends. Whatever her life is to bring, Marietta Machiavelli is a happy woman now.

"So? What's the talk of the council tomorrow? Your idea of a citizen militia is dead, right? You know what they say about taking horses to water. I thought using the fall of Constantinople as an example was a masterstroke. Much better than your usual old Roman comparisons."

Niccolò shrugs. These last few months he has been showering the gonfaloniere's desk with detailed, finely argued briefs drawing on everything that he's learned, the most radical idea being the creation of a standing army to take the place of mercenaries. The problem was always going to be money as much as vision. No government wants to raise taxes to pay for something they hope they will not need. But need it they will, that he knows. And while they had refused him, an idea once seeded and watered now has time to grow. For the moment though, the more pressing question, as ever, is what is going on in the duke's head.

Biagio spears a piece of pecorino with his knife. "It doesn't make sense. He's got half of Italy waiting on his next move, yet he's sitting in Rome running a court and rowing with his father."

He waits. If his boss doesn't have an answer, then who does?

A father who also happens to be the Pope. When Niccolò replays his conversations with Cesare (he holds many word perfect in his mind), it always strikes him how little mention of Alexander there had been. Of course young men would prefer not to be beholden, but . . .

"I think he is occupied with Church business. If the Pope is growing older faster now, as the reports say, then the duke has to have influence over whoever succeeds him. And for that he needs—"

"A lot more cardinals loyal to the Borgias." Marietta is still busy with her darning as she mutters the words under her breath.

"You are talking in your sleep, my dear," Niccolò says loudly. "Go to bed!"

There is barely a woman in Florence who could—or would—dare to talk politics openly, and if he indulges her sometimes—as he does when she pesters him—it is with the knowledge that she will not show him up to others. She gives a big yawn and ducks her head closer to her cloth, the smile shared by her and her stitches. Biagio, who has his back to her, seems not to have heard. But then he is a loyal friend.

A man in love with his wife. Ha! Niccolò clears his throat loudly.

"The appointment of new cardinals will give him votes in conclave, and the money they pay will go straight into his war chest. The Pope has just created eighty new posts to be sold off inside the curia at seven hundred and sixty ducats apiece." He pauses, as if daring Marietta to come up with the mathematics.

"And when all that's done, then he'll go for Arezzo, Pienza, all the other cities in Tuscany? And the French be damned, is that it?"

Niccolò smiles. "Come on, Biagio. The French are damning themselves. You've read the dispatches coming out of Naples. The Spanish are bringing in troops by the shipload. Louis has waited too long to invade. The few fortresses the French still control could soon be in trouble. All this time he's been humoring the Borgias because he needs the Pope's support and the duke's army when he marches south. But what if the Spanish start marching north instead and the Pope switches allegiances? Then Cesare Borgia could walk into Tuscany with a Spanish alliance behind him."

Biagio shakes his head: he has a desk laden with half digested reports, yet this man who has read everything knows the future as well as the past. In the silence that follows, Marietta's gentle snoring marks a return to the status quo of marriage.

When his guest has gone, Niccolò wakes her gently and she rises almost automatically, taking her sewing and moving like a sleepwalker to
the bedroom. Then he goes into his study and gets out a sheaf of papers
from his chest.

He is writing—when there is time—an account of the conspiracy of
Sinigaglia, filling out the details of the things he did not, could not,
know at the time. Livy sits on his shoulder, refining his prose, nurturing
elegance but always careful to let the drama speak for itself. Two of the
rebels—Vitellozzo and da Fermo—had died that night, strangled as they
sat tied back-to-back in their chairs. The others had left the city as prisoners, to be executed later as the army moved through Tuscany, their
bodies on show one morning with ropes dug deep into their necks. In
both cases the talk was of how they had begged for their lives, each man
blaming the other for their treachery. Their cowardice completes the
story, but then how else would the victor choose to tell it?

Niccolò does, however, have one piece of firsthand evidence. That
first morning after the taking of Sinigaglia he had gone out in a freezing
dawn to try to find a rider to take his dispatch. The town had been
subdued—even plunderers have to sleep sometime—and he had been
on the streets talking to whomever he could find when the duke himself
had ridden by with men-at-arms, overseeing the enforcement of calm.
He had been effusive in his greeting, as if he was meeting a long-lost
friend.

"You see how it has come to pass, Signor Smile!" he had said, waving
his hands around him. "This is what I nearly told you that night when
you and your bishop sat with me in Urbino. I said then that I would
bring down all these petty thugs and tyrants who are ruining the country. All I needed was the opportunity. I knew already then that it would
be given to me. There is not a man in Italy who does not think we are
better without them. True or false?"

Ah, the making of history. Biagio is right: he is beginning to miss it.

CHAPTER 34

*F*ortune: the serendipitous collision of time, place and person, the unfolding of opportunity, the seizing of the moment.

It is impossible to know what might have happened if Alfonso d'Este had arrived back in Ferrara earlier. If, for instance, he had cut short his pilgrimage and come back before Lucrezia returned to court. It would have been a fine gesture: the man who had escorted her to the convent gates all the weeks before, now bringing her home.

But any journey that moves into winter is a precarious business. As the weather grew foul, it had offered him a chance to poke his nose into yet more fortresses, since all these campaigns and conspiracies were accelerating defense innovation and rebuilding. And with his brother-in-law's fortunes riding high, it made sense for him to deepen his knowledge of such things; that way any meeting they have in the future will be equally enriching to them both. It is Alfonso's fate to be a man wise about war but ignorant about women. Or at least ignorant about the one in his life that he doesn't have to pay for.

When he does finally get back, he goes first to his father, making an appointment to dine with his wife afterward.

"You haven't seen her yet? You have a surprise in store. Such a glow she has about her now. I must say she is a duchess indeed," Ercole coos. "The wonders of living with nuns, eh? You're a lucky man, my son."

But Alfonso is one of nature's exceptions when it comes to erotic fantasies about convents, and the hint of lust in his father's voice disgusts him. He would like to get up and leave now, but there have been shifts in the political landscape since he has been away and matters of state must come first.

So it is late when he arrives in his wife's bedchamber.

Business as usual in the Este marriage then.

Except not quite.

He has made an effort, bathed again to rid himself of any remaining grime of the road, had his beard and hair trimmed and anointed himself with perfumes.

Lucrezia is not yet in bed. Instead she sits by a fire, with the remains of a meal—now grown cold—in front of her. To pass the time and keep her mind calm she has been reading—well, what else but poetry?—but she puts the pages away carefully when his arrival is announced.

He apologizes for his lateness, and they sit together talking for a while, while the great bed in the corner dances under the light of the candles. His journey has been fruitful. He tells her of his thoughts on her brother's triumph, how everyone says he will be master of Sinigaglia before the snow melts. His admiration is clear, and she listens intently, her cheeks rosy in the candlelight. She is evidently wonderfully recovered.

"My father tells me he's approved your full allowance."

"Yes, it was good of him."

He grunts. Bloody hypocrite, he thinks. He wonders if he should tell her his part in it, but he is no better at paying compliments to himself.

Silence falls. The bed beckons. He has picked up a few tricks of love on the road: women who charged more than he was used to paying and were artful in the taking (or faking) of pleasure, as well as the giving of it. He would like to imagine the same thing could happen here tonight, but already he is not sure. It is not just him; there also seems to be something wrong with his wife. Certainly she is plump and lovely, but she is giving off an air of fragility that he finds most unnerving. And they still have all their clothes on.

Timing. How cruel it is on both sides.

While it is true that Lucrezia is interested in poetry now—is already half in love with the man who composes it—that is not the problem tonight. The problem tonight is that though she looks well, something unpleasant is happening inside her body again.

She sits opposite him, her heart pounding. What can she say? That in recent days she has felt a recurrence of the tenderness that she felt after the stillbirth; so much so that this afternoon, after she had bathed, she had decided to apply a little of the dispensary sister's ointment. But as soon as she slipped her finger inside herself, she had felt a sharp pain, so sharp she had let out an involuntary cry. Is there an obstruction there, or has some fissure opened up again? Why? How? And how will it feel when it is more than her finger pushing inside her?

An army of boys, she thinks, glancing down at his rough hands as the conversation between them starts to fall away. *As soon as you are well we will get on with making an army of boys.* Those had been his words as she lay flirting with death. She had been too far gone to hear him, but her ladies have repeated it often enough since, for they find it romantic in a most manly kind of way.

It is time. He goes to relieve himself, and with the help of Catrinella she prepares herself for bed, choosing a new embroidered shift and slipping between the sheets.

"Put out the candles as you go," she says as she dismisses her lady-in-waiting.

At least this way he will not be able to see the panic on her face.

"Your hands are cold," she mutters with a little laugh when at the first touch she flinches slightly.

He gives a grunting little sound as he rubs and blows upon them. He leans over and moves his lips to hers, kissing slowly, the novelty of little probes before he pushes farther in. For a moment it goes well. For a moment she is there with him.

He moves his lips down onto her neck, then to her breasts, taking a nipple gently between his teeth. Foreplay. That is the kind of thing some women like. (See how he has been thinking of her.) He hears her breathing coming faster now, registers it along with his own. But the minute his hands move lower, searching out her bushy pleat to test her moistness with a playful finger, as he has seen work on other women, her whole body freezes and she gives a half swallowed cry.

He pulls back so fast it feels as if he is the one who has been hurt.

For a moment they both lie in the darkness next to each other breathing heavily. He has made a considerable effort to imagine another scenario here, and he is angrier—or more disappointed—than he understands.

"You . . . you are healed, yes?" he growls, cross both that he cannot say it better and that she makes him say it at all.

"Yes—except . . ." And her voice is shaky. Oh, Sweet Mary, help me, she thinks. "Except it seems . . . in the last day or so—I have some new tenderness where the baby was dispelled. I did not realize it until . . . Oh, I am so sorry."

And she is. *So sorry.*

But *sorry* is not a word that works for Alfonso d'Este in bed. *Sorry* was all he ever heard from his first wife. No. That's not true: after a while she said nothing at all, just lay corpse rigid, fear rising off her like newly applied perfume. Duty between them had been an act of violence, and even in memory he hates her for it.

"Perhaps if we were careful," she says hesitantly.

But *careful* does not work any better, God damn it. His prick now lies flaccid across his groin.

"We will leave it till another time," he says coldly, pulling himself out of bed. "You will let me know when. I will send your ladies to you."

"No, please, Alfonso, stay! We can talk."

He is already half dressed, fumbling at his buttons in cold fury.

"Talking is not what we are about here," he says.

"Oh, but . . . Alfonso, I didn't mean . . . I was much looking forward to your return," she says fiercely, equally upset. "This is not how it should have been."

But he is halfway out the door.

Her sobs have Catrinella up from her bed pallet by the door, barely bothering to knock before she throws herself into the room.

"What is it, my lady? What is it?"

"Oh, we are undone here." She can barely speak inside her tears. What is wrong with her? Could it be that the struggle to expel that sad little corpse from her womb has somehow corrupted her very insides, so that she no longer has the capacity to make children at all? "Help me. Bring me paper and pen. And find a messenger. This must go at dawn."

• • •

In the dispensary of Corpus Domini, the nun sits at her desk in the morning work hour, the letter in front of her.

Renewed tenderness, raw pain on contact. Is this another lesion inside the vaginal passage? How could this be? It is true she has no experience of labor and stillbirth, but she had made it her business to find out. Another wound now. It makes no sense.

She puts her head in her hands, as if in deep prayer.

Unless.

Unless this is a symptom of something else . . .

The world is full of things that it is not a dispensary nun's business to know. And she has never been prone to gossip. But she would have to be deaf and dumb not to have heard stories of this plague that for years has been ravaging its way through Italy. And the court of Ferrara. When had it been? The death of the duke elect's first wife in childbirth, yes? Four, no, five years ago at least. Every courtier had been in mourning, in attendance at the funeral. Except for one. Her husband. The story was the duke elect Alfonso had been too ill with a bout of fever to leave the palace. But the gossip that filtered in spoke of something more shocking: that he was suffering from an attack of the French pox and was too disfigured to be seen outside.

He was not the only one to be so afflicted. If seemed half the city was infected, including two of the duke's younger sons. One of them, Ippolito d'Este, was a cardinal! The Church in Rome, people said, was full of it. The Pope's own son had contracted it, his handsome face so eaten by pustules that he had taken to wearing a mask.

Officially, such things were never referred to inside the convent, except by way of their general prayers for the well-being of the Este family. If the plague was indeed God's way of putting a mirror up to the corruption of the world, then He would surely show the most mercy to those who were prayed for hardest. With so many convents and churches in Ferrara, it seemed He had listened. The duke elect had recovered—though some said his hands still bore the marks of ravaged flesh—and eventually, like all gossip, it was superseded by other news.

But sitting now in front of Lucrezia's letter, Sister Bonaventura is not so sure. The French pox. What does she know about this disease? Only that it had started in the south with the French army and that God had used fallen women as his weapons, so that everyone would know when a man had lain with them by the affliction written on his skin. But what about the women themselves? Those who harbor and carry it. They must suffer its horrors too, for they are at least as guilty as the men. What does it do to them? Pustules on their faces and bodies? Surely not. No man would sleep with such a disfigured woman. In which case what else might they suffer? And if it is so infectious, then why does it pass only one way? Had God decreed that men give it only to other fallen women? For how else had it moved so fast through the whole country? Or . . . or what might happen when those same men come home to their wives? No, it is inconceivable, surely . . .

Lesions inside the vaginal passage. She might work within her dispensary for a hundred years, but there will always be others outside who know more! Humility is a prized quality in a good convent, but it cannot always replace frustration. What about all those doctors at court who had treated the duchess? Wasn't one of them the personal physician to Cesare Borgia himself?

She asks for an interview with the abbess. If she is right, she will need permission for a letter to leave the convent without coming under the scrutiny of the gate mistress, who must read and censor all correspondence.

The abbess listens calmly, the only sign of distress the way her fingers slip between one another as her hands sit entwined in her lap.

"I understand your concern, Sister Bonaventura, but what you ask is out of the question. For a dispensary nun inside a closed convent to write to a doctor in Rome? It cannot be done."

"But—this doctor—he is also a priest."

"That is neither here nor there. Such a communication asking such questions—well, it could only bring scandal down on the convent and the order."

Sister Bonaventura sits staring at the rough weave of her habit, stained with dispensary work. What else had she expected? "The duchess needs our help, Mother Abbess."

"Then we will do what we do best—and pray for her. My decision is clear, Sister. We will not refer to it again." The mother abbess looks at her sternly. "Tell me—this letter, you have already written it?"

The older woman does not meet her eyes. She is not adept at lying.

"Do you have it with you?"

The abbess waits, putting out her hand for the offered package.

Once she is alone she reads the words, once, then twice. She sits for a moment in thought, then moves to her desk, drawing out a sheet of paper and an inkstand. It is a great privilege to be the chosen convent of the Duchess of Ferrara, but with privilege comes responsibility, and that is the business of the abbess, not a cloistered nun. That night she leads prayers for the ruling family: for their continued succession and the well-being of them all.

• • •

In his rooms in Rome, Torella unpacks the chest that contains his archive. Six years of research and correspondence across Italy and parts of Europe. If there is a response to the extraordinary missive he has just received, it will be here. But even before he starts he is confident that he will find nothing.

He had not been present at the symposium on the new pox that had been held in Ferrara in the spring of 1497 (his own patient Cesare Borgia had yet to be infected), but he has heard stories about the Ferrarese court. And of course he had noticed Alfonso's hands; he is an expert on the many ways a man's skin can erupt, leaving irreverent stigmata over the worst-affected areas, areas that, like the disease itself, can change from man to man.

But having studied him as carefully as he could, he is convinced that the duke elect's scars are old but irritated by his work in the foundry, for in every other way he had been a robust, healthy figure. He must be one of those who has naturally thrown off the disease without further damage. Because, as Torella knows better than anyone, its progress does so change from man to man.

From man to man. It is a phrase he has used often in his treatise.

But those same words now take on a different meaning.

> *. . . Having treated our guest in the convent after her illness, my dispensary sister, a most humble and holy sister, intent on finding God's remedies in nature, finds herself in need of advice that only you can give. . . . I beg your leave to ask these questions on her behalf . . .*

Rereading them, he wishes again the earth might swallow him up.

Over the years he and all the other doctors have exchanged notes and experiences, they have studied only men. Of course they have discussed women. But in the abstract, as the carriers who must be controlled: the need to close public brothels, to banish prostitutes from the streets, out of reach of men. He has written such advice on public policy himself. But it has never occurred to him to seek these women out or examine them. Ever since Eve's original sin in paradise, God has used women as the instruments of temptation that man must—but so often fails—to resist. It is the corrupt humors of Eve's most licentious daughters that are the problem now. If these daughters fall victim to their own foulness, it's not something that has concerned him. For they are not—well, they are not women like the duchess.

Mother Abbess, from my considerable work on this disease I can assure you this is not the cause of this patient's distress, which can only be, in some way or another, a further result of the stillbirth she suffered.

He thinks back to those fretful days and nights when there were so many doctors jostling for position, many of them more experienced in women's matters than he. He had been caught between the opinion of Duke Ercole's physician, an expert on fever and pregnancy, and the more subtle diagnosis of the Pope's own doctor, the Bishop of Venosa, who had seen the duchess's distress more in terms of an imbalance of her humors.

"The lady Lucrezia has always been a most emotional creature," the bishop had confided in Torella one day as they sat, fanning away the Ferrarese heat and waiting for the next crisis. "Susceptible to moods and exaggerated feelings. Regular bleeding would do as much as all his stomach poultices."

Moods and exaggerated feelings. They run in the family. He remembers his vigil at her bedside as the stillbirth fever raged. How she had woken and turned to him. *Don't worry. There is no pulse. I am dead.*

There had been such clarity in her fevered confusion.

The patient has been through a testing time, and such trauma can have an effect on spirit as well as body: she may well be experiencing nervous strain, which might explain such "symptoms" emerging now, when she must return to the "duties" you speak of. In such cases, the best redress is further bleeding to rebalance her humors.

Yes, yes, that will do it.

Of course he is right. For if he is not, then his whole treatise must be reconsidered. And then what would it say? That all around Europe women of royal or noble birth, educated in virginity and fidelity, might find themselves suffering internal pustules because their husbands had impregnated them with their sin? Imagine the chaos such information would cause if it leaked out, as it must. It simply cannot be done.

He signs his name, dusts the ink with sand and is about to seal the dispatch when he quickly picks up the quill again.

I reiterate: I have come across no evidence to support such fears. However, given the thirst for knowledge that your humble sister displays, I would offer a few thoughts on the remedies that I with God's grace have gleaned from nature and the ways I have applied them most successfully on the patients it has been my privilege to heal . . .

It is usual for him, as a medical scholar, to archive any letter he receives, along with a copy of his own answer, for posterity. This time, however, he takes no copy, and the page from the convent of Corpus Domini is consigned to the flames.

• • •

Four days later, Sister Bonaventura is called to the abbess's cell and given permission to order certain things from outside her herb garden. She knows something already about the properties of mercury. It is a harsh medicine, and applied to such a delicate place it will need to be tempered and diluted with a dozen other unguents that she already trusts but that she must now test out carefully.

Honored Duchess, she writes, *be certain that I will have something to send to you within a few weeks, and during that time my prayers will work as hard as my hands.*

Fortunately, the duchess has the comfort of poetry to sustain her.

CHAPTER 35

❖

*I*nside the Vatican, with the orgy of revenge now over, Alexander finds himself enervated, almost lazy. He takes to spending time in the garden outside his apartments. The orange trees, shipped from Valencia a decade ago, are mature now and about to burst into flower. It's a moment he longs for every year, and in preparation he has his papal chair brought out so that he might see a few ambassadors and envoys there, though, more often than not, when the time comes he is slumped downward, head on his chest, apparently sleeping soundly. He can stay like this for hours: like a great snake lying in the sun, digesting a prey that has been too big for him. It is as if, having swallowed half of the Orsini family, they are lodged in the distended papal belly.

But he is not always asleep. Sometimes he is caught in daydreams. The arrival of the orange blossom is intoxicating, its fierce tangy sweetness so different from the taste of the fruit that will follow. Such different nutrients: one coursing through the nose, the other exploding onto the tongue. Another of God's miracles, as humble as it is magnificent.

He loves this moment, for it reminds him painfully of Spain and his homeland. There had been orange trees in Xàtiva when he was a child, but he had not been overwhelmed by them until the year he moved to Valencia, into his uncle the bishop's palace, where the courtyard garden had been full of them.

Valencia. No city charms like the one in which a boy reaches his manhood. And for all the bombast and hyperbole about the wonders of Rome, it was Valencia that had made Rodrigo Borgia what he is: a churchman in love with women, wealth, orange blossom and the taste of sardines.

With his eyes closed he could be there now again: blinding summer sun suffused through the alabaster windows, shops overflowing with silk and silver work, the rising smells of grilled meat and fish, new buildings and dark alleys—all rich pickings for a country boy from a good family. Over the years he has had his choice of some of the loveliest women in Rome, beguiled by their plucked smooth skin, their pale complexions and streams of golden hair, but the first real smell of a woman's bush, the dirty earthiness of it, the juice of desire—all this he associates with tangled black hair, sprouting armpits, sallow skin and a mocking laugh. *Little boy from the bishop's palace—how you have grown. A few coins in my hand and I will show you how to grow even bigger.*

How could anything so marvelous be offensive to God? That is what he had thought afterward, and indeed has done ever since. Of course he had gone to confession (he'd not yet been picked out for the Church), but how could he be truly penitent? The seeds of addiction had been sown, and not even the prospect of hell could stop him. With each succeeding sin, absolution had got easier.

Ah, those first women in Valencia. Though Giulia was the greatest prize a man could have, the only one who had really come close, who had the smell of the earth mixed in her perfume, was Vannozza. No wonder their children are so marvelous. Hair tumbling over those lovely ripe breasts as she sat washing his feet when he returned from days of Church business. His very own Mary Magdalene. That was their joke.

And such a laugh she had: like the peal of a church bell, as if her whole body was inside it. Oh yes, Vannozza would have made a splendid Spanish whore. He feels almost young again thinking about her.

"Your Holiness, Your Holiness?"

He is alert at once. "What? No need to shout, man. I am not sleeping, simply sitting with my eyes closed."

"The Spanish ambassador begs an audience as soon as possible. He brings urgent news from Naples. And Duke Valentine asks to visit you straight afterward."

• • •

From his rooms on the upper floor of the Borgia apartments, Cesare has been observing his father's reverie in semidisgust. These recent weeks have seen a sharp deterioration in their relationship. Whatever pleasure he had got from the crushing of the rebels at Sinigaglia, for Cesare it had soon been over. He'd been sending a message about the past to the future, to make sure such betrayal never happened again. The Orsini, old hands at politics, would get it fast enough. The ailing cardinal had deserved to die—he'd known the risks when he put his name to the conspiracy—but his public humiliation and the Pope's conspicuous gloating were, to Cesare's mind, excessive. As he had marched his army toward Rome, they had crossed swords over it yet again, with Alexander sending daily letters demanding that Cesare besiege and take every one of the Orsini fortresses to the north of the city, as if he wouldn't stop till the family had been wiped off the face of the earth. Cesare had ignored him. Over the last months, he has grown adept at listening to his father only when he says something the duke wants to hear.

"We have much to celebrate, but I must say, you have become a law unto yourself these last months." The Pope had greeted his return with ill-concealed rage. "God Himself knows how many dispatches I have sent you throughout this campaign. Yet all I got was thunderous silence."

"I told you what you needed to know, Father. Rome is a sieve when it comes to gossip. And secrecy was vital."

"What? You are saying I have a loose tongue?"

"No." Though of course that was exactly what he meant. "I am saying the more information that was on the move, the more risk there was of interception and the discovery of our plans."

"Bah! In which case there was no such danger when it came to the Orsini fortresses. By then we were at open war with the family. I tell you, your refusal to attack them made me look like a fool."

"You would have looked more the fool if we'd failed to take them. This business with the Orsini is a weakness, not a strength. And we have more important things to do than to waste time besieging castles that could have held out for months."

"What? What is more important than the punishment of the men who killed Juan?"

Juan! The murder of precious Juan! In the end it always came to this.

"Jesu Cristus, Father! Juan has been dead for six years. How long will you stay weeping at his grave?"

"How dare you!" the Pope yelled back. "You will not blaspheme in my presence or speak to me in that tone. Not now, nor ever again, do you understand?"

By now there had been half a dozen Vatican officials hovering outside the door in fascinated horror, trying to decipher the lava flow of Catalan. While Cesare had been away, the Pope had grumbled and raged enough, but no one has talked back to him like this, either in volume or with this fury. In the weeks since Cesare's return a few of the smarter diplomats have started speculating on how the balance of power is changing in this most remarkable of partnerships, whether perhaps the Pope is growing frightened of his own son.

He would not be the only man in Italy to be so afflicted. Now even when Alexander is awake, many of the envoys and ambassadors knock first at the duke's door. He is barely ever seen outside his apartments in the Vatican. The devil has become an overworn comparison, but what else could describe him: this elusive masked creature who lives mainly in darkness, an expert in murder and deceit? Even the glint in his dark eyes suggests a man who has given up feeling in favor of cruelty. The only thing missing is any sign that he might be enjoying it—for isn't the devil supposed to take pleasure in the horror he unleashes?

That day of the argument, Cesare had been the one to make peace, but only because it had been a waste of his time to fight further. The Pope's obsession with the Orsini is another example of how his vision is blurring. Even if they could be wiped off the map, it would only create anxiety in others, leaving no room for the shifting sands of allegiances that, over time, could force even the fiercest of enemies to become allies again. Or vice versa. What a captivating bedfellow fortune is turning out to be.

Cesare's love affair with France, like everything else, has been contingent on what he could get out of it, and it will not cause him much grief to be unfaithful now.

The Kingdom of Naples. Even he, who has never had time for history unless it involves a direct comparison between himself and the other Caesar, knows it to be so troublesome and wild a place as to be hardly worth the effort. The French should have learned that by now; the only thing they had to show for their last occupation, ten years before, was the birth of the pox and a few strategic remaining footholds to hold out against future Spanish aggression. France and Spain. Like some international bout of arm wrestling, the two powers have been locked in conflict over Naples for years. But not, it seems, anymore. It has taken less than six weeks—my God, what timing!—for the French to find their arm being forced inch by inch backward toward the surface of the table. Over half of their fortresses are now in Spanish hands. Even their castle strongholds inside Naples itself are threatened, and no one, certainly not France's most valued allies, the Borgias, can remain unaffected.

From his window, Cesare watches as the Pope, guided by his chaplain, waddles inside to meet the Spanish ambassador. He already knows the news the man will give his father, for these days anyone of any importance visits him first.

The Pope will have something to smile about tonight over his sardines. This long alliance between the papacy and France has been painful for a man of his Spanish blood. He will almost certainly want to move too soon—this latest gain is inside the boundaries of the city itself—but Cesare knows they must be careful. When it comes to arm wrestling, the loser must be screaming for mercy, his forearm slammed hard against the wood, before it is over.

Cesare turns back into the room where Michelotto stands waiting, a rough map of Italy already laid out on the table. At least here there is no danger of loose tongues.

Through the long months of diplomacy and conquest, Miguel de Corella has remained his master's shadow, silent until called upon to speak. Most of the world sees him as a hatchet-faced executioner, more a machine than a man, but those with more discernment recognize a fine soldier with an eye for political strategy. In a government run by Cesare Borgia, he would be the minister of war. It is perhaps not so far away.

"So, these are the strongholds the French still have and need to hold," Michelotto says, ringing three or four fortified castles scattered to the north and east of Naples.

"According to the Spanish ambassador, they will take them all before the summer."

Cesare cuts in. "But he's a diplomat who's never held a sword. He wouldn't have the first clue how to take this one."

Cesare jabs his finger down onto a spot near the sea, about sixty miles north of Naples. The fortress of Gaeta. Both of them remember it from their journey to Naples six years ago, when Cesare was still in the Church and on official business. The city, especially the women, had welcomed him generously, and among the gifts he had left with had been a leaking boil on his penis and a recurring bout of excruciating pustules and pain. Thank God for Torella. He must remember to agree to the man's dedication for his treatise. But even with his groin on fire, he had noticed the fortress at Gaeta. Nothing of import could pass

north—or south—without the agreement of whoever controlled it.
And the French have held it for years, effectively locking the Spanish in.
But if Gaeta was to fall . . .

"How long would it take us if we had our own artillery outside its
walls?" he says. "Two, three weeks?"

Michelotto shakes his head. "More almost certainly. It is well fortified. If the summer is bad enough and one could somehow poison the
wells, they would drop with the heat. But then so would the besiegers
on the other side. I wouldn't want to be the one doing it."

Both men fall silent. They know that when King Louis finally
launches his counterattack on Naples, the Borgia army is bound by the
terms of allegiance to join them. Southern Italy in summer. A man
could fry inside his armor.

"If Louis moves we will have no option," Cesare says, not needing to
clarify the thought. "To turn against the French now would bring Louis's army down on half of our cities in the Romagna. However . . ."

He looks back at the map.

"If they did lose Gaeta, then we could ditch France and make a new
alliance with Spain. God's bollocks, my father's smile would be as big as
the Sistine Chapel! The papacy would give a Spanish army freedom to
pass through Rome, and the French would be shaking in their shoes.
And then, all of this"—he gestures to the southern half of Tuscany—
"all of this, would be ours for the taking."

CHAPTER 36

❖

*I*n Florence, it is a peculiarity of the republic that the men who are elected to govern must leave their houses and live in the fortified town hall of the Palazzo della Signoria for the length of their appointment. Niccolò Machiavelli, employed, not elected, gets to stay at home, though, as ever, he is still at work before any of them.

On this particular morning, the first day of June 1503, he arrives to find the dispatches have been delayed. A peerless blue sky and the promise of heat are more appealing than the pages of Livy, and rather than stay at his desk, he makes his way up through the building to the bell tower, with its fine view of the city. The only finer vantage point is the top of the Duomo itself. As an official of the state, he would no doubt be allowed to climb inside the skin of Brunelleschi's miracle construction, but the prospect of scaling pitch-black vertical tunnels no wider than a coffin has never appealed. He thinks of Michelotto crawling like a worm through the earth under the fortress of Fossombrone. When Florence comes to create her militia, as surely she must, they should pick its commander carefully; men new to soldiering will need a leader who can inspire a little fear along with admiration.

The climb up the bell tower staircase takes him past a single cramped cell built into the walls; it is reserved for the state's more illustrious prisoners. The great Cosimo de' Medici was a visitor here for a few months when his love for the state grew too entangled with his own ambition. If Niccolò had been in government then, he would have offered to be Cosimo's jailer, for there would have been no better conversation to be had anywhere else in the building. He steps inside, and his nose registers the tang of dried urine. How long does a man's piss last, or is this the product of the odd bell ringer relieving himself on the way up and down the stairs? The last occupant had left what—four? no, five years ago now. That man too had loved Florence, though he'd been more interested in saving her eternal soul than in easing her passage through life.

Niccolò had never had any time for his apocalyptic preaching, yet there were those who believed in Savonarola passionately. He had been brought here after the mob stormed the monastery of San Marco and took him prisoner. From one cell to another. But he had found no comfort in these stones. From here they'd taken him for the torture of the strappado: fixing his wrists behind his back and winching him up to a great height, only to release him suddenly to jerk and dangle, his arms straining out of his sockets. With each successive drop they had accused him of treachery against the state and the heresy of false prophecy. His screams could be heard out into the square, where the crowd cheered when it was announced that he had confessed to everything. But when they brought him back, he fell to his knees, broken and shamed, crying out to God, shouting to his jailers that his body had betrayed him and he was and always would be God's true prophet.

So they had strung him up again. And again. And again; finally, he had broken.

When the news reached the tavern where Niccolò and his friends were drinking, none of them had the stomach to celebrate. No man knows how strong he will be until he is tested. Niccolò still thinks about it: did God abandon Savonarola as a punishment for hubris, or had his prophecies been delusion all along? What if he was right and Florence had been so corrupted by the new learning? Might all those newly painted church frescoes peopled with flesh-and-blood men and women in some ways undermine the purity of the Scriptures? Except who could live freely in a city that believed such things?

Whenever such questions assail him, Niccolò goes back to the work of the great Lucretius, his wild, wise outpouring of philosophy and nature; a vision of the world as a seething mass of atoms from which all life, man included, is made: birth, growth, decay, time stretching out before and after like an ever-receding horizon. If you cannot remember yourself before birth, why should you fear what you might feel after death? He can still taste the thrill of the moment as he absorbed that thought. But what excites one man is heresy to another. What makes sense to one man is heresy to another. He barely speaks of such ideas in company, for even the faithful Biagio finds the idea of a Godless universe too shocking to contemplate. Better to talk matters of state.

The cold cell has dampened Niccolò's appetite for fresh air, and he makes his way down toward the offices again. As he does a huge commotion reaches him. While he has been spinning thoughts, the dispatches have arrived, and for once they are worth opening. An official communication from the Vatican, signed by the Pope himself! There is to be an elevation of nine new cardinals to the Consistory, and Florence's own Bishop Francesco Soderini is one of them. A cardinal's hat for the city! The first since Giovanni de' Medici over twenty years before.

When finally the door to his office closes, Gonfaloniere Soderini's smile makes him look ten years younger.

"A cardinal's hat for my brother no less. This day will go down in the history of Florence. It is a great, great honor. A cardinal's hat," he says again. "Even if it is partly a reward for the signing of our treaty, eh?"

Partly, Niccolò thinks. Though possibly also a bribe for something yet to come.

"I have written to Francesco recalling him from diplomatic duty, and when he returns we shall have the whole of Florence on the streets to greet him. It is a long time since the city had something to celebrate."

Soderini sits enjoying the moment for as long as he can. But there is another dispatch, also from Rome, that is demanding their attention.

"And then there is this," he says.

He pushes the paper across the table.

Niccolò's eyes scan it fast. It is a richer as well as a darker piece of news than a cardinal's hat: the strangled body of the Pope's envoy to King Louis was pulled out of the Tiber two days ago.

"So, what do we make of this? The man was an intimate of the Borgia circle for years. He must have smoothed the path between the king and the Pope a dozen times when Duke Valentine's actions overstepped the mark. Yet now he falls so grossly out of favor."

Niccolò dances a little on the spot. His wife is not the only one who has grown accustomed to his quivering. "Perhaps his long closeness to the king compromised his loyalty to the Pope," he says slowly. "If the Borgias are considering throwing over France in favor of Spain, Louis would have paid a great deal of money to know the details."

"You think the man betrayed their plans to the king?"

"The duke has the nose of a hunting hound for treachery, and the garrote is a traitor's death," Niccolò says quietly.

He is thinking again of the arrival in the small town of Sarteano, east of Siena, on the evening of January 18—he had marked the date in his notes. He had watched the two remaining conspirators, Paolo and Francesco Orsini, be pulled from their horses and bundled into the town's small fortress. Next morning their bodies had been on display in the forecourt. The ritual of a bloody necklace; all that was missing was the duke's favorite graveyard, the Tiber.

"So it is Valentine's work, not the Pope's?"

"I think there's nothing to choose between them now."

"In which case, God save the Church. And God save Florence too. Because if Spain is the way the wind blows, it can only bring the duke down on us sooner rather than later. Even with a cardinal in the Consistory. What? Come—I know that look. What are you thinking?"

"I am not sure that's how it will happen, Gonfaloniere. This gift of the cardinal's hat may be less a reward than a way of ensuring our neutrality while he takes everything else in his path. The duke likes to insult us, but he must know that a republican government would be more of a challenge than a dozen corrupt family city-states. For a while we might sit better as an ally at the table than a rebellious meal in his stomach. Also." He pauses. "Also, he must be hoping that a Florentine cardinal will be another vote for whoever is his chosen candidate in the conclave after his father's death."

The gonfaloniere sits back in his chair. There have been moments since his secretary arrived back from his great diplomatic adventure when he wonders whether it is Machiavelli or Cesare Borgia he is talking to.

"Hmm. How long have you been back now, Niccolò?"

"Four months."

"Time to get over your saddle sores?"

Niccolò can feel a pulse of excitement. He would not like to miss the baby's birth. But . . .

"Well, let us all enjoy life a little first. After the bishop, my brother's inauguration in Rome, we will have our own ceremony here in the cathedral. Perhaps then, if events call for it, you might like to go to Rome yourself. Catch up with a few old friends from your days on the road."

Rome! The center of the web, a dozen new strands of history spun every other day.

He thinks of Marietta's face.

Maybe if he could get her a ringside seat at the service it would help.

CHAPTER 37

Yours is the radiance which makes me burn
And growing with each act and gracious work
My joy in seeing you is never done.
. . . And to you I look, as heliotrope looks to the sun.

In Ferrara the rising temperature is matched by the heat of poetry. Radiance which burns . . . Heliotrope to the sun . . . How cleverly he contrasts the parallel worlds of emotion and nature. Lucrezia has been reading widely and understands the language of poetry better now. Along with the heartbeat and blush that come with their meetings, there is now the challenge of argument. She has written a short poem of her own. He praises it too highly, but she is not so much in love that she doesn't see through it and argues back. In her three marriages, her mind was never a considered attribute. A little wit is, perhaps, desirable in a woman, but only for fencing prettily: real swordplay is men's business. Her intelligence is a pleasure for both of them. In this epic poem

of love that he is composing, smart women are the foils to his philoso-
phizing men, and he wants their voices to sing. How better than to listen
to hers?

But it is more than that: when a woman is unobtainable—as Lucrezia must be—then words have to do much of the work of the affair.

The Este marriage, meanwhile, has been restored to life thanks to a
natural fading of tenderness and the arrival of a jar of unguent from her
precious dispensary sister. They have both been nervous, and the different ways in which they have compensated—she too solicitous, he too
polite—effectively doused any spark of passion long before it could be
ignited. The act was accomplished without pain, though with no great
pleasure, and since then, business—the occasional night visit, aug-
mented for him by his ladies and for her by a growing interest in court
matters—has continued much as usual.

She has not let it dampen her spirits. She has come too far in this last
year—is it really only a year since her barge broke through the fog to a
blood orange sun lighting up a city?—to be defeated by the demands of
the marriage bed. Perhaps this is the resilience of survival that Sister
Bonaventura talked about, in which case she is most grateful for it. After
their first night, she had retrieved the pages of the manuscript from
under her mattress and thrown herself into a clever discourse about
love.

In public, she and Bembo remain duchess and poet occasionally
crossing paths in a lively court, while in private they are never left entirely unchaperoned. No child was conceived by the union of meta-
phors, and while her ladies may cultivate a little strategic
blindness—dropping behind in the gardens, or turning their eyes as
the couple's hands join with their words—it is not to the point of reck-
lessness.

But what they cannot hide is the glow that Lucrezia carries about
her. It lights up the whole court. What a marvelous thing it is to have a
duchess so gay and pretty, so eager to enjoy life, while encouraging others to do the same. Her musicians have grown new calluses on their
fingers from all the dance tunes they play, and Tromboncino cannot

keep up with her demand for new frottole and motets. He has a voice with the sweetness and strength of caramel. A drug to the senses. There are times listening to him when she cannot help but slide her eyes toward Bembo. He is a regular at both her own and the duke's soirees now, sitting with Strozzi and a few other scribblers, court perfect in his manner, body upright, profile medallion sharp. Does he feel her glance upon him? Of course he does. An invisible thread of attention is strung taut between them, so that if either pulls on it even by a fraction the other is aware.

The language of their public behavior has developed its own private translation—a certain gesture, a posy of spring flowers hanging from her belt, a new outfit, each casual meeting—can be read in another way . . .

It seems each day to increase my fire, you cunningly devise some fresh incitement, such as that band which encircled your glowing brow today . . .

The words come with the verse, but everything now is subterfuge; poems are dedicated to nobody, and the letters that accompany them are unsigned. They are even addressed to someone else. But underneath the veil of anonymity, what license they take.

Dear FF,

. . . If you do these things, because feeling some warmth yourself, you like to see another burn, then I shall not deny that for each spark of yours untold Etnas are raging in my breast. . . . Let love wreak just revenge for me if upon your brow you are not the same as you are in your heart.

Glowing brows and raging Etnas: the images ignite an excitement to rival his physical presence.

Let love wreak just revenge for me if upon your brow you are not the same as you are in your heart. Perhaps she should show some favor to someone else, just to watch his eyes burn, for she is already alert to the ways he enjoys piquing the pleasure. She goes through her wardrobe in her mind, wondering what she might wear when they next meet. A little doubt, a little jealousy, the suggestion that one loves more than the other? It can only make the fever hotter.

Of course it is wonderful. She is more alive than she had been for years. And yet . . . yet it is not without stress: this wild brightness, the stretched nerves between communications, how when the words do arrive they caress and tease at the same time. Sometimes she wonders if this is a taste of the pain that he writes of, how love turns to obsession. Certainly these days she thinks of little else.

And there is something more. Because at certain moments, even as the joy threatens to overwhelm her, she is assaulted by sudden painful memory. It is so long ago now—a convent garden on the outskirts of Rome; a gauche and flighty young woman (for that is how she sees herself) paddling palms and trading a few kisses with a messenger in her brother's service, a handsome young man in love with love. The dalliance had been so innocent, so forgivable in such a bloody world. But not for Cesare. The young man had ended up in the Tiber, his throat slit open on the blade of her brother's jealousy. And she had swallowed her fury along with her sobs and turned her face to a second marriage, which had brought even worse suffering. No, the truth is love has been a dangerous guest in Lucrezia's life, and she is not so completely in its thrall that she does not appreciate its perils.

The person in her household who understands most clearly of all is the one who knows least of such turmoil of the heart: Catrinella.

Since the arrival of all this poetry, the girl's position has changed. In the past when an evening stretched out before them, Lucrezia might have called her in to talk or play a board game before her husband visited or she settled down for sleep. But now Catrinella is excluded. Instead, she lies on her pallet outside the door, watching the ribbon of candlelight that tells her that rather than sleeping her mistress is reading: newly delivered private letters and a brick-heavy manuscript all about love. She knows this is its subject because it is her business to check that the candles in the room are properly extinguished, and more than once she has had to lift the pages off the bed when Lucrezia has fallen asleep. As she would have fallen asleep too, because when she tried to read the words—she has learned her letters well over the years—they are as knotted as old wood in a fire grate. Yet her mistress cannot seem to get enough of them. Or of the man who writes them.

Of course, a servant to the bedchamber is not schooled in the art of chivalric poetry. Nor is it her place to sit with the higher-class ladies-in-waiting as they gasp and giggle over the wonders of life, love and poetry. But she doesn't need to hear all they say to see that underneath her mistress's brightness she is not entirely happy. And the fault lies with this handsome, strutting poet, who uses pretty words to cover up the usual male stew of lust and leer.

It is late spring when one evening a messenger from Alfonso arrives to say that he has been held up on other business and will not be visiting that night after all. Catrinella uses it as an excuse to gather her skirts and her courage and interrupt whatever may be going on behind her mistress's door.

In the glow of the oil lamp Lucrezia is, for once, not reading but sitting staring out into the room.

"Held up on business," she repeats quietly when Catrinella delivers the news. "Yes, of course."

Recently she has gone out of her way to include Alfonso more directly in her court celebrations: music that calls for him to perform, dances that favor the athletic rather than the elegant. It is not just deceit. Lucrezia is not the only wife to have lain with her husband and imagined another man's body making love to her. It was not something she intended, but when it happened it had been so powerful that she could not help it happening again. Could such a thing really be a sin if it makes the coupling less barren? Mutual pleasure is, after all, one of the sparks of conception. And conception is what this marriage is about.

The second time it happened Alfonso had paid her the compliment of falling asleep afterward, the heavy plank of his arm pinning her body to the bed. As she had waited quietly for the right moment to shift herself, her mind had drifted to heliotropes and radiances and a dozen other weightless images of love. Such poetry seems—well, almost too refined to capture the fleshiness of copulation, the sour tang of men's and women's dark places. Does a great poet make love differently? She thinks of Sister Lucia and her bony, moaning recitations of joy. It is well known that being loved by God is the most sublime union of all. That, after all, is where Bembo's poem will end.

"Are you all right, my lady?" Catrinella is closer now. "You look flushed."

"It must be the rouge on my cheeks," she says flatly, lifting her hand to wipe it off, for she will not need it now.

"No, no, let me." The girl leans over to gently dab her skin. As she does so, she notices a line of tears welling up in her mistress's eyes. Perhaps Alfonso has seen through her deceit. Or perhaps his ladies please him even more. To be so loved and so unloved at the same time is taking its toll.

"Oh, my lady!"

"It is nothing. Nothing," Lucrezia says harshly.

"I think you are not well. We should leave for the country. The weather is turning fast and you will be better out of the heat of town."

"Nonsense. There is no sign of the fever yet."

"Except for the one that you are suffering," the girl mutters under her breath.

Lucrezia turns to look at her. "You are wrong, Catrinella," she says gently. "I have no fever."

"Well, that's not what Angela and the rest of them are saying." And the words tumble out now. "They talk about how you are burning up with it. Nobody speaks of anything else these days."

"Oh." Lucrezia laughs. "Oh no, fire and fever are just images from the poetry we are reading."

"Poetry!" she says as if it were a lump of excrement, and her stern little face does not budge an inch. "Poetry. And is this Laura poetry too?"

"Laura?"

"Yes. They talk all the time about you and Laura, and another woman too—Beatrice."

"Ah—Laura and Beatrice." And despite her sudden melancholy, Lucrezia is charmed by the misunderstanding. "They are both women whom great poets fell in love with and about whom they wrote the most marvelous verse."

"What? Better than the stuff that the Venetian is writing about you?"

"Catrinella—"

"All I can say is I hope it makes more sense than the bits I've read. Because . . . because everyone in the kitchen and laundry is gossiping about the comings and goings of poets and duchesses."

"What?" Lucrezia stiffens a little. "What do they say?"

The girl shrugs. She had not meant to let it slip. "Nothing really. They're like a leaking pump, always needing something to drip on about."

"You know better than to listen to such gossip. This is court business we are talking about. Poets like Ercole Strozzi and Pietro Bembo are a valuable—necessary—adornment for any duchess's household."

Catrinella falls silent for a second, but she has been anxious on her mistress's behalf for too long, and now it comes bursting out. "That's as may be, I am sure. But it fits well enough with what they thought when you arrived. You didn't have to listen to it, my lady, but I was down there all the time and they never stopped teasing me. Telling me how the Este family didn't like fast women and that you wouldn't last long. But when I asked what they meant they said they couldn't tell a pagan like me because black faces didn't understand and everyone knew you were a sinner and a harlot."

"Oh, Catrinella," she says, pulling the girl toward her. "You should have told me."

How old is she now? Barely fifteen. She is such a fighter, it is easy to forget how the color of her skin might make life cruel for her.

"What did you say to them?"

"I smiled at them—like this—"

She breaks away, grinning wildly, her bared teeth like a run of jagged bright blades. "And then I bit one of them. Quite hard. Well, that's the kind of thing pagans do, isn't it? They left me alone after that."

Lucrezia cannot help but laugh. It is a joy to see a spirit so unfettered.

"Well, if you ever hear anything, anything said against me again, you tell them that their duchess is building a court that will make Ferrara the envy of all of Italy. And that if even a scrap of such gossip reaches me they will be out on the streets suffering deeper bites than you can ever inflict."

They sit together for a while, until Catrinella, reassured, breaks away. She settles her mistress, fussing over the covers and the mosquito lamps, before taking her leave.

But at the door she turns again, as if just struck by something.

"This Laura and Beatrice who they gossip about. Were they married to other men too?"

"Yes, yes, they were. But there was no hint of scandal attached to them either. On the contrary, they inspired Petrarch and Dante to turn their love higher, toward God. Which is what our poet, Pietro Bembo, is also writing about. So you see—for a lady to be the muse for such a man brings only good into the world."

"And what happened to them?"

"Laura and Beatrice? They both died young, alas."

"And the poets?"

"Oh, the poets became very famous."

Catrinella gives off a clucking noise, for as far as she is concerned this is not at all a satisfactory ending.

◆ ◆ ◆

It is at this moment that Isabella d'Este—and her considerable wardrobe—arrives in Ferrara for a visit.

CHAPTER 38

❖

For Cesare the sweetest time to be on the streets of Rome is just before dawn.

Having worked through the night, he and his men ride across Ponte Sant'Angelo, through the built-up hub that lies cradled in the crook of the bend in the Tiber, out into the scrubland and wilderness that laps all around. The Colosseum is still shrouded in darkness, its monumental mass more a presence than a sight, but as they pass the Forum a stain in the eastern sky silhouettes a run of columns so that for that moment they do not look like ruins at all but rather the outline of a great city about to come to life with the daylight. Cesare has little time for flights of fantasy, yet this miracle he never fails to notice, for it brings home the sheer scale of Imperial Rome. A city built on and for triumph. His own victory parades have paid homage to it. He has even ridden in a chariot followed by a hundred men-at-arms wearing the name of Caesar emblazoned across their chests. The crowds love it—who would not want to live at the center of an empire?—but the taking of a few city-states could only ever be a shadow of an era when the power was imperial and the right leader could have both people and government at his feet. Even at his most arrogant, Cesare knows he is a man born in the wrong time.

At the hunting lodge outside the southern gate, he is greeted by the clamor of his hounds—they know his smell and his voice and are already mad for the hunt. Together they head off into the forest with the insistent yelping of the dogs as they root and rustle in the undergrowth to pick up the scent. For a few hours he will be free from all concern. Diamonds of morning dew are everywhere. The world is newly made out here, the battle simple. Not every prey is taken: some outrun the dogs or go to earth too cleverly, but there is always the joy of the chase, the welding of thought and action. In the weeks after he had taken Urbino, the greatest celebrations had taken place on horseback as on his daily hunt he explored and mapped the boundaries of his new state. By the end, he had it all in his head: the passes, the roads, the contours of the land, each point of defensive vulnerability or stretch of open ground where he might muster troops for a battle—all these remembered.

They take two boars that morning, but he leaves the messy business of the kill to the dogs. In the Vatican his father will be rising and bathing, ready to put on ceremonial dress for the inauguration of nine new cardinals. He needs to be there too, for they are all his appointments, each man picked for his potential loyalty, even down to Bishop Soderini in Florence, who with his favored elevation will surely help keep the city neutral for a while, when Cesare takes the rest of Tuscany.

When . . . It is hard sometimes waiting on his own destiny.

By the time he gets home the latest dispatches from the Spanish army in the south should have arrived. The French are still hanging on, but the rope is fraying. Two fortresses alone remain: one to the east of Naples and the other at Gaeta. How long will it take them? Not more than a month, surely. But Cesare could do with it coming sooner; this uncertainty is starting to rattle everyone's nerves.

A few weeks before in Milan, where the French army was gathering ready to march, their own envoy to the king had suddenly disappeared. How long had he been lining his purse playing both sides, leaking news of their secret negotiations with Spain to Louis? Such futile greed, for what corpse ever had need of money? It had taken Michelotto ten days to track him down and bring him back to Rome. Where else could it end but in the Tiber with a wire around his neck? How stupid can a man be? Still, the body had caused overcrowding in the Pope's waiting room, and a further fiery exchange of words between father and son.

"He was a traitor, telling—and selling—our business to the French. You knew that as well as I did."

"I am not disagreeing with the why, Cesare, but with the how. The man had fled to Corsica. Why not have him killed there? You harangue me for insisting on public revenge, yet you go out of your way to stage a theatrical execution. This feeding of the fish in the Tiber is a spectacle that always leads back to me, and I am weary of it."

No more than I am weary of you, Cesare had thought coldly. At such times he can barely stand to be in the same room with his father, he seems so myopic and ill tempered. He has aged dramatically in the months they have been apart. He can no longer walk the length of the corridor without help. He sweats faster than he can mop it off, and he barely puts down his fork before his insides are erupting with rancid wind. Sometimes when Cesare looks at him it is as if he is already seeing a dead man, wondering when it will happen and how he will deal with whoever it is who stands in his place.

If asked, he would surely say he loves his father, yet he feels no shame or sorrow when such thoughts come to him, only a sense of impatience about all that must be achieved before the moment arrives. And when it does? That too he has planned in every detail: the clearing of the Vatican apartments, the troops needed to secure Castel Sant'Angelo as his fortified base, further men stationed outside Rome and the final makeup of the list of cardinals, the favors and threats to lobby the factions within the conclave that must follow.

"What? I am talking to myself now? I am grown invisible to my own son?"

"I am sorry, Father. I was thinking."

"About what?"

"About how cardinals behave in conclave."

"Conclave! I am not dead yet!"

"Far from it, thank the Lord," he murmurs with scant gratitude.

"Cardinals in conclave . . . Hmm, certainly it's something you should know. How do they behave? Like animals, most of them—wolves or sheep—though it can change the minute the doors are bolted. Some, who claim they never wanted power, are suddenly rabid for it, while others find their fangs are blunt when it comes to the kill."

As often happens, now he has the floor he is beginning to enjoy himself.

"Luckily there are always sheep, men up for sale as if they had inked the words on their foreheads. All you have to do is negotiate the price. Though, I fear you would be no good at it, Cesare. You know why? Because you don't laugh enough. In my experience men who are selling themselves like it to be to someone who knows how to laugh. It makes them feel lighter, more at ease with their own corruption."

"Except that my buying and selling will have to be done before the doors close, because I won't be there."

"No, no, that is true. You won't."

But then neither would Alexander be. How could such a thing be possible? The gravity of the thought stilled him for a moment.

"So?" Cesare prompted.

"So . . . so it will need more planning, though it's not so hard. This latest batch should put close to a third of the conclave in your pocket, and we can appoint more next year. For the rest . . ." He took another leisurely sip of wine. It was not often that he got to be the one doing the teaching these days. "For the rest, you make friends with everyone and trust no one. And always promise more than you can give. Threats are all very well, but if you lose you cannot keep them, whereas if you win there will always be money to make up for what you give away."

Six mules laden with silver and a Roman palace to go with them.

That is what it had cost him to turn the final vote his way. Cheap at the price.

"But before you start, my son, make sure you remember to weep for me a little. Because, whatever you think now, nothing will be so easy when I am gone."

He started to pull himself from the chair.

"Come, help me up, then pay obeisance and embrace me. Oh, I know, I know, you don't like it, but believe me there will be a time when you will miss my smell."

Cesare had entered that familiar embrace, and the Pope had clasped his arms around him and held him for so long that he had been forced to take a breath.

No, he wasn't dead yet.

Arriving back in the Vatican after the hunt, Cesare finds the morning dispatches have arrived. Castel dell'Ovo, the last French stronghold within Naples, is close to falling. Which leaves only Gaeta. One set of fortress walls between him and the conquest of Tuscany. He can already feel the blood thumping in his head. Once he has wined and dined the new cardinals tonight—they pay him directly for their appointment. Why bother putting it into the papal coffers when it is coming to him anyway?—he will start dispatching his troops out of Rome, ready for the move against the French.

Alexander too cannot wait. It will bring him full circle to the days when he arrived in Italy and his beloved Spain held the south, while across the Alps, family factions in France were still at one another's throats in search of a unified crown. Two French invasions have done nothing but spread discord and violence. And now he, Alexander VI, will go down in history as the pope who threw them out. Not once, but twice.

He is up and dressed in his silk ceremonial undergarments. He will wait till the last minute to put on the heavy robes: the inauguration of cardinals is a lengthy business, and he will die a slow death in this heat.

He says his morning prayers in the Sistine Chapel, for its great space stays cool long into the day. He enters on the arm of his chaplain to a commotion. Sometime in the night a cat had sneaked in through one of the doors and managed to hide herself at the back under the altar table, where she has given birth to a litter of kittens, and the guards are trying to get her out, their angry voices alternating with hissing and mewling from under the gold cloth.

Alexander stands and watches as a heavyset man emerges with scratched arms and two tiny balls of blind fur half crushed in his hands.

"Don't manhandle them, you oaf. They are all God's creatures," he says loudly. "Here, here, give them to me."

They fit in the palm of one hand, curling and squirming as they fumble for the teat. He is reminded of the squalling little bundle Giulia had put into his arms a few months before, when he visited her after the birth. Another boy who likes to yell at his father, he had laughed. Another son to swell the Borgia army. Cesare can argue all he wants, but he, Rodrigo Borgia, Alexander VI, is still the head of this family. You only had to look at Giulia, pale and languid in her cloak of golden hair, to know that. What other seventy-two-year-old man in Rome has such a lovely mistress? He had jiggled his new son up and down a bit, but the angry bee sound had got on his nerves and he had handed him back soon enough.

He pushes a gentle finger into the animals' damp skin. "Such a thirst for life they have when they are young, eh? Our Holy Mother Church offers sanctuary to everything and everyone," he says, rising to his St. Francis moment. "Let them be. I shall enjoy hearing their cries as I pray this morning. Here—put them back with their mother and don't hold them too tight."

The guards stare at him, but do as they are told. Better to humor him and get rid of them later. He will never remember.

He turns away into the body of the great chapel. It never fails to raise his spirits staring up into its majestic vaulted ceiling. This is his hunting moment, a sense of power and beauty combined. By the end of today there will be nine new cardinals ready to take their places in the chapel's pews. Out of thirty-six men who, making up at least a third, will owe their appointments directly to the Borgias. Though how far that sense of duty will survive when it comes to the next conclave is always a question.

Sweet Mary, what wouldn't he give to be there? As long as you don't mind the food and the smell of the latrines, it is the most marvelous entertainment a man can have. He can see it already: the lines of wooden cells on either side of the chapel, their construction so hurried that a man can lose a dozen threads of a robe rubbing against the splintered boards. There will be many more compartments this time, which will make for less open space for mingling. Five times he has done it, and each time he was in his element. Though never more so than eleven years ago, when he could see, almost feel, the tide moving under his command.

My God, it had been hot then too. He sees himself walking down the marble corridor in the middle, passing each of the doors counting off the votes, the abacus in his head adding up the cost of victory while high above him a hundred gold stars stared down from the vaulted ceiling into the nave. If you give this to me, God, he had said, I vow that I will keep Italy safe and bring peace to the warring families of Rome. He had not gone into detail about what he might do for his own family. God ever would know what was in his heart.

And he has not done badly! The Orsini, always the worst of the troublemakers, have been humbled, and another two, three years at most will see it all fall into place: the French will be pushed out of Italy, Cesare's unifying papal state will stretch from the Mediterranean coast to the Adriatic, there will be a brace of boy children in Ferrara securing Lucrezia's place, with her first son, Rodrigo, and Giulia's offspring coming up behind. That is the Borgia future, should the good Lord be willing to grant him just a little more time. No, he might be old, and a little loose in the tongue, but he is far from finished.

Behind him he hears the soft mewling of kittens.

Young life saved by an old man. He decides to take it as God's answer to his prayers.

The guards wait till he has left, then dig out the little parcels of damp warm fur and drown them in the nearest water butt outside.

CHAPTER 39

❖

*P*resents, embraces, compliments, a river of endearments . . . it is
over a year since the two women met, and in that time the Borgias have taken everything in their path. Including Isabella's own son in
the promise of marriage.

"Oh, a most propitious union." Her smile swallows up her eyes in
creases of flesh. "Though, of course, little Federico is so very young yet
and much can happen in the world. Meanwhile, I say again, my sweet
sister-in-law, how overjoyed I am to see how well you look, doesn't she,
Alfonso?" she croons as the three of them sit together waiting for one of
the duke's interminable entertainments to begin.

"Such stories we heard in Mantua about the fever and your closeness
to death. Yet here and now, you seem, well, more in a fever of joy,
wouldn't you agree, Alfonso? I have to ask—forgive me, both of you—
but might it be that . . ."

She leaves a coy pause.

"No," Lucrezia says, putting her husband out of his evident misery.
"No, I am not with child. Not yet."

"Well, it will happen soon enough. I am certain of that, aren't you, Alfonso?" she says, squeezing his arm as in closest confidence. "Oh, don't scowl so, dear brother. There is no one in Italy who doesn't envy you such a . . . a highly regarded wife."

They are excruciating, these evenings. Even if he and Lucrezia were madly in love he would still be surly as soon as Isabella comes near him. Lucrezia does her best, but his retreat is automatic; his eldest sister has been pecking at him ever since he can remember. It doesn't help that the state of his wife's womb is public business. The duke himself never fails to twist the knife in. "Your mother was already carrying your sister by this time in our marriage. I know, I know—but she has been well for months. This is politics not pleasure we're talking about. What are you doing every night? Playing chess with her?"

He spends most of the next week sleeping in his foundry. My God, how he hates his family.

Lucrezia suffers a gentler interrogation from her own father. His letters are filled with yearning for another grandson. How is it between them? Does the duke elect still come regularly to her bed? She will remember how important it is not to turn a husband away.

Of course she does not turn him away. But court life still bores him. He has taken a dislike to the dandified crippled Strozzi, sniffing around women's skirts like a randy dog, and has no time for poetry, which seems to him to epitomize the worst of courtier fakery. Does he have any idea what is going on? And if he did would he let himself care?

Isabella, however, has ideas about everything. She already knows about Bembo's great composition on love and is keen to have him recite parts of it at a soiree of her own, together with music and singing. Of course, Lucrezia is invited. And of course she will not attend. She and Bembo had discussed the possibility of such a gathering before Isabella arrived.

"She collects poets as she collects statues. You had better be careful she does not pack you up in her chest and take you home."

"And why would I go with her, when everything that is important in my life is here?" he had said, entwining his fingers with hers. Their hands have been lovers for a while now.

"Then you had better hide that fact with your life. I tell you, she is a bloodhound for scandal and would do anything to destroy me. I am serious, Pietro. She is a harridan. My brother calls her a jealous cow."

She had paused, inviting him to decorate the attack with more subtle wordplay to show how much he values her over any other woman. But he who was usually so fast and fluent at this game had said nothing.

A cow perhaps, but also one of Italy's greatest patrons, and even a love-struck poet must keep an eye on the future. It was the first time she had thought such a thing, and it sent a chill down her spine.

The morning of the concert she excuses herself with a bout of pollen fever. "I shall ruin everyone's enjoyment by sneezing all the way through." She laughs, having put some effort into blowing her nose for days so that it is red and inflamed. But that evening as she sits in her chamber with her ladies at their embroidery, through open windows every now and then she catches strains of music and laughter, as her needle stabs angrily into the taut linen.

The success of the event is on everyone's lips, along with rumors that Bembo is thinking of setting more of the work to music given the magic that he and the visiting marchesa have made together. But in each other's company, Isabella and Lucrezia do not refer to poetry much. Which is strange, since Isabella's intelligence service—her ladies' noses are known to reach round corners and through closed doors—must be well aware of the interest she has taken in the art form.

When Lucrezia is at her most nervous, she wonders if the absence of the subject is an attack in itself.

In the third week of the marchesa's visit—thank God she will be leaving soon—the two women and their ladies spend the afternoon in the duchess's apartments. Isabella is eagle-eyed for the changes Lucrezia has made. "These new colors are lovely. Lovely. I am sure my father didn't mind. Your pleasure was upmost when he took such trouble over the original decorations before the marriage. What do they call this shade of ocher? It is almost puce, I think. I would look most sickly against its background, but it fits your pallor very well."

Finally she stops talking. The silence grows. The windows are open. The orange blossom from the terrace garden overlooking the moat is fading as spring slips toward summer.

"Such a scent still! I am surprised you can bear it, with your nose as sensitive as it is." Isabella smiles.

"The worst of the malady is past," Lucrezia replies sweetly. "I received a remedy from the nuns of Corpus Domini."

"Ah yes, Corpus Domini," she says quietly. "My mother often visited it, such perfect cloisters. A fine convent, yes."

Lucrezia stares at her. For the briefest moment her adversary seems—what?—almost vulnerable.

"I envy you growing up in a city as lovely as Ferrara," she says generously, for she has thought about it. Sixteen. That's how old Isabella was when she went in marriage to Mantua. Old enough for a rolling landscape of memories. "You must have missed it when you left."

"Of course, I did." Isabella looks at her strangely for a moment. Perhaps she is remembering the pain in her mother's eyes, the stories of how she ordered her daughter's rooms to be shuttered and closed up after she left, as if a death rather than a marriage had taken place.

How would it be if they could find a way to talk honestly to each other, to realize that some of the battles they fight as women and wives are not so very different? But it would take more than a wisp of memory to soften Isabella d'Este now. It's not her fault. She has been trained since birth in the art of dynastic snobbery, and her hatred of the Borgias, in name and in person, is something she cannot let go of.

"But Mantua is a fine city too, and my mother visited me there. Such a marvelous woman she was; the greatest duchess Ferrara will ever have, without blemish of blood, thought or deed."

Unlike you or your own courtesan mother, she does not need to add.

Oh, Cesare is right, Lucrezia thinks. You are a jealous cow.

"And her memory lives on still," she says, nailing on a smile. "The duke, your father, is kind enough to say that when I am on the dance floor he is often reminded of her."

Sweet Madonna, it is like being caught in a catfight, never knowing when the next claw will swipe. The scrapping stops for a moment as they regroup.

In the distance is the rumble of carts and the cries of the minstrels.

"Ah, such a din. It doesn't bother you?"

"Not at all, I enjoy it: the sense of life going on outside."

"Tell me. Do you ever hear anything else?"

"What kind of thing?"

Isabella moves her head a little. It is a gesture Lucrezia is beginning to recognize when trouble is afoot. "Your tower is above the run of the old dungeons. Such horrid places." She shudders.

"There are no prisoners anymore. They were transferred before we moved in."

"Of course. Still, terrible things happened there," she says with a certain relish. She had everyone's attention anyway, but she is good at the theater of timing. "One of the family's greatest tragedies. You must have heard about it many times."

"No. No, I don't think I have."

No one ever says anything bad about the Estes in her presence. They might have lived on a diet of roasted children for the last century and it would somehow have been turned into a triumph worthy of another fresco.

"What? You don't know about the screaming duchess?" Isabella says, leaning in a little in the pretense that the words are just between the two of them.

Lucrezia shakes her head.

"I heard her only once. There was unrest in the city and my mother brought us children from the ducal palace into the fortress for protection. Oh, she was howling and weeping, it was an awful sound."

"Who? Who was she?"

"Well, of course by then she had already been dead for half a century." Isabella takes a breath. "Dear Sister, you really don't know? About the wife of great duke Niccolò, my grandfather? Oh, it is the saddest, most shocking thing you could ever hear. She was his second wife—he had three, you know—a young woman, about your age. Parisina Malatesta was her name, from that scandalous family in Rimini. So clever of your brother to get rid of them in his great campaigns."

Lucrezia has no idea what is going on here, but she knows she must protect herself. The fan of ladies has moved imperceptibly closer, though Isabella's whisper remains loud enough for everyone to hear.

"The duke was a most energetic man, very fond of women. Not the first or the last in that respect, I think." She laughs. "It is a trial the things some wives have to put up with, yes?" she says conspiratorially.

Her husband is in every bed but her own. Cesare's words when Lucrezia was ill come back to her. Except what is unfolding here now has nothing to do with sisterly solidarity. "It seems some men give in to temptation more easily than others, yes," she says, lifting herself up and looking directly into Isabella's eyes.

"And some women too." The answer snaps back, accompanied as ever by the fleshy smile. "Though I suppose one must have a little sympathy. For she must have grown—well, quite lonely."

Ah. Here it comes, she thinks. Well, I am ready. Do your worst.

"However, there was one young man at court who understood and paid her kind attention. Handsome, courteous, quite a charmer by all accounts. And, well . . ." She lifts her hands as if to invite Lucrezia to continue.

But Lucrezia is remembering something now. A story whispered many months ago when she was negotiating her income, about how the duke had pardoned one of his best musicians, a man guilty of murdering his wife and her lover. And someone had mentioned how in Este history marital justice always favored the husband.

"Of course, in the end they could not help but give themselves away. When the duke found them together he went mad with rage. Because . . ."

She pauses for maximum effect. "Not only was she, Parisina, his wife, but her young lover, Ugo, was his own son from another marriage!"

Lucrezia's ladies draw in a combined breath.

"All night the duke raged, while in the dungeons she screamed and sobbed for mercy. At dawn, despite her pleading, they were both beheaded."

"Oh, how terrible!" But even as she whispers the words Lucrezia is thinking of Catrinella's descriptions of her first weeks working down in the laundry and the kitchens. The long dark corridors and the needling gossip. *The Este family don't like fast women.* Had her tormentors also mentioned a screaming duchess?

Lucrezia knows that this story is meant to frighten, even to act as some grotesque warning, but instead it is stirring again a memory of her own past: the young Pedro Calderón, handsome and courteous, whose only crime had been to offer a little romantic comfort during her own loneliness, but who, in doing so, had brought upon himself her brother's furious jealousy.

It does not matter what a woman does. Only what others say about her had been Cesare's furious retort. *Your reputation must be stainless. Stainless, do you hear? Without it you are no use to anyone.*

Reputation: such a sly, partisan word. Men may father a dozen children out of wedlock and be admired for their virility. When Alfonso d'Este openly takes all manner of loose women to his bed, his "reputation" is not affected one jot, but his wife's would be destroyed if it were discovered that she is even thinking of finding solace elsewhere. A dalliance of words, a cache of love letters, an exchange of poetry, and it is as if the deed is already done.

"You look so pale, Sister. I hope I haven't upset you?" Isabella is frowning solicitously. She is always at her most generous when she has got what she wants. "I am sure she has stopped screaming now. At least I pray to God that she has."

. . .

After she goes, Lucrezia banishes her ladies and sits alone in her garden as dusk falls. She takes in deep breaths, a vestige of orange scent and woodsmoke as the city prepares for supper and darkness. Ferrara at its best, spring nudging into summer.

Close by a pigeon lands laboriously on the garden wall, then flaps down again nearer her feet in search of the crumbs that sometimes fall there. It has bright orange beady eyes, and when it walks on pink splayed claws, it juts its head out, as if its body is too cumbersome to accompany it smoothly. She thinks of Alfonso's scaly hands, Ercole's thick torso and Isabella's cold beady eyes, her body encased in vast skirts that come juddering behind her. The Este family as a flock of strutting pigeons! The laugh sticks in her throat.

She puts her head back and gazes up at the sky. High above the battlements, the swifts are coming in, feasting on the wing, dipping and wheeling so high that they resemble flakes of ash tossed by the wind. There is poetry everywhere in the world if you look hard enough. In the year that she has spent living in her castle tower, she has never once heard a woman's screams rising up from the dead. And she does not intend to listen for them now.

SUMMER
1503

Times vary and evil and good fortune do not always remain on the same side.

—Niccolò Machiavelli

CHAPTER 40

❧

*W*ho would make war in such weather? In the great fortress of Gaeta, between Naples and Rome, the besieged French troops stand on the battlements staring down at the Spanish enemy camped beneath. At least inside the walls they have the shade of stone buildings to rest in. Imagine it being too hot for killing, not so much the brutality as the exertion. Cannons pound the walls from dawn until sometime after midday, when the sun overwhelms; then everyone crawls under canvas or carts or trees, anywhere that might offer a little shade. The sea is barely half a mile away, but anyone tempted to find comfort there would be strung up as a deserter when he returned. If only conquest could be left till the autumn. But it can't. Weather and war. History is made of it.

In Florence now the heat is daily gossip. A merchant taking down his stall in the central market at midday drops a basket of eggs on the cobbles and the whites start to sizzle, so that beggars have a free meal alfresco. Then there are the dead, whose bodies stew in the heat so they bloat and start to leak, creating the most dreadful stench in morgues and graveyards. As the fever comes in, the worst job in the city is that of the gravediggers, who must work through the night to keep up with the demand. One man digging a family grave drops the church keys into the earth and, going down to retrieve them, is so overcome by the fumes that when they find him next morning he has become one of the corpses. Digging your own grave. How can it not be true when so many have heard the story, every second one learning it first from someone who swears he knows someone who knew the man personally?

In her house off Via Guicciardini, Marietta Machiavelli, heavily pregnant, is packing to leave for the country. She has put on a lot of weight these last weeks and moves sluggishly, like an overloaded galleon with no wind in her sails, her underbodice and petticoats soaked with the sweat that gathers constantly under her heavy breasts. She is due sometime within the next weeks, though everyone knows that first babies are a law unto themselves when it comes to staging their arrival. In the village of Sant'Andrea in Percussina, midwives and wet nurses have been employed and will be ready.

At first she had not wanted to go. "I am giving birth to a Florentine and his first journey should be with his parents to the Baptistery to be registered. And what kind of wife leaves her husband when the world is being turned upside down?"

"One who cares for him almost as much as he cares for her, which is why he is sending her away in the first place."

She had given a little humph. Who would be married to a diplomat? There is always an answer for everything, and she is not as fast as she was. If the baby is the boy she has prayed for she will soon be outnumbered: two clever Niccolòs in the house. She had better have a few girls quickly to even the score.

But once it is decided she goes meekly enough. In the heat it can be a boon not to share the bed with anyone, and she is feeling the need of safety, like an animal building its nest. Niccolò is amazed, even a little alarmed, at this easygoing new wife of his.

"There will be no fever there, and the women in the village will take care of you. Things are born all the time in the country."

"You are sure you will cope here without me?"

"I shall look after myself very well."

"Or let someone else do it for you," she says gaily, running a careless hand down the smooth nap of his doublet. She is not grown so placid that she is blind to those nights when, he claims, the council has kept him at his desk till dawn. "I only hope she does it as well as me."

He is rearranging his face in response when Marietta laughs.

"Oh, don't worry. I am not upset. On the contrary, it is better for a wife to know that her husband is cared for. And we are married almost two years now, remember? It is fine—I do not expect you to recall the date. It is not Roman history after all. Marriage is marriage. People tell me this is how it is and that I should get used to it. Though they also tell me it is better not to mention it, but, well, I am doing my best, wouldn't you say?" She looks up at him almost coyly. Her face is plump, like a full moon. When she smiles it gives her dimples. It is true that in recent weeks her whale proportions have dampened his desire, and there have been other attractions elsewhere. He knows himself too well to expect it to be any different. As does she.

"My mother said I would never find a husband because I spoke my mind too much."

"Now you tell me! I should have known this during the marriage negotiations."

"Oh, you still got a bargain." She turns away, busying herself with her bags. "I have always known that you were a man with more on your mind than your wife. We will let it rest at that," she says, thinking how proud she will be of herself, making so light of difficult things. "And don't forget that it is also your job to keep Florence safe for your family. God knows what we would do if Duke Valentine invades—"

"I have told you—whatever happens he will not make a move against Florence."

"That is what everyone said about Urbino," she says, for it is still her pleasure to try to keep up with him. "And what about Sant'Andrea in Percussina? That is south of here. Are you sure he won't come there?"

He laughs. "I think if I tell him you are in residence he'll give it a wide berth. Marietta, we agreed that such things are not for you to worry about."

"Still I cannot help it if I do. It is your fault: all those thoughts you have leaking out from your head into mine. I was never so concerned about the world before I met you."

"And you need not be now. Just remember what the cardinal said to you."

She smiles. Such a wonder it had been. Francesco Soderini's elevation had been celebrated throughout the city: a procession and a special service in the Badia for the clergy, followed by the new cardinal himself saying mass for everyone. The whole of Florence had been trying to get into the church, but as wife of the secretary who had accompanied Soderini on diplomatic missions, she, Marietta Machiavelli, had been reserved a place in the center of the pews. She had sat stuffed into her best dress (made from the bolt of red silk, because the color does so suit her), her stomach straining hard against the stitches, a pomade to her nose to cut out the worst of the crush of bodies. And afterward, the cardinal himself had come up and spoken to her, giving his blessing both to her and to the child in her belly, and telling her she had the most worthy husband and that Florence owed a great debt to him. She had blushed so much that it had made him smile and he had told Niccolò what a lucky man he was.

Oh, a woman could die happy with such honor heaped upon her. Except that dying would not get this baby born.

"Come, Wife, if you don't leave now the heat will be chasing you all the way into the hills."

He watches till the carriage disappears down the cobbles, on its way past the Palazzo Pitti toward the southern gate of Porta Romana. Next time he sees her there will be a child. If fate is kind enough to give him a boy, he will have him reading Latin and Greek by the time he is ten. If the republic lasts he might find a way for him to be employed in government early. A privilege he was not allowed, as Florence had spun into the chaos of invasion and pious tyranny. Would he be a better diplomat now if he had had more experience? Or did those years standing on the sidelines watching madness unfold give him the means to see it in a different perspective?

If the republic lasts . . . By the time he enters the side entrance of the Palazzo della Signoria, Marietta is already long forgotten. He has chosen to keep the latest developments from her because no pregnant woman needs to know that Italy is now teetering on the edge.

Three days before news had come that Cesare Borgia was moving his troops—five thousand of them—out of Rome toward Viterbo, on the northern border of the papal state and Tuscany. The pretense is that they are on maneuvers, ready to join with the French and therefore no threat to anyone. But Niccolò is not the only one who is not fooled. The morning's first dispatch brings news from Milan. The French army— twice as many men—is on the march into Lombardy.

He sits at his desk conjuring up distances and timings. If Gaeta doesn't fall within the next seven or eight days, the duke will face a stark choice: either to keep his pledge to join King Louis's attack on the Spanish or stand against him and risk the security of his own towns as the French march south to confront him. He and Biagio already have half a month's salary wager on which it will be.

Though he has kept his preparations a secret from Marietta, Niccolò is already packed and ready. He has another half month's salary riding on whether he will be in Rome before or after he becomes a father.

He needs to win at least one bet, because a birth with all the trappings, feasts and ceremonies will be a costly business.

CHAPTER 41

❖

With Isabella's departure, the atmosphere in the Este court changes.

Alfonso, like a cat chased from his house by a visiting dog, appears back at more court functions, and Lucrezia joins him. He has never been a man interested in gossip, and whatever he might think of her recent commitment to poetry, in the company of his overbearing sister she has always quietly taken his side. If he were better with words, he might try to tell her how grateful he is, for he has noticed how she has blossomed these days. Along with the furnaces and the casting pit, there is a kiln in which he has been known to fire bowls and jugs that he has designed and then decorates himself. And the foundry men who work with him have noticed that he has been busier on such things in the last few months.

The tenderness of pots: it is hardly the stuff of epic poetry.

Except that poetry is not as satisfying to Lucrezia as it once was. After so many words, so much quivering flirtation and drama, what is left to be said? And then there is the leaking poison of Isabella's story. Though there is still no trace of screaming to disturb her sleep, there are moments when Lucrezia thinks she sees courtiers looking at her differently, waiting till she turns her back before they speak to each other. Perhaps she is picking up tension from her ladies. Certainly they are more flighty, with more whispered conversations in corridors and outside rooms. As ever, it is left to Angela to say the unsayable, though not when their mistress is present.

"What happened to Parisina's ladies-in-waiting?"

Could it be there is such a thing as too much intrigue?

The city is starting to swelter when Bembo arrives back from a brief visit to the country, coinciding with the end of Isabella's stay. Though his presence in a crowded room still blazes through her body, she finds herself hesitant, even standoffish. She avoids his eyes, finds reason to talk to others. By the time they meet—the excuse is a newly delivered volume she has ordered from Venice—it feels as if they have had a lovers' tiff even though they are not lovers.

"You grow more radiant with every absence," he says when they take their customary break for refreshment, her ladies settled in a circle at the other end of the room, eyes intent on their embroidery. "Everyone speaks of your brilliance as a hostess."

"Strange. All I hear is the brilliance of your evening of poetry and song."

"An entertainment, that's all. The room was empty without you."

"And the offer the marchesa made you to visit her in Mantua?"

He smiles. Though in the gardens of Asolani the men do most of the talking, when they stop it is almost always to find the woman has arrived there before them.

"It was, as you predicted, graciously put. And graciously declined."

"How?"

"I spoke of her father, the duke, who has been generous to me for many years and whose hospitality I could not turn my back on." He pauses. "However tempting her offer." He has recently been refining Perottino's thoughts on the many ways love can hurt, and the sweet poison of jealousy is much in his thoughts.

"My lady." He brings his head closer. "I told you, you have nothing to fear from her. You eclipsed her as effortlessly as Venus nightly eclipses every star in the sky as she rises."

"Then it might have been better if Isabella had been Venus on Tuesdays and Thursdays," she says tartly. "That would have made my life easier."

He glances back to where her ladies sit, eyes down, ears sharper than their needles. "This time has been difficult for us both. Might we be alone for a moment?"

She looks behind him to the circle. Oh, how tired I am of being watched, she thinks.

"Ladies, Signor Bembo is in need of paper and ink. Go to my study and find them for me, please," she says gaily.

Camilla looks up with a question in her eyes. But Lucrezia stares her down.

As the door closes, they sit for a moment.

"Ah, Lucrezia," he says, leaning over and taking her hand. "I have missed you so much."

"How much?" she says lightly.

He laughs. "It would take me days to fashion the right words."

"So try a few wrong ones."

How he loves her sense of mischief and flirtation. It has been a stalwart defense when intimacy threatens to overwhelm them. But this . . . this feels a little different.

"I have come to ask you something: I want to dedicate my poem *Gli Asolani* to you."

Whatever she had expected, it is not this.

"*Gli Asolani*? But it's not finished."

"No. Nor will it be for a year or so. However, when it is . . ."

"You are sure that is wise—I mean—it is a poem about—"

"Believe me, I have considered it carefully. There is nothing but honor attached. It is about love in all its forms, explored and presented through a series of evenings at court. For that reason, and given its scope and ambition, it is only right and proper that it should be dedicated to a great duchess at a great court. And who else could that be?"

In the shiver of the pause that follows, it is hard not to feel the name of Isabella d'Este hanging in the air.

The work that will alter the course of Italian poetry. That is what Strozzi says about it. *Gli Asolani,* dedicated to her, Lucrezia Borgia, for so long reviled as a murderous, incestuous whore.

"You had written so much of it before you met me," she says quietly.

"That may be true, but knowing you has changed it into something infinitely richer."

"Then . . . then how can I possibly refuse."

He moves her hand toward his lips again and kisses it, palm open now, gently.

Each time he woos her back it gives him greater pleasure, for she always grows more lovely. The air stills around them, and he feels the parasite of desire dig a little farther into his entrails. Yes indeed, *parasite* is the right word. She will always be his greatest muse, for each meeting sends him spinning back to his own ideas.

But Lucrezia has had enough of poetry.

She leans toward him and their mouths meet, sending a shock through her body. I will have none of you, Isabella d'Este, she thinks angrily, I am the daughter of a pope and the sister of a soldier. And I will not be crushed by your malicious gossip. The kiss deepens as their tongues start to play. Borgia bravery: always at its fiercest when most threatened. Whatever happens now, it is her choice. She is nobody's victim.

His hand is kneading at her breast and a raging Etna is rising in both their groins, when suddenly he moans and pulls away.

"Ah, my sweet lady," he whispers, cupping a hand under her chin so he can hold her close and yet a little away. "Ah, you are too lovely."

She sits frozen, her lips still parted, her breath coming fast.

"You are my siren, my muse—" He breaks off, as if this is too much for even his poetic skills. "But—"

"But?" she echoes. "I am the Duchess of Ferrara. Is that it?"

He shakes his head as if it is too painful to even think about.

"And if I was a siren married to someone else?"

He drops his eyes. "You are not," he says simply.

"No, you are right. I am not."

She hears herself laughing, a light frivolous sound. "Of course you know the story of Parisina and Ugo?"

He sits staring at her. It is so unlike him to be lost for words.

"Duke Niccolò's wife and son?" she pushes. "Both of them executed because of their great affair. He was a most handsome, courteous man, they say, though not, I think, as talented with words." And she is suddenly quite angry, though she does not understand why.

"Lucrezia, this has nothing to—"

"Do with us now? Of course not! For we are not adulterers, are we? Only courtiers. We make love with words, not bodies. Because if we did, if we did . . . who knows where it might take us?" Her voice is icy.

He winces. "You are laughing at me."

"Oh no, Pietro. On the contrary, I am very serious. I am a woman who has the capacity to destroy any man I love."

And though she is looking at him, she is seeing someone else; equally handsome, full of life and laughter. But the image turns and now she is looking at a body dragged from its bed, the face swollen and purple from the garrote of Michelotto's hands. Not even marriage had saved Alfonso from her brother's wrath.

She pulls herself out of his grip. "You will find it hard to change the course of Italian poetry with your neck wrung like a chicken's."

She is up and moving toward the door, calling loudly for her ladies. Outside they are standing far too close—paper and ink held out as their lame excuse for having just arrived. The alarm in their eyes brings her to her senses a little.

"Signor Bembo will need some time alone to put his thoughts onto paper," she says firmly. "He will be leaving now."

And she bows her head, offering him her hand to show that the audience is over.

He stands for a moment, caught between shame and confusion.

"My dear duchess," he says with almost theatrical dignity before he turns. "The time I spend in your presence is more precious to me than life itself. There is no greater muse in my work and no sweeter woman walking the earth. *Gli Asolani* is your poem. It will never be anybody else's."

She does not cry for long. And when it is over she feels lighter, as if she has been wearing a bodice so tight for so long that it has begun to feel like her skin and only now, with it taken off, can she breathe freely again.

She retires to bed early, dismissing Catrinella. It is a balmy evening, and through the windows she can hear the bright strains of trombone and bombarde from Ercole's palace. The duke may be a miser, but he is lavish with the things he loves. She had turned down tonight's invitation on the excuse of a welter of correspondence to catch up with since the marchesa's going, but now she wishes she was there.

The drum is beating the tempo of a saltarello. She taps her feet on the floor, humming the music line to herself. It is months since she danced to this tune. Such a different language one speaks on the dance floor. When the body is talking so loudly, there is little room for the mind. It is one of the reasons she loves it so.

She moves into the middle of the room, pulling herself up through her spine, her head floating back in readiness, adding an inch to her height so that the hem of her voluminous night shift lifts around her ankles. Unencumbered by shoes, her bare feet make contact with the grain of the wood floor. She holds her arms up high, crossed at the wrists so her hands are like twin birds rising in flight in front of her. It is a dance she loves, the saltarello, for it moves so easily between earth and sky; gliding, prowling, twirling and skipping, drawing geometric patterns inside and between a dozen dancers. She places them in her mind, marking out her path to come. With a rising shoulder and a grace-

ful, infinitely slow unfolding on one arm in the direction of the imagi-
nary partner to her left, her feet begin to move.

After a while the strains of music end, but she dances on, conjuring
up the bright commands of trombone and drum to control her steps.
She adapts joyfully to the lightness of her dress, moving more freely, her
bowing and twisting exaggerated, her skipping taking her higher off the
floor.

*Yours is the radiance which makes me burn . . . my joy in seeing you is never
done.*

Bembo's words twirl with her, shining like phosphorescence in a
night sea. Her loosely braided hair has come undone and is dancing
with her now. She tosses her head to feel its thick whip across her face.
The other dancers in her mind have all fallen away, yet she continues.

*And to you I look, as heliotrope looks to the sun . . . for each spark of yours
untold Etnas are raging in my breast . . .*

It is not that he does not love her. She knows that. How can one
blame a man whose weapons are words if he chooses to move out of
range of cannon fire? She claps her hands fast, increasing the tempo of
her steps. Whatever pain has passed between them is being washed
away in the dancing. She registers a familiar film of sweat on her skin
and tightness in her calves. She stretches higher and feels the space
under her ribs expand so that with the next breath she seems to lift off
the floor.

Ah. My lady, there are times when I swear you are dancing on air.

Those had been Stilts's words to her in Spoleto. Or was it Gubbio?
The towns and dance floors have all blurred together now. He wasn't
the first to offer such a compliment. When she had danced with her
brother at the Este betrothal celebrations in Rome, the whole of the
Ferrarese entourage had whooped and applauded. She had never been
more unhappy, the memory of Alfonso's body still thick in her blood,
but under her smile no one had noticed, and if she was truthful, for that
moment too she had felt released.

She executes a final energetic series of turns, her breath catching in
her throat, and comes to rest, bringing her hands back to the position

where they started, before executing a deep theatrical curtsy in the direction of an empty chair.

Who else could be sitting there but her father?

He has always been her greatest audience. The greatest and the first. How clearly she remembers the joy of his visits when she was a child: how he would sweep into the house, inviting them to climb all over him as he handed out presents amid gales of laughter. Later, when the boys had yelled and screamed their fill, she would dance for him; spreading her skirts in a wide curtsy before flouncing round the room, her childish face screwed up in concentration at the latest steps she had been taught.

"God has given you golden feet and a swallow's grace," he would say. "But there is one last thing you have yet to learn." And he whispered the word in her ear.

When he had returned a week later, her head was high and her smile was a sunburst directed at any and all who watched her.

"Brava, bravissima. They will be queuing up for your hand in marriage. But I will never let you go."

He had been right about the first, though that had more to do with his becoming pope than with her dance steps. But he had also, in his way, been right about the second.

It will be two years next winter since they said their goodbyes, she riding out in the snow and he rushing from window to window along the Vatican corridor to wave to her. Once this mad contest between Spain and France is decided, perhaps they could arrange a visit. Ferrara would put on a rich show for him: their Pope and their duchess's father. How much she misses him.

The Mantuan viper has been visiting Ferrara, she writes before she goes to bed.

> *But I have not let her fangs pierce my skin. The redecoration of my apartments is almost complete and I am ordering new editions from Manutius's printing press in Venice for my library. The viper is of the opin-*

ion that his prices are too high, but he is the best in the city and her collecting is known to be profligate in other ways. With my full allowance now paid, I have commissioned more music, and the Venetian poet Bembo is enjoying court hospitality as he works on his much anticipated dialogues on the nature of love. With God's help, I intend to build a court here to rival any that Italy has seen. When you come I know it will please you. I pray for you every day and cannot wait until we might be in each other's company again. For though I may be Este in name and proudly hold the title of Duchess of Ferrara, in my heart I remain forever,

Your loving daughter,
Lucrezia Borgia

CHAPTER 42

❖

August, and in Rome it is getting hotter. The Pope and the Vatican court should have been in the country long before now, but who can go anywhere when two armies are at a standoff in the north and the news from the south is that Gaeta can't hold out for more than a few days?

In Alexander's bedchamber, the windows are flung open and he is covered only by his shift, but night brings little respite. He has a cramp in his left leg, his gut is grumbling and his farts are a long way from the scent of orange blossom. The sounds and smells of old men: such things had been repugnant to him when he was young and he feels no differently now. He heaves himself over onto his other side, his stomach collapsing like a small landslip next to him. How did he, who eats less than many thinner men, grow so fat?

Still, he is not the fattest. These days Rome is full of spreading prelates who like nothing more than to sit in front of full plates belching their pleasure for all to hear.

He had dined with some of them only a few days ago, he and Cesare guests of honor at a supper party at the country villa of one of the newly appointed cardinals, Adriano de Corneto. It had been an alfresco banquet, a groaning table underneath a loggia: roast pigs and pastas, rich sauces and sugar and ice statues melting fast in the thick clammy air. All he had been able to think about was going home.

Let us raise our glasses to the greatest family Rome and the Church have ever seen.

The sun had set and the candles been lit, though the heat was still unbearable, when their host had offered up the toast.

He had acknowledged it with a lazy fixed smile, but inside he'd been fuming.

The greatest family Rome and the Church have ever seen. What? They think he doesn't read the insult in such craven flattery?

Sniveling hypocrites, all of them! Fifteen years ago he wouldn't even have warranted a place at this table. If he had the energy he would get up and tell them what he really thought. For years most of you couldn't bring yourselves to say the name Borja without hawking up spit. Yet now we are the greatest family the Church and Rome have ever seen! How stupid do you think we are?

A most memorable toast for a most memorable moment, gentlemen.

Cesare had been on his feet, glass raised high. Alexander had never seen him in such exuberant spirits, wine flowing, food untouched, laughing and talking with anyone and everyone, as if they were all long-lost brothers. He grew tired just looking at him.

As leader general of the papal army and on behalf of our loving pontiff Alexander VI, I offer another toast: To the Borgias and their allies.

"The Borgias and their allies." The words rang out in a chorus of voices.

"What is wrong with you, Father?" Cesare had hissed angrily as the cheers rang out around them. "We are celebrating here."

"What? With these oafs? They're all made of straw. Bought and sold. Bought and sold . . . Not a real man of God among them."

"Well, that's what the Church is, Father. No point shitting on what you've made."

Alexander had glared at him, fury tightening his chest. Father and son. Was this what it had come to: profanity and insolence? He will not stand for it. But in this heat he was suddenly too exhausted to fight.

"Get me a plate of sardines," he growled.

That had been five days ago, and he has not felt well since. Yesterday— the eleventh anniversary of his accession to the holy throne—he had been too tired to mark the occasion. It must be the tension of waiting on Gaeta. There is a joke going round the Vatican (of course he is not supposed to have heard it) that if only they had launched the Pope instead of cannonballs, the city would have fallen immediately. It is the kind of thing he would have laughed at normally—everyone knows him as a man who prefers to be in good humor rather than bad—but instead it had left him depressed and surly. A man who has vanquished so many of his enemies ought to be savoring life more.

He moves his head onto the cool of another pillow. If only Lucrezia were here. She always found something to make him smile. Even after all this time, the missing of her is still a splinter in his soul. Those tight-fisted Este! He has given them a jewel and they treat it like a glass fake. Her last letter had brought tears to his eyes. Of course, she will have a great court of her own, and if her allowance is still not enough he will send her money of his own. No daughter of his will ever have to stoop to ask.

Such a boost it would give him to see her. It had been written into the original marriage contract that they would meet within the year at the shrine of Loreto, but all the fighting and her illness had made that impossible. In which case they will do it next year instead. She will be pregnant by then, for what man could resist such a wife? And how well it will suit her. She had been a beauty when she was carrying Rodrigo.

Just like her mother. He tries to conjure them both up in his mind, but their faces keep dissolving. He has not seen Vannozza for years—though she is surely still a handsome woman. And Lucrezia—well, the only likeness he has of her is in Pinturicchio's fresco in the Hall of the Saints as a young Santa Caterina, and she had been little more than a child then, all puppy fat and earnest shyness. I should never have let her leave me, he thinks. I will ask for a portrait. Though everyone complains that Venice sucks in the best painters, there must be a few artists still worth their salt in Ferrara. Yes, yes, a portrait would help.

But what would help him more is to sleep. Around the four posters of his bed the winter curtains have been replaced by wet sheets that the servants change every few hours in an attempt to keep the temperature down. It works for a while and there are moments when he is almost dozing off, but then he hears the angry drill of mosquito flight. The morning after the banquet his face had been like a pincushion. This summer they are more plentiful and insolent than ever, and there is a limit to the number of smoking pomades that a man can bear in hot weather. He imagines the insects gathering like flying artillery, ready to attack, his body a banquet laid out in front of them, the courses going on forever. He lifts himself farther up the pillows and hears the creak and snort of boards above. Cesare must have company tonight. Such stamina! He used to be the same not so long ago: ruling Christendom in the day with the same energy with which he entered heaven at night.

But these days Alexander doesn't long for women's flesh. Only a cooler place to put his own.

• • •

In the rooms above, Cesare is not between the sheets. He is the soldier not the lover now, and women have become a part of the catering, a dish to be delivered when he feels hungry, then removed as soon as he is finished.

"I shall not be available for a while," Fiammetta had told him as she plaited her hair and fixed it up under her silken hood and cloak before leaving his apartments a few weeks before. "It is hot and I shall be going to the country."

"What if I need you?"

"You don't need me, my lord; you just need a hole to put it in. I can think of a dozen others that would serve you as well. Perhaps when your taste becomes more refined again . . ."

It is not easy for anyone who serves him. As the rest of the world grows slower, stunned by the heat, he is speeding up. By night he works on the business of the Romagna: reading and composing reports for the governors who are overseeing his cities. Administering peace is more time-consuming than waging war, and he has his eye on everything, already impatient for the reply to his dispatch, which they will not receive till the day after tomorrow.

At dawn he still hunts, the morning air briefly wiping clean the headaches that Torella's potions now seem unable to touch, before returning to the military and political reports of the day. He is poised to leave Rome the minute the news he is waiting for arrives. But still Gaeta does not fall. In the worst heat of the day he may lie down for an hour or so, though not to sleep because he is thinking too hard, and then comes the entertainment; a snatched female meal or a banquet, such as the one he and his father attended a few days before, and from there back to the night dispatches. He is like some street juggler, moving twirling torches through the air so fast that they resemble a circle of fire.

Torella watches from the sidelines, hawkeyed. He has seen this manic energy before, during the dark days of the conspiracy in Imola, and while he knows better than to interrupt, he is also wary of letting it continue unchecked. Finally he requests an audience. He is refused, only to be pulled from his bed before dawn the next day with the news that the duke will see him now.

"I wanted to know how you are, my lord," he says, having doused his head into cold water to seem more alert.

"Never better. Can't you see?"

"Except you've not slept for more than a few hours for almost a week. It is not usual for a man. I am wondering how your head is."

"As clear as a bell, even when it chimes too loud. You should be pleased. Your cure has made me twice the man I was. I would let you patent it, only who needs stronger enemies?"

And he laughs, for this is surely the best joke in the world.

"The real question is not why I do not sleep, but why other men sleep so much? Explain it to me if you can. Why are we not awake all the time? We would get so much more done."

"Sleep is a mystery that no one understands, my lord, though there are many who believe that man needs time for dreams, for they seem both to cleanse the mind and to offer us advice and guidance for our own behavior."

"Rubbish. They are a waste of time. Useless! Dreams are useless. Even the word is guilty. Dreams are what men use to comfort themselves when they cannot get what they want. It is my conjecture that the great men of history did without sleep. Ride through Rome in the mornings and you can see it. As the sun comes up behind those columns and temples, look at it all. We're dwarfs compared with them. I tell you, Rome was built not on naps and dreams but on energy, action, war."

So many words from a man who at other times barely speaks. Torella is doing his best not to let his concern show. He glances at the table strewn with papers. "You are indeed busy, my lord. May I ask how it goes in the south?"

"Beh! They lack the appetite for conquest. The cannonballs pound the walls of Gaeta, yet still it doesn't fall."

"That must cause problems for Your Lordship's plans."

"What plans are they, Torella?" he says sharply.

The physician shrugs; everyone knows that the duke's army is half-way to Tuscany poised for attack. "Whatever you feel moved to tell me, my lord."

Another mirthless laugh. "You're a loyal man, and so I shall indeed tell you. King Louis is even now marching south with the excuse of taking Naples, but of course it is really to stop me, for he knows too much of my business thanks to that bastard traitor envoy of ours. So, we must change our plan a little. Yesterday I sent the king a message explaining that my troops are only waiting to meet with his, offering him my undying support in his fight against the Spanish. You're wondering how I will take advantage of this setback? I shall tell you. As we get closer to Naples I will make sure the king pays dearly for my allegiance, or . . ." He pauses. "Or, I will offer my army to the other side. Ha! A brilliant move, yes?"

Torella is now thoroughly alarmed. Not only is the duke talking too much and too fast but he is saying things that can only be secret.

"I tell you, war is like dancing. No, no, not dancing. No. More like jumping from one moving horse to another. I used to do it often, you know. And each time you could see men's faces staring, as if I had defied the gods, for it is something they would never dare to do. But that is exactly the trick, Torella. To dare. To put your hand up underneath Fortune's skirts and play with her till she is dripping for you. What? Does my soldier's language upset the priest in you?"

"No, my lord, not at all. My thought is only . . . well, perhaps I might suggest a palliative for your head, for you may find—"

"There is nothing wrong with my head," he yells. "Though I have aches again in my limbs."

"In your limbs. Which—"

"It is of no importance. The fact is most men are simply weak. Whereas I am forged from metal. You have played your part in that. And you will be well rewarded for it. What is it, Michelotto?" he says, eyes in the back of his head as the door opens behind him.

"The French ambassador is here."

"No one saw him enter?"

"I guided him myself via a side door."

"And my father?"

"Is still in bed. The chaplain says he is sleeping badly."

"No metal in him, see." He grins, dismissing Torella with a wave. "Right, bring him up and let's get this done."

In his room, Torella retreats to his notes, writing fast, his own hand trembling a little: *A sixth day without sleep. Aching limbs. Speech and laugh-ter rapid. Good humor verging on mania and small tremor movements in his hands and feet when he talks, as if he is dancing, but does not seem to notice it. An unexpected manifestation of the pox or some kind of derangement of the brain.* He looks down at the words, then puts a question mark at the end.

CHAPTER 43

❖

*T*he Pope is raving. There is no other way to describe it.

It has come upon him suddenly. He had risen that morning exhausted and despondent, taken a little watered wine and fruit, seen a few envoys, and was dictating a letter to Lucrezia when he was seized by a violent attack of vomiting that lingered long after there was anything left to evacuate. By the time they had got him to his bedchamber, the fever had already descended.

Within the hour the Bishop of Venosa and half a dozen other doctors are everywhere. The papal bedchamber, the apartments, even the doors to the Vatican itself are sealed off.

By the evening he is burning up, crying out that his body is on fire and that he must have more water. But when it arrives he is thrashing so wildly that he knocks the jug out of their hands. They hold him down and apply wet compresses. He has drunk barely a few sips when he starts throwing up again.

"It's a bad month for fat men. I knew it . . . I knew it . . ." he shouts when he finally falls back onto his pillows, his eyes glazed with effort.

Everyone knows what he is referring to: the death of his nephew, the most corpulent Cardinal Juan de Borja Lanzol, felled by the same fever less than a week ago. At the funeral two of the coffin bearers had fainted from the heat—or perhaps it was the weight. Watching the procession pass, Alexander had been noticeably morose.

"Poor Juan. He should have prayed more and eaten less. August is a bad month for fat men."

At that very moment, a young crow, mistaking its flight path in the thick air, had careered in through the open windows, smashing itself frantically against the walls, until it fell flailing like a small black-winged demon at Alexander's feet. There is not a language in Europe that does not fashion such a thing as a harbinger of death.

Summer fever; carried on bad air rising out of the marshlands and sweeping through the city like an invisible fog. All through his seventy-two years, Rodrigo Borgia has watched younger, fitter men drop around him. But this summer has been different right from the start, death cutting down anyone and everyone indiscriminately. As the doctors gather at the end of his bed, the Bishop of Venosa puts into words what they already fear: in all the years he has treated the Pope he has never seen him this ill, and if his fever has not lessened by tomorrow they must bleed him.

The next day they take ten ounces of blood. Near on enough to kill a smaller man. He comes to life while the leeches are drinking their fill, stuck like small black turds on his vast chest. He cries out in horror, trying to pluck them off. Again they have to fasten his hands with straps.

"It is for your own good, Your Holiness."

"For my own good? Good?" He stares up into a circle of worried eyes. "You're bloodsuckers, vultures all of you. If you let me die, I swear, I will be waiting for you in eternity."

"You will not die, Your Holiness," the bishop says cheerfully. "Just let the humors take their course."

"Lucrezia," he mutters as he lies limp when the bleeding is over. "I need Lucrezia. Is there a letter yet? I must have word of her."

"Your letter was dispatched only yesterday, Your Holiness. Any reply will take days."

"And Cesare. Where is Cesare? Send for him now."

The doctors look at each other nervously.

"He . . . the duke is not in the Vatican at the moment, Your Holiness." The bishop speaks for all of them.

"Not in the Vatican. Then where is he?" The Pope rallies enough to be indignant. "Has he gone to join the army without discussing it with me first? I want him brought back now. How dare he!"

There is a small silence.

"Ah, Sweet Mary and all the saints, that boy will be the death of me."

As he closes his eyes it is not clear whether he has heard his own words.

When the leeches are removed, he dozes fitfully for a while. Burchard, who has been waiting outside while the doctors do their best—or worst—is now brought in, in the hope that a familiar face might reassure him.

"How is Your Holiness?" he says gently.

"I tell you, never trust doctors. Their job is to keep you ill so they have employment." He grabs Burchard's clothing, pulling his Master of Ceremonies closer. "My God, Johannes, what has happened to your face? I have told you before you should not smile. It does not suit you."

Everybody laughs a little. Alexander himself even smiles at his own joke as he pumps Burchard's hand. Perhaps the bleeding has worked. Perhaps the worst is passed.

That night he sleeps like the dead, and the next morning the fever seems to have abated. He is recovered enough to sit propped up against a bank of fresh pillows, his jowls reaching down to his neck, his eyes rheumy with age and sickness. He orders one of his chaplains to play a game of cards with him. But he finds it hard to remember when it is his turn and his hands shake as he reaches out to place the card and he is soon dozing off again.

"How do you feel, Holy Father?" the bishop asks gently as he probes for the pontiff's pulse.

"How do you think I feel?" he says irritably. "What is that sound? They are ringing the bells! Why are they ringing the bells? Do they think I am dead?"

"It is the Feast of the Assumption, Holy Father. August fifteenth."

"The Assumption! Ah, yes, yes, Our Blessed Lady enters heaven this very day." He stares up into the ceiling, his eyes glazing over. "This very day . . . yes. See—see how she rises, surrounded by angels. Ah, such beauty! If only my body were so light. How I would like to be with her." And the tears are now pouring from his eyes. "If only she would take me with her."

Even the bishop feels a lump in his throat, for he has never known a churchman who loves the mother of Christ quite as much as Rodrigo Borgia.

Meanwhile outside, Burchard is busy trying to placate a crush of envoys and ambassadors desperate to know what is happening.

"Nothing serious, gentlemen, I assure you. The Pope is simply a little indisposed."

Indisposed. It is the word of the moment. But overused. Most important men who are "indisposed" for longer than three days in Rome are dead by now.

"The Holy Pontiff has the fever, yes?"

"No, no, the doctors say he caught a slight chill when he supped at the cardinal's house last week."

It is not only Burchard's abject inability to lie that is the problem here. The fact is the Pope is not the only one to have reacted badly to the evening. The cardinal himself is stricken with fever. Along with two other guests. This is surely the fault of eating and drinking to excess in such heat. Rome is fast becoming a morgue.

"And Duke Valentine?"

"Is not available right now."

They know that anyway, since any attempt to get into the building has been met by armed guards. But with Cesare Borgia, nothing is ever what it seems. It would suit him to pretend he is in residence when he is not, and they all know the stories of him and his beloved Michelotto racing around the country disguised as a beggar or a holy knight of St. John of Rhodes.

"Is he with his father?"

"Has he left the city?"

"Is he on his way to his troops?"

As the questions fly, Burchard waves his arms as if to show that with the duke anything and everything is possible.

In the rooms above the Pope's apartments, Gaspare Torella is a man sorely tested. Over the years he will ask himself again and again if there was something he missed that night when he offered the garrulous duke a palliative for his head. There had been no sweat, nor chill, nor any sign of fever. Had he been so fixated on the symptoms of his precious disease that he had missed the obvious killer?

As with the Pope, it had hit like a thunderbolt. Michelotto had been dozing in a chair outside early one morning when he heard cries and moans, rushing in to find Cesare fully clothed on the bed, wrapped in linen and blankets, rolling and juddering, teeth chattering uncontrollably, like a madman. For what other kind of person could be so cold in the middle of such heat?

From chills to fever and back again. He is so ill so fast there is no time to rail against fate or doctors. As his temperature soars he shouts and raves, immediately incoherent. They close the windows to muffle the noise, which makes it hotter. Not that he would notice. By the evening his body is a furnace, his forehead so hot that Torella is barely able to hold the back of his hand there. Sweat streams off him, and whatever liquid he takes in he throws it up again. It is almost as if this man of metal is melting.

At the end of the second day, when there is no change, Torella answers the silent question that Michelotto has been asking. "Those who are fittest often get it the worst."

Or perhaps they simply fight it harder, he says to himself. God knows the duke is strong. He has never known anyone stronger. But he has not slept for days or eaten for almost as long. Had the illness already been at work stripping him of his armor? Torella thinks back to Ferrara and Lucrezia's battle the summer before; the way the fever had gulled both her—and them—one moment making her better, the next worse. But there is no sense of play at work here. This feels like business. And the business is death.

Huddled in an antechamber, the Pope's and the duke's doctors meet along with Burchard and a few trusted chamberlains. Father and son stricken at the same time; this cannot, on any account, become public knowledge. But of course it cannot be stopped. Envoys and ambassadors are men with eyes and spies everywhere, and as another new doctor is spotted sneaking in through a side entrance, conclusions draw themselves. Three of the last four popes have died at exactly this time of year. And if Cesare were not dying too, then surely it would be him now controlling the news.

"There is nothing to alarm yourselves about, gentlemen. Both men are on the mend."

Burchard's assurances next morning confirm it. Suddenly there are not enough dispatch riders in Rome to handle the business: Alexander and his son are felled by the fever, with the added whisper that the duke is hit worse than his father.

No one has expected the Pope to live forever.

But Cesare Borgia . . .

What happens if . . . ?

As word filters out past the Vatican gates, the rumors breed like flies. The Borgias are dying of their own venom. That supper party in the country had been a front for them to gather a dozen cardinals and kill them all for their money. But they had made a mistake with the glasses and had drunk most of the poisoned wine themselves. No matter that it had taken so long to have its effect. Such death reflects the cunning nature of Borgia cruelty. Meanwhile, there are others who are more interested in talking up dead crows and the devil, as if it is more than just illness that has taken up residence in the Vatican at this most important moment in history.

• • •

Across the country, another decrepit old ruler is sitting in a city infected with illness. The fever this summer in Ferrara is mild, perhaps because Duke Ercole has his holy nun to intercede for him. Her new convent is almost finished, and he is just back from inspecting the work—what honor it already brings to them all—when the urgent dispatch from his ambassador in Rome arrives. He reads it quickly, greedily, then more slowly, tasting each detail. The Vatican is in lockdown, and while everything is denied, it is clear that both Borgias are fevered nigh unto death.

What with the convent and Isabella's visit, the duke has not spent much time with his daughter-in-law recently. But he has no doubt about the effect such news will have on her. The dispatch is dated almost two days before. Two days. What might already have happened, or be happening at this very moment? The rider had been in relay, picking up the message at the way station outside Bologna. When questioned, he swears he does not know what it contains. Such news always leaks out, despite an unbroken seal, but it will take time. And right now, in Ferrara, Ercole d'Este is the first to know. "Did you," he asks lightly, "pass any dispatch rider for the duchess?" The man shakes his head. With panic in both Vatican households and the outcome so uncertain, it is possible no one has thought to inform her.

As her father-in-law, it's his duty to make sure she knows. And yet, what could she do with such grave tidings, except to grow frantic with worry? Better to wait until there is firm news one way or the other. For if they were both to die . . .

As it happens, she has only just left the city for her country villa and, dutiful as ever, she had come to bid him goodbye before she went. He cannot deny that she is a most courteous young woman. A court like Ferrara needs to inspire men of letters, and she has gone out of her way to make men like Bembo welcome. He's heard only the highest praise for this epic new poem, which he will surely dedicate to the duke himself, as he has hosted his visits for years. If only his own sons might enjoy such a grasp on culture. Instead, he has sired a line of uncouth, lascivious, quarrelsome boys, with the most uncouth of all his eldest, the cannon maker. Still, there is no honor in the young anywhere these days. It is a sign of the times; Italy is consumed by corruption, and what examples do they have except whoring and warring to guide them? The fault for which lies squarely inside the Vatican.

No, he will keep the dispatch to himself until he knows what the future holds. He takes himself to his newly decorated chapel and falls on his knees in rapt prayer, calling on God and all the saints to have mercy on Ferrara and the whole of Christendom and rid them of the scourge and scandal that have taken root in the Holy See, both the father and his violent bastard pup.

The duke is wrong about Lucrezia. A message from Rome has been dispatched and is waiting when she returns. She is in the highest spirits. She has been talking to the duke's newest musician, Josquin des Prez. His first work for the court, a setting of the Fifty-First Psalm, is one of the loveliest pieces of music she has ever heard, and she is eager for him to compose for her musicians too. She had even had an encounter with Bembo, both of them careful, kind with each other, the feeling sweeter if less charged.

And now news from Rome! A letter no doubt from her father, whose reply she has been expecting for some days now. But when she picks it up, it is not his personal crest on the paper but rather that of his doctor, the Bishop of Venosa.

His words scrape out the lining of her stomach with a burning spoon.

Ill but not dead. Both of them. *Ill but not dead.*

She calls for her confessor, closing the door against everyone else. By the time he reaches her, she is hunched on her knees like an ancient nun at prayer. Bembo, Alfonso, Ercole, Ferrara, it has all fallen away.

Ill but not dead. Does God watch and judge a family? Could her own carefree behavior somehow have anything to do with this?

"Father, will you hear my confession?"

Within the hour the household is gathered at vigil in the chapel, a host of young women's voices rising up like the choir of Corpus Domini in deepest intercession for the lives of the Pope and his son Duke Valentine.

During the night that follows, great multitudes of swifts, so high on the wing that they are invisible to the human eye, pass over a dozen cities where by now urgent dispatches have been opened and read, and where prayers are also rising into the air; most of them are tipping the scales away from recovery, toward death and revenge.

CHAPTER 44

❖

*T*he Pope's rally does not last. On the morning of the sixth day, he
begins to lapse in and out of consciousness. A few words pass his
lips, garbled references to orange blossom and his beloved Mary covered
in gold on a throne, but Cesare is no longer mentioned, nor even a
thought for his beloved daughter. Rodrigo Borgia has moved beyond
family.

The Bishop, a second doctor, the papal treasurer and two chamberlains are all that are left in attendance. Most cardinals flee Rome in summer, and any remaining, even Borgia supporters, are too canny to show
their faces. There is some talk about bleeding him again, but no one is
willing to take the risk. Their faces speak their fears. Should Duke Valentine survive his father, they would not want to be accused of causing
him further weakness.

Better now to leave it to God.

. . .

Meanwhile, the man who used to be Cesare Borgia is hovering somewhere between life and death. Torella is close to his wit's end. Four days
of pouring sweat have sucked half the duke's body weight from him. He
lies, mouth open, lips cracked, panting slightly, his skin as dry as it was
once wet, his heart rate that of a man running for his life. At the end of
the bed, Michelotto stands silent sentry, watching, waiting; if death
brings the scythe anywhere near, it will have to cut him down first.

When the fitting starts again, the convulsions lift the duke's body
half off the bed, his arms and legs flailing in all directions like those of a
man in battle with an invisible devil. Torella watches as they struggle to
restrain him. If nothing is done to bring down his temperature, the duke
will be dead before his father. There is one possible way forward. It is a
decision Torella would prefer not to make alone. He approaches Michelotto. There is no one else and no one better.

Michelotto listens, the expression on his fierce scarred face unchang-
ing. "It might kill him."

"Yes," the doctor says immediately. "But this"—he gestures to the
body convulsing on the bed—"this will kill him sooner."

The empty wine barrel is brought up from the cellars, the top sawn
out of it, and a relay of servants start moving buckets of cold water up
the stairs from the pumps. The process is painfully slow, but gradually
the water level rises. Then comes the ice. It takes six men to carry the
hessian-wrapped boulder upstairs, water dripping a dark trail on the
pale stone behind them. Once the mass is uncovered, men get to work
with hammers and chisels, steaming chunks flying everywhere, people
running to collect them with bare hands and throwing them into the
barrel.

If Cesare were conscious, it would be like a man watching the inquisition lay out the tools of torture. But he does not care. On the bed he
lies twitching, eyes closed, breath coming fast like that of a panting dog.
Is this too late? Torella is thinking. Is he already dying?

The barrel is finally close to full. Torella tests it with his hand, holding it deep inside until the count of ten, the pain written on his face.

He gestures to Michelotto. "It's ready. Get him up."

Two other men stand by, but Michelotto pushes them aside. He leans over the bed, holding Cesare's head still between his hands and talking in a low, urgent voice. Does the duke hear him? It barely matters: the intimacy between these two men has always been deeper than words.

Now together, he and the men strip the duke of his few clothes. As they lift him up, Cesare snarls and struggles, then falls back barely conscious. Michelotto heaves the body up and across his shoulders as if the duke was a sack of peat or, already, a corpse. They have dragged a chest next to the barrel for better leverage, and Michelotto clambers upon it until he stands above the water. For a second he seems to hesitate.

"Now." Torella's voice is urgent.

He throws the body off his shoulders into the barrel.

"One, two . . ."

The duke's screams rend the air as his burning flesh hits the icy water.

"Three, four." Torella is counting.

Cesare is thrashing furiously, jolted back into consciousness by the shock.

"Aaaaaaagh. Aaaaagh." The shock and the pain.

"Five, six."

Ice water is everywhere, the duke's cries lost for a second as his head goes under, then comes gasping up for air. The men are exchanging worried glances. Is he going to drown?

"Seven, eight." Torella's voice is shaking. They should get to ten, but he doesn't have the courage.

"Nine. Get him out. Get him out now!"

Michelotto is already there. With the help of the others, he manhandles the duke out of the freezing water, his body rigid, almost catatonic with shock. His skin is mottled purple, his eyes wide and mad, too stunned for pain, too stunned for anything.

"On the bed. Get him covered." Torella is like a general on a battlefield.

Cesare is barely breathing now, the look on his face sheer terror. Maybe those staring eyes are seeing something. Faces of all the men he has killed, or the furnaces of hell. They wrap him round in a bolt of silk, like a great child in swaddling. He is shaking like a mad dog, but when Torella feels the pulse in his neck, it is no longer racing, and after a while the duke drops into what seems like a deep sleep.

Torella would like to remove the wrapping, but he does not want to disturb the healing stillness. Eventually, they unwind him gently; the skin is blistering, and strips of it peel off stuck to the silk. This body, once so perfect that it might have been a model for some newly un-earthed Roman sculpture, is now pitted with the pox and scalded by ice and fire. But he is not dead. Not yet. That is the best that can be said.

As they open the windows to allow in some fresh air, Michelotto hears the sound of men's voices chanting from the floor below. Though Cesare remains unconscious, he does not need the order to be given again. What he must do next has been discussed and decided long ago.

• • •

Though Cesare's screams send shivers through the doctors and priests around the bed, Alexander remains unmoved. Within that huge frame there is now barely a flicker of life. Earlier he had regained conscious-ness enough to mumble a last confession—no place for detail, just a general plea for forgiveness—and received absolution, after which they anointed him with holy oil as the ceremony of extreme unction was conducted over his bed.

Later, the world will be full of stories of this moment: how the chamber had been invaded by seven cavorting demons, poking and prodding the body, reminding him of the pact he had made, selling his soul to the devil to rule Christendom for eleven years, and that now he was four days overdue. And he had screamed and begged for mercy, promising all manner of evil if he could be given just a little more time. More time . . .

But for those who are with him, Rodrigo Borgia's passing is an alto-gether gentle affair. Whatever matters there are to be settled between him and God—or the other—must wait until later. The bishop sits closest, every now and then pressing a damp cloth across the mighty forehead, but the gesture goes unnoticed.

When the day is moving toward its hottest, Rodrigo lets out a small cry and opens his eyes wide, staring up into a ceiling crowded with gilded crests of the Borgia bull that has rampaged its way through Italy. But there is no sign that he recognizes them or anything else, and when his eyelids shut he does not move again.

His breathing now is stuttered and harsh, as if each gasp of air must be fought for, held on to for fear that it will be the last before finally reluctantly released. Silence. Until it starts again. Time passes. Venosa starts the prayers, and their voices meld into a melodious hum, to help the Pope on his way.

When the end comes, it is almost unnoticeable: a final constricted intake of air, held and then exhaled so gently on the longest sigh that it takes time to realize there will not be another. How long must they wait? At last, Venosa raises himself from his knees and, from a silver box by the bed, lifts out a white dove's feather that he holds directly under the Pope's nose, watching carefully as the fronds remain undisturbed in the still air. After what feels like a small lifetime, he takes the feather away and replaces it in the box.

The Borgia Pope, Alexander VI, is dead.

CHAPTER 45

✦

*T*he news is formally announced just after four o'clock in the afternoon.

On the status of the duke there is only a silence as deep as death. Every gate and road out of Rome is now choked with dust from horses' hooves. There will be madness everywhere soon, with every man looking out for himself and some who already have. But there is one notable exception.

Ceremonies: the life of a pope is full of them, complex choreographies of tradition, status, precedence, detail. And after life comes the business of death. The bells of St. Peter's are striking the hour, and Johannes Burchard is deep into his books on the other side of the Vatican, checking and double-checking details he already knows, when he hears footsteps approaching. It is not his role to be there at the passing of the pontiff, and work has kept his mind clear of any thoughts he might have, but for a while he has been aware of a rising level of noise.

"How long ago?" he asks as two armed guards enter, clearly confused and hurried.

"We were told to fetch you only now," one of them mumbles.

"Then you are in breach of papal rules. When a pope dies I should be the first to be informed."

The urgency and speed with which they escort him through the back corridors toward the Borgia apartments increase his anxiety. There is always an element of chaos after the death, even a low level of plundering by the Pope's own household. But nothing has prepared Burchard for what he finds now.

Every room in the papal apartments has been ransacked: chairs, tables, cushions, tapestries, curtains, ornaments of any kind, all gone; the chest where special vestments and papal jewels were kept is overturned and emptied, strongboxes prized open, or missing altogether, silver and gold chalices removed, all manner of sacred objects, anything and everything of value gone! Even the papal throne. The papal throne! Sacrilege as well as anarchy, and not a single culprit in sight.

"Where are the bishop and the chaplains? Where is the papal treasurer?"

And for a man who never raises his voice, it is sword sharp.

"It is an outrage! Who did this?"

The two guards lift their hands in surrender, as if it is impossible that he doesn't know. "The duke's soldiers, my lord."

The Pope had barely been declared dead when Michelotto and his men smashed down the doors, holding a dagger to the treasurer's throat and threatening to slice his head off if he didn't open the chests. Burchard can see the old cleric's eyes popping with terror as he fumbled for the keys. Corruption is a breeder of cowardice. But would he have done any differently with a knife at his bulging vein? He glances nervously upward to the apartments. "And the duke himself?"

They shrug.

"What does that mean?" he snaps.

"No one knows, my lord. They left soon after. All of them. There was a stretcher covered by a sheet but . . ." They trail off.

A sheet for a corpse, or to cover an invalid who no one must recognize? He does not need to ask where they have gone. When a pope dies, the safety of the Vatican palace dies with him. But Castel Sant'Angelo is a fortress with barricades and cannons, and the overhead corridor that leads to it is protected from the outside world. He can still recall the edge of panic as the Pope and his chamberlains had rushed through it when the French army invaded the city ten years before. He has a vision of a clumsy procession: men laden with stolen papal gold and jewels, keeping pace with stretcher bearers, Michelotto, sword drawn, at the back. God will do with them as He sees fit. They are not Burchard's concern anymore.

"And His Holiness's body?" he asks, steadying himself for further horror.

They are only too eager to show him. The bedchamber, like every other room, is denuded and deserted, the air sticky with the sweetening smell of death, but the body at least remains untouched, its only wealth, the rings on his fingers, protected by bulging flesh.

For a moment Burchard is struck dumb. He has seen dead men before, is accustomed to the intangible sense of loss when the soul vacates the body, but this, this somehow is more disturbing. A few sheepish souls are now returning. He rouses himself, barking out orders: pails of water and sponges for the washing and anointing, the ceremonial vestments, prepared and stored long ago in another part of the palace. Once the bier has been delivered, he locks the doors, stationing the soldiers outside.

"If you let in anyone, anyone—" He hesitates. So many threats over so many years. "I will find you a place in my own household if you keep the room secure," he says drily. It is time for the violence to stop.

Inside, the men grunt and swear under their breath as they labor to undress and wash this mountain of dead flesh. Burchard looks on appalled: it is clear that the body is already in rigor mortis, which means the Pope must have died hours ago, lying here alone while the vultures helped themselves to whatever was left. They must move him fast if they are going to move him at all.

Once the body is dressed—pristine white satin robes—Burchard rounds up enough men to push, pull, shift, and heave it onto the bier. Then, under buckling shoulders, they carry it through the apartments to the Hall of the Consistory. How many plots and meetings, feasts and entertainments have these walls witnessed in this last eleven years? For the next few hours the bier will rest here and the Master of Ceremonies will stand sentry over the dead, so that any family, if they so wish, should visit the late Pope. Then the body will be taken to the basilica for a day of public lying in state before burial. This is what ceremony demands and this is how it will be, for he, Burchard, will be there at every stage.

He might have wished for better circumstances, but he is satisfied that all is as it should be now.

He sits alone in a corner of the room reciting prayers for the dead, his eye running over the bier to check the details: the crimson satin cloth that makes up the bed, the flowing robes, the intricate pattern of the antique Persian carpet, which, by tradition, has now been laid over the body.

As the Latin words flow automatically, his mind goes back to that moment when he had first walked in on the newly elected pontiff. His job then too had been to oversee the ceremonial dressing, only Rodrigo Borgia had been too excited to wait. He was already clad in the new silk robes and was leaning over, peering into the surface of a great brass vase, trying to settle the biggest—but on him still small—papal cap onto his tonsured head.

The grin on his face as he turned round had been one of pure joy. He had been so beside himself that for a moment Burchard was terrified he might try to physically embrace him, and so the Master of Ceremonies had fallen to the floor and prostrated himself in order to kiss Alexander's feet. As ceremony demanded.

As ceremony demanded.

And so it has been for the last eleven years.

We have things in common, you know. We are both foreigners. Both from somewhat humble backgrounds—though yours is more humble than mine—

and both masters in our own way: I of the Church in its time of trouble, and you of its rituals and traditions. I always knew we would get on well.

He would not call it *well*. Though some ceremonies were orchestrated correctly, others Burchard had had to invent: marrying the Pope's daughter in the Vatican, inaugurating his bastard son as a cardinal, then uninaugurating him a few years later. Never in the history of the Church . . . And God willing, never again.

And throughout, he had weathered the storms of the Pope's moods: joy, fury, petulance, love, grief. Such grief. If he closes his eyes now he can still hear the endless wailing coming from the pontiff's bedchamber, as if along with a broken heart he was suffering disemboweling as well.

Corrupt, venal, vain, carnal: the man now lying in front in him had been all those things. He had bought his way to power and used the papacy as a war chest to enrich his family and carve a state for his son out of what ought to be papal lands. Never in the history of the Church . . .

And yet, and yet . . .

Burchard sees him sitting alone at the table with a slab of bread and a plate of marinated sardines, a glass of rough Corsican wine in his hand and a smile on his ruddy face, like a peasant back from the fields.

"Here! Taste it, Burchard," he had said once, offering him a fillet in greasy fingers. "The sea's most humble harvest. I think Our Lord might have eaten like this when he and his disciples walked through Galilee. Pope Alexander and Our Lord eating together! Does the idea shock you? I know, I know, I am not a man without stain. But which man is? Would you rather some thin-lipped cleric who never laughed or broke wind? I tell you if della Rovere was in this chair, he would be blasting the world with cold fury. Better someone who smiles as well as rages, eh?"

Giuliano della Rovere. Is that who will come next? Burchard sees again the figure of the cardinal, tall and stringy, marching out of the Sistine Chapel, incandescent with fury when the last vote had gone against him. He would have wrung necks then if he could, one after the other in the same order they had changed their minds. Giuliano della Rovere. There will be no problem with the protocol of ceremonies under his pontificate. Burchard's own life will surely become easier. Only the thought of it now makes him almost distressed, as if he will miss the madness and anxieties of these last years.

He hears again the Pope's booming voice, sees the deep laughter lines decorating his eyes. Even when he was raging, Burchard thinks, he seemed to be enjoying life. It is a trick he himself has never quite mastered. Might he have felt more if the Pope had felt less? He stares at the body on the bed. It seems impossible that all that energy is no more. He calls up his voice again, for the silence in the room is very deep.

When it comes to it, you will oversee my funeral too, yes? I would have no one else.

"You are not to worry, Your Holiness," he says, "I shall see to everything." And he is embarrassed to find he has spoken the words aloud.

He settles himself further into his chair. The Pope is dead and it is his job to keep vigil, not to try to bring him back to life. He starts the recitation of prayers, closing his eyes so that he can concentrate better.

Is it possible he dozes off? He would not like to think so. There is noise somewhere? A small rushing sound. Gone now. The light outside is fading. It is time to move the bier. He takes a sniff of the pomade he has kept next to him, for the smell from the body seems to have grown worse.

He will call the guards after he has done a last check of the vestments.

He starts with the feet, smoothing out the satin beneath the velvet slippers. They are newly made, but they are no longer the right size, for small mounds of flesh, like discolored rising dough, are overflowing the edges. Farther up there is no definition between foot and ankle. He pulls at the hem of the robe to try to cover the distressing sight. The mountain of silk hides the rest of the torso well enough, and it, in turn, is covered by the carpet. As ceremony demands. It would be a fine thing in winter, but in this heat? Still, it cannot be taken off. He moves along the body toward the head, preparing himself for the shock of the grimace he will find there, for the features of a face can go violently rigid at this stage of death. He has attended the lying in state of one dead pope and a good many cardinals, and has trained himself not to be affected by such things.

But Johannes Burchard has never seen anything like this.

The stage of rigor mortis is long past. In its place, the Pope's face appears to have exploded. The flesh is the color of a split plum, with every feature appallingly bloated. Neck and chin have become one, the blown nose has spread into the jowls, while the lips, thick as eels, have forced the mouth open, and the tongue pokes out, livid and fat. From below there comes a slight gurgling sound. Burchard takes an involuntary step back in horror. Rodrigo Borgia is decomposing in front of his eyes. If there were no devils at the deathbed, they have surely crawled inside his body now, speeding its decay as they make him their own. Heaven protect them all!

He moves swiftly down the corridors. "Get guards in here now!" he shouts, his voice trembling. "We must move the bier to the basilica at once!"

Custom demands that the Pope be on show in St. Peter's for a day. But is that possible? And if it is not, what will he do? Must he cut short the lying in state in order to have His Holiness's body buried before it explodes?

Even in death this pope will break every rule.

For the first time in his long life, Johannes Burchard feels defeated. His eyes start to sting as tears form. His vision blurs, and he stops to try to collect himself, but the tears keep on coming. Soon it becomes clear, even to him, that he is crying.

Mourning. It is an essential part of the ceremony that accompanies the death of a pope.

CHAPTER 46

❧

*L*ucrezia is sitting with her ladies over her embroidery, her needle moving in and out of the green stem of a lily, in search of the tranquillity of Corpus Domini. But the set of her face tells another story, and with every footstep or clatter of horses' hooves, she is halfway out of her seat in anticipation.

When the dispatch comes, she reads its contents in the set of the rider's face even as her fingers break the seal. It is in the Bishop of Venosa's own hand, a hurried scrawl before he fled the scene: the language of the priest taking over from the doctor.

She folds the paper carefully, strangely calm. "And my brother?" she asks. "This says nothing of him."

The man shakes his head. The only news is conjecture: that and the story of screaming. But if it is not written, he cannot tell it.

After he has gone she turns to her ladies.

"Our good father and our Holy Pontiff passed peacefully into the hands of Our Redeemer Lord God, on the afternoon of the eighteenth of August," she says, the first tears sliding down her cheeks. "We were at vigil in the chapel here at that very time." She stops to catch her breath. She is trying so hard. "I—I believe our prayers may have soothed his going."

She attempts a smile, but it dissolves as the tears take over. They rush toward her, but she pushes them away.

"Leave me! Leave me be!" she says, almost angrily.

They stand helpless.

"Did you hear me?" she cries out suddenly. "Go to your duties. Put the house into mourning. Close the shutters, cover everything in black and bring me a bolt of the darkest cloth you can find. Go!"

They do as they are bid. When they return she has sunk to the floor and is sitting in a balloon of skirts as the sobs come.

"My lady, please. Don't send us away. Our hearts are broken too," Angela begs.

But Lucrezia will have none of it. She winds the black cloth around her. The fabric is hot and the crying makes it hotter, but she does not care. The Pope, her father, is dead. The man whose arms were always open to her, whose love encircled her like a golden fortress, is gone, and if that is not enough, her brother is dying too. What use her ladies now? They cannot protect her, for they are all abandoned. With each sob she swallows more sorrow until it feels as if her whole body is overflowing. Perhaps she will drown in it. Why not, for what else is there to live for now? Her father and her brother dead. A future without their love. Better to cry forever than face that.

Camilla, who has been with her the longest, looks on from a half closed door. She has seen this disintegration of grief once before, three years ago when her lady's husband Alfonso had been murdered. For days she had sobbed, lying in a shuttered room refusing all nourishment. They had finally tempted her back to life with her baby son. But there is no child here yet, more's the pity. And with no pope to protect her . . .

"Send for Pietro Bembo," she says.

Whatever the risk, the alternative is worse.

. . .

The horse takes longer than the wings of love, and he is not yet fully recovered from his own bout of fever, but they crowd around him when he enters, clasping his hands. "Please. Please. She will listen to you. This way she will make herself ill."

Her crying fills the house. He approaches the door, opening it quietly, his eyes finding her in the gloom, a figure huddled on the floor, rocking to and fro. Oh, but she is consumed by sorrow. A woman's tears: there is nothing, nothing that rends the heart more. The ancients knew it best: Andromache wailing as the body of Hector is dragged through the dirt around Troy; Phaeton's sisters, weeping so much they are turned into willows forever, dipping their fronds into a river of tears. Such is the power of a woman's grief. He must go to her.

He sees himself holding out his hands, taking her into his arms, caressing her hair, kissing away the salt on her cheeks as his own eyes weep for her sorrow. Two lovers melting into each other's tears. And then? What then? He cannot stay. Others will be coming soon enough, and for her sake he cannot be found here. This is not only personal sorrow she is suffering. The Pope's death is the stuff that states and wars are made of. And she will be most vulnerable now, for she has lost the very men who have insured her position in the world.

He has never associated her, this sweet gentle soul, with the stain of Borgia corruption. How could he? But in others' minds the crimes run thick in the blood. Everyone knows how much Duke Ercole loathes the family. How will he look on her now, when both the incentive and the threat are dissolved?

Her crying tears at his heart. He must go to her.

And yet he hesitates. Perhaps she would not thank him for seeing her in such despair, so utterly undone. What if he could not find the right words to bring her back? Women's tears; a man might drown in them.

I will write to her, he thinks. Compose the finest letter, drawn from the connection of our souls and a love deeper than any tears can wash away. And in this way I will also be able to advise her. For when her tears eventually dry, she will need to look out for herself.

He turns from the door and walks quietly out of the house, out of sight of the ladies.

He labors over it long and hard. It is indeed a beautiful, beautiful letter: compassionate, poetic, wise.

Platonic love has its limits.

In town, Alfonso has been pulled from his smelting to talk politics with the duke. A worker had been badly scalded, and he is busy seeing to him when the summons comes. The man's wounds are still on his mind when he enters the ducal salon, to find his father exultant, scribbling at his desk.

"Ah, Alfonso! Such news, yes? This is a great day! A day of honor for Our Lord God and the universal welfare of Christendom. I am writing those same words to King Louis even now. Shall I add something in your name? For we can say what we like now that Satan has taken his own. The word is that it was not fever, but poison. They had set out to murder the new cardinal at the lunch he gave for them, so they could grab his fortune, but they got the glasses mixed and drank it themselves. Ha! And at the end, his bedchamber was filled with devils, dozens of them, tormenting him with pitchforks. Thank the Lord, our prayers have not been in vain."

Yours perhaps, Alfonso thinks, for such ferocious piety has never left much room for anyone else's intercession. "What about Duke Valentine?"

"Nigh unto death and fading fast." Can a man's smile grow any wider? "Even if he survives, without the Pope's money and protection he is nothing. It is over. Finished. Everything he owns will be taken from him."

"Does Lucrezia know?"

Ercole shrugs. "I would think so by now."

"You have sent no message of condolence?"

He shrugs again.

"She will be much affected by this. It will plunge her into mourning."

"Then she will find herself alone," Ercole retorts fiercely. "There will be no black worn in my court. No public mourning of any kind. I have made that clear in my letter to the king. This is God's will. And it comes not before time."

Alfonso drops his eyes. How he hates his father's mean spirit; so many years of praying, yet it has never come close to softening the heart of stone. A man would have needed to be a saint to earn his approval.

"But we must still note her loss. I will go and see her now."

"Then you be careful what you say. Everything is changed by this, Alfonso. Montefeltro will be back in Urbino, the alliance between the children of Mantua and the duke is over, Venice will take whatever of his towns she can—and we may use it too."

"And in what way would we do that, Father?" he asks coolly.

"You need an heir!"

"Lucrezia has already conceived once."

"It died," he says flatly. "And there's no sign of another."

My God, Alfonso thinks, is this an insult to both of them or only to him?

"We are still married."

"Beh! You can always be unmarried. With the right pope it happens often enough."

"I thought Ferrara despised Church corruption, Father," he says, the sarcasm now heavy in his voice.

"Don't lecture me on the Church, Alfonso! Without me this city would be half heathen. Anyway, why should you mind? From what I hear you still spend more time with your whores than with your wife."

No, the injury had been intended for him. Every time he opens his mouth it is to deliver another insult.

"Was there ever a moment when I did not disappoint you, Father?" he mutters under his breath.

"What? What is that?"

"I asked you if you could ever afford to pay back the dowry," he says with no attempt to hide his anger.

Rodrigo Borgia and Ercole d'Este, Pope and duke; both born in the same year, both living through tumultuous times and both growing more intransigent as they move toward death. How might it have been if the fever had been worse in Ferrara this summer? Alfonso is thinking as he leaves the room.

• • •

Lucrezia's cries have not stopped. On the other side of the door, her ladies hover, pale and lost, faces streaked with tears.

"Why is no one with her?"

"She won't have us, my lord. She won't have anyone. She has been locked in there for hours, ever since the news came."

He has ridden straight from the palace with no time to wash or dress himself, the dust of the road now adding to the grime. He takes an offered bowl and wipes a wet cloth over his head and neck. The ladies' faces act as his mirror. Well, it has never been his destiny to comfort women with his looks. His eyes slide past them to the closed door. As to what he will do or say next, he has no idea.

Her keening voice fills the shuttered darkness of the room.

"Lucrezia?" he says tentatively as he moves toward the crumpled heap on the floor. She does not seem to hear him.

"Lucrezia."

He is in front of her now, but though his voice is louder there is still no sign of recognition. He can stand at the mouth of an open furnace for hours without any ill effect, but he has never been able to handle a woman crying. Yet his disgust at his father's lack of pity leaves him no option.

He lowers himself onto the floor, curling his legs to one side awkwardly, until he is on a level with her. He can feel the warmth coming off her even from here. She cannot fail to notice him now.

"I am most sorry for your father's death. It is sad news and I have come to offer my condolences." He waits. "If, if I . . . can be of help to you in this . . ."

She puts some effort now into holding back her cries, succeeding enough to look up at him. He sees her face, hot and swollen ugly by the flood of tears, a trail of mucus running from her nose to her mouth and a mass of wild tangled hair. The black cloth has fallen from her shoulders and her breasts are heaving with the force of her sobs. No sign of refined courtly beauty here. She looks more like a woman of the streets.

"Lucrezia—"

"No, no!" She lifts up her hands in front of her face as if to ward off some threatened violence. "No, go away. Go away, please. Don't look at me. I am undone and not fit to be seen."

"I can't see you anyway," he lies with surprising ease. "It's too dark in here."

At the same time his eye picks out a run of tiles on the floor nearby where the grouting is uneven. The palace was finished fast, another of his father's instant extravaganzas. Such waste. When he has the time . . . And the power . . .

The sobbing has taken her again, rocking her backward and forward. It feels as if her heart must break such pain is she in. How deeply this family feels toward one another, as if they are connected by more than blood. Everyone knows how the Pope wept for days after the murder of his son. At least this grief shows how much you loved him, he thinks. When my father dies I will struggle to find a single tear to mark his going.

Except it seems he may have said the words out loud, because she is looking at him again, more directly now.

"Oh, yes, you are right, I did love him," she says almost angrily. "So much. No one will ever understand. He was not the monster everyone says he was. Not to me. Not ever . . . How could anyone—" And she turns away as the flood breaks through again.

"No, I don't think he was a monster either," he says firmly. "I only met him once. I was barely old enough to tie my own breeches. But he was most gracious to me, spoke highly of Ferrara. He seemed a man happy with his state. The whole of Rome was celebrating, processions, fountains flowing with wine. And you and that fancy Farnese woman were like his handmaidens, such golden beauties both of you. Everyone was amazed. I remember thinking how much I envied my brother Ippolito, to become a cardinal in a city with so many pretty women." He laughs bitterly. "In all my life it's the only time the Church has ever appealed to me."

He wonders if he is telling the truth. Had he really felt those things? Does it matter? Certainly these are the sweetest words he has ever spoken to her. She is staring at him, the tears held back in a series of small snorts. Now she gives a much louder one. The kerchief she has grasped in her hands is soggy with tears. He digs out his own, clean enough except for the usual grime, and hands it to her. She takes it and blows her nose. Such a deeply unpoetic noise. He risks it all now on a single gesture, putting his arm awkwardly around her shoulders. To his astonishment she does not resist. He pulls her a little closer until he is holding her against his chest. She is crying again and her flesh is moist and hot and her smell most particular: the morning's perfume overwhelmed by hours of summer sweat. It makes him feel almost comfortable, for the women he frequents don't bother with sweet smells.

He holds her tighter, his other hand hovering in the air, as if it might complete the circle of the embrace, but in the end he leaves it where it is. It does not seem to matter; she makes no move to pull away. She is weeping a little less now; perhaps it is the way she is crushed to his chest or perhaps there is something strangely familiar for her here too: a reminder of all the times she had been half smothered inside her father's sweaty embrace, his great bulk clutching her to him as if he would never let her go.

No one ever holds her like that. No one.

He lifts his other hand again, and this time it connects, so that she is inside both his arms. Her body sags against his. It is as if she had asked without words and he had heard without listening.

Time passes. He sits, trying to ignore the rising cramp in his leg. No chance of moving it now. No, like being the blast of the furnace, he will stay for as long as it takes to get the work done.

. . .

In the antechamber, the ladies wait, straining their ears to detect any change in her sorrow. Catrinella sits huddled in a corner, her hands half over her ears so she does not have to hear the distress.

Eventually, the door opens and Alfonso comes out, brushing down his clothes and frowning, as if he is somehow embarrassed by his success.

"I think you may go to her now," he says curtly, not directly looking at anyone, for he has never been at ease with these giggling, flirtatious girls.

Outside, he waits on the portico for the groom to deliver his horse.

"My Lord Alfonso?"

He turns to find Catrinella, standing small and upright, in front of him, too close for courtesy.

"I have something to say," she announces loudly, like a defiant child, taking a hurried breath and talking before anyone can stop her. "You should come to her more often at night. That is the only way now."

He stares at her dumbfounded. But by the time he has thought of any response, she has turned and disappeared back into the darkness of the house.

Later, as the stories of the Pope's death grow as rank as his body, Alfonso will think back to his father's talk of devils cavorting with pitchforks and he will see again Catrinella's small fiery blackness and it will make him smile. Such courage. She would not be out of place in his workshop, for they are familiar with the skin tone of devils there.

After he is gone Lucrezia agrees to take a little food but refuses all attempts to be led out of the room, insisting instead on sleeping on the floor, her head on a pillow they bring her, with Catrinella on guard in a corner. With the dawn she lets them bathe and dress her in black, before inspecting the decorations in the house for the mourning. At each stage she falls easily into tears, and she spends hours in the chapel praying. But she is no longer undone.

The composition arrives early from Pietro Bembo. She reads it once, twice, alone, sheds a few more tears, then folds it up and puts it away in the box where she keeps their correspondence, locking it with a small silver key. But she does not return to it, as she has done to so many others of his letters.

Later something else is delivered. It must be from him too, some gift—a book perhaps to help move her mind toward sweeter things, except it is not the right shape for a book. She sends her ladies away—their incessant fussing is more than she can bear—and lets Catrinella unwrap it.

Inside, carefully protected by cloth, is a majolica vase, finely shaped and decorated in green and blue washes: a scene of hunting, a man and woman on horseback chasing something into the undergrowth. The draftsmanship is artless, but there is a certain life to the figures. Whoever painted them knows what it is like to be on horseback.

And with it, a folded piece of paper.

Catrinella waits shyly, slyly, saying nothing. Lucrezia stares at it for a long time.

"It is from my husband," she says at last.

Catrinella nods. "He makes things like this in his workshop," she says casually.

"Does he?"

"That's what they say."

"Who says?"

"Kitchen gossip. One of the women has a son who works with him in the foundry. They all love him, she says, because he has no airs or graces."

Lucrezia's finger traces the figure of the woman on horseback, her fair hair caught up in a net. She is remembering their early hunts around Ferrara: the cold soup of fog and the warm blanket of horseflesh. It is the first time she has ever received something from him that was not part of a preordained ceremony. She is on the edge of tears again.

"Well, we must put it somewhere," she says, distracted.

Catrinella takes it from her hands, sending a fast glance down toward the letter still resting in her lap.

"He asks to visit me tonight. Of course it is impossible. I am in mourning." She frowns. "What?" she says as she realizes the girl is talking.

"I said I think he was moved by your grief, my lady. When he left, I noticed he had tears on his cheeks." For one who was not born into Christianity, she has never quite understood confession—what was there in her life that she needed to confess? But she knows the difference between a venial and a mortal sin. And a lie like this does not, on its own, merit hell. "I think he would have preferred it to have been his own father who'd died. Everyone knows how badly he gets on with him, the pious old goat."

"No! You must not say such things," Lucrezia tells her with sudden ferocity. "Not say them, nor even think them. Especially not now, do you hear me?"

She has not been in such grief that she doesn't see the traps ahead. Her first marriage had been annulled even though everyone knew it had been consummated. With the right pope and with a king behind him, the duke could do whatever he wanted now.

"But my la—"

"Don't you understand, you stupid girl, we are not safe in Ferrara now. Without my father's protection Duke Ercole could easily get rid of me."

"Not if you were with child, he couldn't," Catrinella says bluntly.

Lucrezia stares at her. *With child.* No. If she were with child he would do nothing.

When my father dies I will struggle to find even a single tear to mark his going.

He has shared so few intimate thoughts with her, but one thing she knows without being told: he would not want another marriage. How could he? It would mean leaving his precious foundry, dressing up and sitting through all those interminable ceremonies again. Even if he cared nothing for her he would hate that with a vengeance. She puts her hands over her stomach. This time last year she was nursing a dead baby in her womb. But they would make an army of boys together. He had promised her that, as if, then too, he had really cared.

You must make sure your husband comes to you every night . . . every night. Open your arms to him, make him welcome and never complain when he leaves you.

Her father's advice, delivered in the last bear hug between them, feels like a lifetime ago. *You are a Borgia and deserve to be worshipped— but . . . well, it is how men are.*

Drowning in this river of sorrow, she has not heard him once: but he is back again now, strong and clear in her mind, that rumbling dark voice always as close to laughter as it was to shouting.

You are a Borgia . . .

If Cesare is dead, she is now the only one. Who will hold the family fortune now? There will be no marriage of his baby daughter to Mantua. Even her own son will be cast aside—another stab of pain—though perhaps she might plead to have him come to stay with them. But not yet. To ask for anything, first there must be an heir.

The fate of the family lies in her loins. She will grieve later.

She writes a short note and seals it fast.

"See that this goes at once. And organize supper to be delivered to my room."

Catrinella cannot contain her joy. "Oh, it will be a boy this time, my lady, fine and healthy, I am sure. The first of many."

"You are sure of that, are you?" She cannot help but smile. "Tell me how it is that the most committed virgin in Ferrara knows so much about these things?"

Catrinella shrugs, pursing her mouth so that her lips look like the sweetest pinkest rosebud in the world. She has never been so pleased with herself.

Lucrezia stares at her. *Tears in his eyes.* Had she really seen that?

"I think, Catrinella, that you may be the oldest young woman I have ever known," she says, and she opens her arms toward the girl.

As they embrace, Lucrezia buries her face in the rough frizz of black hair. She thinks back to the image of a child holding her train in the palace of Rome, tongue caught between her teeth in fierce concentration. She remembers the fearful expression as the young girl washed her body after the wedding night, and hears again her tirade against poetry and the fate of Laura and Beatrice.

My father is gone; my brother may be dead, she thinks. But I will not die for lack of love. And neither will I let my family down.

That night, Catrinella lies on her pallet looking up into the darkness.

The noises she hears from inside the bedchamber are familiar ones: rising grunts and pants and little half throttled cries. She has heard such things a number of times: from this same room, or from the basement, where one of the laundry girls brings a boy who has promised to marry her, or in the antechamber, where Angela hides herself with the duke's bastard son. Some women say that it makes their stomachs curdle with envy to hear such sounds, while others claim to feel only relief that it is not them. Lucrezia's voice flutes upward, gasping, stopping, dying away. Now it is his turn. Such a meal he makes of it. Always has done and no doubt always will. It is hard to tell if it is pleasure or pain. No, she has no need of it, whichever one it is. Eventually it is over. She lies still, listening for the door to open and for him to leave. Tonight of all nights she must check to see how her lady is. But there is no noise, except perhaps the quietest mumble of voices. She waits some more. Nothing. Could it be that the duke elect will stay with his wife tonight?

She curls in on herself like a small animal ready for sleep. How long before they are duke and duchess together, governing Ferrara with a string of children at their feet? Because even the most cantankerous old men must die eventually. Birth, coupling, death. The more she thinks about it, the more it seems that that is all there is: a wheel turning over and over, moving so fast that sometimes you cannot even make out the spokes. It is a wonder there is any room for poetry.

TEN YEARS LATER

Wishing to present myself to Your Magnificence with a token of my deepest respect . . . I have found among my possessions nothing that I value higher than my knowledge of the deeds of great men . . . a knowledge acquired through my long experience of modern affairs and a lifelong study of ancient times.

—Niccolò Machiavelli,
The Prince,
1513

Epilogue

*W*hen evening comes, Niccolò Machiavelli puts on a clean undershirt and a velvet tunic, deep burgundy, with embroidered sleeves. It had been made for him at great expense—the cloth alone cost four and a half ducats—while he was on an embassy to the emperor Maximilian in Germany some years before, and though the nap has worn thin in places, it is barely noticeable in lamplight and it pleases him to be well dressed when he is in esteemed company.

He has spent the day, as he does most days now, in country matters: walking his small estate, catching thrushes, discussing the price of firewood, reading poetry and playing tic-tac at the local tavern across from the farmhouse, but as the sun sets he returns to eat with his family; such joyful chaos the children bring. Then, when they are in bed—more often than not Marietta falls asleep settling the sickly new baby—he takes the lamp and makes his way to his study. A stone sink carved out of the wall nearby marks where visitors once washed their hands for dinner, but a man in political exile hosts no suppers, and these days he uses it only to clean the ink stains from his fingers.

Not that he is lonely. Not at this moment certainly; for once he is settled at his desk, his precious books lined up like a cohort of soldiers in front of him, the room will start to fill with ghosts, men summoned from history to help him in the composition of a short treatise on the government of principalities and the skills needed in a prince to be a secure and prudent ruler.

He plans to dedicate the work to Lorenzo de' Medici, the new ruler of Florence since the fall of the republic last year, in the hope—though hope is in short supply in his life these days—that it may find favor enough to get him back into government, the Eden from which he has been so violently ejected.

Alexander the Great; King Darius; Spartan, Greek and Roman generals; emperors and philosophers, they have all visited him during this long summer and autumn, their exploits, successes and failures placed alongside those of figures of recent history; kings, popes, dukes and the power blocks of Italian families and factions. For though the past has long been his teacher, it is Niccolò's intention in his book to illuminate the present and parlous state of Italy: the work of a diplomat whose career in politics and observations of power have given him a great many "opinions" of his own.

Tonight he is working on a chapter about the place of fortune in men's lives. How far she, Lady Fortuna—for throughout history she has always been a she—can be seduced or resisted. How, like many women, she seems to respond best to rough handling from energetic young men. But how she can also turn against them, and that when she does, it is like a tumult of nature, a river in such full spate that it breaks everything in its path, for a man's essential character makes it hard for him to adapt or change his stroke and so he often drowns in the flood. Such ideas and images have been percolating within him for many years. The irony is that now, at the age of forty-four, Niccolò Machiavelli can bear painful personal witness to fortune's power.

His own fall had been as brutal and undeserved as the torture inflicted upon him in Florence's Bargello prison: the strappado, the same device they used on Savonarola, a wooden crane that hoists a man high into the air by his wrists, only to drop him so violently that his arms are half torn from their sockets.

From the moment the aging della Rovere Pope had turned his snarling, warring face directly against the French and her allies, fomenting Medici opposition inside Florence, the fall of the republic had been predictable. Not even Michelangelo's herculean statue of David, which amid much civic celebration had replaced Judith on the plinth outside the Palazzo della Signoria, could help stem the tide and a year ago this November Niccolò had found himself dismissed from government. His closeness to Gonfaloniere Soderini would always have compromised him in the eyes of the next administration, but who but Lady Fortuna could have known that his name would be found on a scrap of paper in the pocket of a man arrested as a conspirator against the new Medici state? He had been entirely innocent. But that did not stop them from inflicting six drops of strappado to make him confess. *No man knows how strong he will be until he is tested.* Two of the convicted conspirators had gone to their deaths while he sat in a cell that stank of his own despair, the walls alive with lice as big as butterflies. His silence under torture and the lack of any other scrap of evidence had saved him. But it has done nothing for the recurring ache in his soul when he contemplates his future.

At least such blows of misfortune put him in interesting company, and tonight he will again spend some hours with that most complex of characters, Cesare Borgia.

It is not the first time the two have met here in this room. Though the duke himself is long dead (killed six years ago in a skirmish in Spain, where he spent the last years of his life as a prisoner), there are many things about his astonishing flight toward the sun that mark him out as a most effective prince.

There will be those who will find Niccolò's admiration startling, for in recent years the Borgias' name has grown even blacker, dragged deeper into the mud by the enemies who survived them. But the pain in his shoulders is its own reminder—should he need it—that history is only and always the story of human nature in action, and that in an imperfect world, men who set out to make their mark must work with what is, rather than what one might like it to be. And judged against this backdrop in an Italy riven with violence, factions and foreign invaders, it is his belief that Duke Valentine was, for a time at least, a remarkable player, a warrior and a prince who combined the strength of the lion with the cunning of the fox.

Tonight, however, the encounter between them will take a different tone. For in the greatest test of all, when Lady Fortuna had turned her capricious face against him, Cesare Borgia had not fared well at all.

◆ ◆ ◆

I tell you, I had given attention to everything that might happen in the case of my father's death; had prepared for all of it, except this one thing: that I myself would be brought nigh unto death at the same time.

How clearly he remembers the duke's words from their first meeting in Rome. It was October 1503 and the eve of the papal conclave following the Pope's death. What a time that had been. He had left behind him a wife and his new baby son (*he is white as snow but his head is like black velvet and he is hairy just like you and so he seems beautiful to me, though he fills the whole house with noise*) and was heading for the city of his dreams. Yet, there had been no chance to savor it, such was the mayhem and violence everywhere. The Borgia duke and his bodyguard of men were holed up in Castel Sant'Angelo, while armed gangs of the Orsini and the Colonna stalked the streets, searching out anyone with a sniff of Borgia loyalty to skewer on their swords.

They had not seen each other since the campaign of Sinigaglia, and Niccolò barely recognized the man who sat in front of him. Half dead with the fever, that was what everyone said. Looking at him, he would have put it closer to three quarters, for this most manly of figures had been quite eaten away. The full-length robe worn to disguise his gauntness only showed it up further. His head seemed too big for his body, his hair and beard were wild and his skin waxy yellow, eyes dull in sunken sockets. The most handsome, the most feared man in Italy. Where was he now?

"Signor Smile." His voice had been breathy, as if his lungs could no longer pull in enough air. "You're surprised to find me thus, yes? It is not often a man rises from the grave to fight again, but I am proof it can be done. Did you pass the Spanish cardinals on your way in? No? They are here all the time, eager to find out how I would have them vote, for in this papal election there is no greater kingmaker than I."

Except Niccolò's briefing the night before, from Florence's own Cardinal Soderini, had told a different story. While the duke might not yet be utterly defeated—he still had troops outside Rome and a war chest plundered from the papal apartments—he had no cards left to play. Half of his cities in the Romagna had been retaken by Venice, drawn like a vulture to the smell of carrion, and those cardinals whose votes he did control—seven, eight at most—were all Spaniards, and like the French could have no ambition for themselves.

After a decade of invasions and wars, neither the Church nor Italy would stomach another foreign pope. Which left the Italians. And out of them, just one had the requisite purse and ruthlessness to take the crown. Giuliano della Rovere needed only a handful of extra votes to turn the tide his way. And he'd waited too long for this moment to let a weakened Cesare Borgia stand in his way.

"He can't do it without me, but I tell you, I do not sell myself cheap. In return for my cardinals' votes, della Rovere has promised to confirm me as the captain general of the papal forces and guarantee the security of my cities in the Romagna. A fair deal, wouldn't you say?"

Niccolò had been so stunned he had found it hard to reply. What man in his right mind would keep such a promise against a sworn enemy once he had the prize in his hands? Cesare Borgia would not have done it, that was for sure. Not now, not once, not ever. In which case, how could he possibly believe it of another?

"What, Signor Smile? No thoughts on this? Perhaps you think I cannot win back my states? Give me six weeks and even half my men, and they will be mine again. Della Rovere needs a warrior to push back the Venetians, and he knows there is no better one than me."

No man in his right mind . . .

As he listened, Niccolò had noted the sweat building on the duke's forehead. Raving for six days. That is what all the dispatches had said. Six days of boiling blood before his doctor finally saved his life by plunging him into iced water. Violence to defeat violence. Had it been the fever or the cure that curdled his senses most? Or could this be the impact of fortune's blows on a mind not accustomed to losing?

It was the shortest conclave in Church history. The next day the doors of the Sistine Chapel had barely been locked before they were opened again and Giuliano della Rovere walked out as Pope Julius II. Since Castel Sant'Angelo was now his official property, his first action was to offer the duke visitors' rooms in the Vatican. With the Orsini still on the streets, where else could he go? But was he a guest or a prisoner?

As order returned to the city, Niccolò had spent his days jostling with Venetian envoys in the Vatican waiting rooms, both cities falling over themselves to convince the new pontiff of their undying loyalty.

That first meeting had made his spine tingle. Tall and string thin, with snow white hair and beard, the della Rovere Pope sat stooped on his throne, head to one side like a brooding eagle, eyes cold as flint. The gossip was that he was prone to fits of rage, exploding out of nowhere like spirits thrown onto a fire. You would not want to be in the room with him then. There was not a hint of compassion in this man. No one in his right mind would expect him to keep a promise that went against his own interests.

When he was not in waiting rooms, he was out gleaning information or composing epic dispatches home. The councils of Florence needed to know anything and everything, and it was his job to make sense of a whole new landscape of power. So when a few weeks later Cesare Borgia had issued an invitation for him to visit, the fact that he was having to do the asking was its own sign of weakness.

On his way in, Niccolò had passed a man in priest's dress coming out, too wrapped up in his own thoughts to greet him. He had thought then that it must be the duke's doctor, for his had never been a household to set any score by God.

Inside, Borgia greeted him with a body hug—a crush of bones as much as flesh—and a torrent of talk: how Florence had always been his greatest friend. Unless of course she was again his enemy. That this Pope was a slimy one, for there was no sign of confirmation of his office, and with each passing day the wolves howled at the gates of yet another of his towns.

"I should be out leading an army, but how can I leave Rome now? What news do you hear on the matter? Nothing? Are you sure? Well, never mind. I have another, better plan now, which is why I have brought you here."

At the back of the room Michelotto stood sentry as always. A few times Niccolò had tried to catch his eye, but his gaze was fixed on the floor. He must know. How could he not?

Another plan. Niccolò could barely believe his ears.

In return for safe passage for him and his men into Tuscany, the duke would become Florence's protector, which she needed now since Venice was a hyena and the King of France's days were numbered, for this new Pope held a grudge against everyone. Italy would come to rue his election and only he, Cesare, could save the day. How quickly could Niccolò guarantee his safe passage, for there was no time to lose.

Thinking back on it ten years later, Niccolò can still remember the mix of pity and excitement he had felt as he wrote that night's dispatch, describing an inconstant, irresolute man whose fortunes were moving from bad to worse; this once consummate strategist who would never tell a soul what he might be thinking was now shouting to everyone about things he could not possibly achieve.

What had Biagio once said to him? *Your beloved Valentine.* Had Niccolò misjudged his character totally, or was this what happened when a man was overwhelmed by fortune?

Niccolò had known Florence would refuse safe passage, but he had told the councils plainly that he thought the duke would send his men anyway and so they should be on the lookout. Two weeks later, a Florentine force had captured Valentine's soldiers, arms and baggage, along with the prize catch of Michelotto himself.

Inch by inch Cesare Borgia was slipping into his grave.

Beautifully put, Biagio had told him later over a stoop of wine, though the image had given him no pleasure.

In his study, Niccolò leans back in his chair. As so often happens, his thoughts have wandered. His fingers are cramped from his grip on the quill, and his damaged right shoulder is growling in memory of the strappado, as it does more often now the weather has turned cold. History; everyone builds up their own. And this, until now, has been his.

The fire in the grate is almost out. If it were summer he might go now and sit on the stone terrace that looks north toward Florence and wait for the dawn, for it can be a lovely sight, the color returning to the land, a mixture of God's wonder and Lucretius's pulsating, all-encompassing nature. During the first months of his exile, such beauty had acted as balm on his soul. With autumn and the denuding of the trees, he had discovered that in a certain spot, over to the right, he can just make out the top of Brunelleschi's great dome rising from the valley floor six or seven miles away: a small distance, but a long journey for him now. He chooses not to look for it anymore, for it reminds him of everything that he has lost.

There will be no place in his little book for the end of the duke's story, for it is too protracted and bitter: how Pope Julius had reeled him in on a long line—promising, cajoling, threatening and finally imprisoning him. Any dream of a Borgia state in the Romagna was long dead, and the Pope was one of many waiting to pick up the pieces, but there had been a few cities that had stayed loyal in memory of fair government, refusing to open their gates to anyone without the agreed password.

In the end, Cesare Borgia had given Julius the magic words in return for his freedom. Except that there was nowhere in Italy that would have him, and when at last he fled to Naples on the promise of safe haven from the Spanish commander, he was betrayed by an arrangement between the Pope and the Spanish monarchy. He had been shipped to Valencia, arriving as a prisoner at the same port from where his father had so optimistically departed for Italy half a century before. A family come full circle.

He died making an escape attempt from the last of his many jails. Those who witnessed it spoke of a suicide rather than a battle, a man charging straight out into a line of soldiers, cut down before he killed even one of them. Niccolò had been in the field inspecting local troops when the news had come. A Florentine militia! His greatest ambition had become a reality, though even then he could see how a part-time army brought with it its own problems. At first, he had felt very little—in his heart Cesare had been dead for a long time—but in the coming days memories flooded back: the magnificence of the taking of Urbino, the sly triumph of Sinigaglia, the compulsive, almost violent charm of a man with no illusions about greed and fickleness, who thought he could never lose. If Cesare was here now, his mind clear again, what conversations they might have about the strategy of soldiering.

No, whatever the indignity of his final years, the duke's passing had been something to be mourned. Niccolò would have been the only one to do so, except of course for his sister, Lucrezia, who according to the envoys from Ferrara, took the news very badly indeed.

Lucrezia Borgia-d'Este. Though their paths had never crossed, Niccolò has followed her fortunes with interest. After the death of Duke Ercole, she and her husband had forged a strong partnership as the winds of war brought first the Venetians, and then the forces of the choleric Pope himself, down upon Ferrara. She gave the Este family the heirs they needed, and when Duke Alfonso was away fighting for their state's survival, she ran the government in his stead, playing host to diplomats, overseeing civil justice and bravely keeping up the appearance of a humanist court, even when the sound of the cannons could be heard in the distance. There was gossip, of course: that she had once had a passionate affair with her own brother-in-law, the ruler of Mantua. If that were true, their mutual positions of power had kept them safe, though it would no doubt have enraged his wife, the Marchesa Isabella, for it was common knowledge the two women had never got on.

Borgia blood. It seems it runs strongly in her veins too, and though her sons and daughters would be d'Estes, they will carry a line of Borgia blood with them into history. It is all that is left of a family that was once poised to take half of Italy.

Niccolò closes his notebook and cleans his pen. When he finishes this work of his—and it will not be long now—there will be nothing to write but letters. Better to eke it out a little longer. He already knows how it will end. A final chapter with some judicious hyperbole and deference is called for: a call to arms for a new prince to free Italy from her invaders and take the country into a new golden age. Who better suited for the job than the new Medici ruler of Florence, a man from a family that has already tasted greatness? If Biagio were here, he would no doubt mock him for such toadying, but it is only a necessary veneer of flattery, another example of how man's nature, for good and ill, lies at the wellspring of politics.

And because he has leaned so heavily on the lessons of history, Niccolò will leave the last words to the past: the voice of the fourteenth-century Tuscan poet Petrarch looking back to the glory days of Imperial Rome:

> *Prowess shall take up arms*
> *Against brutality, and the battle will be swift;*
> *For ancient Roman bravery*
> *Is not yet dead in Italian hearts.*

The sentiment is more optimistic than he feels, but sometimes it is necessary for a man to dissemble in pursuit of the best end. He still has a few friends on the edges of power. If they can help get his work noticed, then surely it might act as his calling card back into government. For what would his life be like without it?

Historical Note

The last five novels I have written have been the fruit of a double passion: for history and for storytelling. I first encountered the power of the past by reading historical fiction as a teenager. It lit a fire in me that took me away from fiction and into serious historical study, and by the time I left university I was convinced that no novel (or certainly not one that I could write) could do justice to the complexities, nuance and depth of the process of history.

When I returned to challenge my conviction sixteen years ago, it was the Italian renaissance and its profound impact on Western culture, politics, religion and art that propelled me. Being a child of my age, I was also fascinated to find out what, under a roll call of famous men, might have been the experiences and achievements of women. The stories that my research threw up, much of it the work of recent scholars, gave me vibrant material for a trilogy of novels, whose plots were fiction, but whose characters, along with the texture, experiences and details of their lives, were rooted in historical fact.

In 2010, I turned my attention to the Borgias. Here was the biggest challenge of all. In the 1490s, this Spanish family, led by Pope Alexander VI, set out to found a dynasty and a new power block in a fragmented Italy. Their methods were often corrupt and brutal, much like the society they lived in. As foreigners they were insulted and reviled, and when their ambitions failed, the historians who followed them continued the

process of deceit. I wanted to set the record straight, most especially
with regard to the character of Lucrezia, who, over the centuries
through novels, operas, films and multiple television series, has become
a symbol of a villainous vamp and guilty of incest, and lust, intrigue,
murder and poison.

In the Name of the Family, like *Blood and Beauty* before it, sets out to
tell the truth—or at least as much of it as we know—about this colorful
family; from the political manipulations of the Pope to his love of sardines and the Virgin Mary; from the volatile brilliance of Cesare Borgia
to his battle with the pox and his near demise in a barrel of icy water;
from Lucrezia's arguments with her father-in-law over money to the
words *I am dead*, which she is reported to have said during her illness.
Firsthand sources are woven everywhere into the story, gleaned from
ambassadors' reports, the diaries of Johannes Burchard, the surviving
correspondence between Pietro Bembo and Lucrezia, the many letters
of Isabella d'Este, and the penetrating dispatches and writings of Niccolò Machiavelli, whose experiences as a diplomat during these years
helped inform his views on human nature and his works on political
philosophy. (This extraordinary man never did get his job back. But his
misfortune was history's gain since it gave him the time and the impetus
to continue writing, not only about history and politics, but also two
comic, bawdy and illuminating plays.)

In all these cases I am beholden to the various translators and scholars whose work I used, all noted in the bibliography, but especially
Deanna Shemek, professor of literature at the University of California,
who allowed me to quote from a new translation of a selection of Isabella's letters before the volume is published.

These then were my sources. There are, however, a few places where
the demands of storytelling won out over what we know from history.
Not every letter quoted in this novel is verbatim (not every piece of correspondence survived), though the events or feelings that they describe
are rooted in fact. At a more serious level, I have taken liberties with the
following:

We have no direct proof that Lucrezia Borgia suffered from syphilis (the correspondence between the convent Corpus Domini and Gaspare Torella is entirely my fiction), but there is clear documentation that Alfonso contracted the disease in 1496–1497. His marriage to Lucrezia took place when he would still have been infectious, and her stillbirths, illnesses and early death at the age of thirty-nine during childbirth all suggest that she too had fallen victim to it. Whether she had any suspicion of this we will never know. The disease was young and mutating, doctors were reeling from its impact, and, from the evidence we have, they were much more concerned about its effect on men than women.

After Pope Alexander VI died in August 1503, there was a brief interregnum pope (ailing and old, Pope Pius III lasted only twenty-two days), while the power vacuum in Rome sorted itself out. It seemed just too confusing to include all the machinations surrounding that conclave, so I have left it out. I have also changed the timing of the birth of Niccolò's son, described in the letter from his wife. This is the only direct example we have of Marietta Machiavelli's voice, and it is so immediately engaging that one can feel her character shining out from it.

Finally, while Machiavelli's dispatches and letters are compelling reading, I have taken the liberty of giving him one observation: "The conspirators have taken a dose of slow acting poison." That actually belonged to the Venetian ambassador to the Vatican, Antonio Guistinian. It seemed just too good to miss.

All these "mistakes" are deliberate. There will be others, I am sure, that are not, for which I apologize in advance.

I leave you with one last historical fact. Though the Borgia project effectively ended with Alexander's death, the family does deliver one final famous figure—the pope's Spanish great-grandson, St. Francis Borgia, who became head of the Jesuit order and was canonized soon after his death. A Borgia saint. Perhaps the reason I remain intoxicated by history is that it so often trumps anything a novelist's imagination could come up with.

Acknowledgments

Books take years to write and help comes in many different forms.

I owe a debt to Vicky Avery, curator of Renaissance Bronzes at the Fitzwilliam Museum in Cambridge, who helped me with sixteenth-century foundries, the properties of bronze and the forging of cannons (as well as letting me into the museum storeroom to get my hands on a few stilettos and swords).

As already mentioned, a special thanks goes to Deanna Shemek for the translations of Isabella d'Este's letters. To musicologist professor Lauri Stras for her expertise on the court of Ercole d'Este, and alerting me to the arrival of Josquin des Pres just in time for him to make his way into the text. To the professor and historian Lauro Martines for conversations on the nature of the Florentine state, and to professor Kate Lowe, who I can confidently say knows more about Bishop/Cardinal Francesco Soderini than anyone else in the world.

Karen Gelmon and Eileen Horne were astute readers of early drafts, and Tim Demetris, while trying to finish a PhD in fifteenth-century papal politics, did a detailed reading of the text, pointing out numerous small mistakes, as did James M. Bradburne, director of the Pinacoteca di Brera gallery in Milan.

My agent, Clare Alexander, was with me every step of the way, most especially when the going got rough, and Lennie Goodings in London, Iris Tupholme in Toronto, and Susan Kamil in New York were creative, committed editors. If I ever bared my teeth at them it was only because we all cared equally intensely about the novel I was writing.

And, finally, of course, there is my companion, Anthony, a man who knows more about the Borgias than was ever his intention, but who kept me as sane and as happy as it is possible for a writer to be.

Sarah Dunant

Florence

August 2016

Bibliography

For translations of the original Italian I am grateful to:

Shankland, Hugh, *The Prettiest Love Letters in the World: Letters Between Lucrezia Borgia and Pietro Bembo 1503 to 1519* (London: Collins Harvill, 1990).

Shemek, Deanna, *Isabella d'Este, Selected Letters* (Academic Press and Arizona Center for Medieval and Renaissance Studies, 2017).

The following works were important in my research, and are recommended for those who would like to dig deeper into this fascinating time of history:

Arrizabalaga, Jon, John Henderson and Roger French, *The Great Pox: The French Disease in Renaissance Europe* (New Haven: Yale University Press, 1997).

Bellonci, Maria, *Lucrezia Borgia* (Phoenix: Phoenix Press, 2003).

Black, Robert, *Machiavelli* (New York: Routledge, 2013).

Bobbitt, Philip, *The Garments of Court and Palace: Machiavelli and the World That He Made* (New York: Grove Press, 2013).

Bradford, Sarah, *Cesare Borgia: His Life and Times* (London: Weidenfeld & Nicolson, 1976).

————, *Lucrezia Borgia: Life, Love, and Death in Renaissance Italy* (New York: Viking Press, 2004).

Brown, Kevin, *The Pox: The Life and Near Death of a Very Social Disease* (Stroud: Sutton Publishing, 2006).

Burchard, Johann, ed. and trans. by Geoffrey Parker, *At the Court of the Borgia* (London: Folio Society, 1963).

Cartwright, Julia, *Isabella d'Este, Marchioness of Mantua* (New York: AMS Press, 1974).

Castiglione, Baldassare, trans., and George Bull, *The Book of the Courtier* (New York: Penguin, 1967).

Chamberlin, E. R., *The Fall of the House of Borgia* (New York: The Dial Press, 1974).

Chambers, David. "Papal Conclaves and Prophetic Mystery in the Sistine Chapel." *Journal of the Warburg and Courtauld Institutes* (1978).

Cummins, J. S. "Pox and Paranoia in Renaissance Europe." *History Today* (1988).

De Grazia, Sebastian, *Machiavelli in Hell* (New York: Vintage, 1994).

Gilbert, Allan, trans. and ed., *The Letters of Machiavelli* (Chicago: University of Chicago Press, 1988).

Greenblatt, Stephen, *The Swerve: How the Renaissance Began* (London: Bodley Head, 2011).

Gregorovius, Ferdinand, trans. by J. L. Garner, *Lucrezia Borgia* (London: John Murray, 1908).

Grendler, Paul F., *Schooling in Renaissance Italy: Literacy and Learning, 1300–1600* (Baltimore: Johns Hopkins University Press, 1989).

Kidwell, Carol, *Pietro Bembo: Lover, Linguist, Cardinal* (Montreal: McGill-Queens University Press, 2004).

Lev, Elizabeth, *The Tigress of Forlì: Renaissance Italy's Most Courageous and Notorious Countess, Caterina Riario Sforza de' Medici* (New York: Houghton Mifflin Harcourt, 2011).

Lowe, K. J. P., *Church and Politics in Renaissance Italy: The Life and Career of Cardinal Francesco Soderini, 1453–1524* (Cambridge: Cambridge University Press, 1993).

Machiavelli, Niccolò, *The Art of War* (Mineola: Dover Publications, 2006).

————, *The Prince* (Chicago: University of Chicago Press, 1998).

————, *The Discourses* (New York: Penguin Classics, 2003).

Majanlahti, Anthony, *The Families Who Made Rome: A History and a Guide* (London: Chatto & Windus, 2005).

Mallett, Michael, *The Borgias: The Rise and Fall of a Renaissance Dynasty* (Chicago: Academy Chicago, 1987).

Marek, George R., *The Bed and the Throne: The Life of Isabella d'Este* (New York: Harper and Row, 1976).

Nicholl, Charles, *Leonardo da Vinci: Flights of the Mind* (New York: Penguin, 2004).

Partner, Peter. "Papal Financial Policy in the Renaissance and Counter-Reformation." *Past and Present* (1980).

Pastor, Ludwig, *The History of the Popes from the Close of the Middle Ages* (London: Kegan Paul, Trench, Trubner and Co., 1899–1908).

Pitkin, Hanna, *Fortune Is a Woman: Gender and Politics in the Thought of Niccolò Machiavelli* (Oakland: University of California Press, 1984).

Pizzagalli, Daniele, *La signora del Rinascimento: Vita e splendori di Isabella d'Este alla corte di Mantova* (Milano: Bur Saggi, 2013).

Ray, Meredith K., *Daughters of Alchemy: Women and Scientific Culture in Early Modern Italy* (Cambridge: Harvard University Press, 2015).

Ridolfi, Roberto, trans. by Cecil Grayson, *Life of Niccolò Machiavelli* (Chicago: University of Chicago Press, 1963).

Rolfe, Frederick (Baron Corvo), *A History of the Borgias* (New York: Modern Library, 1931).

Roo, Peter de, *Material for a History of Pope Alexander VI: His Relatives and His Time* (Spain: Desclee, De Brouwer, 1924).

Rowland, Ingrid D., *The Culture of the High Renaissance: Ancients and Moderns in Sixteenth-Century Rome* (Cambridge: Cambridge University Press, 1998).

Ruggiero, Guido, *Machiavelli in Love: Sex, Self, and Society in the Italian Renaissance* (Baltimore: Johns Hopkins University Press, 2010).

Sabatini, Rafael, *The Life of Cesare Borgia: A History and Some Criticisms* (London: Stanley Paul & Co., 1926).

Setton, Kenneth M., *The Papacy and the Levant, 1204–1571* (Philadelphia: American Philosophical Society, 1976).

Shaw, Christine, *Julius II: The Warrior Pope* (Hoboken: Blackwell, 1993).

Stinger, Charles L., *The Renaissance in Rome* (Bloomington: Indiana University Press, 1998).

Taylor, F. L., *The Art of War in Italy, 1494–1529* (Cambridge: Cambridge University Press, 1924).

Tuohy, Thomas, *Herculean Ferrara: Ercole d'Este and the Invention of a Ducal Capital* (Cambridge: Cambridge University Press, 1996).

Viroli, Maurizi, trans. by Antony Shugaar, *Niccolò's Smile: A Biography of Machiavelli* (New York: I. B. Tauris and Co. Ltd., 2000).

About the Author

SARAH DUNANT is the author of the international bestsellers *The Birth of Venus, In the Company of Courtesans, Sacred Hearts,* and *Blood and Beauty,* which have received major acclaim on both sides of the Atlantic. Her earlier novels include three Hannah Wolfe crime thrillers, as well as *Snowstorms in a Hot Climate, Transgressions,* and *Mapping the Edge.* She has two daughters and lives in London and Florence.

sarahdunant.com
Facebook.com/SarahDunantAuthor
@sarahdunant

About the Type

This book was set in Dante, a typeface designed by Giovanni Mardersteig (1892–1977). Conceived as a private type for the Officina Bodoni in Verona, Italy, Dante was originally cut only for hand composition by Charles Malin, the famous Parisian punch cutter, between 1946 and 1952. Its first use was in an edition of Boccaccio's *Trattatello in laude di Dante* that appeared in 1954. The Monotype Corporation's version of Dante followed in 1957. Though modeled on the Aldine type used for Pietro Cardinal Bembo's treatise *De Aetna* in 1495, Dante is a thoroughly modern interpretation of that venerable face.